Praise for Federico Moccia and the Rome Novels

"Federico Moccia has touched the romantic heart of a whole generation."
—*Il Giornale* (Italian newspaper)

"Federico Moccia is the romance king of the Mediterranean bestseller."
—*Woman* (Spain)

"Federico Moccia knows how to get straight to the heart of all young readers. His words always hit the right spot."
—*TTL* (Italian newspaper)

"With his novels, the writer Federico Moccia has revolutionized young people."
—*Glamour*

"Federico Moccia is an author who writes about love, and he wins the hearts of a broad and diverse audience—the teenagers of today and the teenagers of yesteryear."
—*la Repubblica* (Rome newspaper)

"Federico Moccia is a household name for millions of readers."
—*Revista Universitarios* (Spain)

"The Roman writer has managed to connect with an audience who have become dedicated fans and who are eager to read his novels, great romances with vital teachings."
—*El País* (Spain)

"His novels of young love are sold by millions around the world."
—*El Mundo* (Spain)

"Italian writer Federico Moccia brings the reader an updated version of the classic tale of star-crossed lovers, separated by differences in social class and learned attitudes. A tautly paced novel with intense action and unpredictable twists and turns."
—*5 o'Clock Books* (Romanian TV show)

one step to you

FEDERICO MOCCIA

TRANSLATED BY ANTONY SHUGAAR

New York Boston

This book is a work of fiction. Names, characters, places, and incidents are the product of the author's imagination or are used fictitiously. Any resemblance to actual events, locales, or persons, living or dead, is coincidental.

Grand Central Publishing
Hachette Book Group
1290 Avenue of the Americas, New York, NY 10104
grandcentralpublishing.com
twitter.com/grandcentralpub

Originally published in 1992 as *Tre metri sopra il cielo* by TEA Libri in Italy
First U.S. Edition: March 2021

Grand Central Publishing is a division of Hachette Book Group, Inc. The Grand Central Publishing name and logo is a trademark of Hachette Book Group, Inc.

The publisher is not responsible for websites (or their content) that are not owned by the publisher.

The Hachette Speakers Bureau provides a wide range of authors for speaking events. To find out more, go to www.hachettespeakersbureau.com or call (866) 376-6591.

Library of Congress Cataloging-in-Publication Data
Names: Moccia, Federico, author. | Shugaar, Antony, translator.
Title: One step to you / Federico Moccia, [translated by Antony Shugaar].
Other titles: Tre metri sopra il cielo. English
Description: First U.S. edition. | New York : Grand Central Publishing, 2021. | Series: The Rome novels ; 1 | Originally published in Italian as Tre metri sopra il cielo in Italy, 1992.
Identifiers: LCCN 2020042933 | ISBN 9781538732779 (trade paperback) | ISBN 9781538732755 (ebook)
Classification: LCC PQ4913.O23 T7413 2021 | DDC 853/.92—dc23
LC record available at https://lccn.loc.gov/2020042933

ISBN: 978-1-5387-3277-9 (trade paperback), 978-1-5387-3275-5 (ebook)

Printed in the United States of America

LSC-C

Printing 1, 2021

To my father, a great friend,
who taught me so much

To my beautiful mother,
who taught me to laugh

Chapter 1

S*ophia's ass is Europe's finest.* That bright red graffiti, the work of some stealthy hand armed with a can of spray paint in the dark of night, now gleamed in all its brazenness on one of the massive columns lining the Corso di Francia bridge.

Nearby, a Roman eagle, carved long ago, had doubtless seen it all, but wasn't about to name the guilty party. Just beneath the fearsome bird of prey's marble talons, like a baby eaglet sheltering in its protective shadow, sat the boy.

His hair was short, practically a buzz cut, with a high fade at the nape of the neck like a US Marine.

His dark Levi's jacket was missing a button, scraped off along with a stretch of blue paint when he and his motorbike had wiped out on the asphalt of a curve that turned out to be tighter than expected.

Collar turned up, smoldering Camel dangling from his lips, and a pair of wraparound Ray-Ban Baloramas—these accessories all buttressed his tough-guy pose, but none of it was really necessary. He had a dazzling smile, but only a select few had ever had the pleasure of seeing it.

He glanced down the span of the bridge to the cars poised menacingly at the stoplight. Lined up, waiting motionless, like race cars at the starting line, except no racetrack had ever seen such a motley assortment of makes and models—a Fiat 126, a VW Beetle, a Ford Fiesta, some other nondescript American car he couldn't identify, and an Alfa Romeo 155.

He smiled.

A few cars back, in a Mercedes 200, a slender finger with a badly bitten nail gave a gentle push to a cassette tape protruding slightly from the latest-model Alpine stereo. The sound of a tiny motor seized the tape and drew it into the tape deck. From the twin Pioneer speakers in the doors, a young female vocalist's voice burst suddenly to life.

The Mercedes gently moved forward, following the flow of traffic. The scent of the driver's aftershave wafted through the air in the car's interior.

The girl in the passenger seat mused to herself that, even if she'd wanted to, there was no one she could tell, "Go away, love," like the words to the song. If anything she'd have happily kicked her sister out of the car rather than listen for one more second to her pestering demands for a different song: "Change it to Eros, come *on*, I want to listen to *Eros*."

The Mercedes rolled past precisely as the cigarette, smoked down to the butt, was hitting the sidewalk, propelled through the air by an expert flick of forefinger against thumb and lofted a little bit farther by a chance gust of wind. The boy strode down the marble steps, adjusted his 501s, and swung one leg over the saddle of his dark blue Honda VF 750 custom motorbike, with a few slight dents and scratches on the front mudguard. He twisted the key, barely tapped the ignition button, and pushed down hard on the kick-starter.

Suddenly the green light vanished from behind the NEUTRAL on the instrument cluster and, as if by magic, he found himself moving through the line of cars. His right boot shifted through the gears, reining the engine in or letting it roar, as its torque shoved him powerfully forward like a breaking wave, sliding now right, now left. He leaned gently into each curve, slaloming through the narrow spaces between one car and the next like a series of ski gates.

The sun was rising, it was morning, a bright beautiful morning. She was on her way to school; he was still up from the night before. It would have been just another day if that morning, at that stoplight, they hadn't come to a halt side by side.

Red light.

He glanced over at her. An ash-blond lock of hair fluttered out the open car window. As the hair tossed gently in the morning air, it intermittently left her neck uncovered, revealing a faint golden down that followed the direction traced by the wind. Her determined profile was punctuated by the blush of her cheeks and the blue of her eyes, gentle and serene, as she listened dreamily, half-lidded, to the second song, "La vita mia." The sight of such tranquility struck him forcefully, and maybe that's why:

"Hey!"

She turned to look, caught off guard, opening her large, innocent bright blue eyes a little wider. She stared at him. A stranger, stopped beside her on a motorcycle, with broad shoulders, his hands too tan for the mid-April sun. His eyes, concealed behind sunglasses, would surely have had something to add to the already utterly shameless face.

"You want to go for a ride with me?"

"No, I'm on my way to school."

"So just pretend to go, why don't you? I'll swing by and pick you up out front."

"Pardon me." She gave him a tight, forced fake smile. "You must have misunderstood. What I meant to say was, 'No, I do *not* want to go for a ride with you.'"

"No, listen, you'd have fun—"

"I very much doubt that."

"I'd solve all your problems."

"I don't have any problems."

"Okay, now it's me who very much doubts that." Green light.

The Mercedes 200 shot forward, leaving the boy's confident smile anchored to the spot. Her father turned to give her a glance. "So who was that? A friend of yours?"

"No, Papà, just some idiot..."

A moment later, the Honda motorbike pulled up next to the pretty girl for a second time. This time, the boy reached out and grabbed the open windowsill with his left hand, revving the motor slightly with his right hand, just enough to keep from having to lean too hard on the moving car, though that shouldn't have been a challenge for those sixteen-inch biceps.

The only one who seemed to be struggling with the situation was the father. "Hey, what's that reckless fool up to? Why is he driving so close to the car?"

"Don't worry, Papà. Let me take care of this—"

She swiveled decisively around to glare at the boy.

"Listen, don't you have anything better to do?"

"Nope."

"Well, find something."

"I already have."

"You have?"

"Yes. I want to take you for a spin. Come on, we'll go for a fast ride on the Via Olimpica, open her up so you see what this bike can do, then I'll take you somewhere nice for a quick breakfast and drop you off right in front of your school. I promise."

"I doubt your promises are worth very much."

"True, true." He smiled. "So you see, you already know all about me. Admit it, you like what you see, don't you?"

She laughed and shook her head.

"All right, that's enough now." She opened a book she'd just pulled out of her Gherardini bag. "I need to think about my one and only real problem."

"Which is what?"

"My Latin test."

"I thought it was sex."

She turned toward him, shocked. This time, without a smile, not even of feigned courtesy.

"Get your hand off my window."

"Why, where do you want me to put it?"

She pressed a button. "I can't tell you, my father's listening."

The power window started to close. He waited until the last second and then, yanking his hand out of the narrowing gap and shooting her one last glance, pulled away from the car. "See you later."

He didn't stick around to hear her curt reply: "Oh, no

you won't." He leaned slightly to the right and veered away. As he took the curve, he shifted gears and revved the bike's engine, accelerating sharply until he'd vanished into the line of cars. The Mercedes continued straight ahead, with no one left to interfere as it carried the two sisters to their school day.

"Wait, you know who that guy is?" Her sister's head suddenly popped forward between the two front seats. "They call him A-Plus."

"As far as I'm concerned, he's nothing but a moron."

Then she opened her Latin textbook and started reviewing the construction of the ablative absolute. Suddenly, though, she stopped reading and gazed out the window. Was this really her only problem? Certainly not the one that guy had said. And anyway, she'd never see him again. She went back to her textbook with renewed determination. The car turned left, on its way to Falconieri High School.

"That's right, I have no problems, and I'm never going to see him again."

Little did she realize how wrong she really was. About both things.

Chapter 2

Their motorcycles were powerful and so were their muscles. Step, Pollo, Lucone, Hook, the Sicilian, Bunny, Schello, and lots of others. All with unlikely names, and challenging histories. Statuesque and smiling, quick with a wisecrack, their rough hands bore a few extra marks, reminders of past brawls. Okay, so maybe some of them didn't have much money in their pockets, but they knew how to have fun and they were friends. That was enough.

They were stopped there, in Piazza Jacini, most sitting on their Harleys, old 350 four-strokes with the original array of four exhaust pipes or with the classic four-in-one, which made a lot more noise. Motorcycles dreamed of, yearned after, and finally obtained from their parents after endless, relentless begging. Or else by making sacrifices out of their own pockets.

Step smiled. "I hear that there's a party on the Via Cassia."

"Where?" the Silician asked.

"Number 1130. It's an apartment complex. Wanna go?"

"But will they let us in?"

Schello reassured them. "I know a girl who'll be there."

"Who's that?"

"Francesca."

"In that case, they won't let us in," the Silician said.

Everyone broke out laughing.

"Oh yeah? Wait and see. We'll get in, and we'll liven up the place!"

"Come on! That's the spirit," Schello shouted like a lunatic. "Let's go!"

Everyone in the piazza exploded in tune with that shout, starting up their motorcycle and Vespa engines, honking horns, shouting.

The windows of the buildings all around the piazza started creaking open. A distant burglar alarm began to blare. Old women in their nightgowns shuffled out onto balconies, shouting in worried voices, "What's going on?" A voice yelled for everyone to shut up. A woman who believed in law and order threatened to call the police.

As if by magic, all the motorcycles moved at once. Pollo, Lucone, and the others took running starts, leaping onto their seats as the mufflers spewed out white smoke. A few beer cans rattled and crashed as they rolled along, and the girls all went home.

The other motorcycles joined formation, occupying the whole street, indifferent to the occasional car that ran up fast next to them, overtaking and honking loudly. Schello stood up on his beat-up oversized Vespa. Laughing, they all downshifted, practically in unison. Slamming on brakes, fishtailing across the asphalt, they all turned a sharp left. One or two popping wheelies as they went, all of them ignoring the red light. Then they roared up the Via Cassia at top speed.

~

At the sound of the buzzer downstairs, Roberta, euphoric for her eighteenth birthday and for the party that was going perfectly, ran to the intercom.

"You're here to see Francesca who?" Roberta asked the male voice over the speaker.

"Giacomini, that blonde. I'm her brother, and I have to give her some keys."

Roberta pushed the button inside the intercom once and then, to make sure she'd opened the door, pushed it again. She went into the kitchen and pulled two big Coca-Colas from the freezer. They were cold enough, so she shut the freezer door with her right foot and turned to go back to the living room. There she crossed paths with a blond girl who was talking to a boy with his hair slicked back with gel.

"Francesca, your brother is coming upstairs. He's bringing you your keys."

"Ah..." was all that Francesca managed to reply. "Thanks." The boy with the slicked-back hair lost a little bit of his stiffness and allowed himself a faint sound of amusement.

"France, is something wrong?" Roberta asked.

"No, nothing's wrong, aside from the fact that I'm an only child."

The Sicilian and Hook were the first to read the nameplate on the fifth-floor doorbell. "Here it is. This is the place. Micchi, right?"

Schello reached the doorbell and pressed the button. The door swung open almost immediately.

Roberta stood in the doorway and looked out at the

group of young men, muscular and unkempt. *They're certainly dressed rather casually* struck her as a good thing to think. "Can I help you?"

Schello stepped forward. "I was looking for Francesca. I'm her brother."

As if by magic, Francesca appeared in the doorway, accompanied by the boy with the slicked-back hair.

"Ah, there you are. It's your brother." Roberta turned and walked away.

Francesca gave the group a worried look. "Which of you is supposed to be my brother?"

"Me!" Lucone put his hand up.

Pollo raised his hand too. "So am I. We're twins, just like in that Schwarzenegger movie. He's the dumb one." They all laughed.

Francesca took Schello aside. "What on earth were you thinking when you invited all these people, huh?"

"This party strikes me as a morgue. At least we can liven it up a little bit. Come on, France, don't get pissed off."

"Who's pissed off? I just want you all to leave."

"Excuse me, coming through, pardon me . . . " Inexorably, one after the other, they all went through, Hook, Lucone, Pollo, Bunny, Step, and the others.

Francesca tried to stop them. "No, Schello, come on. You can't go in."

"Come on, France, don't be like that. You'll see, nothing bad will happen." Schello locked arms with her. "In any case, you're not at fault here. It's all your brother's fault, for letting all these people tag along." Then, as if he were worried about letting in another group of party crashers, he shut the door politely behind him.

Almost immediately, Lucone and the others mingled with the real guests, or at least tried to. They spread out in the living room.

There are certainly some strange folks at this party. That was the most common thought but also the most secretly kept one. In fact, it passed through many heads but passed not a single pair of lips.

~

Expensive electric appliances had been arranged at the corners of a modern kitchen. The refrigerator door hung open.

"Remember to close the door after getting something out of the fridge..." That's what Signora Micchi would always say, scolding her children when they loitered too long in front of the open refrigerator at snack time. If, however, Signora Micchi were to come face-to-face with the owner of these Adidas and his friends, sitting there with their feet up on the table and her daughter's eighteenth-birthday cake before them, she probably wouldn't have the nerve to say a word to either of them.

"No, I want to blow out the candles," Hook said.

"What the hell right do you have?" the Sicilian asked. "I was the one who found the cake."

"True, but I lit the birthday candles." Hook proudly brandished his Zippo.

The Sicilian looked at him and then smiled. "But there's one thing you haven't considered."

"And what's that?"

"The fact that it's going to be my birthday soon." He blew hard on the cake, extinguishing all the candles. Admittedly, this wasn't his actual birthday, and that was certainly not the appropriate number of candles. The Sicilian looked a far sight older than eighteen, but still a happy smile wreathed his face.

Hook flipped open his Zippo and almost simultaneously gave the flint wheel a sharp spin with his thumb. Then he ran the big flame over the top of each birthday candle, leaving a smaller flame flickering on the various wicks.

"What the fuck are you doing now?" the Sicilian asked.

"Now it's my turn to blow them out."

"Hey, no fair. You can only blow a cake's birthday candles out once."

"Says who?" Hook asked.

"Says me!" The Sicilian stuck his stubby hand into the icing, ruining the perfectly round shape of the eight marking Roberta's new age, to lick the frosting off.

"But I've never blown out a cake full of birthday candles in my life."

"Well, shit, why don't you just blow out the candles on your own side?"

"No, now you've ruined it, and I don't give a damn about it anymore," Hook said.

"Here, why don't you just take back your damned cake!" With those words, the Sicilian got rid of the clumps of frosting that still clung to his hand, flipping them accurately onto Hook's jacket.

In response, Hook grabbed a handful of cake and tried to fire back. Instead, it hit the housekeeper, who had just entered the kitchen.

Hook and the Sicilian called a truce to their cold war and burst out laughing.

Petty thief that he was, Pollo immediately went looking for the mother's bedroom. He found it. It had wisely been locked. Double-locked, in fact, but unfortunately, they'd left the key in the lock. Naively.

Pollo opened the door. The girls' purses had all been left there on the bed in perfect order. He started opening them, one after the other, taking his time, really. The wallets were nearly all full. It really was one fine party. All of these people were high class, no two ways about that, as far as Pollo was concerned.

He was just about to leave when he noticed a handbag dangling from the armrest of a chair off to one side, hidden by a jacket draped over it. He picked up the bag. It was a handsome article, elegant and heavy with a woven leather strap and two fine lengths of deerskin lacing to fasten it. It must be richly stocked if its proprietor had taken such care to hide it.

Pollo started unknotting one of the two deerskin laces, cursing his habit of chewing his nails down to the bloody nub as he did so. At last, he managed to get the knot undone. And just as he did, the door swung open. Pollo hid the purse behind his back. A dark-haired young woman with a dazzling smile walked in, unruffled. When she saw him, she came to a halt.

"Shut that door."

The young woman did as she was told. Pollo swung the handbag around from behind his back and started rummaging through it. She put on a shocked expression.

"So, are you going to tell me what you want in here?" he asked.

"My purse."

"Well, what are you waiting for? Go ahead and get it, why don't you?" Pollo pointed to the bed covered with purses he'd already emptied.

"I can't."

"Why not?"

"A young thug has it in his hand."

"Ah." Pollo smiled. He took a closer look at the girl. She was very attractive, with black hair and side-swept bangs that mirrored the twist of her mouth in a vaguely irritated grimace.

Pollo found her wallet and pulled it out of the purse. "Here..." He tossed her the purse. "You only had to ask..."

Pallina caught the purse neatly and started rummaging through it. "You know that you're not supposed to poke through a young lady's purse, right? Didn't your mother ever tell you that?"

"I've never actually spoken to my mother. Hey, you know what, you should have a chat with yours," he said.

"Why's that?"

"Well, there's no way she should be letting you go out in public with nothing more than twenty bucks in your purse."

"That's my weekly allowance."

Pollo pocketed the cash. "It *was*."

"God you're stupid!" She found what she'd been looking for and set down her purse. "Then, once you're done, put my wallet back inside. Thanks." She turned to leave.

"Hey, hold on a second." Pollo caught up with her. "What did you just take out of your purse?"

"I'm sorry, I would happily have offered you one but..."

She showed Pollo the cigarette. "It was the last one..."

Pollo started laughing. "Oh, don't worry...worst case, we can share it."

"Ah, no." And Pallina gave him a sarcastic smile before turning to leave.

Pollo stood there, unsure what to do now. In any case, it never occurred to him to put back the twenty bucks.

~

The DJ, a music-loving guy, whose hair was slightly longer than the others' as a way of signaling his artistic temperament, flailed and shook in time to the beat. His hands moved the records backward and forward on twin turntables while a large pair of headphones over his ears let him hear first to avoid an awkward mix.

Schello walked over to him. "Hey, boss, would you put this tape on for me?"

The DJ, reading his lips more than hearing his words, took the cassette and slid it into the player next to him. He pushed a few buttons, sending the music into his headphones. Schello stood there watching him with a broad smile on his face. The DJ's expression suddenly changed. The contents of the tape had just entered his headphones. He held out for just a handful of seconds.

"Are you insane?" he asked, taking the headphones off and, immediately afterward, removing the cassette from the tape deck. "That's a tape by Anthrax. Most of the people in here would stampede out of the place, and the rest would have their hair standing on end. This stuff causes heart attacks. Here, take it," he said, handing back the cassette. "Put it on at your house sometime, when you're looking to cause yourself some harm."

"You want to know the truth? I fall asleep to it."

~

Step was wandering through the party, looking around him, distractedly listening to the stupid chatter of eighteen-year-old girls about expensive dresses they'd spotted in shop windows, scooters their parents had refused to buy for them, impossible boyfriends, definite betrayals, and frustrated aspirations.

Not far away, against a background of magnificent paintings and photographs of a healthy, wealthy society, someone was stumbling along as if wrecked. It was Bunny. Their eyes met. Bunny returned his smile and then stole an ashtray with a sudden move, just as a cigarette, with a long column of ash at the end, was coming in for a landing. The ash, which had teetered successfully in perfect vertical equilibrium, collapsed right where the ashtray had been until just a few seconds earlier. The smoker was embarrassed in front of the young woman he was talking to, and Bunny gained another piece of expensive silver. But the biggest loser was certainly the tablecloth.

Step crossed the living room. From the window at the far end, the one overlooking the terrace, came a breath of wind. The curtains were tossing lightly in the breeze, and then, as they settled back to vertical, two figures took shape beneath them. Hands could be seen trying to open the curtains. A handsome, well-groomed young man was soon successful, finding the right opening in the draperies. A few moments later, a young woman appeared at his side. They were laughing happily, amused by that minor mishap. The moonlight from behind faintly illuminated her dress, rendering it translucent for an instant.

Step stood there staring at her. The girl shook her hair, smiling at the guy. She displayed a mouthful of beautiful white teeth. Even from a distance, it was possible to sense the intensity of her light blue eyes. Step remembered her, remembered their meeting. Or perhaps, more than a meeting, their argument.

The young man and young woman near the curtains said something to each other. The girl nodded and followed the boy over to the drinks table. Suddenly, Step was thirsty too.

~

Chicco Brandelli led Babi through the guests. The palm of his hand barely brushed her back, and with every step, he savored a whiff of her light perfume. He and Babi greeted a few of their friends who'd arrived while they were on the terrace. They chatted at the table covered with drinks.

Suddenly a guy stood face-to-face with Babi. It was Step.

"Well, I can see that you listened to my advice, and you're trying to solve your problems." Step tilted his head in Brandelli's direction. "I understand he's just a first rough attempt. But he could work. For that matter, if you haven't found anything better, he'll have to do..."

Babi looked at him, faintly uncertain. She didn't know who he was but she didn't much like him. Or did she? What was familiar about this guy?

Step refreshed her memory. "I accompanied you to school one morning, not very long ago."

"That's impossible. My father always takes me to school."

"You're right. Let's just say that I escorted you. I was holding on to your car."

Babi realized who he was and gazed at him in shock.

"I see you've finally remembered."

"Sure, you were the guy who was spouting all those dumb lines. You haven't changed, have you?"

"Why should I? I'm perfect." Step threw both arms wide, displaying his physique.

Babi decided, at least from that point of view, she couldn't argue. It was all the rest that didn't work. Starting with his clothing and ending with his behavior.

"You see, you didn't say no."

"Because I'm not even talking to you."

"Babi, is this guy bothering you?" Brandelli had the ill-advised impulse to step in at this point. Step didn't even look at him.

"No, Chicco, thanks," Babi said.

"Well, then, if I'm not bothering you, it must mean you like me."

"I'm completely indifferent. In fact, I'd say that you bore me and annoy me a little, to be exact."

Chicco tried to cut off the discussion by speaking directly to Babi. "Would you care for something to drink?"

Step answered in her place. "Yes, thanks. Go ahead and pour me a Coca-Cola."

Chicco ignored him. "Babi, do you want something to drink?"

For the first time, Step looked at him. "I said, yes, a Coke. I already told you that. Now get on it."

Chicco stood there, looking at him, with a glass in his hand.

"Leave him be." Babi intervened, taking the glass out of Chicco's hand. "I'll do it."

Babi finished pouring and set down the bottle. "Here, and make sure not to spill any." She threw the glassful of Coca-Cola right in Step's face, drenching him from head to foot. "I told you to be careful."

Chicco started laughing. Step gave him such a powerful shove that Chicco flew onto a low coffee table, knocking over everything on top of it. Then he grabbed the ends of the tablecloth and gave it a hard yank, trying to do the trick that certain prestidigitators know how to pull off, but it turned out badly. A dozen or so bottles overturned, flying onto nearby sofas and guests. A few glasses shattered. Step wiped his face dry.

Babi looked at him in disgust. "You really are a filthy beast."

"You're right. What I need is a nice hot shower because I'm all sticky. And that's your fault. I'm going to find a bathroom, and then I'll be right back. Don't go away, all right?"

The music of Anthrax filled the living room, and many of the guests had stopped talking.

Roberta, worried, stopped in the doorway, gazing out appalled at her devastated living room.

"Excuse me, where's the bathroom?"

Roberta pointed Step to it. "That way."

Step thanked her and continued in the direction she'd pointed him.

Next Brandelli went over to Roberta. "Where's the telephone?"

"That way." Roberta pointed in a different direction, the opposite way from the bathroom. She felt like a cop trying to direct traffic, trying to manage the terrible outburst of chaos that was unfolding in her own living room. Unfortunately, she lacked the authority to write them tickets and kick them all out.

A few people, either smarter or more cowardly than the others, came over, planting kisses on her cheek. "Ciao, Roberta, happy birthday. We're so sorry, but we're going to have to leave, okay?"

"That way." By now in a bit of a fugue state, Roberta pointed to the front door of the apartment. If it hadn't been her home, in fact, Roberta would gladly have fled through the door herself.

Step entered the bathroom and pulled open the pebbled-glass door to the shower. He took off his T-shirt and started to rinse off with the shower spray.

Just then, Babi walked in, slamming the door behind her.

"So you just can't resist. You're compelled to follow me everywhere I go."

"Do you mind having a word with your friends?" Babi asked. "They're destroying my girlfriend's apartment, and you started the whole thing—"

"Me? You were the one who threw a Coke in my face, weren't you?"

"Okay, I was wrong to throw it."

"Yeah, I know that you were wrong."

Step took the shower spray in hand. "It's too late now. The damage is done. This is all your fault. You should have kept your cool, and above all, you should have kept a handle on your hot temper...Sometimes the best thing in these cases is an ice-cold shower!"

And with those words, he turned on the spray and drenched her.

"You idiot!" Babi twisted and struggled, trying to avoid the water, but Step managed to grab her hand before she could run out of the room and made sure she got wet all over. "Let go of me!"

"Trust me, a shower does you a world of good. It can clear your mind. It improves your circulation, you get more blood to your brain, and that helps a person understand that they need to act nice to others...that they need to be nice and drink a glass of Coca-Cola, not throw it in someone's face."

Schello entered at that very moment.

"Come on, Step. Let's go. Some guy called the police."

"How do you know?"

"I caught the guy on the telephone. I heard him with my own ears."

Step turned off the shower and let go of Babi's hand. Babi, her hair hanging forward, drenched to the bone, said, "I hate you..."

Step looked at her with a smile. "Come on, no you don't...I know you don't. Anyway, you should dry off, otherwise you'll catch your death."

Babi lifted the long, wet hair that draped over her face. She uncovered her eyes. They were angry and determined.

Step acted afraid. "Uh-oh, pretend I didn't say it. I understand, you wanted to take a shower with me, and now you're mad because you had to take one alone. Maybe we can do it some other time."

Step took a towel and gave it to Babi, who threw it at him.

Step laughed. "What manners . . . you're never nice to me!"

"Fuck off."

"What vulgar words you use! How could that be, a nice young woman like you spouting things like that? Remember that, the next time we take a shower together, I'm going to have to wash your mouth out with soap. Understood?"

He wrung out his T-shirt and tied it around his waist. Then he left the bathroom.

Babi watched him go. On his still-wet back, a few drops of water slid around sinews and bundles of muscles, taut and clearly delineated. Babi picked up a bottle of shampoo that she found on the floor within reach and hurled it after him.

Hearing the noise, Step ducked instinctively. Babi hadn't managed to hit him, even though his broad shoulders presented an easy target.

Step bent down to pick up the plastic bottle bearing the image of a pretty blond girl with long, lustrous hair. "Hey, now I understand why you're so mad. I forgot to shampoo your hair. I'll be right back, okay?"

"Get out of here! Don't you dare . . . " Babi quickly yanked the glass door, shutting herself in the shower.

Step looked at her small hands, pressed against the glass. "Here!" He tossed her the shampoo over the top of the shower stall. Then, with a shameless laugh, he walked out of the bathroom.

~

At the sound of the word *police*, there was a stampede for the door in the living room while Roberta sat sobbing in a corner.

Bunny, with the strange clanking sound of silver, went out at a dead run, a little heavier than usual. Behind him came Pollo, silent as he ran because what he had in his pockets might have made less noise but it held a lot more value. The Sicilian was next through the door, followed by Step and Schello. They galloped down the steps quickly, making the railing shake where they placed their full weight on it as they jumped down the last clusters of steps.

They all reached the ground-floor atrium, everyone laughing, and they strode off into the night.

~

Out of the front door at number 1130 on the Via Cassia emerged a group of guests. They were all discussing what had happened. After a number of stupid and pointless questions, the police had finally left Roberta's home. The only one who knew anything, a certain Francesca, had made her escape as soon as she saw that the party was skidding off the rails, taking with her an emptied purse and the names of the guilty parties.

In the midst of the general mayhem, Babi, completely drenched, had lost her sister, Daniela. On the other hand, Roberta had found Babi a pair of shorts that fit her perfectly, as well as her older brother's sweatshirt, in which she could easily swim.

"You really ought to go to parties more often dressed like that. You're captivating," Chicco teased Babi.

"Chicco, do you still feel like joking around?" The two of them walked out the front door. "I can't find my sister, and I've ruined the Valentino dress." She held up an elegant plastic shopping bag emblazoned with a name that was different from that of the drenched dress but still every bit as famous. "And as if that weren't enough, if my mother catches me coming home with wet hair, I'm in trouble."

"There he is. That's the one who made the call." From behind the dumpsters, Schello confidently pointed at Chicco Brandelli.

Step looked at him. "Are you serious?"

"As a heart attack. I heard him with my own ears."

Step recognized the girl who was with that stinking rat. You don't soon forget a woman who insists relentlessly on taking a shower with you. He smiled at his friend. "Let's go tell the others."

Babi and Chicco turned down a narrow street. "But what about you? Why didn't you say anything when that idiot put me under the shower?"

"How was I supposed to know? Right then I was in the hall, calling the police."

"Ah, so that was you?"

"Sure. I could see the situation was getting out of hand... Did you see the fat lip that someone gave Andrea Marinelli?"

"Yes, poor guy."

"Poor guy? It's the best thing that could have happened to him, are you kidding? I can't even imagine the stories he'll tell. All alone, taking on the barbarian horde. The hero of the night. Here we are, this is it."

They stopped when they got to a car. The emergency lights flashed rapidly, and the door locks popped open in unison. The security system was a fairly common model but the same couldn't be said of the brand-new BMW.

Chicco opened the passenger door for her. Babi peered in at the pristine interior, the dark wood paneling, and the soft leather upholstery.

"Do you like it?"

"Yes, a lot," Babi said.

"I bought it just for you. I knew I'd be driving you home tonight."

"You did?"

"Of course I did!" Chicco said. "Actually, the whole thing was planned down to the last detail. I actually hired that gang of idiots. Just think, the whole mess was contrived just so I could be alone with you."

"Well, then, you could have skipped the part with the shower because, at least for once, my clothes weren't up to the occasion."

Chicco laughed and shut her door and then walked around the car and got in on the driver's side. He put the key in the ignition and turned it. The powerful engine immediately roared to life. A small hatch slid down at the center of the dashboard, revealing an expensive car stereo that had been concealed from thieves until that moment. A song started up, smooth in all its tones, in complete fidelity to high notes and low. The car pulled away silently.

"All things considered, I had a lot of fun this evening. If

it hadn't been for that crowd, it would have been the usual grim funeral," Chicco said.

"I doubt that Roberta feels the same way." Babi carefully laid the plastic shopping bag at her feet. "They wrecked her house!"

"Oh, come on, it's no big deal, strictly minor damage. She'll just have to have the sofas scrubbed and send the carpets to the cleaners."

A loud, sharp thump erupted, shattering the atmosphere of elegance and harmony inside the car.

"What just happened?" Chicco looked in his side mirror. Suddenly, he glimpsed the face of Lucone, almost completely filling the disk of glass. He was laughing like a maniac. Behind him, Hook climbed onto the motorcycle seat and, standing upright, delivered another kick to the bumper of the car.

"It's those lunatics! Hurry up, step on the gas," Babi said.

Chicco shifted gears and hit the accelerator. Behind him, the motorcycles immediately picked up speed, and he was unable to shake them. Worried now, Babi turned to look behind them.

They were all there, Bunny, Pollo, the Sicilian, and Hook, and in the middle of the pack was Step. His leather jacket flapped in the rushing wind, opening up and revealing his bare chest. Step smiled right at her.

Babi turned away and looked straight ahead. "Chicco, drive as fast as you can. I'm scared!"

Chicco said nothing and continued driving, pressing down hard on the gas, downhill along the Via Cassia in the chilly night. But the motorcycles were still there, buzzing along on either side of him, glued relentlessly to the hurtling car.

"Chicco, don't you dare think of stopping or those guys will start wrecking *you*."

"No, I can still try to talk to them." He pushed the button that electrically lowered the window and opened it halfway. "Listen, guys," he shouted while trying to remain calm and stay on the road, "this car belongs to my father and..." A gob of spit caught him right in the face.

"Yahoooo, bull's-eye, a hundred points for me!" Pollo got to his feet on the saddle behind Bunny, raising both arms straight up in the thrill of victory.

In despair, Chicco wiped his face with a chamois cloth that was more expensive and more authentic than Pollo's gloves. Babi looked on in disgust at that stubborn gob of spit, and then she pushed the electric button, closing the car window again before Pollo's unerring aim could hit anything else.

"Just try to make it to the center of town. Maybe we'll run into the police there," Babi said.

Chicco tossed the chamois cloth into the back and kept on driving. He thought about the thousands of lire in damage to the car and the endless dressing-downs from his father. At that point, in a surge of sudden rage, he jerked the steering wheel, swerving suddenly to one side.

The car scythed across the road, to the right and then to the left, and smashed into the motorcycles. The Sicilian shot off to the left, winding up in the other lane, which was fortunately empty. Bunny slammed on the brakes, narrowly managing not to be run off the road.

Chicco started laughing, as if caught up in a hysterical jag. "So they want war? Fine, they can have it! I'll crush them like the rats that they are!"

He gave the steering wheel another twist, causing the car to lurch off to the right. Babi clutched tight to the door handle in utter terror.

When Step saw the car heading straight for him, he braked and veered away, downshifting at the same time. The motorcycle slowly veered back to the center of the road, right behind the car.

Chicco peered into the rearview mirror. The group was there, behind him, still glued to his tail. "Scared, are you? Good! Then take this." He suddenly jammed on his brakes. The ABS cut in. The car screeched to an almost complete halt.

The motorcycles on either side managed to veer away and avoid the car. Schello, who was right in the middle, did his best to brake, but his oversized Vespa, with little or no tread, fishtailed wildly and slammed into the rear bumper. Schello hit the pavement.

Chicco took off again, tires screeching, at top speed. The motorcycles stopped to lend aid to their wounded friend.

"Fuck that son of a bitch!" Schello got to his feet, his pants torn over his right knee. "Look at this."

"No surprise, the way you flew you're lucky that's all that happened. You didn't hurt yourself at all. You just have a scraped knee," Bunny said.

"What the fuck do I care about my knee? That asshole ruined my Levi's, and I bought them just the other day."

Everyone laughed, amused and, at the same time, relieved for their friend, who'd lost neither his life nor his willingness to joke about it.

Step watched the BMW vanishing into the distance, far away at the end of the street by now. Between the lines of trees that narrowed to a slender gap, he could see clouds scudding quickly past in the sky. A large, bright moon rode high in the darkness. That moon was the one thing truly out of reach.

Then the BMW veered to the right and pulled onto Corso Francia. "Wahoooo, I fixed those bastards, but good." Chicco was pounding both hands on the steering wheel in delight. He glanced quickly at his rearview mirror. Nothing but a car far behind him. He felt reassured. There was no one in pursuit. "Assholes, assholes!" He bounced excitedly in his seat. "I did it!"

Then he remembered Babi, sitting beside him. "Are you all right?" He turned and gazed seriously at her, expressing his concern.

"Better now, thanks." Babi detached herself from the car door she'd been crushed against and got more comfortable, sitting up normally. "But now I'd like to go home."

Chicco downshifted and took a right turn, heading down the hill. "I'll take you right away."

He came to a quick halt at the stop sign and then continued over the Ponte Milvio. Chicco looked at her again. Her hair, still wet, hung over her shoulders. Her blue eyes gazed straight ahead, still tinged with a look of fright.

"I'm sorry for what happened. Did that scare you?"

"Yeah, pretty much."

"Do you want to get something to drink?" Chicco asked.

"No, thanks."

"But I'm going to need to stop for a second."

"If you want."

Chicco made a U-turn. He pulled over next to a public drinking fountain in front of a church and splashed a few handfuls of water onto his face, rubbing away the last possible traces of human enzymes from Pollo's saliva. Then he let the cool night breeze caress his face and relaxed.

When he finally opened his eyes again, he was looking reality right in the face. His car, or actually, his father's car. "Fucking hell!" he whispered to himself, circling the car and assessing the damage.

Chicco tried to pretend he wasn't in the depths of despair. But in reality, he definitely was. His father had an obsession with cars, and that one in particular, considering how long he'd had to wait before finally taking delivery. Almost as long a wait as it felt for Chicco himself, earlier that evening, in his bedroom, trying to work up the nerve to ask to borrow it.

He gave Babi a forced smile. "Well, the car's going to need a little work. It's got a few bumps and scratches."

He had barely finished the sentence before a dark blue motorcycle, which had followed him all this way with its headlight off, pulled up just inches from him, engine rumbling. Chicco hardly had a chance to turn around before he found himself shoved onto the hood of his car, denting the sheet metal badly. "Help! Help!"

"Maybe next time you'll learn to keep your damned mouth shut, you disgusting piece of shit!"

Babi got out of the car and, in the throes of rage, started pounding away at Step, slamming her plastic bag with the wet clothing inside over his head. "Let go of him, you coward! Stop it!"

Step turned around suddenly, and Babi went reeling back, tripped over the curb, and lost her balance entirely, landing on the ground. Step stood there looking at her in surprise.

Chicco took advantage of that moment. He got up off the hood and shook his head, trying to collect his thoughts. Then he tried to climb back into the car but Step was too fast for him.

Step gave the car door a quick shove, and Chicco called out, helpless and wedged in place between the car and the door.

Babi got up off the ground, smarting from the impact. She, too, started yelling for help.

Just then, a car went by. It was the Accados, friends of Babi and Daniela's parents. "Look, Filippo! What's going on? Why, that's Babi, Raffaella's daughter!" Marina Accado said.

Filippo slammed on the brakes and got out of the car, leaving the door wide open.

Babi ran toward him, shouting, "Separate them. Hurry, they're killing each other!" Even if that wasn't exactly an accurate description of the situation. "Let go of him!"

Filippo threw himself on Step, restraining him from behind. Then Chicco thrust the car door open, sending Step flying into Filippo, before getting back behind the wheel and escaping at top speed.

Step, wrenching free from the arms of Signor Accado, turned to see that the back of his head had struck Filippo's face during the fall, breaking his nose, which had begun bleeding. Now Filippo staggered to his feet, both hands on his nose and with no idea of where to go.

Marina hurried to her husband's side. "You criminal, you miserable wretch! Don't get any closer. Don't you dare touch him!"

Step stood in shocked silence, observing the screaming woman.

"Do you hear me, you little thug? This doesn't end here!" Marina helped her husband into the passenger seat and then started the engine and pulled away.

Babi stood boldly in front of Step. "You disgust me! You have no respect for anything or anyone."

He gazed at her with a beaming smile. "Do you mind telling me what you want from me?"

"Nothing. What could I possibly want from you? What can you expect of a filthy beast? You injured a man, someone much older than you."

"First off, if he hadn't grabbed me from behind, I never would have struck him. Second, too bad for him, he should have just minded his own business."

"Oh, really? So if someone doesn't mind his own business, you hit him in the face?"

"Again with this bullshit?" Step went over to his motorcycle and climbed aboard. He started the motorcycle, and for a moment, he lit up Babi with his headlight. She partly shut her eyes. Step put the bike in first gear. The headlight swept away. "Well, so long."

Babi looked around. There was no one in sight. The piazza was deserted. "What do you mean, so long?"

"All right, I take it back. I won't even say *so long*."

Babi heaved a sigh of annoyance. "What about me? How am I supposed to get home now?"

"How the hell should I know? You could have asked your friend to drive you, couldn't you?"

"Impossible, you beat him up and made him run away."

"Oh, so now it's my fault."

"Whose fault if not yours? Come on, let me get on." Babi went over to the motorcycle and lifted her leg to one side, ready to climb on.

Step let out the clutch. The motorcycle moved slightly forward. Babi looked at him. Step turned his head and looked back. Babi tried to get on again, but Step was too fast for her, and once again darted forward.

"Stop it, hold still. What's the matter with you?"

Step looked at her with that arrogant smirk on his face. "You can't be thinking of accepting a ride from someone as awful as me."

Babi half shut her eyes, this time because of how much she hated him. Then she went walking off, with great determination, down Via della Farnesina.

Step twisted the accelerator and caught up with her. He was rolling along beside her, sitting on his motorcycle. "Forgive me, but I'm doing it for your sake. Otherwise you'd be bitter about having had to compromise. No, far better that you stick to your guns and get home on your own two feet. Agreed?"

Babi crossed back over to the other side of the street. Step followed her. He rose up off the seat of the motorcycle as it bumped down off the sidewalk. He reached out with one hand and grabbed her sweatshirt. "Come on, get on."

She tried to walk past him but he yanked her close to him. He looked into those pale blue eyes, clear and deep, as they stared at him. He carefully released her, and then he smiled gently. "Come on. Let me take you home. Otherwise you'll get in a fight with half the city before the night is through."

In silence, without a word about where she lived, she quickly grabbed her shopping bag from where it had fallen and climbed up behind him. The motorcycle took off, lunging forward. Babi shot backward. Instinctively, she threw her arms around him. Her hands wound up, unintentionally, under his jacket, which had puffed up in the blast of wind. His body was warm in the cool of the night. Babi felt clearly delineated muscles slip beneath her fingers, shifting with every slight movement he made. The wind ran over her cheeks; her wet hair fluttered in the air.

The motorcycle veered to one side, and she clung tighter to him and closed her eyes. Her heart started pounding harder. She wondered if it was merely fear.

She heard the sound of other cars. Now they were on a larger street, it wasn't as cold, and she turned her face and laid her cheek on his back, still without looking, allowing herself to be lulled as the bike rose and fell, at the powerful sound she could feel roaring beneath her.

They were racing faster and faster, overtaking cars, leaning right and then left, whizzing between the vehicles, downshifting again to climb hills, higher and higher, a climb and then nothing. Absolute silence.

Babi opened her eyes and recognized the shops, closed now all around her, the same ones she'd seen every day for the past six years, ever since her family had first moved there. She got off the motorcycle.

Step heaved a deep sigh. "Well, that's a relief. You were crushing me to death!"

"Sorry, I was afraid. I've never ridden behind anyone on a motorcycle."

"There's always a first time for everything." Then he put the bike into first gear and, with a mocking "arrivederci," roared away into the night.

~

That night, a great many people slept poorly, some because they were at the hospital emergency room, others because of their nightmares. Among the latter was none other than Chicco Brandelli. He was going to have to face up to his father, exactly as Roberta had been forced to do that same evening with her parents. Babi was in bed, exhausted from the evening. She decided that the blame for everything belonged to that half-wit, that uncouth oaf, that wild animal, that filthy beast, that violent roughneck, that rude bumpkin, that arrogant, smirking idiot. Then, when she stopped to think it over more carefully, she realized that she didn't even know his name.

Chapter 3

Step poured himself a beer and switched on the TV set. He turned it to channel 13. On Videomusic, an Aerosmith video, "Love in an Elevator," was playing. Steven Tyler was getting a very warm welcome by an insanely hot babe. Tyler, with a voice ten times better than Mick Jagger's, was showing the proper appreciation for the young woman.

Step thought about his father, sitting right across from him. Who could say if the old man appreciated her too?

His father picked up the remote control lying on the table and switched off the television. "We haven't laid eyes on you for the past three weeks, and first thing you do is turn on the TV. Let's talk, all right?"

Step took a drink of his beer. "Sure, why not? Let's talk. What do you want to talk about?"

"I'd like to know what you've decided to do."

"I don't know."

"What do you mean, you don't know?"

"I mean that I still don't know."

The housekeeper came in with the pasta. She set the serving bowl down at the center of the table.

Step looked at the TV, switched off and silent now. He

wondered if Steven Tyler had taken his signature backflip at the end of the video. Forty years old and look at the shape the guy was still in. An incredible physique. A force of nature. Step was going to be in even better shape than that when he was forty.

He looked at his father. Step tried to imagine him doing a backflip just a few years ago. Impossible.

His father passed him the serving bowl of pasta. It was seasoned with bread crumbs and anchovies. That was the kind of pasta he loved best, the kind his mother always made him. It didn't have a special name. Just spaghetti with bread crumbs, period. Even if it had anchovies too.

Step served himself. He remembered all the times he'd eaten at that same table, in that dining room, with his brother Paolo and his mother too. Usually extra sauce or seasonings were brought to the table in a small porcelain bowl. Paolo and his father never wanted extra, so Step always ate it. His mother would flash him a smile and pour the rest of the bowlful onto his pasta.

He wondered if his father had made his favorite pasta intentionally. He decided not to bring it up. That day, the porcelain bowl wasn't on the table. In fact, lots of other things weren't there anymore either.

His father politely wiped his lips with his napkin. "How'd dinner turn out?"

"It was good. Thanks, Papà. It turned out great."

And it hadn't been bad, truth be told.

"The only thing is, can I have another beer?"

His father called the housekeeper. He waited for Step to take a drink before resuming the conversation.

"Not trying to be a pest here, but why don't you enroll at the university?"

"I don't know. I'm giving that some thought. And anyway, I'd have to decide what major."

"You could study law, or business, like your brother. Once you've finished school, I could help you find a job."

Step imagined himself dressed like his brother, in his office, with all those file folders. "I don't know. It doesn't appeal to me."

"Why would you say such a thing? You were good at school. You shouldn't have any difficulty with it. Your score at the final high school exam was a forty-two."

Step drank another swig of beer. His grades would have been even better if it hadn't been for all that craziness. After what happened, he'd never opened a book again.

"Papà, that's not the problem. Maybe after this summer, but right now, I just don't want to think about it."

"What do you feel like doing now, huh? You're always out starting trouble. You're constantly on the street, and you get home at all hours. Paolo tells me about it."

"What the hell does Paolo know about it? What did he say?"

"No, maybe he doesn't know anything, but I do. Maybe it would have been better if you'd done a year of military service. At least you could have gotten your head on straight."

"Yes, that's the one thing I needed, a year in the army."

"Well, if I managed to get you an exemption just so you could hang out on the street and get in brawls, then you'd have been better off in uniform."

"Who told you I'm getting in brawls? Come on, Papà. You're obsessed!"

"No, I'm scared. Do you remember what the lawyer said after the trial? 'Your son needs to be careful. From this day on, any police complaint, any trouble of any kind, the judge's decision automatically goes into effect.' "

"Of course I remember. You must have pounded it into my head at least twenty times. By the way, have you seen that lawyer since?"

"I saw him just the other week. I paid him the last installment on his fee."

He said it grudgingly and emphatically, as if to point out how expensive it had been. When it came to these things, he was exactly the same as Paolo. They were always counting money down to the last penny. Step decided to ignore it. "Was he still wearing that blindingly ugly tie?"

"No, he's managed to get himself another one that's even uglier." His father smiled. That's how badly he wanted to cajole Step along.

"Oh, come on, that hardly seems possible. With all the money we've given him." Step corrected himself. "Sorry, Papà, with all the money *you've* given him, he might be able to buy some decent ties."

"As far as that goes, he could revamp his entire wardrobe."

The housekeeper cleared away their dishes and returned with the main course. It was a steak, done rare. Luckily, that didn't trigger any memories.

Step looked at his father. There he sat, bent over his plate, slicing the meat. Untroubled. A long time ago, that terrible day, he'd been pacing in that same room.

~

"What do you mean, just because! Because you felt like it? Because in that case, I have a violent hooligan for a son, a guy who doesn't think. You ruined that young man. Do you understand what you did? You could have killed him. Or don't you even understand that?"

Step was sitting there, looking at the floor, saying nothing.

The lawyer broke in. "Signor Mancini, at this point, what's done is done. There's no point shouting at the boy. I believe that there are reasons for it, even if they're not obvious."

"All right, counselor. You tell me what we need to do now."

"In order to construct a line of defense, in order to have an argument when we get to court, we need to find out what those reasons are."

Step looked up. What was this guy saying? What did he know?

The lawyer looked at Step with an understanding expression. Then he leaned toward him. "Stefano, there must have been something behind this. Some trouble in the past. An argument. Something this young man said, something that made you...In other words, what triggered that outburst of rage?"

Step looked at the lawyer. He was wearing a horrible tie, adorned with gray diamonds against a shiny background. Then he turned to look at his mother. There she sat, in a corner of the living room. Elegant as ever. She was calmly smoking a cigarette. Step looked down again.

The lawyer continued to look at him, remaining silent for a moment. Then he turned to look at Step's mother and smiled at her in a diplomatic manner. "Signora, have you ever heard that your son had any contact with this young man? Had they ever had any disagreements?"

His mother remained silent for a few seconds and then replied in a firm, confident voice, "No, counselor. I don't think so. I didn't even know they knew each other."

"Signora, Stefano is going to have to go to court. He's been reported to the police. There's going to be a judge, a trial, and a verdict. With the injury that young man suffered, it's going to be serious. If we have nothing to offer in court, no evidence—I mean anything would do, the faintest shadow of a justification—then your son is going to be in real trouble. Very serious trouble."

Step sat there, head hanging low. He looked down at his denim-clad knees. Then he shut his eyes. *Oh God, Mamma, why don't you say something? Why don't you help me? I love you so much. I'm begging you, don't leave me.*

"I'm sorry, counselor. I don't have anything to tell you. I don't know anything."

At his mother's words, Step felt a stab of pain in his heart.

"Do you think that, if I had anything to say, if there was anything I could do for my son, I wouldn't do it? Now, excuse me, I need to go."

Step's mother got to her feet. The lawyer watched as she left the room. Then he made one last appeal to Step. "Stefano, are you sure you don't have anything to tell us?"

Step didn't even reply. Without so much as a glance at him, Step went over to the window. He looked out at that top floor, right across the way. He thought about his mother. And at that moment, he hated her, just as he'd loved her so much in the past.

Then he shut his eyes. A tear rolled down his cheek. He couldn't seem to choke it back, and he suffered like he'd never suffered before, on account of his mother, on account of what she hadn't done that day, on account of what she had done.

Chapter 4

There were lots of young people lining the sides of the broad road with the steep uphill curve on the Via Olimpica in Rome. Young men whose hair looked like it had been dyed blond, all strikingly similar in appearance with American T-shirts and baseball caps and tan, muscular physiques, were pretending to be genuine surfers and health nuts as they struck statuesque poses and handed each other beers.

A short distance farther on, next to a convertible VW Beetle, another small group, much less ambitious in their beliefs, were hunched over, busily rolling a joint. A guy with long hair and a happily dazed look on his face had just burned his hand with a lighter. A young woman with a premature smile plastered on her face was rolling up a small piece of cardboard that featured a winking black bird. Precut joint filters that only a club like Le Cornacchie—literally "The Crows"—would hand out to its customers, encouraging them, as if there had been any need, to get high.

There they were, lining the road and watching the racers risking certain death on their motorcycles. Always them—only them—inept spectators in life as well.

Farther along, a few gentlemen out in search of a thrilling evening were clustered around a Jaguar. Near them, another couple of friends were watching an absurd procession in amusement. Scooters popping wheelies, motorcycles roaring past at blinding speed, and screeching brakes, guttural exclamations. Young men riding past, standing on their foot pegs, craning their necks to see if there was anyone they knew, and others waving to friends. Some of the luckier ones were focusing on a new girlfriend.

Babi rode up the gentle slope with her little souped-up Vespa. When she got there, she was speechless. The panorama that stretched out before her was incredible. All kinds of different horns were honking, some deep, others shrill, in a deranged symphony. Roaring engines called out to each other in corresponding dull rumbles. Headlights glared, colored in different hues by indelible felt-tip pens, navy blue, yellow, or red, contrary to the rules of the road and, for that reason, even nicer to look at, lighting up the road as if it were one huge discotheque.

She proceeded slowly, descending the slope with her engine revving gently. There were a few Nissan four-wheel-drive jeeps with their doors wide open, blaring music toward the sky. Girls crammed into jeans that were too tight danced sensually, the owners of that small patch of space. Bad boys, young but utterly convincing, were smoking cigarettes, like models in a commercial, except that nobody was paying them to be there.

Babi continued rolling along. Every yard of forward progress was greeted by a different piece of music. Different cars, different tastes of their various owners. Rock music by the German band the Scorpions and, directly after it, the latest piece by Phil Collins. From a bright yellow Golden Eagle with a ragtop, there was no mistaking the voice of Madonna.

In front of that car, a young woman all in black, with a skimpy top and a stretch skirt very similar to the attire of that singer, was hanging off her boyfriend's neck. The young man smiled at her. The young woman smiled back. She craned her neck in search of a kiss. He leaned down, complying with her request. He touched her short, soft, blond hair with a slight permanent designed to make her more closely resemble the famous singer. Their tongues started up in a frenzied byplay, taking turns burrowing into the other's mouth.

Babi looked ahead on her left, where the fence surrounding the villa had been ripped open. There was a group of guys. They were on a slight rise. Some of them were seated while others stood around talking.

There, in that small open space, was one of those stands in a trailer that sold cold drinks and hot sandwiches. It was doing a booming business. Babi continued in that direction. Far away in the distance, motorcycles arrived, competitors and rubberneckers for that strange event. Babi looked around, distracted. She bumped into a guy with a buzz cut, wearing a black leather jacket and a single earring in his right ear, who seemed to be in a tremendous hurry.

"Watch where you're going, okay?"

Babi apologized. At a certain point, she saw Gloria, the Accados' daughter. There she was, sitting on the ground, on a jean jacket. Nearby was Dario, her boyfriend.

Babi walked over to them. "Ciao, Gloria."

The young woman turned to look at her. "Ciao, how are you doing?"

"Fine, thanks."

"Have you met Dario?" Gloria asked.

"Yes, we've seen each other around."

They traded smiles, trying to remember where and when.

"Listen, I'm so sorry about what happened to your father," Babi said.

"Oh, really? Well, I don't give a damn. Serves him right. Maybe getting beat up will teach him to mind his own business, for once. He's always meddling. He always wants to have his say."

Dario lit a cigarette. "I agree. In fact, why don't you give Step my thanks? Although if I was the one who'd headbutted him, it would have been a bad situation for me." Dario burst out laughing.

Gloria took a drag and then glanced at Babi with a smile. "So, what, are you dating Step?"

"Me? What, are you crazy? I've got to go, take care. I need to find Pallina."

Babi kept on walking. Finally, she saw one of Step's friends. He was sitting on a powerful motorcycle, chatting cheerfully with a young woman whom he held tightly between his legs. The young woman was wearing a navy-blue baseball cap with a visor and the NY logo in front. Her black hair, tied in a ponytail, stuck out the back of the cap, through the space above the strap. She was wearing a jacket with patent leather white sleeves, like the typical American cheerleader. Her Camomilla double belt, a pair of dark blue leggings, and a pair of Superga shoes in the same shade made her look a bit more Italian.

That lunatic who kept laughing and twisting her head around to kiss him every so often was her best friend Pallina! She'd finally found her. Babi walked over to her.

Pallina saw her coming. "Hey, ciao, what a surprise!" She ran straight over and threw her arms around her. "I'm so happy that you came."

"Not me. In fact, I can't wait to get out of here!"

"Then what are you doing here? Didn't you say that only idiots go to the races?"

"In fact, you're definitely an idiot. I came to tell you that your mother called my house to check up on you."

"No! What did you tell her?"

"That you were asleep and couldn't come to the phone," Babi said.

"And she believed you?"

"Yes."

Pallina whistled. "That's lucky!"

"Yes, but she said that tomorrow morning she's going to come by and pick you up early because you're going to have to get some blood work done, so you'll be missing our first class."

Pallina leaped for joy. "Yahooo!" Her enthusiasm soon waned, however, the minute she remembered their weekly schedule. "Couldn't she have made it Friday, when I have Italian?"

"Well, whatever, she's coming by to pick you up at seven so make sure you get back early, okay?"

Pallina locked arms with Babi and dragged her over and introduced her to Pollo.

"What time are you guys going to be done here?" Babi asked.

Pollo smiled at Babi, who greeted him with some reserve.

"Early, at the very latest, two o'clock, and this will all be done. Then we can go get a nice hot pizza, right?" Pollo asked.

Pallina looked at her girlfriend eagerly. "Come on, don't worry. Won't you come get a pizza with us?"

"Pizza? No, I'm tired, and I want to go home," Babi said.

"Don't be such a pain in the neck!" Pallina said.

Pollo smiled and lit a cigarette. "Come on, Step will be there too. He'll be happy to see you."

"Yes, but I'm going home. Pallina, try to get in early. I don't want to get in trouble with your mother on your account."

Babi looked at Pallina, shook her head, and then turned away. She noticed a plaque nearby on the ground, right on the edge of the road. In the center, there was a photograph of a young man, and next to that picture was a circle, half in black and half in white, with two dots of the opposite color in the two different halves. The duality of life. That same life the young man no longer possessed.

"How am I supposed to like a place like this? Bouquets everywhere to commemorate where young people were killed in crashes, for no good reason, for no real benefit. They just died for fun." Babi realized that the flowers were the reason they called this the Greenhouse.

She walked over to the plaque and read the words that someone had etched into the wood.

> HE WAS STRONG AND HE WAS FAST, BUT THE LORD ALMIGHTY WASN'T KIND TO HIM. HE WOULDN'T LET HIM HAVE A REMATCH.
>
> —HIS FRIENDS

"Nice friends. And they think they're poets! I'd rather be all alone in life than have a bunch of friends who help me to kill myself."

Babi turned on her heel and started to leave. But a hand stopped her.

"Why is it that you always seem to be picking fights with everyone?"

It was Step. Standing motionless, facing her with his brazen smile, and his motorcycle nearby. "Is it really possible that you can't manage to get along with anyone? You really have a difficult personality, you know that?"

"It just so happens that I get along with everyone. I've never had occasion to argue or fight in my life, but that may be because I've always associated with a certain level of person. And lately, it turns out, I've started mixing with a lower quality of individual, and I'd put the blame on someone in particular..."

She gave Pallina an allusive glance, causing her friend to roll her eyes and heave a sigh of annoyance. "I knew it. No matter how you spin the dice, it always turns out to be my fault."

"Well, I mean, didn't I have to come down here to warn you?" Babi asked.

"Wait, didn't you come to see me?" Step turned to face her again. "I was sure that you'd come to watch me race." He leaned forward, coming in dangerously close with his face, almost brushing hers.

Babi darted around him. "Why, I didn't even know you were here." She blushed.

"You knew, oh, you knew. You just turned red as a tomato. You see, you shouldn't tell lies. You're no good at it. Tell the truth. You couldn't resist, and you came running to watch me race, didn't you?"

Babi remained silent. She inwardly cursed that damned blush and her heart that, disobediently, continued to pound. Step slowly came closer. His face was once again dangerously close to Babi's.

He smiled at her. "I don't understand why you get so worried. Are you afraid to admit it?"

"Me, afraid? Afraid of who? Of you? You don't scare me. You just make me laugh. You want to know something? Earlier this evening, I reported you."

This time, it was she who pushed her face close to Step's. "You understand? I said that you were the one who hurt Signor Accado. The one you headbutted, just to make it clear who I'm talking about. I told them your name. Just think how scared of you I must be."

Pollo got off his motorcycle and strode fast and menacingly toward Babi. "You damned..."

Step put out a hand. "Calm down, Pollo, calm down."

"What do you mean, calm down, Step? She's ruined you! After everything that's happened, if you have another report on you, you'll have to face the music for everything else. You'll go straight behind bars, direct to prison."

Babi was stunned. She didn't know that part of the story.

Step reassured his friend. "Don't worry, Pollo. That won't happen. I won't wind up in prison. Worst case, I'll have to go to court. But it'll all end there. Nothing bad's going to happen."

Then he turned to look at Babi. "What counts is what actually gets said at the trial, when you're called to testify against me. When that day comes, you won't say my name.

I'm sure of that. You'll say it wasn't me. That I had nothing to do with it."

Babi glared at him with a look of defiance. "Oh, really? Are you so sure of that?"

"Positive."

"Are you trying to scare me?"

"Absolutely not. When that day comes, when we both go to court, you'll be so crazy about me that you'll be willing to do anything, anything at all, to save me."

Babi remained silent for a moment and then burst out laughing. "You're the one who's crazy, if you've talked yourself into believing that nonsense. When the day comes, I'll say your name. Loud and clear. I swear it."

Step smiled at her confidently. "I wouldn't swear if I were you."

There was a long, determined whistle. Everyone turned around. At the center of the road was Siga, a short man, about thirty-five. He wore a black leather jacket. He was respected by one and all, in part because word was that, under that jacket, he was packing a gat.

He raised his arms. This was the signal. The first race, the one with the chamomiles.

Step turned to look at Babi. "Do you want to ride behind me?"

"So you see, it's really true. You're crazy."

"No, the truth is something quite different. The fact is, you're afraid," Step said.

"I'm not afraid!"

"Then why don't you ask Pallina to lend you her belt?"

"I'm opposed to these idiotic races on principle."

Step moved closer to Babi. "Too bad, you would have

enjoyed yourself. Sometimes fear is a nasty enemy. It keeps you from enjoying the best moments in life. It's like a curse, if you can't figure out how to beat it."

A dark blue Boxer stopped right in front of them. It was Maddalena. She lifted her jacket. "Do you want to take me, Step?" She showed off her double Camomilla belt.

She greeted Pallina with a smile, and then she saw Babi. The two girls exchanged icy glares. Their eyes spoke volumes, saying much more than their sealed lips.

Babi pulled Pallina's jacket open. "Come on, give me this belt."

"What? Wait, are you kidding?"

"No, come on, give it to me. If it's so darned exciting to be a chamomile, then I want to try it." She pulled it out through the belt loops and put it on. She wrapped it around twice and tightened it to her waist.

Step smiled at her. *He does have a perfect smile*, thought Babi, *but I hate him when he's like this*. "I'm not scared."

"Good, so much the better. You'll see. It'll be fun, so get on."

Babi had some difficulties getting onto the motorcycle facing backward, so Step helped her. Babi undid the belt, letting Step take it and wrap it around his waist. Then he handed the other end back to her. Babi fastened the belt, making sure it wasn't too tight on her.

Maddalena smiled at her. "You'll see, you'll have the time of your life. Step can really pull wheelies like nobody's business. Of course, that's if the chamomile riding on back isn't afraid, because if she moves, she'll knock him over."

But Babi didn't have time to answer her. Step twisted the

gas and shot forward. She barely had a chance to glimpse Pallina sitting on the low wall, waving goodbye.

The motorcycle screeched to a halt. The inertia knocked Babi back, slamming her against Step's shoulders. It was impossible to hold on tight with her legs facing the wrong way.

"It's going to be a walk in the park." His deep, warm voice was supposed to reassure her, or at least that's how he thought it should work.

In fact, it had entirely the opposite effect. *Omigod*, Babi thought to herself, *those are the famous last words where practically anything can happen. This must be a nightmare. I've never worn a Camomilla belt in my life, not even when it was in fashion.*

She looked at the people around her. Everyone was shouting. There was a maddening swirl of confusion. *What on earth am I doing in a place like this?* She felt like crying.

Then Step accelerated out to the middle of the road, ready for the race. He raised his right arm.

Suddenly, four other motorcycles appeared out of nowhere and merged toward the center of the road. All of them had a young woman sitting on back, facing backward.

The chamomiles were looking around them. A crowd of young men and women were watching them in amusement. Some of the girls who recognized them pointed at them and shouted their names. Others waved at them, trying to attract their attention.

But the chamomiles made no response. They all were holding their arms back behind them, clutching the drivers for fear of being shaken loose when the bikes started. Two chamomiles who knew each other nodded smiles and greetings, giddy and excited.

Siga collected the bets. The older gentlemen standing around the Jaguar bet more than everyone else. One of them bet on Step. The other one bet on the rider closer to him, on the colorful motorcycle. Siga wrapped up all the cash and stuck it into the front pocket of his jacket. Then he raised his right arm and put his whistle in his mouth. There was a moment of silence.

The young men on the motorcycles were all leaning forward, ready for the start. Their motorcycles roared. Four left feet pushed the gearshifts down. With a single noise, four bikes shifted into first. They were ready.

Siga dropped his arm and blew the whistle. The audience screamed. It was basically the roar of one single voice.

The motorcycles all shot ahead, almost immediately rearing up in wheelies, fast and loud. Babi immediately tightened her grip on Step in sheer terror as all the chamomiles held on to their men. Their faces turned down toward the asphalt, they watched as the road streamed past beneath them, hard and terrifying. Holding their breath, their hearts pounding at two thousand rpms, their stomachs in their mouths. Yanked backward at sixty, seventy-five, eighty-five miles an hour.

The first bike on the left broke its wheelie. The front wheel slammed down onto the surface, hitting loudly, crushing its shock absorbers toward the ground. The fork trembled, but nothing happened.

The bike closest to Step accelerated too hard. The motorcycle reared up, and the young woman, sensing it was practically vertical, screamed. The young man, frightened now, maybe because he was dating her, let up on the gas and hit the brakes. That huge beast of a Bol d'Or motorcycle, all seven hundred pounds of it, glided smoothly as if on command. It lowered its nose, touching down, like a small wingless airplane.

Step continued the race, leading the last competitor, playing expertly with brake and gas. His motorcycle, lunging forward, seemed motionless, as if held up by a transparent thread in the dark of night. It just flew along like that path, hanging from the stars.

As Babi watched, the white stripes of the road were almost invisible as they blurred together. She tried to shout as the motorcycle roared and the wind tossed her hair, but nothing came out of her mouth. She looked around. By now, the people were just a distant knot of figures, colorful, faintly blurry. All around, there was only the wind rushing and the noise of the other motorcycles.

Step was winning. So she was winning. Babi was stunned.

Step passed the finish line to the shouts and screams of joy from his friends looking on and the happiness of the man who had bet on him.

Pollo embraced Pallina, lifting her off the ground and swinging her through the air. Then, still holding her up, he kissed her. He held her up like that for a few seconds while her feet dangled, just brushing the ground, and her jacket, creasing here and there, climbed up.

When Pallina got back to solid ground, she tugged and patted herself all over and adjusted her hat. After that, she turned, slightly embarrassed, toward Babi. "It was an amazing race, wasn't it?"

Babi said nothing. Step, still bursting with excitement at his victory, had screeched to a halt in front of the group.

Dario, Schello, and a few other friends rushed down to wish him well and congratulate him.

A brotherly hand, mingled indistinctly in the midst of the group, reached out to offer him a still-cold beer. Step grabbed at it and took a long drag. "You were great. You never moved once. You were a perfect chamomile."

Babi freed herself from the grip of the Camomilla belt but Step tried to stop her. "Hold on, where are you going? Stay here with me..."

"I need air," Babi said as she got off the motorcycle. Her first few steps were hesitant. She was shaking so much in fear that she could hardly stand up. She melted into the crowd. She didn't know anyone.

At a certain point, she heard another whistle. Longer, this time. What was that? Was another race starting? Everyone started running in all directions. People were banging against her. Motorcycles and scooters went hurtling past.

She heard the wail of sirens. Not far away, a line of cars appeared. Blue emergency lights were flashing on their roofs. The police. That's the one thing that was missing.

She needed to find her Vespa. All around her, young people were running. Someone started screaming, others were smashing into each other recklessly. One young woman on a scooter toppled over just a few yards away. Babi started running. More city police cars braked to a halt all around.

There it was. She saw her Vespa, parked in front of her, just a few yards away. She'd been saved. Suddenly, someone grabbed her by the hair. It was a city traffic cop.

Babi shouted in pain when suddenly, the traffic cop

released her. A boot to his belly had folded him in two, loosening his grip on her hair. It was Step.

The cop tried to fight back. Step gave him a violent shove that knocked him to the ground. Then Step helped Babi to her feet, hoisted her onto the motorcycle behind him, and took off at top speed.

The traffic cop recovered, climbed into a car nearby with a fellow cop behind the wheel, and they took off in hot pursuit. Step wove easily through the people and motorcycles that the city traffic cops had pulled over. He passed a number of photographers who had been given advance notice of the roundup and were busy snapping pictures.

Step popped a wheelie and accelerated. He went by another policeman, this one with a red stop paddle, waving for him to pull over. All around them, photographers' flashbulbs were going off.

Step turned off the lights and bent low over the handlebars. The city traffic squad car with the cop who'd been kicked in the gut veered around the group and, siren wailing, was right behind them. Step shifted and leaned into the curve, racing toward Piazza Irnerio.

Babi held tight to him. She was even more terrified than before. This was worse than being a chamomile. The squad car fishtailed out of control as it tore into the curve. It recovered and started gaining on Step.

When Step reached the top of the slope, he shot the wrong way down a one-way street and veered off to the left, down Via del Casaletto. In the left side mirror, a few seconds later, the flashing blue light appeared again. They were still after him.

"Cover the license plate with your foot."

"What?"

"Cover the last digit of the license plate with your foot."

Babi extended her right leg backward, doing her best to cover the license plate. She slipped twice. "I can't do it."

"Really? Are you fucking with me?"

"It just so happens that I've never tried to run from the police on a motorcycle before. And if I'd had any say in the matter, I'd certainly have avoided the privilege today."

"Maybe you'd have preferred to have me leave you in the hands of that cop who wanted your scalp?"

Step downshifted and made a right turn. The rear wheel slid slightly, screeching across the asphalt.

Babi held tighter to him and shrieked, "Put on the brakes!"

"Are you joking? If those guys catch us, they'll confiscate my motorcycle."

The squad car veered into the narrow street, fishtailing. Step flew down the steep street at 185 kilometers per hour. He could hear the siren echoing in the distance. They were gaining on him.

"Put on the brakes, I'm begging you. I can already imagine what I'm going to read in the papers tomorrow. 'Young Woman Dies in High-Speed Chase with City Traffic Cops.' "

"But if you're dead, how are you going to read the newspaper?"

"Step, slow down! I'm scared! Those guys might start shooting at us."

Step downshifted again and suddenly swerved left. They emerged onto a semideserted country road. There were a few villas with a high wall and a palisade. They had only a few seconds to spare. Step screeched to a halt.

"Hurry up, get off. Wait for me here and don't move. I'll come back and get you the minute I manage to shake them off..."

Babi hopped off the motorcycle in a flash, and Step took off at top speed. Babi flattened herself against the wall near the villa's front gate. And just in the nick of time. The squad car appeared at that exact moment. It went screeching past the villa and tore off in furious pursuit of the motorcycle.

Babi clapped both hands over her ears and shut her eyes to keep out the piercing sound of that siren. The car vanished into the distance, homing in on that tiny red taillight. That was Step's motorcycle, which, outdistancing all pursuit, was racing along through the dark night.

Chapter 5

Pollo stopped his motorcycle in front of Babi's apartment building. Pallina got off and went over to the doorman. "Excuse me, but has Babi come home yet?"

Fiore, who'd been half-asleep, had a hard time recognizing her at first. "Ah, ciao, Pallina. No. I saw her go out on her Vespa, but she hasn't come back yet."

Pallina went back to Pollo. "Nothing doing."

"Don't worry, if she's with Step, she's fine. You'll see, she'll be home soon. Do you want me to stay with you and keep you company?"

"No, I'll go up. Maybe she's in trouble, and she might try calling home. It'll be better if there's someone there to answer the phone."

Pollo started his motorcycle. "The first one who gets any news can call the other."

Pallina kissed him and hurried off. She ducked under the gate-arm and headed up the ramp to the apartment building. When she was halfway there, she turned around. Pollo waved to her. Pallina blew him a kiss and then turned left, up the steps. Pollo put his bike in first gear and drove away.

Pallina lifted the doormat. The keys were there, as promised. It took her a little while to pick out the one for the front door. She climbed up to the second floor and slowly opened the door. A voice came down the hallway. She recognized it. It was Daniela's. She was talking on the telephone.

"Dani, where are your folks?"

"Pallina, what are you doing here?"

"Answer my question. Where are they?"

"They're out."

"Good! Get off that call, and quick. You need to leave the line free."

"But I'm talking to Marcello. And where's Babi? She came looking for you."

"That's why I need you to get off the phone. Babi might call. The last time I saw her, she was on the back of Step's motorcycle being chased by city traffic cops."

"No!"

"Yes!"

"My sister is just too cool."

~

The dust had slowly settled. Low, gray clouds were floating up above in the moonless sky. Everything around her was silent. Not a single light. Except for a small spotlight in the distance, fastened high on the wall of a house.

Babi stepped away from the wall and crossed the road. It was hard to walk on that uneven old cobblestone surface. She took a few steps.

From a distance came the sounds of the countryside. She caught a strong whiff of manure scattered on the fields. A faint breeze moved the branches of the trees. She felt alone and lost.

She was afraid. If for no other reason than that she really didn't want to be forced to spend the night in this place.

Who could say where Step was. Had he eluded their pursuit?

Babi headed toward the little spotlight. She was walking slowly along the wall, with her hand flat on the fence, careful where she put her feet, among tufts of tall wild grass. Could there be snakes here? An old memory from her science textbook reassured her. Snakes aren't out at night.

But rats are. There must be plenty of them around there. And rats bite. Urban legends. She remembered someone, a friend of a friend, who'd been bitten by a rat. He'd died very quickly. Lepto-something. Terrible. She veered away from the tufts of grass, dangerous hiding places for death-dealing rats. Darn that Pallina.

Babi walked to the center of the road, dragging her feet, her hands out in front of her. Suddenly she heard a sound off to her left. Babi stopped. Silence.

Then a branch snapped. Something came moving fast toward her, running, panting, through the shrubbery. Babi was terrified. Motionless, paralyzed in the middle of that dark road.

Out of the dark patch of vegetation in front of her came a big dog with a black coat, snarling. Babi saw its silhouette come barking toward her, moving at top speed through the night. Its baying bark echoed ominously over the solitary hills.

Babi turned and started to run. She slipped and nearly fell on the cobblestones. She recovered, stumbling through the darkness, hurrying forward, unable to see where she was going.

The dog was right behind her. It was galloping menacingly, gaining ground. Snarling and barking ferociously. Babi reached the palisade. She found a gap, up high. She stuck in her hand, then the other hand, and finally found a foothold. Right foot, left foot, and up and over. Leaping into the void, barely eluding the sharp white fangs behind her.

The dog slammed against the fence. It bounced off with a dull, hollow thud. It started running back and forth, barking, searching in vain for an opening, a space through which to reach his prey.

Babi got back up. She'd hit her hands and knees falling face forward in the dark. She'd landed in something warm and soft. It was mud. It slid slowly down her jacket, down her jeans. Down her aching hands. She tried to move. Her legs sank into the mud up to the knee. She almost tripped and fell. She regained her balance. She stood still. The dog was running far away along the palisade. *Let's just hope there's not a way through.* She could hear it barking, even more ferocious than before because it couldn't get to her. Well, better this mud than a dog bite.

Then, all at once, an acrid odor, with a hint of sweetness, swept over her. She put her filthy hand up to her face. She sniffed at it. For a moment the countryside seemed to envelop her and make her its property. A shudder ran down her spine. Manure! That turned out not to be such a great trade after all.

Pallina stepped out of the front door, letting it shut gently without clicking locked. Then she took the keys out of her pocket, bent over, lifted the doormat, and put them back in the agreed-upon spot.

Babi hadn't phoned yet. But at least this way she wouldn't have to ring to get in.

Just then, Pallina heard the sound of a car. From the curve in the courtyard, a Mercedes 200 appeared. She recognized it. It was the same car that often brought Babi to school in the morning. Her parents.

Pallina let the doormat drop and ran toward the front door. She let it slam behind her. She took the stairs at a run, went inside, and shut the door behind her.

"Quick, Dani, your folks are home."

Daniela was standing in front of the refrigerator in the throes of the usual terrible hunger that visited her at two in the morning. For that one time, she'd have to go to bed hungry. She slammed the refrigerator door. She ran to her room and shut herself in.

Pallina rushed into Babi's bedroom. She took off her shoes and hid them behind the curtain near the window. Then she lowered the shutter and slipped into bed, fully dressed. Her heart was pounding. She lay still and listened. She heard the noise of the roller gate in the garage being shut. It was a matter of minutes now.

Then, in the dim light of the bedroom, she saw the school uniform draped over the chair. Babi had prepared her attire for the following day before leaving. She'd expected to be home early. What a good girl she was, poor Babi.

But this time, Babi was definitely in deep shit—literally.

Chapter 6

Step raced down Via Gregorio VII at top speed. He shot past the Samoto dealership, the same place he'd bought his Honda. He shot past Gregory's Jazz Club. The different sound of his tires gave him some information. He'd left the asphalt and was now running on cobblestones.

He downshifted without touching his brakes. He quickly checked the traffic light. He looked right and then left. He shot into the tunnel.

Right after him came the city traffic cops' squad car. The siren howled louder as it echoed off the tiles, a prisoner of the rounded walls. The light blue flashing lights spread, alternating, across those horrible yellow walls.

Step came hurtling out of the tunnel, practically leaping. He downshifted and hit the brakes before veering off to the right, along the Lungotevere riverfront. He accelerated and slalomed past two or three cars. Then he put the bike into third gear, accelerating and gaining speed.

If Step could make it to Piazza Trilussa, he'd be safe. In his side mirror he could see the police car getting dangerously close.

Two cars were ahead of him. He upshifted and poured on

the gas. Third gear. The motorcycle lunged forward. He just managed to squeeze between the car doors. One of the two vehicles veered away from the other, frightened. The other just sailed along down the middle of the road. The driver, in a daze, hadn't noticed a thing.

The city traffic cops passed on the far right. Their cars rose, thumping and springy, on the low curb of the sidewalk.

Step saw Piazza Trilussa straight ahead. He shifted again. He veered across the road, from right to left. The dazed driver slammed on the brakes. Step shot straight down the narrow street across from the fountain that joined the two riverfront roads, the two Lungoteveres. He raced between the low marble traffic barriers. The city police were forced to brake, marooned there by the barriers. They couldn't get through.

Step accelerated. He'd made it. The two cops got out of their car. They only had time to glimpse a pair of young lovers and a group of panicked youngsters hopping onto the narrow sidewalk of that side street to let the lunatic on the motorcycle with his headlights off roar past. Step appeared at top speed in their midst and then shot away to the far side of the Lungotevere. He curved to the left. He continued to race along for another short while. Then he looked into his side mirror. Behind him, all was clear. Only a few cars in the distance. The usual traffic at this time of night.

No one was following him anymore. He turned on his headlights. That would be the one thing he needed: to be stopped for riding without his lights on. Then he took a deep breath. He'd done it.

He just prayed that they hadn't managed to read his license plate. But he didn't think so. He'd almost never used his brakes for that exact reason. The brake lights would have lit up the license plate too.

He upshifted again and twisted the throttle. Now he needed to turn around and go pick up Babi. He'd take the long way around. He didn't want to run into that squad car full of city traffic cops again.

After all, Babi could wait. She was safe.

~

Babi's father, Claudio, opened the refrigerator and poured himself a glass of water. Her mother, Raffaella, went down the hall, to the girls' bedrooms. Before going to sleep, she always kissed her daughters good night, in part because it was a habit and in part because it was a good way of checking up to make sure they'd returned home.

That evening, they weren't supposed to have gone out at all. But you never knew. Better to check.

She went into Daniela's room. She walked soundlessly, taking great care not to trip over the edge of the carpet. She put one hand on the nightstand by the bed. She put her other hand against the wall. Then she leaned forward slowly and let her lips brush that cheek. She was asleep.

Raffaella tiptoed out of the room. She softly shut the door. Daniela slowly turned over. She sat up, her weight on one side. *Here comes the good part*, she thought.

Raffaella silently turned the handle and opened Babi's door. Pallina was in the bed. She saw the wedge of light from the hallway that slowly projected itself across the wall, spreading wider. Her heart began to race. *And what am I going to tell them now, if they catch me?*

Pallina lay there on her side, trying not to breathe. She heard a sound of necklaces, pieces of jewelry hitting each other. This had to be Babi's mother. Raffaella went over to the bed, bent slightly forward. Pallina recognized her perfume. It was her all right. She held her breath and then felt the kiss brush her cheek. It was a mother's soft and affectionate kiss. It's true. Mothers are all the same. Worried and kindhearted.

But are their daughters the same to them too? She hoped so. At that moment, the one thing she hoped against hope was to resemble Babi as much as possible. To have her hair, her build. Raffaella tidied the covers, delicately tucking the edge of the sheets up around her. Then she smoothed them lovingly, eliminating even the faintest creases and wrinkles. But suddenly she stopped. Pallina lay there, motionless, waiting. Could Babi's mother have detected something out of place? Had she recognized her? She narrowed her eyes, her ears pricked up, straining to detect every last tiny sound, even the smallest imaginable movement.

She heard a slight creaking. Raffaella had bent over. Now she could sense her warm breath coming closer. But then she heard light footsteps moving away across the wall-to-wall carpeting. The faint light in the hallway disappeared, as if she were taking it with her until the last little click of the door.

Silence. Pallina slowly turned over. The door was shut. At last, she breathed. It was over. She looked down. Why had Babi's mother leaned over? What had she done?

In the dim light of the bedroom, her eyes, accustomed to the darkness, immediately spotted the answer. At the foot of the bed, perfectly lined up, were Babi's slippers. Raffaella had set them in their place, in orderly fashion. Ready to welcome her daughter's feet, still warm from the night's sleep, when morning came around.

Pallina wondered whether her own mother would have done such a thing. No. It wouldn't have occurred to her. On more than one evening, Pallina had lain awake, awaiting her kiss. She had waited in vain. Her mother and her father had come home late. She'd heard them talk, walk past her room, and continue on. Then that click. Their bedroom door shutting. And with that closing door, her own hopes vanishing.

~

Step emerged onto the narrow road. He pulled up to the gate where he'd left Babi, and applied the brakes. A cloud of dust rose behind him. It climbed slowly into the dark sky, spreading as it went. The taillight illuminated the cloud of dust, tingeing it a faint red.

Step looked around. Babi wasn't there. He honked his horn. The sound of the horn spread, echoing across the countryside. He switched off the motorcycle. No answer. He tried calling her name: "Babi."

He called her name over and over again. He turned his headlight so that it illuminated the whole area. Nothing. She'd vanished. He was about to start the motorcycle when suddenly he heard a rustling sound on his right. It came from behind the palisade.

"I'm right here."

Step peered through the dark wooden planks. "Where?"

"Here!" A hand reached through an open space between

one plank and the other. It fluttered up and down, signaling her location.

"Oh, there you are. I figured you'd caught a ride and gone home."

"Sure, I caught a ride all right!" Babi said.

"What are you doing back there?"

Step saw her big blue eyes. They were peering out, just a little above her hand, in the slightly wider space between two other planks. Those eyes were illuminated by the faint moonlight, and they seemed frightened.

"Babi, come out of there."

"I can't. I'm afraid!"

"Afraid of what?"

"There's an enormous dog right back there, and he doesn't have a muzzle."

"Where? I don't see any dog around here," Step said.

"Well, there was one before."

"Well, listen, it's nowhere to be seen now. So either you come out from back there or I'll leave you here all alone."

"Even if the dog isn't here, I still can't come out," Babi said.

"Why not?"

"I'm embarrassed."

"What are you embarrassed about?" Step asked.

"Nothing. I don't want to talk about it."

"What happened? Did you fall and bump your head? Well, anyway, I'm sick and tired of this. I'm going to start my bike and go." Step kick-started his motorcycle.

Babi slapped her hand on the fence. "No, wait."

Step turned the motorcycle back off. "Well?"

"I'll come out now, but you have to promise not to laugh."

Step looked through that strange wooden palisade into those bright blue eyes. Then he put his right hand over his heart. "I swear it."

"You swear it, right?"

"Yes, I just told you so..."

"So, you promised, okay?"

"For sure."

He heard an extended rustling sound behind the palisade. He saw a pair of hands pushing through the gaps, careful to avoid any splinters or chunks of sharp wood. A throttled "Ouch!" told him that those hands hadn't been sufficiently careful though. Step smiled.

Babi's silhouette appeared at the top of the fence. She straddled it, then started down the near side. When she was almost to the ground, she jumped. Step turned the motorcycle's handlebars in her direction. The beam of light caught her in full. Except for her face, Babi was filthy from head to foot.

"What happened to you?"

"I was running away from the dog, so I jumped over the fence and I fell."

"So now you're covered with mud?"

Babi remained silent. "I wish...No, this is manure."

Step burst out laughing. "Oh my God, manure...No, this just can't be." He couldn't stop laughing now.

Babi lost her temper. "You promised not to laugh. You promised."

"Yes, I did, but this is too much. Manure! I can't believe it. You, falling into manure. It's too perfect. It's the best!"

"I knew that I couldn't trust you. Your promises are worthless." Babi stepped closer to the motorcycle.

Step stopped laughing. "Halt! Not an inch closer. What do you think you're doing?"

"What do you mean? I'm getting on."

"Have you lost your mind? You think I'd let you get on my motorcycle in the state you're in?"

"Of course you will. Otherwise, what am I supposed to do, strip naked?"

"Ah, that I couldn't say. But you're not getting on my nice clean motorcycle in the shape you're in. You're filthy, and what's worse, you're covered with manure!"

Step burst out laughing again. "Oh God, I just can't help it..."

Babi looked at him, exhausted now. "Listen, you're joking, right?"

"Absolutely not. If you want, I'll give you my jacket and you can use it to cover yourself. But get that clothing off you. Otherwise, I swear, you're never climbing onto this bike."

Babi heaved a sigh of rage. She was beet red with anger. She walked past him, coming within reach. Step held his nose, overdoing his disgust. "Oh God... that's just intolerable..."

Babi smacked him and walked behind the motorcycle. "Listen, Step. I swear to you that if you turn around while I'm taking my clothes off, I'll jump all over you with every ounce of manure on my body."

Step sat facing front. "Fine. Just tell me when you need me to hand you the jacket."

"Believe me, I'm not kidding around. I'm not like you. I keep the promises I make."

Babi checked one last time to make sure Step wasn't

turning around. Then she took off her sweatshirt. She pulled it off slowly, taking great care not to get any manure on herself. Under her clothes, there was practically no manure on her. She was sorry she hadn't worn a T-shirt.

She looked at Step again. "Don't turn around!"

"I wouldn't dream of it!"

Babi leaned forward. She took off her shoes.

It only took a second but Step was lightning quick. He twisted the left side mirror, tilting it toward Babi so she was perfectly framed.

Babi stood up. She hadn't noticed a thing. She quickly glanced back to check on him. Fine. He hadn't turned around.

In reality, though, Step was watching her, unseen. She was a reflection in his side mirror now. She was wearing a bra of translucent lace and had goose bumps all up and down both arms. Step smiled. "Could you step it up? How much longer will this take?"

"I'm almost done. Just don't you turn around!"

"I told you I wouldn't. Come on, quit dragging this out."

Babi undid her jeans. Then, slowly, doing her best to keep from getting it all over her, she bent forward, lowering her pants to her feet, bare by now on those dusty cold rocks. Step tilted the side mirror downward, following her with his eyes. The jeans descended slowly, revealing her smooth, pale legs in that faint nocturnal light. Step sang "You Can Leave Your Hat On," imitating the voice of Joe Cocker.

"Forget about *Nine and a Half Weeks* . . ."

Babi whipped around. Her eyes, illuminated by the faint red taillight, met Step's amused glance as he smiled mischievously in the side mirror.

"I didn't turn around, did I?"

Babi quickly got rid of her jeans and hopped up behind him on the motorcycle, in her bra and panties.

"You miserable sneak, you're a bastard!" She pounded him with her fists on his shoulders, neck, back, and head.

Step curled forward, doing his best to find whatever shelter he could. "Hey, that's enough! What did I ever do to you? I just peeked a little, but I kept my word... Ouch, keep this up and I won't give you the jacket."

"What? You won't give it to me? I'll go get my jeans and rub them all over your face. You want to test me?"

Babi started tugging on his jacket, pulling on the sleeves.

"All right. All right. Enough's enough," Step said. "Calm down. Come on, stop it. Here, I'll give it to you now."

Step let her pull his jacket off. Then he started the motorcycle.

Babi hit him one last time. "You filthy pig!" Then she put on the jacket, covering herself up as much as she could. The results weren't much to look at. Both her legs were exposed, right up to the edge of her panties.

"Hey, you know that you aren't bad? You just ought to try to wash yourself more often... But you really have a nice ass... I'm not kidding."

She tried to hit him on the head. Step ducked, laughing. He put the bike into first gear and took off. Then he pretended to sniff at the air. "Hey, do you smell this odd odor too?"

"Idiot! Just drive!" Babi yelled.

"It smells like manure..."

Just then, from a bush on the right a short distance ahead, a German shepherd emerged. It came running at them, barking. Step went straight at him with the motorcycle. The dog stood still for a second, blinded by the light. Its red eyes glittered angrily in the night. Its teeth appeared, snarling, sharp, and white.

That fleeting instant's delay was sufficient. Step upshifted. He twisted the throttle and veered the motorcycle wide. The dog took off immediately. It barely missed the motorcycle, leaping sideways, jaws wide open.

Babi screamed. She pulled up her bare legs and grabbed tight to Step's shoulders.

The dog fell just a hair short.

The motorcycle accelerated. First gear. Second, third. Off they went, with the throttle open wide. The bike roared off into the night.

The dog ran after them, snarling furiously. Then it slowly started to lose ground. It went on running for a little while longer. At last, it stopped. It vented its rage by continuing to bark from afar. Then it was slowly swallowed up by a cloud of dust and shadows, vanishing as quickly as it had appeared.

The motorcycle continued its journey through the chilly damp of the green countryside. Babi still had her legs wrapped around Step's waist. Little by little, the motorcycle slowed down.

Step reached up and caressed her right leg. "That was close, wasn't it? It would have meant a sad end to those lovely thighs of yours! So your story about the dog was true after all..."

Babi took his hand off her leg and let it drop to one side. She scooted back on the seat, putting her feet back on the pegs, and zipped up the jacket. "Don't touch me."

Step put his hand back on her leg.

Babi took it off again. "I told you not to touch me with that hand!"

Step smiled and changed hands. He put his left hand on the other leg. Babi took that hand off too.

"I can't even touch you with that hand?"

Babi snapped, "I don't know which is worse, the dog that was chasing me or the pig who's sitting in front of me on this motorcycle!"

Step shook his head and accelerated. Babi zipped up the jacket. How cold it was! What a night! What a mess! Darn that Pallina.

They flew through the night. Step tore along like a lunatic. Babi held on tight, arms wrapped around him and trying to cover herself up as best she could.

At last, they arrived safe and sound at her apartment building. Step stopped in front of the gate arm. Babi turned to look at Fiore. She waved to him. The doorman recognized her and raised the gate arm. The motorcycle raced through as soon as was possible, without waiting for the gate arm to finish rising to the top of its arc. Fiore couldn't resist taking a peek at Babi's fine legs, which were sticking out, chilled and bare, from under the jacket. The things he saw on this job. In his day, no young woman went out wearing a miniskirt like that.

The motorcycle ran the circuit of the courtyard. Babi saw that the garage's roller gate was lowered. Her folks had come home. One less danger. She wondered what she could possibly have said if they'd caught her at that very moment, riding behind Step on his motorcycle. In panties and bra. She preferred not to think about it; she wasn't really that fanciful.

She got off the motorcycle. As she stood up, she tried to cover herself up as much as was possible with the jacket. But it was no good. It barely reached down below the hem of her panties.

"Well, thanks for everything. Listen, I'll toss the jacket out the window."

Step looked at her legs. Babi squatted down. The jacket hung a little lower, but it still wasn't covering up much.

Step smiled.

"Maybe we could see each other again sometime. I see that you have some very interesting topics to discuss."

"I already told you that you're a pig, right?"

"Yes, I seem to remember something of the sort. So, I'll come pick you up tomorrow evening."

"I don't think so. I doubt I could survive another night out like this one."

"Why? Didn't you enjoy yourself?"

"I had a great time! I always let the police chase me for a while, then I hop off the motorcycle while it's still moving in the middle of the godforsaken countryside, I let a rabid dog chase me, and just to polish things off, I take a nose dive into a patch of manure. I wallow in it for a while, and then I come home in just my bra and panties."

"And with my jacket covering you."

"Oh, right... I almost forgot."

"And one thing above all else..."

"What?"

"You did all this with me."

Babi looked at him. What a character. He had a beautiful smile. Too bad about his personality. But she had no complaints about his body. Quite the opposite.

She decided to smile at him. It didn't take much of an effort. "Yes, you're right. Well, good night."

Babi turned to leave but Step took her hand. This time, gently. Babi put up a bit of resistance, but then she let herself go.

Step pulled her toward him, drawing her closer to the motorcycle. He looked at her. Her hair was long and messy, blown back by the night wind. Her skin was white and chilled. Her eyes were blue and intense and kind. She was beautiful.

Step let a hand slide under the jacket. Babi opened her eyes, slightly frightened, deeply moved. She felt his hand rise inside the jacket, along her back, higher and higher. His hand stopped when it reached the hook to her bra. Babi quickly put her hand behind her. She put it on his hand and stopped him.

Step smiled at her. "So it's true that you're not afraid of me. Are you going to report me to the police?"

Babi nodded. "Yes." She practically whispered it.

"Seriously?"

Babi nodded her head.

Step kissed her on the neck, once, twice, three times, delicately. "Do you swear it?"

Babi nodded again and then shut her eyes.

Step continued kissing her. His kisses climbed her face, brushing over her cool cheeks, her chilly ears. A warm, provocative gust of breath gave her a shiver farther down. Step approached the pinkish corner of her lips. Babi sighed tremblingly. Then she opened her mouth, ready to welcome his kiss.

At that moment, Step pulled away. Babi stood there for

an instant like that, mouth open, eyes shut, dreaming. Then she suddenly opened them.

Step was standing in front of her, arms crossed. He was smiling. He shook his head. "Babi, Babi. This isn't right. I'm a pig, a wild animal, a filthy beast, a violent thug. That's what you say, you never tire of repeating it, but then, in the end, you give in... You're willing to let me kiss you. You see the way you are? You're full of contradictions!"

Babi went beet red with rage. "You really are an asshole!" She started pounding him with a hail of punches.

Step did his best to ward off her fists as he laughed. "You know what you reminded me of, earlier? A goldfish I had when I was little. You were just standing there with your mouth open, gasping. Just like the goldfish whenever I changed the water and he fell out into the sink. Ouch, that's enough."

Babi had hit him dead center with her fist.

Step touched his cheek, amused. "You know that's wrong, don't you? Nothing good ever came of violence. You're always telling me that! It's not as if I'm going to kiss you if you beat me. I might, if you promise you're not going to report me to the police..."

"Oh, but I *am* going to report you to the police. And how! You'll see. You'll wind up behind bars, I can swear to that."

"I already told you that you should never swear to anything. You never know what's going to happen in life..."

Babi hurried away. The jacket rode up as she went, revealing an attractive derriere covered by a skimpy pair of light-colored panties. She tried to cover herself as she inserted the wrong key in the front door.

"Hey, I want my jacket back now."

Babi glared at him furiously. She took off the jacket and threw it on the ground. She stood there in bra and panties, in the cold, with tears in her eyes. Step looked at her appreciatively. She had a nice little body. He picked up the jacket and put it on.

Babi cursed those keys. Where was the one to the front door?

Step lit a cigarette. Maybe he'd made a mistake when he decided not to kiss her. Oh well, it would be for some other time.

At last, Babi found the key, opened the door, and went through.

Step walked toward her. "Well, little fish, aren't you going to give me a kiss good night?"

Babi practically slammed the door in his face. Through the glass, Step couldn't hear what she was saying but had no trouble reading her lips. She was advising him or, really, ordering him to go straight to a place far underground. He watched her stomp away. Then he started his motorcycle and rode away.

Babi slowly opened the door to the apartment, slipped inside, and shut it behind her without making a sound. She tiptoed down the hallway. From the living room came the unmistakable colorful glow of the television set. Her father was sitting there. He was watching a fat man with a mustache discussing interesting topics with a number of unfamiliar characters. He was the same man who appeared in a commercial for a brand of shirts, wishing everyone could have one. She wondered if the people talking to him knew that. How can you take someone seriously who goes on TV and says, "Happy new shirt to you all"? Her father took the guy seriously. He seemed to be fascinated by him. Maybe he'd even bought one of those shirts.

Babi silently walked around behind his back. The guy on television, dabbing at a spot of sweat, pointed at her father and said, "And now a message from our sponsors." Maybe tomorrow Claudio would buy something else.

Babi opened the door to her room and slipped inside. Safe and sound!

Pallina turned on the little lamp on the nightstand. "Babi, it's you! What a relief, I was so worried! What are you doing tricked out like that? Did Step take your clothes off?"

Babi looked in her dresser drawer for her nightgown. "I wound up falling in manure!"

Pallina sniffed the air. "You're right, I can smell it. You can't imagine how scared I was when I saw the police come!"

Babi silenced her with a frosty glare. "Pallina, I don't ever want to hear another word about Pollo, races, or anything else like it. You hear me? And for right now, you'd probably better just keep your mouth shut, or I'll kick you out of my bed and make you sleep on the floor or, actually, I'll just kick you out on the street!"

"You'd never do it!"

"You want to test me?"

Pallina looked at her. She decided she'd better not try and find out. Babi walked away, heading for the bathroom.

"Babi."

"What is it?"

"Tell the truth though. You had the time of your life with Step, didn't you?"

Chapter 7

A persistent noise. The alarm clock.

Pallina turned it off. She slipped out of bed without making a sound and got dressed. She looked down at Babi. She'd barely moved and was still fast asleep, belly-up.

Pallina walked over to the little wooden bookcase on the wall full of cassette tapes. Boy George, Supertramp, Elton John, Michael Jackson, New Kids on the Block, U2, and Duran Duran. It needed to be something really special.

There it was. She slid the tape out of the bookcase. She pushed the STOP-EJECT button. A slowly grinding electric motor opened the gaping mouth of a rectangular Aiwa tape deck nearby. Pallina slid the cassette tape into the slot and shut it again.

She checked the volume and, guessing at it, turned it down a little. Then she lightly touched the PLAY button. Tears for Fears started singing softly. The volume was perfect. Babi opened her eyes. She turned on her pillow and lay belly-down now.

Pallina smiled at her. "Ciao."

Babi turned away from her. Her voice came out, slightly muffled: "What time is it?"

"Five to seven."

Pallina leaned over and kissed her on the cheek. "Truce?"

"At the very least, you'd need to bring me a chocolate pastry from Lazzareschi."

"There's no time. My mother will be here any minute, I have to get my blood drawn."

"In that case, no truce."

"You were incredible yesterday."

Babi turned to look at Pallina. "I told you I never wanted to hear about any of that again."

Pallina threw both arms wide. "Okay, whatever works for you. Hey, what should I say to your mother if I run into her on the way out?"

"Try 'Good morning, Signora Gervasi.'" Babi smiled at her and pulled the blanket up under her chin.

Pallina took the bag with her books and threw it over her shoulder. She was happy they'd made peace. Pallina softly shut the door behind her, quickly tiptoed down the hallway, and made it to the apartment door. It was still locked. She twisted the dead bolt, and just as she was easing through, she heard a voice behind her, "Pallina!"

It was Raffaella in a pink dressing gown with her face stripped of makeup, slightly faded but, most of all, astonished. Pallina decided to follow Babi's advice and, with a bright "Good morning, Signora Gervasi," she fled down the stairs.

Babi walked into the bathroom. She caught a glimpse of her face in the mirror. It wasn't her best look, she had to admit. She turned on the cold tap, let it run for a bit, and then put both hands under the stream and vigorously scrubbed her face.

Daniela appeared behind her.

"Tell me all about it! How did it go? How was the Greenhouse? Is it really as much fun as people say it is? Did you meet any girlfriends of mine?"

Babi opened the toothpaste tube and started pressing on it from the bottom, doing her best to make Daniela's thumbprint disappear from where her younger sister had squeezed it, right at dead center.

"It's a completely stupid activity. A group of lunkheads risk their lives for no good reason, and every so often one of them manages to lose their life doing it."

"Yes, okay, but were there lots of people there? What do they do? Where do they go afterward? Did you see the chamomiles, and weren't they awesome? Weren't they courageous? I'd never be good enough to be a chamomile!"

"Oh, it's really nothing special, I can assure you, and now I've got to get ready."

"There, that's what you always do! There's just no satisfaction with you. What good is it to even have a big sister if she won't tell you a thing that happens? Anyway, Marcello and I have already decided that next week we'll go too! And if I feel like it, I'll be a chamomile!"

Daniela left the bathroom snorting with anger. Babi smiled to herself, finished brushing her teeth, rinsed her mouth, and after drying off, picked up the hairbrush.

Daniela reappeared from behind the door.

"What did you do with the pair of Superga gym shoes I loaned you last night?"

Babi set the hairbrush down on the edge of the sink. "I threw them away."

"What do you mean, you threw them away? My brand-new Supergas...?"

"You heard me, I threw them away. They wound up deep in manure, and so they were so messed up I had to throw them away. Also because, if I hadn't, Step would have refused to take me home."

"You wound up in manure, and then Step took you home?" Daniela followed Babi into her bedroom. "So, Babi, are you or aren't you going to tell me what happened?"

"Listen, Dani, I promise to tell you every last detail later, okay?"

Dani heaved a deep sigh of discontent. "Okay." Then she went back to her bedroom.

Babi put on her uniform. She'd never tell her a single word of it, she knew that.

Raffaella walked into Babi's room. "So, Pallina slept here?"

"Yes, Mamma."

"But where?"

"In my bed."

"How could that be? When I came in to kiss you good night last night, you were all alone."

"She showed up later. She couldn't stay at her house because her mother was throwing a dinner party."

"And where had she been before that?"

"I don't know."

"Babi, I don't want to be responsible for her too. Just think if anything had happened to her, and her mother thought that she was here at my house the whole time..."

"You're right, Mamma."

"Next time, I want to know in advance if she's coming over to sleep at our house."

"But I even told you she was coming, before you went over to the Pentestis' place, don't you remember?"

Raffaella stopped to think for a moment. "No, I don't remember."

Babi smiled at her naively, as if to say, *So what am I supposed to do about that?* She knew perfectly well that her mother had no way to remember such a thing. She'd never said it, after all.

"I'd never want to have a daughter like Pallina. Always out and about at night, up to who knows what. I don't like that young woman. She'll come to a bad end, wait and see."

"But, Mamma, she never does anything bad, she just likes to have fun. I assure you, she's a good girl."

"Maybe so, but I still prefer you." Raffaella smiled at her and caressed her under the chin before leaving the bedroom.

Babi smiled. She knew how to handle her mother. But lately she'd been telling her too many lies. She resolved to stop.

Poor Pallina, even when she had nothing to do with it, she turned out to be guilty. Babi decided to forgive her entirely. Certainly, there remained the whole Pollo problem to solve, but to everything, there is a season.

She slipped on the uniform skirt. She stood in front of the mirror, pulled up her hair, uncovering her face, and fastened it in place with two side hairclips. She stood there, staring at herself and, while the latest song by Tears for Fears poured out of the stereo nearby, Babi noticed how much she looked like her mother. No, even if she managed to figure out everything Babi had got up to, Raffaella could never think of trading her for Pallina because there were too many similarities between mother and daughter.

~

The sun filtered cheerfully in through the kitchen window. Babi finished eating her whole-wheat biscuits and drank the last drop of milky coffee that she'd saved at the bottom of the mug until then.

Daniela was digging to the very bottom. Her spoon probed anxiously against the edge of the plastic container of a small pudding as she tried to scrape up every last bit of defiant chocolate hiding down there in the furthest nooks and crannies.

Raffaella went to her bedroom, taking with her a demitasse of black coffee, still steaming hot. Claudio was happy. Maybe because of a positive horoscope, certainly because of the coffee he'd at long last been able to enjoy.

"Babi, it's a beautiful day today. The sun is out. And I don't think it's even particularly cold. I talked to your mother about it just now, and we're in agreement. Today you can take the Vespa to school!"

"Thanks, Papà. You're both super nice. But you know, after what we said the other day, I gave it some more thought, and maybe you do have a point. Going to school together in the morning, you, me, and Daniela, well, it's become sort of like a ritual, a kind of good-luck charm. Plus, it's kind of a special moment because we can talk about anything and everything. Starting the day together is much better like that, don't you think?"

Daniela couldn't believe her eyes or, actually, her ears.

"Babi, excuse me. Let's take the Vespa. We can talk to Papà whenever we want. We can linger over dinner with him in the evenings, or Sunday mornings."

Babi grabbed her by the arm and clenched it, squeezing a little too hard. "Oh, no, Dani, seriously, it's better this way. Let's go with him." She clenched her arm again. "Plus, I'll remind you of what I said last night. I wasn't feeling very well. Starting next week, maybe, we can take the Vespa, when it's warmer."

That final squeeze left no doubts that Babi was trying to send her a message. Daniela really was an intuitive young woman, more or less. "Yes, Papà. Babi is right. We'll come with you!"

Claudio happily threw back his last sip of coffee. It was great to have two such wonderful daughters. It's not often that you feel so beloved. "All right, girls, let's get going or we'll get you to school late." Claudio went down to the garage to get the car while Babi and Daniela waited outside the apartment house door downstairs for him to drive around.

"Well, you finally understood! What was I going to have to do, break your arm?" Babi asked.

"Well, you could have told me earlier, no?"

"How was I supposed to know that today of all days he was going to give us permission to take the Vespa?"

"But why don't you want to take it?" Daniela asked.

"That's easy enough, because it's not there."

"The Vespa isn't there? Then where is it? Didn't you take it last night when you went out?"

"Yes," Babi said.

"Well? Did you drive the Vespa into the manure, too, and then you had to throw it away?"

"No, I left it out at the Greenhouse."

"I don't believe you!"

"Believe it."

"I don't want to believe it! My Vespa!" Daniela said.

"Well, as far as that goes, I was the one they gave it to."

"Yes, but who paid to soup it up? Who had the new carburetor and intake put in? Next year, Papà and Mamma were going to buy you a car, and then it would have been mine. I just can't believe it."

Claudio stopped right in front of them. He rolled down the electric car window.

"Babi, what happened to the Vespa? It's not in the garage."

Daniela shut her eyes. Now she had no choice but to believe it.

"Nothing, Papà, I just put it back in the courtyard. It bothered you so much when you tried to get the car into the garage. I thought it might be more convenient just to park it outside."

"Are you kidding? Put it back inside right away. What if it gets stolen? Believe me, your mother and I have no intention of buying you a new one. Run and put it inside immediately. Here, take the keys."

Daniela got in the back seat while Babi walked off toward the garage, pretending to pick through the bunch, hunting for the right key. Once she arrived back in the courtyard, Babi started thinking. *So now what am I going to do? I need to find the Vespa by tonight or else I'm going to have to come up with some other solution. Darn that Pallina, she's the one who got me into this mess, and she's going to have to get me out of it.*

Babi heard the sound of the Mercedes arriving in reverse. She ran toward the garage. She leaned down in front of the roller gate. Just in time because the Mercedes emerged from around the corner and came to a halt right in front of her. Babi pretended to shut the garage, slid the key into the lock, mimed turning it, and then pulled it back out and walked smiling toward the car. "All done. I put it away."

She decided that she was quite the mime, but that the best solution would be to find the Vespa as quickly as possible. As she was getting into the car, Babi felt she was being watched. She looked up. She was right.

The boy who lived on the third floor was looking down. He must have seen everything. That is, he hadn't seen anything, which is why he had that puzzled expression on his face. She smiled, trying to reassure him. He smiled back, but it was perfectly clear that something was mystifying him. It would have been impossible for anyone to make heads or tails of it.

The Mercedes drove off. Babi gave the keys back to her father, and she smiled at him. "I just wanted to make it easier for you to park."

"I know, and I thank you, but it's better this way. Did you put it good and solid against the wall?" her father asked.

"Good and solid. It can't get in your way." Babi turned to look at Daniela. She was sitting with her arms crossed tight across her chest. She was in a foul mood.

"Come on, Dani. We can ride the Vespa to school next week!"

"I really hope so."

Babi went back to sitting normally. She looked straight ahead. Yes, they had to find a solution as quick as they could, absolutely.

The Mercedes stopped at the front entrance to the apartment building, right in front of the gate arm, which slowly began to rise. Claudio waved to the doorman, who gestured for him to wait a minute. He emerged from the booth with a package in his hand.

"Good morning, sir. Excuse me but someone left this for Babi."

The doorman handed over the package. Babi picked it up, her curiosity piqued. The Mercedes moved away slowly as the car window rolled up. Babi opened the package. Daniela leaned forward, consumed by curiosity. Claudio, too, rose up slightly in his seat to see what it could be. Babi smiled. "Who wants a piece? It's a chocolate pastry from Lazzareschi."

Babi tore the pastry apart with her hands. "Papà?"

Claudio shook his head.

"Dani?"

"No, thanks." Maybe she'd been hoping that the package contained some news about "their Vespa."

"So much the better, I'll eat it all myself. You have no idea what you're missing, you guys..."

Pallina really was a sweetheart. She knew how to win your forgiveness. Now all she needed to do was find Babi's Vespa for her by no later than eight o'clock.

Chapter 8

In front of the school, the girls were chatting cheerfully, waiting for the bell to ring. Babi and Daniela got out of the car and said goodbye to their father. The Mercedes moved off into the traffic around Piazza Euclide. A group of girls immediately surged in Babi and Daniela's direction.

"Babi, is it really true that last night you were at the Greenhouse?"

"Is it true that you had to escape from the city traffic cops on a motorbike?"

"Is it true that traffic cop grabbed you by the hair and then Step knocked him down and you both got away on his motorcycle?"

Daniela listened in astonishment. So the loss of the Vespa hadn't been a completely pointless sacrifice. This was true glory.

But Babi couldn't believe her ears. How had they already managed to find out everything? Not actually *everything*. The story about the manure, luckily, still seemed to be a secret.

The sound of the bell saved her. As she was climbing the steps, she gave vague answers to some of the questions from her least obnoxious friends. Well, it was done. That day, she was a celebrity.

Daniela waved a fond goodbye. "Ciao, Babi. See you at recess!" Incredible. In all the years they'd been going to school together, she'd never uttered those words

She watched Daniela walk away, surrounded by all her friends. They were all walking around her, asking a thousand questions. She, too, was savoring this moment of extreme notoriety. After all, it was only fair. She'd had to sacrifice her Supergas. Babi just hoped that Daniela said nothing about the manure.

The first period was ancient Greek, and Signora Giacci was testing. She was about to put an end to the last quarter before the final exams of high school. Once the list of subjects was posted, there would be no more pop exams. Babi checked the little checkmarks on the list she kept in her notebook. There were just three missing to complete the set of exams. These would be the "lucky girls." Babi read the names. Once again, Silvia Festa. Poor thing.

Babi called to her as the students entered the schoolroom.

Silvia heard her. "What is it?"

"Listen, Signora Giacci is going to test you in Greek today."

"I know." Silvia gave her a quick smile. "I'm reviewing."

Babi smiled at her. For all the good it was likely to do her. Because, in cold hard fact, only a miracle could save her now.

"Ciao, Babi!"

"Pallina! How are you today?"

Pallina set her book bag down on Babi's desk. "Fine, but with a quart of blood less than I started the day with!"

Pallina rolled up the light blue blouse of her uniform, displaying her pale white arm. "Look here!" She pointed to a bandage that was ever so slightly stained blood red at the center. "That's nothing. You can't imagine, that doctor, the work he had to do to find my vein. He stabbed me all over, pinching my arm because he said that would help to bring the vein out.

"The only positive thing about all this is that, afterward, my mother took me out for breakfast at Euclide café. I had a delicious maritozzo pastry with whipped cream. By the way, did you get my package?"

"Yes, thanks!"

"Well, it's just that your doorman has the expression of someone who always wants to know what's in every package you drop off for him. He's worse than an X-ray machine. So he didn't eat the Lazzareschi pastry?"

Babi smiled. "No."

"Have I been forgiven?"

"Almost."

"Why almost? What, was I supposed to get you two pastries?"

"No, you need to track down my Vespa by eight o'clock."

"Your Vespa? How am I supposed to find your Vespa? Who knows where it is. How am I supposed to know?"

"Don't ask me. You always know everything. You're well connected in the circuit. You're Pollo's woman, after all. One thing is certain, when my father gets home at eight o'clock tonight, that Vespa has to be in the garage..."

"Lombardi!" Signora Giacci was at the door. "Go to your seat, if you please."

"Yes, excuse me, teacher." Pallina picked up her book bag.

Babi stopped her. "I have an idea. I don't need to find my Vespa anymore, at least not right away."

Pallina smiled. "That's good. It would have been impossible anyway! But how are you going to handle it? When your father returns home and doesn't find the Vespa in the garage, what are you going to tell him?"

"But my father *is* going to find the Vespa in the garage."

"How is that going to happen?"

"Simple, we'll put yours there."

"My Vespa?"

"Sure, as far as my father's concerned, they're all identical. He won't notice a thing."

"Okay, but how am I going to..."

"Gervasi! Come on up and let me see your signed notebook."

Babi brought her the notebook, already open to the signed note. Signora Giacci checked it. "Well, what did your mother say about your failing grade?"

"She grounded me." It wasn't true, but she might as well let Giacci think she'd had a full, crushing win.

In fact, Signora Giacci swallowed the bait hook, line, and sinker. "Well, good for her." Then she spoke to the class. "It's important that your parents appreciate the work we teachers do and that they support it wholeheartedly." Nearly every girl in the class nodded in agreement.

She turned back to Babi. "Your mother is a very understanding woman. She knows perfectly well that, what I do, I'm doing entirely for your own well-being. Here." She handed back her notebook.

Babi went back to her desk. *A strange way of looking after my well-being, flunking me on my Latin test and sending home a disciplinary note*, she thought to herself.

Signora Giacci reached into her old suede briefcase and pulled out the Greek assignments, folded in half. Those papers unfolded, reckless and rustling, on the teacher's desk, spraying over the class the magical thought that they might all have received at least a passing grade. "Let me warn you all that it's been a bloodbath. You should all just hope that Greek isn't one of the subjects at the final high school exams."

Everyone relaxed. They all knew for certain that the subjects this year were going to be Italian, Latin, mathematics, and philosophy. They all pretended not to know though. In reality, they could just as easily have been a class of consummate actresses. Dramatic roles, assigned by the situation of the moment.

"Bartoli, F. Simoni, F. Mareschi, D." One after the other, the girls went to the teacher's desk to retrieve their assignments in silent resignation. One of them went back to her desk with a smile. It wasn't clear why. Maybe she was just putting on her game face.

"Alessandri, D. Bandini, D plus." There was a sort of funeral procession. They all went back to their seats and immediately pulled out the paper, trying to figure out the reason for all those red marks. Most of the time it was a pointless exercise, just like their utterly unsuccessful stabs at translation.

"Sbardelli, C minus." A young woman got up, making a V for victory. In fact, for her it was. She regularly got Ds for her classwork. That half a grade higher constituted a major achievement for her.

"Carli, C." A pale young woman, with thick-lensed eyeglasses and greasy hair, invariably accustomed to getting at least an A minus, turned pale. She got up and walked slowly to the teacher's desk, wondering what she could have gotten wrong.

A thrill of joy ran through the line of desks. She was one of the class grinds, and she never let anyone copy.

"Come on!" Pallina whispered to her as the poor thing trudged past her.

Signora Giacci handed Carli her paper. She seemed sincerely chagrined. "What happened to you? Maybe you weren't feeling well? Or has this class full of illiterates finally managed to infect you too?"

The young woman forced a smile. And with a faint "I wasn't at my best" went back to her desk. One thing was certain. Now she really did feel bad. Carli, who could rattle off the most challenging translations, with a big fat C. She opened her assignment. She scanned it rapidly and immediately spotted her tragic error. She slammed her fist down on her desk. How had she managed to get that wrong? She put her hands in her hair, clearly distraught.

The class's glee and happiness reached incredible peaks.

"Benucci, C plus. Salvetti, B minus." And that was that. The students who hadn't yet picked up their classwork heaved a sigh. By now, they had definitely received a passing grade. Signora Giacci always handed back the assignments in order of grades, from worst to best. First the failures and then, in a slowly rising crescendo, up to passing grades and then the various A minuses and As. Although an A was something of an event.

"Marini, B plus, Ricci, A minus." A few of the girls

were waiting calmly to receive their grades, accustomed as they were to occupying the high end of the rankings. But for Pallina, this was a genuine, full-fledged miracle. She couldn't believe her ears. Ricci, A minus? Then that meant she must have received at least that grade, if not higher. She dreamed of being able to go home to her mother for lunch and tell her, "Mamma, I got an A minus in Greek." Her mother would flat-out faint.

"Gervasi, A minus."

Pallina smiled happily for her friend. "Go, Babi."

Babi turned to look at her and waved a greeting. For once, she wasn't going to have to feel bad about having gotten a better grade than Pallina.

"Lombardi." Pallina leaped out of her desk and headed straight toward the teacher's desk. She was euphoric. By now she must have at least an A minus.

"Lombardi, D." Pallina stood speechless. "Your paper must somehow have wound up in this stack by mistake," Signora Giacci apologized with a smile.

Pallina took her assignment and trudged back to her desk, devastated. For a fleeting instant, she'd believed it. How great it would have been to get an A minus. She sat down.

Signora Giacci glanced at her, still smiling, and then went on to read the grades on the last few papers. She'd done it on purpose, the old bitch. Pallina felt certain of it. Her surging rage caused her eyes to fill with tears. Damn it, how could she have fallen for it? An A minus on a Greek translation: impossible. She should have realized immediately that something wasn't right.

She heard a whisper on her right. She turned around. It

was Babi. Pallina tried to smile but without much success. Then she sat up, running the back of her hand under her nose. Babi showed her a handkerchief. Pallina nodded. Babi knotted it and tossed it to her. Pallina caught it in midair.

Signora Giacci glanced at her with a look of annoyance. Pallina raised her hand apologetically and then blew her nose. Taking advantage of the handkerchief in front of her face, she made a face as well as a rude noise. A few of the girls around her noticed and laughed in amusement.

Signora Giacci slammed her fist down on her desk. "Silence!"

She handed back the last few papers and then opened her ledger, ready to test some students. "Salvetti and Ricci."

The two girls went up to the teacher's desk, handed in their notebooks, and waited by the wall, ready for the ensuing firing squad of questions.

Signora Giacci looked down at her ledger again. "Servanti."

Francesca Servanti stood up from her desk, stunned. That day it really wasn't her turn. Giacci was supposed to be testing Salvetti, Ricci, and Festa. Everyone knew it.

She walked in silence to the teacher's desk and handed over her notebook, doing her best to conceal her outright desperation. Actually, though, it was plain to see. She was entirely unprepared.

Signora Giacci gathered the notebooks and laid them one atop the other, squaring them up with both hands. "All right, with you three, I'm done with this round of testing, and then I hope to set aside Greek for a while. We'll be able to focus on Latin. Well, I'm going to tell you right now.

Almost certainly, that'll be one of the subjects that's going to be on the final exam..."

Well, tell me something I don't know, most of the class thought inwardly. One young woman had another thought on her mind. That was Silvia Festa. She was afflicted by quite another order of worries, far more personal to her own situation. Why hadn't Signora Giacci called her? Why wasn't she being tested, instead of Servanti, as she ought to have been? Could Signora Giacci have something else in mind for her?

And yet her situation was far from ideal. She already had two Cs on the books, and she really couldn't afford to do any worse.

That said, the teacher could hardly have made a mistake. Signora Giacci never made mistakes. That was one of the golden rules there at Falconieri High School.

Everyone knew Signora Giacci. She lived on in the memories of the school's graduates for the rest of their lives, for better or worse. Especially for worse, given that no one had ever told or heard a single story or anecdote that featured Signora Giacci helping out a student in dire straits.

If you were having difficulties, then Signora Giacci would pounce on you, finish you off, terminate you. If you were doing well, on the other hand, Signora Giacci would sing your praises and, if she could, at the final exams see to it that your grade was pumped up by a point or two.

Which meant, in practical terms, that she never did a lick of work. If a student was doing well, she didn't need anyone's help. But if a student was doing poorly, then she needed everyone's help, including all the saints on the calendar. In fact, especially the help of the saints. What Silvia

Festa needed, more than anything else, was the score from her third test, and what's more, she had the right to it.

Stealthily, she called out to Babi. Babi replied by shrugging helplessly. Babi, too, had noticed that something wasn't right. But she couldn't figure out what had happened. She gestured to Silvia to wait a second.

Silvia sighed impatiently. Babi rechecked her notebook. No doubt about it. Her little dots and checkmarks were all where they were supposed to be. To finish the round of testing, Signora Giacci was supposed to summon Salvetti, Ricci, and Festa. Servanti had already been tested three times, and most recently on March 18, to be exact.

Signora Giacci must have made a mistake. But it wasn't a very good idea to bring that point up to her. Babi knew the golden rule of Falconieri High School as well as everyone else. She decided it was better not to get involved. There are rules you'd best not break.

She called out to Silvia. "I'm sorry, I don't know what to tell you. According to my notes, you were supposed to be tested too."

"So what are you saying? That Signora Giacci made a mistake?"

"Maybe. But you know the way she is. Better not say anything."

"Yes, but unless I say something, they're not going to let me take the final exams."

Babi threw both arms wide. "I don't know what to do..." She really was sorry. But it just wasn't a good idea at this point to set out to collect more disciplinary notes. Her school notebook and, most of all, her mother wouldn't be able to withstand the impact of another one.

She started the test. Silvia fidgeted nervously at her desk. She didn't know what to do. In the end, she decided to speak up. She raised her hand.

Signora Giacci saw her. "Yes, Festa, what is it?"

Silvia started to speak, and then she remembered. She stood up with alacrity. She did her best to infuse her tone of voice with as much respect as possible.

"Excuse me, teacher. I don't want to bother you. But I'm afraid I've never had my third test." Festa smiled, trying desperately to conceal the fact that she was accusing her of having made a mistake.

Signora Giacci heaved a sigh of annoyance. "Let's just take a look." She pulled out two notebooks to aid her in her research. She laid them out on the Ancient Greek class ledger and cross-referenced them until she found the last name Festa and the corresponding third test. "Festa... Festa... Here you are, tested on March eighteenth, and naturally it's a C. Satisfied? Actually... " She checked the other grades. "I'm not sure you'll be admitted to final exams."

A weak "Thank you" emerged from Silvia's mouth as she turned to go back to her desk.

With an aloof air of competence, Signora Giacci went back to her testing.

Babi rechecked her notebook. March 18. In fact, that was the date that Servanti had been tested. There could be no doubt about it. Signora Giacci must have made a mistake. But how could she prove it? It would be her word against the teacher's. Which amounted to guaranteeing another disciplinary note.

Poor Festa, she really had bad luck. This seriously meant that she'd flunk the year.

Babi opened to the pages with the other subjects. March 18. That was a Thursday. She checked for all the other classes. How strange though—on that day Festa hadn't been tested on any other subjects. Maybe it was just a coincidence, or maybe not.

She leaned over the front of her desk. "Silvia."

"What is it?" Silvia looked devastated. She wasn't wrong, poor thing.

"Would you give me your notebook?"

"What for?"

"I just want to see something," Babi said.

"See what?"

"I'll tell you after I check it... Come on, hand it over."

For a moment, a tiny spark of hope glittered in Silvia's eyes. She handed Babi her notebook. Babi opened it. She went to the back pages. Silvia gazed at her hopefully.

Babi smiled. She turned to her and handed back the notebook. "You're a lucky girl!"

Silvia shot her a sketchy smile. She wasn't all that sure it was true.

Suddenly, Babi raised her hand. "Excuse me, teacher..."

Signora Giacci turned around to look at her. "What is it, Gervasi? Haven't you been tested either? Oh, you're really pains in the neck today, all you girls. Speak up, what is it?"

Babi stood up. She remained silent for a second or two. The eyes of the class were all pointed right at her. Especially Silvia's.

Babi looked at Pallina. She, too, like all the other girls, was waiting curiously. Babi smiled at her. After all, it was only right what she was doing. Signora Giacci had intentionally put Pallina's paper in the stack with the ones that had been marked A minus.

"Well, Gervasi, what is it?"

"I just wanted to tell you, teacher, that you made a mistake."

A general murmur washed over the class. The girls seemed to have lost their collective minds. Babi was unruffled.

"Silence!" Signora Giacci turned red before regaining her self-control. "Oh, really, Gervasi, about what?"

"You couldn't have tested Silvia Festa on March eighteenth."

"What do you mean? It's written right here, in my class ledger. Would you care to take a look? Here it is, March eighteenth, a C for Silvia Festa," she said. "I'm starting to think that you really enjoy receiving disciplinary notes."

"That grade is for Francesca Servanti. You made a mistake, and you put it down for Festa."

Signora Giacci seemed to explode with rage. "Oh, really? Well, I know that you mark down everything in your notebook. But it's just your word against mine. And if I say that I tested Festa on that date, then that's the way it is."

"And I say it's not. On March eighteenth you couldn't have tested Silvia Festa."

"Oh, really? Why not?"

"Because Silvia Festa was absent on the eighteenth of March."

Signora Giacci blanched. She pulled out her general ledger and started leafing back through it.

Sitting at her desk, Silvia Festa opened her notebook. She turned to the last pages, where her justified absences were all noted. That's what Babi had wanted to see. She leafed through it rapidly. The whole class sat in silence, waiting to learn whether that final confirmation would be forthcoming.

Silvia found her mother's signature. There it was, gleaming in all its reality, on March 19, the day after her absence.

Signora Giacci stopped and stared at the page in the ledger that bore that awful date: March 18. She frantically checked the absences. Benucci, Marini, and then, there she was. Signora Giacci slumped onto her desk. She couldn't believe her eyes. Festa. That surname, written in her own hand, stamped before her in letters of fire. Her agonizing shame. Her mistake. Nothing more was needed. Signora Giacci glanced at Babi.

Babi slowly sat down. All her classmates turned to look at her. A general buzz of voices stirred in the classroom: "Good job, nice work, Babi, good job."

Babi pretended not to hear. But that soft buzz of whispers reached Signora Giacci's ears, those words as chilling as needles of ice hitting her, cold and cutting, like the burden of that defeat. Looking like a fool in front of the class. In front of *her* class. And then the words that issued from her lips, so heavy and painful, to underscore her mistake. "Servanti, please be seated. Festa, come up to be tested."

Babi lowered her eyes to her desk. Justice had been done. Then she slowly lifted her face to look at Pallina. Their gazes met, and a thousand words flew silently between those two desks. Starting today, it was possible for Signora Giacci to make mistakes. The golden rule had been shattered. It collapsed before them, crumbling into thousands of shards like a fragile crystal glass slipping out of the hands of a young and inexperienced waitress.

But Babi didn't see anyone step forward to dress her down. Everywhere she turned, all she saw were the joyful eyes of the other girls in her class, proud and entertained by her courage.

Then she looked farther on. And what she saw terrified her. There sat Signora Giacci, staring at her. Her gaze, devoid of any expression or sign of life, was as hard and grim as a slab of gray stone on which someone had labored mightily to carve the word *hatred*.

Chapter 9

It was noon. Step walked into the kitchen wearing a sweatshirt and a pair of shorts, ready for breakfast. "Good morning, Maria."

"Good morning, sir." The housekeeper immediately stopped washing the dishes.

Step took the coffeepot and the pan of hot milk off the stove and sat down at the table, but then the doorbell started to ring. Step lifted a hand to his forehead. "Who the fu..."

With tiny footsteps, Maria hurried to the door. "Who is it?"

"It's Pollo! Would you let me in, please?"

Maria turned to look at Step with an inquiring expression. Step silently nodded his head so Maria opened the door.

Pollo came rushing in. "Hey, Step? You don't know what an incredible thing! A fairy tale, the coolest shit ever!"

Step cocked a brow. "You brought me sandwiches?"

"No, look at this." He showed him that day's edition of *Il Messaggero*.

"I already have the newspaper." He lifted a copy of *La Repubblica* from the table. "Maria brought it to me. By the way, you haven't even said good morning to her."

Pollo turned to look at the housekeeper impatiently. "Morning, Maria."

Maria smiled. "I'll go and tidy up your room, sir." And she left the kitchen.

Step sipped his hot coffee. Pollo opened the newspaper and laid it out on the table. "Have you seen? Take a look at this unbelievably cool picture! A legend. You're in the newspaper."

Step put his hand down on the page with the local news. It was true. It was him on his motorcycle with Babi on back as they were pulling a wheelie in front of the photographers. Perfectly recognizable, but luckily it was impossible to see the license plate. Otherwise there would have been bitter repercussions. There was a whole article. The illegal street races, the surprise arrival of the police, some of the names of those arrested, and a description of the chase that ensued.

Pollo looked enthusiastically at his friend. "Did you read it? You're a legend, Step! You're famous now! Fuck, if only I could have an article like this."

Step smiled at him. "You can't pull wheelies as well as I can. Oh, it really is a nice picture! Did you see how good Babi looks?"

Pollo nodded glumly. Babi really wasn't what he would have defined as his ideal woman.

Step held up the newspaper in both hands and gazed at the photograph in a state of bliss. "No doubt about it, my motorcycle really looks great here!" He wondered if Babi had already seen their photo. Almost certainly not. "Pollo, you need to take me somewhere. Here, have some coffee while I take a shower." Step went into his bedroom.

Pollo took his seat. He looked at the photo. He started

rereading the article. He lifted the coffee cup to his mouth. Yuck! Oh, that's right. Step always took his coffee without sugar.

Step's voice arrived muffled from the shower: "What time do the shops close?"

Pollo put his third teaspoon of sugar into his coffee. Then he looked at the clock. "In less than an hour."

"Then, fuck, we'd better get moving."

Pollo tasted his coffee. Now that was the way it should be sugared. He lit a cigarette.

Step appeared in the doorway. He was wearing a bathrobe, and with a small hand towel, he was vigorously massaging his short head of hair. Soon, his head was nice and dry. He turned to look at Pollo again and then gazed at the photo. "So, what's it like to be friends with a living legend?"

~

The motorcycle, with Pollo sitting on it, sat motionless, parked on its kickstand on Viale Angelico. When Step walked out of the print shop, Pollo kicked over the motorcycle engine and revved it.

Step climbed on behind him, being careful not to crease the poster. "Oh, Pollo, drive carefully. I put the poster right between us."

"How much did they charge you?"

"Twenty-two thousand lire."

"Son of a bitch. I wanted to do the same thing with my picture, but does it have to cost that much?"

"Practically speaking, they print it, plus they laminate it too. That's not much, if you stop to think about it."

"I don't want to stop, and I don't want to think. Where are we going now?" Pollo asked.

"To Piazza Jacini."

"What for?"

"That's where Babi lives."

"Not seriously! And you've never seen her place?"

"Never."

"Life is funny, isn't it?"

"Why?" Step asked.

"Well, at first you never see someone at all, and then you start seeing them practically every day."

"Yes, strange."

"Then it's even stranger how, after you start to see them every single day, you start to bring them sweet little presents too." Pollo felt the sharp slap of Step's open hand on his neck. "Ouch!"

"Are you done? You're like one of those pain-in-the-ass taxi drivers who never stop talking while they take you to your destination and then they ask you a bunch of questions. All you're missing is a crackling radio, and you'd be identical."

Pollo started driving cheerfully and then twisted his mouth into a strange grimace to turn his voice rasping and metallic in imitation of a taxi radio. "*Ktchsss* Piazza Jacini for Pollo Forty, Piazza Jacini for Pollo Forty," he said, shouting at the top of his lungs.

Step gave him another smack on the neck but Pollo continued in the voice of the taxi radio. And so they kept going, laughing and shouting, zigzagging through the traffic with all the cars around them slamming on their brakes to avoid them.

They approached a real taxi. Pollo shouted into the driver's window, "Piazza Jacini for Pollo Forty." The cabbie almost had a heart attack, but he said nothing. As their motorcycle roared off, the taxi driver raised his hand, gesticulating at them and shaking his head. It was perfectly clear that this taxi driver's idol could, at the very most, be Alberto Sordi, certainly never Robert De Niro.

"Piazza Jacini to Pollo Forty, arrived at destination!" Pollo's motorcycle stopped, roaring, in front of the lowered electric arm in front of Babi's apartment building.

Step waved hello to the doorman, who waved back and let them through. The motorcycle climbed the ramp. The doorman watched those two muscle-bound arrivals, vaguely perplexed.

Pollo turned to speak to Step. "Oh, then you've been here before. The doorman recognized you."

"Stop here and wait for me." Step hopped off the motorcycle.

Pollo revved the engine and switched it off. "Make it snappy. The thingy that tells you how much to pay is running..."

"The meter."

"Whatever the fuck it's called, that's what it's called. Get moving. Otherwise I'm leaving."

Step picked up the poster and then went to the doorbell. He found the right surname and rang. A voice replied with a Sardinian accent, "Who is it?"

"I need to deliver a package for Babi."

"Second floor."

Step went upstairs. An overweight housekeeper with features as unmistakably Sardinian as her accent was standing in the doorway.

Step walked toward her. "Good morning. Here you are. I need to leave this for Babi."

The housekeeper took the poster in her strong, healthy hands.

"Be careful, please. You'll ruin it."

A voice came from the far end of the apartment hallway. "Who is it, Rina?"

"A young man brought something for Babi."

Raffaella appeared behind her. She came walking toward him, her eyes taking in the young man in the doorway with broad shoulders and short hair. That smile, she'd seen it before but she just couldn't remember where.

"Buongiorno, signora. I'm Stefano Mancini. I brought this for Babi. It's nothing, just a trifle. Would you mind seeing that she gets it when she returns home from school?"

Raffaella was still smiling. She hadn't really focused yet. Then, all at once, she realized. Step noticed, too, when it happened.

Raffaella was no longer smiling. "You're the one who assaulted Signor Accado."

Step was surprised. "I didn't think I'd become so famous."

"In fact, you're not famous. You're just a miscreant, a thug. Do your folks know what happened?"

"Why, exactly what's happened?"

"You've been reported to the police."

"Oh, that's no problem. I'm used to it." He smiled. "And after all, I'm an orphan."

Raffaella stood there awkwardly for a moment, suddenly embarrassed. She didn't know whether to believe him. And she was right to doubt. "Well, in any case, I don't want you around my daughter."

"Actually, she's the one who always turns up wherever I go. But I don't mind, it doesn't bother me. But promise me this, don't yell at her, don't scold her—she doesn't deserve that. I can appreciate her motives."

"Well, *I* can't." Raffaella looked him up and down, trying to intimidate him.

But she was unsuccessful. Step smiled. "I don't know why it is, but mothers never like me. Well, signora, please excuse me, but now I really have to get going. I have a taxi downstairs waiting for me. It's costing me an arm and a leg."

Step turned around and started down the stairs. He leaped down the last few steps just in time to hear the door slam hard behind him. He turned and looked back up. How that lady resembled Babi. It was astonishing. Her eyes had the same shape and angle, and her face had the same geometry. But Babi was prettier. He hoped she was also less eager for a fight. No, the resemblance extended to that aspect as well. For a moment, he yearned to see her again.

Then Pollo leaned on his horn. "Oh, you want to get a move on? What the fuck are you doing, are you in some kind of trance?"

Step climbed on behind him. "Could you possibly be even worse at being a cabbie than everything else you do badly?"

"Screw you and your whole family. What were you up to?"

"I talked with her mother." Suddenly a thought occurred to Step. He looked up. In fact, it was just as he expected. Raffaella was there, looking out the window. She recoiled suddenly, trying to get out of sight. But it was too late. Step had seen her.

He smiled up at her and waved. Raffaella didn't respond in any way. She slammed the window shut as the motorcycle disappeared around the curve. Pollo came to a halt when he reached the gate arm. Step greeted the doorman. It was good to make friends with someone in that apartment building.

"So you talked to the mother? And what did she say to you?" Pollo asked.

"Oh, nothing. We had a little bit of a quarrel but actually she adores me."

"Step, be careful." Pollo took off.

"About what?"

"About everything! This is the classic story that goes sidewise."

"Why?"

"You bring her gifts. You talk to her mother. You've never done these things. But what about Madda?"

"What does Madda have to do with it? That's another story."

"So wait, do you want to be exclusive with Babi?"

"Pollo..."

"What?"

"Did you hear that yesterday someone killed a guy right near where you live?"

"Seriously? I don't know anything about it. How did it happen?"

"They cut his throat." Step suddenly put his arm around Pollo's neck and tightened it.

"It was a taxi driver, and he asked too many questions."

Pollo tried to wriggle out of that grip but to no avail. So he decided to turn it into a joke and went back to making the crackling staticky voice on the radio. "Pollo Forty, message received. *Ktchsss.* Pollo Forty, message received."

Chapter 10

Raffaella unrolled the poster. She recognized Stefano on a motorcycle with its front wheel in the air. What a brazen smirk that boy always seemed to have on his face.

But riding behind him was her daughter. Who had taken that photo? It was a little out of focus. On the top left someone had written on it by hand, with a felt-tip pen. No doubt, it had been that same boy. There were a few printed words: THE PHOTO OF THE FUGITIVES. What was that supposed to mean?

"Signora, it's your husband on the telephone."

Raffaella went into the other room. "Hello, Claudio?"

"Raffaella!" He seemed horrified. "Have you seen today's *Il Messaggero*? In the local news section, there's a photo of Babi..."

"No, I haven't seen it. Let me go and get it right away."

"Hello? Raffaella?" But his wife had already hung up. Claudio looked at the silent receiver. His wife never gave him the time to finish speaking.

Raffaella hurried down to the newsstand in front of the apartment building. She took a copy of *Il Messaggero* and paid for it. She opened the paper without even waiting for her change.

She turned to the local crime news. There it was, the same photo. She read the banner headline "The Pirates of the Road." Her daughter. The roundup, the city traffic cops, the high-speed chase. The arrests. What did Babi have to do with all this?

The lines of print started to dance before Raffaella's eyes. She felt she was about to faint. Then she took a deep breath. Little by little, she started to feel better. She took her change.

Seeing her look so pale, the news vendor expressed his concern. "Signora Gervasi, what is it? Are you feeling ill? Have you had some bad news?"

Raffaella turned away, shaking her head. "No, it's nothing."

She left the newsstand. What could she have told him? What would she say now to her girlfriends? To the other tenants? To the Accados? To the world?

It was going to be hard to wait for the school day to end.

~

The voice on the intercom said, "Signor Mancini, it's your father on line one."

"Thanks, signorina!" Paolo pushed the button marked L1. "Hello, Papà."

"Have you seen today's *Il Messaggero*?"

"Yes, I have the photo of Step right in front of me."

"Have you read the article?"

"I read it."

"What do you think?"

"Well, there's not that much to think. I think that, sooner or later, this is going to go in a bad direction."

"Yes, I think the same thing. What can we do?"

"There isn't much to be done, if you ask me."

"When you get home, would you speak to your brother, please?"

"Yes, I'll speak to him. For all the good it will do. But if it makes you happy, I promise I'll do it."

"Thanks, Paolo." His father hung up the telephone. *Happy. What's supposed to make me happy? Certainly not an article like this one about one of my sons.* He picked up the newspaper in both hands. He looked at the photo. *God, how handsome he is. He takes after his mother completely.*

And a faint smile appeared on his weary face, incapable of erasing that age-old stab of pain. And for a moment, he told himself the truth. He finally realized what could have made him happy.

~

Pallina pulled a pack of Camel Lights out of her purse. She took one out and stuck it in her mouth. She looked inside the cigarette pack. It would take three more before she got to the one turned upside down, the last cigarette, the one you could make a wish on. Almost always for the man of your dreams.

Then she started rummaging around in the purse. Finally, she found her lighter and lit her cigarette.

Babi watched her. "Hey, didn't you say that you were going to quit smoking?"

"Yes, I said I was. I'll quit on Monday."

"But wasn't it supposed to be last Monday?"

"That's right. I quit on Monday but then I started again yesterday."

Babi shook her head and walked down the last few steps. Then she looked around, and she saw her mother's car parked on the other side of the street. "What are you doing, Pallina? Are you riding with us?"

"No, I'm waiting for Pollo. He said that he'd come by and pick me up. He might be coming with Step. Why don't you stay here and wait with me? Come on, tell your mother that you're coming over to my house for dinner."

Babi stood in silence for a moment. She hadn't thought about Step since that morning. Too many things had happened. She thought about how they'd said good night yesterday. How he'd said that she was full of contradictions. Just crazy. She wasn't inconsistent, and she didn't want to be.

"Thanks, Pallina, but I'm going home. Plus, like I've already told you, I don't have any real desire to see Step. So don't keep on with that refrain, or you and I really will have to fight about it."

"As you wish. All right then. See you at five o'clock at Parnaso—" Babi tried to answer back, but Pallina was too fast for her. "Yes, with my Vespa."

Babi smiled at her.

Pallina watched her walk away. Who knows why she was playing so hard to get. That was her business. Maybe it was a plan, she thought. Well, in any case, she liked Babi just the way she was.

Plus, she liked anyone who could put Signora Giacci in

her place like that. She decided that it was time to start spreading the word a little. She walked over to a group of younger girls who were in ninth grade. "Did you hear about what a fool Signora Giacci made of herself?"

"No, what happened?"

"She was about to flunk Silvia Festa, a girl in my class. She'd gotten confused and given another girl's grade to Festa."

"Do you swear it's true?"

"I do, but luckily Babi noticed."

"Wait, which Babi? You mean Babi Gervasi?"

"The very same."

A girl with *Il Messaggero* in her hands glanced over at the other girls with a curious look on her face. Some of them nodded at her. The girl worked up her nerve. "Listen, Pallina, but isn't this her?"

Pallina tore the newspaper out of her hands. She read the article rapidly. The other girl, still intimidated, went on. "We'd heard that the two of you went to the races, but we didn't believe it. But instead, it turns out it's true."

Oh, it's true, and then some, Pallina thought to herself, *as true as this article*. She folded up the newspaper and glanced toward Babi. By now, she'd almost reached her mother's car. Pallina shouted at the top of her lungs but the traffic noise drowned out her voice. By this point, there was nothing more to be done.

Babi stuck her head in the car, pushing the seat forward to get in back. "Ciao, Mamma." She leaned forward to give her mother a kiss. An open hand slapped her right in the face. "Ouch!" Babi fell back, flat on her butt, onto the rear seat. She rubbed her stinging cheek, and as a red patch appeared on it, a sullen scowl spread over her face.

Daniela got in the car. "Hey, have you seen this cool thing? Babi's in the newspaper..."

She looked around. The heavy silence. Raffaella's expression. Babi's hand massaging her stinging cheek. It was all clear in a flash.

"Let's forget I ever mentioned it," Daniela said.

They waited, arguing, for Daniela's friend Giovanna to arrive, and as usual, she was late. In the meantime, Raffaella was shouting like a madwoman. At last, Babi understood the whole story, and she tried to explain. Daniela testified in her favor but Raffaella got even more upset and angry. Pallina became the lead defendant. Even though she was found guilty out of hand, she could not face prosecution because she wasn't there. Daniela, who was within reach and available to have her face slapped, decided it would be wise to say nothing.

Babi was grounded. But not before she got a glimpse of *Il Messaggero*. When she saw the photo, she smiled because she really looked good in that shot. However, she decided to keep her opinion to herself.

At last, Giovanna arrived with her usual "Sorry I'm late" and got in back. Daniela pushed the front seat back in place and got in, and the car pulled away. The rest of the trip unfolded in utter silence. Giovanna decided that this situation was too tense. That said, the sisters had really overdone it this time.

In the end, Giovanna managed to work up the nerve to speak. "Well, at least today I wasn't very late, was I?"

Daniela burst out laughing. Babi controlled herself for a minute or two, and then she let loose too. Even Raffaella smiled.

Chapter 11

The old black leather purse was clamped tight under Signora Giacci's arm. A cloth jacket, mustard yellow. Short, drab hair that looked as weary as her gait. The dark brown opaque stockings made her look a few years older than she actually was, and the worn loafers with low heels and beat-up toes were making her feet ache. But that hurt was nothing like what she felt inside. Her heart must have been wearing shoes two sizes too tight.

Signora Giacci opened the glass door of her apartment building. The hinges squealed but that didn't surprise her. She stopped in front of the elevator and pushed the button. A red light lit up faintly. Signora Giacci looked at the glass fronts of the letter boxes built into the wall. Some of them were unmarked. One of the little doors didn't even have a glass pane and hung off-kilter, missing one of the two screws, imparting a sense of chaos and disorder and neglect, as did the apartment of Nicolodi, the owner. *Is it people's possessions that grow to resemble their owners, or is it the owners who grow to resemble their property?*

Signora Giacci wouldn't have known how to answer that question. Maybe the blame belonged to both owners and possessions. She stepped into the elevator and reminded herself to tell Nicolodi to fix that mailbox.

The elevator started up. There was graffiti carved into the wood. It was especially easy to read the name of some past love. Higher up, the symbol of a political party was perfectly etched by an optimistic sculptor. Down below, on the right, a male sex organ had turned out slightly inaccurate, at least to the best of her recollection.

When she reached the third floor, she opened the elevator's metal grate. She reached into her purse for a bunch of keys and inserted the longest key in the middle lock. She heard a sound behind the door. It was him, her beloved, her one and only. Her reason for living.

She opened the door with a shy smile. "Pepito!"

A little dog came running toward her, barking as he came. Signora Giacci leaned down. "How are you, sweetheart?" The dog leaped into her arms, tail wagging. He started eagerly licking her. "Pepito, you can't imagine what they did to your mamma today."

Signora Giacci shut the door behind her, set down her purse on a cold marble table, and took off her jacket. "A silly girl dared to upbraid me in front of everyone in the class, can you imagine… You should have heard the tone she took with me."

Signora Giacci went into the kitchen. The dog trotted along after her. He seemed sincerely interested.

"I just made a stupid, miserable mistake, and now she's ruined me, you understand? She humiliated me in front of the whole class." She turned an old faucet, and water ran through a rubber hose, yellowed by the passing years. The water sprayed chaotically onto a white rubber grate with odd, imprecise outlines. It had been cut by hand to fit the kitchen sink.

"She has it all. She has a beautiful place to live, someone who is making her lunch right now. She has nothing at all to worry about. By now, she's probably not even thinking about what she did. Right, why should she care?"

Signora Giacci reached into a cabinet full of glasses, each different from the others. She chose a glass at random and filled it with water. Even the sides of the glass seemed to be showing the signs of the passing years. She put a kettle full of water on the stove to boil and went into her small living room. The dog followed her obediently.

"And you should have seen all the other girls. They were overjoyed. They were laughing at me behind my back, so happy to see that I'd made a mistake..." Signora Giacci pulled open the door of a cupboard. She reached into a drawer and pulled out some homework and sat down at a table. She started correcting the papers. "She shouldn't have done it." She drew and redrew a bright red line under the mistake some girl had made. "She shouldn't have made me look ridiculous in front of all the girls."

The dog leaped up onto an old crimson velvet armchair and curled up on the soft cushion, by now well accustomed to his little body.

"You understand, how on earth am I going to be able to go back and face that class? Every time I give someone a grade, someone might very well ask, 'Are you sure you gave that grade to me, teacher?' And they'll laugh, just know they'll laugh..."

The dog shut his eyes. Signora Giacci put a red D on the paper she was correcting. The poor innocent girl might even have deserved a slightly higher grade. But Signora Giacci continued talking to herself.

Pepito fell asleep. Another paper was immolated on the altar of her indignation. On any more peaceful day, it might easily have cleared the bar and collected a passing grade.

Signora Giacci picked up another paper. The following day was going to be one of weeping and moaning for that class. But in this room, a woman sitting at a table covered by an old oilcloth had provided an answer to the question practically all on her own: It is people who make their possessions resemble them. Because for an instant, everything in that apartment seemed grayer and older. Even a beautiful Madonna hanging on the wall seemed to become a little cruel.

Chapter 12

A cheerful voice on the radio listed the American hits of the moment. Babi, sitting at the desk facing the window, was attempting to study, unsuccessfully. She leaned back in her chair and looked out, trying to concentrate.

On the terrace of the apartment across the way, a man was standing in bright sunlight, fixing something. Things didn't seem to be going all that well for him either.

Babi tried to repeat the latest algebraic formula she'd just studied. After mentally opening and closing a pair of round parentheses, she was no longer all that certain of what she had put inside them. She looked down and checked in the book. As expected, she'd got it wrong.

The man on the terrace across the way was gone. Babi went back to her formulas. She continued repeating them aloud, checking them now and again in the textbook. She guessed a few of them right and then got tired of doing it.

She picked up a pen that was lying on the desk. It had an odd cap. She looked at a couple of photos that were underneath the desk's glass top. She and Pallina hugging, sun kissed in a mountain meadow in Cortina. A beautiful postcard from the beach. She remembered it. Pallina had sent it to her the time she'd gone to the Maldives. Or had it been Seychelles? She leaned closer to the postcard but it didn't help much. The sea on a postcard always looks the same. More or less. She wished she were there, wherever it turned out that beach might be.

She smiled. Up above it was one of those little pictures you get in a photo booth on the street. She and Pallina holding ice cream cones. There was even a caption on it: *The Gluttons*. The handwriting belonged to Pallina. The gelato, on the other hand, came from Giovanni's shop. She could remember that day perfectly. The taste of the gelato. She was suddenly hungry.

She went into the other room. It was empty because Daniela was studying in her bedroom and her mother had gone out to play cards. She opened the fridge. A meager display. Skim milk, a few cheeses wrapped in wax paper. Fruit. Vegetables still bundled, not yet washed. A few bottles of Vitasnella diet water and some low-fat puddings. Terrible stuff.

She opted for a low-fat yogurt. She pulled off the paper top, and as usual, the last piece of paper remained stuck to the edge of the container. Without even licking it, she let the paper lid drop into the plastic shopping bag hanging from the handle of the window. If only it had been a fruit yogurt...

She dipped in a spoon and put it in her mouth. A bitter shiver ran all the way down to her feet. What torture.

She went back to her room. She'd dip in for a spoonful of yogurt now and then, and took just the bit from the end of the spoon. That day nothing seemed to suit her. What was wrong with her?

Then she saw it... and understood instantly. There was the poster, hung up on her armoire. Step seemed to smile at her in amusement with his motorcycle rearing up on just one wheel.

And there she was, behind him with both arms wrapped around his waist, holding on for dear life. With the wind in her hair. Her blue eyes seemed bigger. She didn't recognize herself. For a moment, she forgot the fear she'd experienced and wished she could be behind him on that motorcycle again. Right then, so she could hold tight to him.

A cruel fate by the radio's programming chose a new song, the latest by George Michael, and it spread through the room, magical and romantic. A shiver, this time of delight, traveled down her back, and her eyes, full of desire, wandered over the large photo until they halted on the phrase written in felt-tip pen at the top right. *Legendary pair!* And that exclamation point. Step had written it.

Babi looked below that phrase, at the hands gripping the handlebars. The right hand in particular. It had been its fault, it was the guilty one. It had caressed her that night on her bare back; it had attempted to undo her bra. And her own fingers had stopped it. Crazy fingers. She wondered if the left hand was more innocent. She hoped not.

She looked at the clock. It was five o'clock. Time to go. And as she was putting on her sweatshirt, she finally understood. Pallina was right. Daniela was right; her mother and Step were both right. She felt herself being enveloped by a strange warmth of sincerity. And for a moment, she was no longer a liar. Just full of contradictions. But true to her heart.

~

Pallina, Silvia, and a few other girls from Falconieri High School were sitting on a chain that groaned, suffering beneath their weight, stretching from one low marble post to another. They swung and swayed, laughing and talking about the topics of the day: Signora Giacci's snafu, yesterday's race, Babi's photo in today's newspaper.

"There she is." Silvia pointed to Babi as she approached the Parnaso Restaurant. She greeted them with an amused smile.

Pallina ran to greet her. "Ciao." They exchanged kisses, affectionate and sincere. The exact opposite of most of the kisses exchanged at the tables of the restaurant where elegant girls were sitting and chatting, luxuriating in the warm sun of that spring afternoon.

"That was an exhausting walk. I didn't think it was this far!"

"You came on foot?" Silvia looked at her, appalled.

"Yes, since I no longer have my Vespa." Babi gave Pallina an arch glance.

"Plus I just felt like stretching my legs. But maybe I overdid it a little. I'm not going to have to walk all the way back, am I?"

"No." Pallina heaved an annoyed sigh. "Here." She gave Babi a key ring. "My Vespa is at your disposal." Babi looked at the large light blue rubber *P* in her hands. Then she glanced over at Pallina's Vespa, parked a short distance away.

"Any news about what might have become of mine?"

Pallina tilted her head toward a group of boys.

"Pollo said he doesn't know anything about it. That means no one stole it, otherwise they'd have heard about it first thing. The police must have taken it. He said that they'll alert you after a while."

"Just think if they wind up talking to my folks." Babi looked over at the group of boys. She recognized Pollo and a few of Step's other friends. One guy with a patch over his eye smiled at her. Babi quickly looked away. She hoped that Step was with them.

A waiter was standing by a table, hoping for a generous tip. A young man leaned forward in his seat in order to extract his wallet from his trouser pocket. An embarrassed young woman pretended not to know how much the order was going to cost. Actually, though, that same young woman came to Parnaso practically every day and always ordered the same thing. The only thing that seemed to change on a constant basis was the young man taking her to dine there.

Babi continued looking around. A number of motorcycles roared to a halt nearby, and Babi turned hopefully to look at the new arrivals. Her heart pounded furiously. But to no avail. These were just random young men, as far as she was concerned, and they walked to their tables calling greetings. None of them resembled Step in the slightest.

"Who are you looking for?" Pallina's tone of voice and expression left no doubts. She knew.

"No one. Why?" Babi put the keys in her pocket without looking at Pallina. She was sure that her eyes, honest to a fault, would give her away.

"Nothing, it was just that I thought you were searching for someone...," Pallina persisted. Babi wondered how much she knew. And she glimpsed herself, stunned. Her lips were slightly parted, her eyes rapt and dreamy, and that shattered her reverie, that kiss not given.

"So long, girls." Babi said a hasty farewell as a blush spread over her cheeks. And it was no longer just the recent effort of the walk.

Pallina went with her to the Vespa. "Do you know how it works?"

Babi smiled. She undid the steering lock and turned on the ignition. She gave it a push forward. The kickstand retracted with a screech of springs.

"What are you guys doing this evening?" a man's voice asked.

Pallina raised her eyebrows. "Hey, this is a new twist. Are you deigning to go out with us?"

"You sure do like to argue. I just asked what you're up to!"

"Oh, I don't know. If you like, I'll phone you or have someone phone you." Pallina glanced at Babi archly, and looking past her, Babi suddenly glimpsed him. Step. His dark eyes, his bronzed skin, his short hair, and his hands marked by shattered smiles, broken noses, and other facial features that had once been intact.

His voice. *Full of contradictions.* He'd been right. A flash of pride took hold of her.

"No thanks, don't worry about it. I'll see you tomorrow after school," he said. "It was just idle curiosity."

"Whatever you think is best..." The Vespa carried Babi off quickly before that weak dam of pride could be shoved aside by a dangerous and stormy flood of emotion.

Pallina watched her go. The sweet way she used her shoulders to shift the gears. That faintly determined head, the hasty way she fled the scene. Pallina finally knew exactly what Babi wanted.

"Excuse me, girls." Pallina turned and reached in her pocket to pull out two hundred-lire coins and flipped them in the air. "I have a mission to perform . . . I have a phone call to make." She snatched the coins out of the air and, with the attitude of a tough broad, strode into the bar. "Ah, if it wasn't for me . . . "

She picked up the receiver. On the display at the top right appeared a number: ₤100. Someone hadn't used all their money. That small savings already struck her as a good sign. Cheerfully, she dialed the number. It rang. This mission was destined to be successful.

~

Babi parked Pallina's Vespa in the family garage. It was perfect. Her father would never be able to see the difference. She pushed it even closer to the wall so he wouldn't have anything to complain about.

She looked at her watch. A quarter to seven. Holy moly! She went galloping up the steps. "Ciao, Fiore."

The doorman didn't have time to return her greeting before Babi hastily opened the door. "Dani, is Mamma back?"

"No, not yet."

"Well, that's good." Raffaella had grounded her. Babi wasn't allowed to go out until next week, and it struck her as a bit much to violate parole on the very first day.

Daniela looked at her with annoyance. "So, still no news about our Vespa?"

"Nothing. The police must have it."

"What? Oh great! What are they using it for, high-speed chases?"

"They tell me that, sooner or later, the police will call us to give it back. We just have to make sure we intercept the phone call before Mamma and Papà..."

"Easier said than done. What if they call in the morning?"

"Then we're done for. But for now, Pallina gave us her Vespa. I put it in the garage, so when Papà comes home, maybe he won't notice a thing."

"Oh, speaking of which, Pallina called."

"When?"

"Just a little while ago, when you were still out. She said to tell you that they're going out and they're going to Vetrine. That she'll wait for you, not to act all difficult and just come. She said that she knows everything. And then she said something else, ummmm, it was like the name of an animal. Puppy, little mouse...Oh, right, she said, 'Say hi to the little fish for me.' Who's the little fish?"

As Babi turned to look at Daniela, she felt wounded, found out, betrayed. So Pallina knew.

"Oh, nothing. It's just a joke of ours."

It was going to be too complicated to explain. Too humiliating. Rage swept over her for a second and followed her silently into her bedroom. In the sunset painted on the glass panes of her window, she glimpsed the arc of that story. Step's mouth, his amused smile, the story, and Pollo next to him, his laughter and then Pallina and who knows who else.

She'd been stupid. She should have told her girlfriend. *She* would have understood her and consoled her. She would have been on her side, as always. Babi had no doubt about that. And this, at least, was nice.

Then she looked at the big photo on her armoire. And for a moment, she felt a stab of hatred. But only for a fleeting instant. Slowly, her arms dropped to her side, silently, weakly. Pride, dignity, fury, and indignation overcame her as she approached his image.

For a moment, they seemed to smile at each other. Arms wrapped around each other in the setting sun, close even if different. He was made of laminated paper; she was filled with clear-eyed emotions, finally lucid and sincere. They looked at each other.

Then she shyly lowered her eyes and, without wanting to, found herself facing the mirror. She looked at herself, and in that moment, she failed to recognize herself. Her eyes dancing, smiling, that luminous flesh... Even her face seemed different to her.

She pulled her hair back, and for an instant, she was someone else. She smiled happily at what she'd never been before. A woman in love, uncertain and worried about how to dress that evening.

~

Later, after her folks had given her yet another dressing-down and had then gone out for one of their usual dinners, Babi walked into Daniela's bedroom. "Dani, I'm going out."

"Where are you going?" Daniela asked.

"To Vetrine." Babi pulled a few sweaters out of Daniela's drawers and threw open the doors of her armoire. "Listen, where did you put the black skirt... the new one..."

"I'm not lending it to you! If I do, you'll throw that one away too! No way."

"Oh, come on. It was just bad luck that time, no?"

"Yes, but tonight you might have more bad luck. You might wind up in a mud puddle. No, I'm not lending you that skirt. It's the only one that actually fits me. I really can't let you have it, no kidding."

"Right, but then when I race as a chamomile or get my picture in the newspaper, then you boast to all your friends and tell them that you're my sister. But you don't tell them that you refused to lend me your skirt!"

"What does that have to do with anything?"

"It has everything to do with it, believe me. You just need to ask me a favor."

"All right, go ahead and take it."

"No, now I don't want it anymore..."

"No, now you have to take it..."

"No, now I don't want it..."

"Oh, really? Then unless you're wearing my skirt when you walk out that door, I'm going to call Mamma right up and let her know."

Babi swung around angrily on her sister. "You're going to do what?"

"Exactly what I just told you."

"I'll slap your cheeks red as a tomato..."

Daniela made a funny face, and at last, they both burst out laughing. Daniela went into her bedroom and opened the closet.

"Here." She laid the black skirt on the bed. "It's all yours. Dive into mud with it, if that's what makes you happy."

Babi took the skirt in both hands and held it up against

her belly. She started trying to imagine what she could wear over it.

The telephone rang. Daniela went to answer it. "Hello? Oh, hi..."

In her room, Babi turned up the radio. The music inundated the apartment.

Daniela put down the receiver. "Marcello, hold on for a second." She shut the door to the hallway and then resumed talking, relaxed now.

Babi turned her bedroom upside down. The armoire stood open, all the drawers spread out on the floor. There was clothing on the bed. Indecision.

She went to her mother's bedroom. She opened her big armoire. She started rummaging. Every so often she'd remember something. Could that be right for the black skirt? She opened the drawers. She was careful where she put her hands. Things had to go back where they belonged, otherwise her mother would notice. Mothers notice everything, or practically everything. Even Raffaella had overlooked Pallina's Vespa.

But never send a mother to buy the same kind of jeans you saw your girlfriend wearing. They'll always bring you the kind that the biggest loser in the class wears. She smiled.

A sky-blue angora sweater. Too warm. A silk blouse. Too fancy. A black jacket with a bodysuit underneath it. Too funereal, too somber. But the bodysuit wasn't bad. Bodysuit under a blouse? *Let's give it a try.*

She shut the drawers again. She started back to her bedroom. She'd left a red sweater on the bed. She'd be caught. She put it back. Would her mother notice? Enthusiasm won out over fear.

"Who the hell cares!" The threat of punishment vanished, disintegrating in the mirror. Babi stared at herself, puzzled. *Bodysuit under blouse, no, and Dani's skirt doesn't work with any of this anymore. So much the better.*

But what am I going to wear? Denim overalls? She hastily pulled open the bottom drawer. She pulled it out, faded, short, and rumpled: *Exactly the way my mother hates it most.* Exactly the way he would love it most, she felt certain. Rapidly, she slipped out of her clothing. In a split second, she was ready. She looked at herself in the mirror. Perfect. She put on the faded jeans shirt, tucked it down into the pants, and then pulled up the suspenders. She flopped down onto the bed, picked up the short gym socks and put them on, and then put on her high-top All Stars, navy blue, the same shade as the elastic headband she found in the bathroom. She brushed her hair and pulled it back. A pair of fish-shaped colorful earrings, looking as if they'd come from the South Seas. She straightened the collar of the shirt.

Then she started putting on her makeup. The music was pounding at full volume. A black line made her eyes look wider. The gray eyeliner pencil made them look smoky, in an attempt to make them look even more beautiful. Her white teeth were scented with mint. A delicate sheen of pink covered her soft lips. While her cheeks, naturally apple red in color, were tinged to perfection of their own accord.

Daniela was still on the phone when the music suddenly stopped. As the hallway door slowly opened, Daniela turned around. Babi appeared in the dim light. She took a few steps and then stopped. The glow from the nearby living room enveloped her completely.

Daniela stopped talking into the telephone. "Wow, you look gorgeous!"

Babi smiled at her. Then she put on her dark denim Levi's jean jacket. "Do I really?"

"You're superhot!"

"Thanks, Dani, but your skirt was just a little too serious." She gave her a kiss.

Dani watched as she walked away. For a moment, she doubted that this was really her sister. She wondered if she, too, would become so beautiful as she grew up.

Babi pulled the Vespa out of the garage. She started the engine and put it into first gear. She rolled down the ramp, slipping quickly out into the cool of the evening. Her French Caron perfume mixed with the scent of the native jasmine flowers in a delicate blend. She waved goodbye to the doorman.

Then, driving in the middle of traffic, she smiled as she remembered Daniela's opinion. Babi didn't feel ordinary, as she usually did. She wondered what Step would think of her. Would he like it? What would he say about her denim overalls? And her makeup? And her shirt? Would he notice that it was the same shade as her eyes?

Her little heart started beating hard. Pointlessly worried. She would very soon have all her answers.

Chapter 13

Babi locked the Vespa. Around her, a number of young people were sitting on their scooters or else lazing against a low wall, chatting about a love story gone wrong. Two guys dressed in punk getups were sitting on the steps. One of the two licked a cigarette and opened it, skillfully emptying all the tobacco into his hand. Then he reached into his jacket pocket and pulled out something. He looked around. No one was watching. In front of the club door, a big guy with a small earring in his left ear and a smashed-in boxer's nose was making a group of people wait.

Babi got in line. Nearby, there were two girls, too heavily made up, wearing light cloth coats. Their companions were two young men wearing fake camel hair jackets. One of the two guys had a golden pin in his buttonhole in the shape of a sax, at least as improbable as the idea that he knew how to play one. One of the two young men was betrayed by his light leather loafers with fringe. The other was undone by the heavy white socks that appeared boldly beneath the hem of his trousers when he reached into his pocket for a pack of cigarettes. That Marlboro in his mouth wasn't going to save them. They weren't getting in.

The bouncer spotted Babi and pointed to her. "You." Babi walked past all the other girls with their poufy, layered hair, a couple that was far too well dressed, and two or three other losers from out of town. Everyone envied her. There was one guy who grumbled, who tried to complain, but only under his breath. In reality, he just wanted to let his buddy hear what he had to say.

Babi smiled at the bouncer and went in. He decided that he'd chosen well. He went back to gazing grimly at his small flock, his face decisive, his brow furrowed, ready to crush any rebellion. But there was no need. Everyone continued to wait in silence, exchanging glances, but with that half smile that was worth a complete sentence, thinking, *We don't count for shit*.

Two enormous subwoofers were pounding high above the club, putting out a bass line to die for. At the bar, young men and women were shouting at the tops of their lungs, trying to make themselves heard and laughing. A guy with a funny face and little round glasses was sitting perched on the edge of a stool. He was happily chatting with a beautiful girl whose hair was long and blond. In fact, she was waiting for her boyfriend. He seemed not to understand her, or maybe he was just pretending not to. The girl shrugged her shoulders and let him buy her a gin and tonic. He paid for the round. He'd heard exactly what she'd said, but he was hoping against hope that the other guy would simply not show up.

Babi leaned against the glass. She was looking down at the big dance floor. Everyone was dancing like they'd lost their minds. At the sides of the floor, even the calmer club-goers were starting to be swept away by the beat of the house music.

She searched for Pallina and the others but she couldn't seem to spot them. She moved to the left. She really liked Vetrine. You came in and looked down through that glass floor at the people dancing beneath you. Then, if you wanted, you could go down there, too, throw yourself into the frenzied crowd, and be watched by others, a tiny, colorful spectacle.

Babi gazed down and ran her eyes over the whole dance floor. Two young men were dancing with each other, out of control. A few girls were waving their hands in the air. Another was jumping up and down, amused and laughing with a girlfriend, with their skimpy spandex black-and-white tops and their narrow-waisted shorts. Some had bare midriffs and brightly colored jeans, slightly flared at the leg, fastened with a long handkerchief at the waist. A solitary girl dancing on a podium thrashed away with her eyes closed, with a well-mannered gentleman in a coat and tie doing his best to hook up. A lunkhead who thought he was a latter-day John Travolta, with a headband and a loose shirt, was lit up by the flashing lights every so often, almost invariably high energy and out of control as the smoke poured near and far with a hiss, enveloping one and all. One couple was trying to say something to each other. Maybe he was suggesting a more sensual dance they could try at home with a gentler, softer music. She laughed. Maybe she was going to accept. Or maybe they were talking about something entirely different.

But no sign of Pallina, or Pollo, or any of their other friends, and especially not him, not Step. Maybe they hadn't come? Impossible. Pallina would have let her know.

Then Babi sensed something. An odd sensation. She'd

been looking in the wrong direction. And as if guided by a divine hand, by the gentle push of destiny, she turned around. There they were. In the very same room. Not far away, sitting in a corner at the far end of the club, right up against the last sheet of plate glass. The whole group was there. Pollo, Pallina, the guy with the patch, other young guys with short hair and bulging biceps, accompanied by smaller, cuter girls. There was Maddalena and her round-faced girlfriend.

And then there he was. Step was there. He was drinking a beer from a clear glass with a colorful trademark emblazoned on it, and every so often he'd look down. He seemed to be looking for something or someone. Babi felt her heart race. Could he be looking for her? Maybe Pallina told him that she was going to be there.

Slowly, she looked down again. The dance floor seemed blurry behind the glass. No, Pallina couldn't have told him that.

She turned her gaze in his direction again and smiled to herself. So strong, with that bad-boy attitude, his hair short, in a fade at the back, his jacket zipped up, and that way he had of sitting, like a confident hero.

And yet, there was something kind and good about him. Maybe it was the look in his eyes.

Step turned in her direction. Babi whipped away, frightened. She wasn't ready for him to see her, so she melted into the crowd and moved away from the glass. She went to the far end of the club where the staircase led down to the dance floor. She pulled her leather wallet out of the back pocket of her overalls. A short, stout guy stopped her. She gave him ten thousand lire. The guy handed her a yellow ticket and waved her through before going back to talking with a young woman wearing her cap sideways.

Babi hurried down the steps. Downstairs, the music was much louder. At the bar, Babi asked for a Bellini because she liked the taste of peaches. From that corner, she looked up and saw them. Step had stood up, and now he was leaning against the glass, braced with both hands. He was moving his head up and down in time to the music. Babi smiled. He couldn't see her from there, so she stayed and watched him.

Behind the bar, a slightly older young woman caught her attention. Her Bellini was ready. Babi gave her the yellow ticket. The young woman handed her the glass, and the Bellini was consumed just as quickly as it had arrived. Without letting herself be seen, Babi went around the dance floor from behind, going over directly beneath them.

She felt strangely euphoric. The Bellini was starting to take effect. The music took hold of her and she let herself be swept away. She shut her eyes and very slowly, dancing, she crossed the dance floor. She moved her head to the beat, happy and slightly drunk, surrounded on all sides by strangers. Her hair was whipping around.

She climbed onto one of the higher walls on the side of the dance floor. She clenched her hands and started dancing with her shoulders, mouth shut, dreamily, and then she opened her eyes and looked up. Through the glass, their eyes met. Step was there, staring at her. For a moment, he didn't recognize her. Pallina saw her too. Step turned to Pallina and asked her something. From down there, Babi couldn't hear, but she easily guessed at the question. Pallina nodded. Step looked down again. Babi smiled at him and then looked down and went back to dancing, caught up in the music.

Step moved away fast, indifferent to everything and everyone. Pollo shook his head. Pallina leaped onto her man, gleefully embracing him and kissing him on the lips like any woman in love.

The bouncer at the stairs let Step pass without paying. He greeted him respectfully and went back to necking with the young woman whose cap was on sideways. Life at Vetrine went on.

Step stopped. Babi was face-to-face with him. A lunkhead with long hair in a pageboy cut was dancing around her, interested in a potential hookup. Once he saw Step, he turned to go just as he had arrived, acting all casual now. Babi continued dancing, looking Step in the eyes, and in that instant, he lost himself in that sea of blue, in that inviting music. Slowly, his body came to life. He stepped up onto the raised side of the dance floor next to her, and silent and smiling, they danced side by side. Joining their gazes, their hearts.

Babi moved, swaying. Step leaned in closer until he could smell her perfume. She raised her hands, putting them in front of her face, and she danced behind them, smiling. She had surrendered.

He looked at her, captivated. She was beautiful. He'd never seen such a naive, innocent pair of eyes. That soft mouth, in a pastel hue, that velvety skin. Everything about her seemed fragile but perfect. Her hair hung free under the headband. They were dancing enthusiastically, shifting from side to side, as he admired her smile. With her fore-head, smooth and high, and that petite, narrow nose, and those rosy cheeks, she seemed like a baby doll. Step took her by the hand, pulled her close to him, and caressed her face. Babi looked at him, and for a moment... he trembled at the idea that, if he did anything more, she, fragile dream of china that she was, would vanish into a thousand shattered pieces.

Then he smiled at her and took her away with him. Carrying her off from that confusion, that frantic crowd. Everyone seemed to spin out of control as they went by. Step led her through that forest of flailing arms, protecting her from sharp human edges, holding her tight, warding off dangerous elbows pointed by the rhythm and pounding footsteps of human joy.

Farther up, Step carried her behind the glass. Pallina watched Babi vanish with him, her friend finally following her heart.

Maddalena watched him go, Step guilty only of not having loved her or of ever letting her think that he did. And while the couple, freshly in love, went out onto the street, Maddalena let herself collapse onto the sofa nearby. Sitting there with an empty glass in her hands and something much more difficult to fill inside her. She, mere fertilizer for that plant that so often blooms upon the grave of a withered love. That rare plant whose name is happiness.

Chapter 14

Youthful and covered in denim, they were better than a real-life commercial. Riding on the midnight-blue motorcycle, Babi and Step melted into the city, laughing all the way. Talking about everything and nothing, smiling at each other in the rearview mirrors. She, leaning on his shoulder, letting herself be carried along like this, buffeted by the wind and by that new power: freedom.

Via Veneto, Piazza Barberini, Via Nazionale. They went to the Angeli Theater. They sat upstairs and watched a movie on the big screen. They were thrilled more by the simple chance contact of their bodies than they were by that music video by an American rock star. They didn't even recognize him, rapt as they were in the same thoughts. And yet he was rich and famous. But right then and there, they were much more important than he could ever hope to be.

Via delle Quattro Fontane. Piazza Santa Maria Maggiore. Right turn. A small pub. An English guy at the door recognized Step and ushered him in. Babi smiled. With him, she could get in everywhere. He was her key to every door. Her key to happiness.

She was so happy that she didn't even realize she was

ordering a dark ale, she who couldn't even stand the lightest of blond beers, so dreamy that she shared a bowl of pasta with him, forgetting her diet. With the words rolled out leisurely, she realized that she was telling him about everything, that she had no secrets from him. He seemed intelligent and strong to her, handsome and sweet.

They played darts and she hit the target high. She turned jubilantly to him. "Pretty good, huh?" He smiled at her and nodded his head. Babi tossed another dart, but her blue eyes didn't notice that she'd already hit the bull's-eye.

Carried off again. Willingly kidnapped. Via Cavour. The Pyramid of Cestius. Testaccio. Little Vito, dispenser of cheer, was checking the crowd of people waiting at the entrance to Radio Londra. When he saw Step, he waved at him from a distance. He made some of the young people move aside to let him through. Vito raised the rope. Step gave him a friendly slap on the shoulder and then, holding hands with Babi, walked into the club. A few of the girls waiting outside watched enviously as Babi went by, and not just because she'd been allowed in. Frankly, given the guy she was with, they'd have happily waited outside.

Everyone in the club seemed to know Step. They walked past him, saying hello and slapping him on the back or just brushing close. A few young women walked over to him. Babi felt a strange emotion, new to her. One of the women gave Step a kiss on the cheek and tried to strike up a conversation. Now she knew what that feeling was. Jealousy.

But Step didn't even give her the time to realize it. He put a quick end to the conversation with the young woman and dragged Babi out into the middle of the dance floor. They danced together to the pounding beat of the house music. Then, smiling and sparkling like fancy champagne, they drew close in a small, passing toast.

Later, they exited, sweaty and laughing. They said good night to Vito, as they were once again envied by those who were still waiting outside. They left as they'd arrived, on that roaring motorcycle that they'd parked right in front of the club. They roared uphill in second gear at top speed, savoring the cool breeze of that night in late April.

When they reached the intersection, they turned left and took the main thoroughfare. Step put the bike into third gear and then fourth. The traffic light at the intersection was blinking yellow. Step went through the light. Suddenly, he heard a screech of brakes. The sound of rubber scorching as it dragged across the asphalt. The sound of fine gravel. A Jaguar Sovereign was coming from the left at full speed.

The Jaguar tried to brake hard. Step, caught off guard, also braked and sat there, motionless, in the middle of the intersection. The motorcycle coughed and died. Babi held on to him tight. The car's powerful headlights were reflected in her frightened eyes as it hurtled toward them.

The snout of the big, wild cat rebelled against the crude application of the brakes, and the car fishtailed. Babi shut her eyes. She heard the roar of the engine being reined in, the ABS perfectly controlling the wheels, the rubber tortured by the brakes. Then nothing.

She opened her eyes. The Jaguar was there, just inches from the motorcycle, motionless. Babi heaved a sigh of relief and released Step's jacket from her terrified grip.

With an impassive face, Step gazed at the car's driver. "Where do you think you're racing to, asshole!" Then he started the motorcycle back up.

The guy, a man about thirty-five with a perfectly groomed head of hair, thick and tightly curled, lowered his electric car window, displaying his angry face. "Excuse me? What did you just say to me, kid?"

Step turned off the motorcycle. He smiled as he got off. He knew this type of guy. He must have a woman sitting beside him and didn't want to come off looking like a fool. Step walked over to the car. Sure enough. Through the glass, he saw a pair of feminine legs next to the man. A pair of shapely hands crossed on an elegant black evening bag and a fancy evening gown. He tried to glimpse the woman's face, but a streetlight reflecting on the glass concealed her. *Kid. He called me kid. Wait until you see what this kid does to you.*

Step opened the guy's car door very politely. "Come on out, asshole. Maybe you'll be able to hear me better."

The man started to get out. Step grabbed him by the jacket and dragged him hurtling out of the car. He slammed him down on the Jaguar's head. The short antenna of his telephone vibrated. Step cocked his fist back, poised in midair, ready to slam down.

"Step, no!" It was Babi. Step turned to look at her. For a second, he'd completely forgotten about her. He saw her standing next to the motorcycle, her gaze filled with concern, her arms hanging helplessly at her sides. "Don't do it!"

Step released his grip, and the guy took advantage immediately. Free now and a coward at heart, he punched Step in the face. Step's head rocked back. But only for a moment. Surprised, he raised his hand to his mouth. His lip was bleeding. "You filthy son of a . . . " Step lunged at him.

The guy threw his hands up and dropped his head, trying to flee in fright. Even he didn't know why he'd dared to hit Step. Step grabbed him by his curly hair, yanked his head down, ready to slam his knee into the guy's face, when suddenly he was hit again. Differently, this time harder, a blow that went straight to his heart. A short, sharp jab. A mere word. His own name.

"Stefano..."

The woman had stepped out of the car. Her handbag was sitting on the hood, and she was nearby. Step looked at her. Then he looked at her bag but didn't recognize it. He wondered who'd given it to her. What a strange thought.

Slowly he opened his fist. The lucky curly-haired guy was suddenly free. Step stood gazing at her in silence. She was as pretty as ever. A faint "Ciao" issued from his lips.

The guy pushed him aside. Step moved back, letting himself be pushed.

The guy got back into the Jaguar and started the engine. "Come on, let's get out of here."

Step and the woman stared at each other for one last instant. Between those two similar pairs of eyes, a strange magic unfolded, a long history of love and sadness, suffering and the past. Then she got back into the car, beautiful and elegant, and as quickly as she had appeared, she left him there on the street, with his lip bleeding and his heart in pieces.

Babi ventured closer to him. Worried about the only wound she could see with her eyes, she delicately dabbed at the blood with her hand.

Step recoiled from that kind touch, so filled with a new burst of love. He mounted his motorcycle in silence and waited until she was seated behind him before he took off, in anger. He shot forward. The motorcycle tried to resist at first but soon, docile and submissive, it veered to the right, turning onto the Lungotevere. Step upshifted. Then he twisted the throttle, and the motorcycle shot out onto the road, the rpms climbing steadily.

Without thinking, Step started racing. He left old memories behind him, accelerating to outrun them. Eighty kilometers per hour, ninety. Faster and faster. The chilly air pricked at his face, and that new source of suffering seemed to provide some relief. Ninety-five, a hundred. Faster and faster still.

With his turn indicator blinking, he went racing between two cars side by side. He almost brushed against them as his half-open eyes looked elsewhere. Happy images of that woman filled his tangled mind.

A hundred five, a hundred ten, a gentle rise and the motorcycle practically flew through an intersection. A stoplight that had just turned red. The cars on the left honked their horns, stopping short just after starting up at their green. Obeying the dictates of that arrogant, bullying motorcycle, as fast and dangerous as a navy-blue chrome-plated bullet.

A hundred ten, a hundred twenty-five. The wind was whistling. The road, its sides blurry now, merged at the center. Another intersection. A distant stoplight. The green vanished. The yellow appeared. Step pressed his thumb down on the small button on the right, marked in English as the HORN. The horn sounded its voice in the night like the scream of a wounded wild animal, galloping to its death. Step shouted into the darkness, like an ambulance siren, piercing as the shout of the wounded man it was carrying. His scream came out loud and deep, a suffering mirror of what he was feeling.

Closer and closer now. The traffic light changed again. Red light.

Babi started pounding her fists against his back. "Stop, stop."

At the intersection, the cars started up. A wall of metal, dozens of colorful, expensive bricks, was suddenly erected, loud, in their path. It drew closer and closer, dangerous and insurmountable.

"Stop!" That last scream, that cry for life. Step suddenly seemed to snap out of it. The throttle, suddenly released, quickly dropped to zero. The engine downshifted under his domineering foot.

Fourth gear, third, second. His left hand clenched down hard on the steel brake handle, practically bending it. The motorcycle shook as it braked to a halt, as the RPMs dropped dizzyingly, in a rivalry with the speedometer to drop to zero. The tires left two deep, straight stripes on the asphalt. The smell of burning rubber swirled around the smoking pistons. Motionless.

The cars went rolling past just inches from the motorcycle's front wheel, just beyond the white stripe, the limit line. None of the drivers had noticed a thing.

Only then did Step remember Babi. He turned around. She'd dismounted. He saw her there, leaning against a wall at the side of the road.

He put the bike on the kickstand and got off, crossing the street to join her. Fragile cries were emerging from her chest, unrestrained like the tiny tears that streaked her pale face. Step didn't know what to do now. Standing there, facing her with his arms spread, fearful even of touching her, afraid of the idea that those faint nervous hiccups might be transformed by his mere touch into an unstoppable wave of sobbing.

Nevertheless, he dared to touch her. But her reaction was unexpected. Babi pushed his hand away forcefully, and her words came pouring out in something approaching a shout, broken by her cries.

"Why? Why are you like this? Are you insane? What made you think you needed to drive like that? So reckless, so crazy?"

Step didn't know what to say to her. He looked at those eyes, so big and glistening, bathed in tears.

How could he explain it to her? How could he tell her what lay behind this? His heart tightened into a silent vise grip.

Babi looked at him. Her suffering, inquiring blue eyes sought an answer in him, a tranquil beach where it was possible to lie comfortably in satisfied peace.

Step shook his head. *I can't*, he seemed to be repeating deep inside. *I just can't.*

Babi sniffed loudly and then, as if gathering her strength, launched into it again. "Who was that woman? Why did you change all of a sudden? Step, you have to tell me. What was there between you two?"

And that last phrase, that huge mistake, that unthinkable misunderstanding seemed to hit him full on. In an instant, all his defenses collapsed. The constant, powerful guard he always kept up, trained by an enduring silence, day after day, suddenly fell. His heart let go, for the first time unafraid and tranquil.

He smiled at that naive young woman. "So you want to know who that woman was?"

Babi nodded.

"That was my mother."

Chapter 15

Just two years earlier, Step was pacing back and forth in the privacy of his room as he tried to go over his chemistry lesson. He leafed back through his notebook full of notes. It was no good. Those formulas just didn't want to enter into his head.

He let himself fall back into his chair and went on studying, with both elbows braced against the table, fists driven into his forehead, determined to do well on that exam. It was his last year of high school at Villa Flaminia.

Suddenly, from the top floor of the building across the way, loud music started up. It was Lucio Battisti, singing loud and clear, *You come back into my thoughts, sweet as you are...*

Step looked up. *Lucky you,* he thought. *Nothing comes back into my thoughts, and I hate chemistry.*

Then, seeing that they were really determined to make him listen to the whole album, he lost his temper. *They're out of their minds!* He slammed both hands down on the table. *That's the last thing I needed.*

He stood up and looked out the window. Nothing. In the building across the way, there was no sign of anyone.

He opened the window. "Are you done listening to that music?"

For a second, Step thought he saw a curtain move in one of those windows. Then he decided that he'd been seeing things. "Hey! Would you turn it off!"

Slowly, the volume of the music was lowered. "Those idiots." Step went back down and focused on those rumpled sheets of notes from his notebook.

A few minutes later, the telephone rang. He looked at the clock. It was almost four. That must have been Pollo. He went to the telephone to answer it. He picked up the receiver. "Hello?" On the other end of the line, silence. "Hello?" Still more silence, then a simple click. Someone had just hung up. They hadn't liked his voice. Stupid crank calls. He slammed the telephone receiver down.

"Stefano..."

Step turned around. His mother was there, right in front of him. She was wearing a dark brown fur coat with stunning highlights, light and golden. Her legs peeked out from under a burgundy skirt. They were sheathed in fine stockings that vanished into a pair of elegant, dark brown high-heeled shoes.

"I'm going out, do you need anything?"

"No thanks, Mamma."

"Well, we'll see you this evening then. If Papà calls, tell him that I had to go out to take the papers he knows about to the accountant."

"All right."

His mother came over to him and gave him a soft kiss on the cheek. From the curls of her black hair, slightly long and twisted, came a caress of perfume. Step decided that she'd put on a little too much. He also decided not to tell her so. Then, watching her as she left, he realized he'd made the right decision.

She was perfect. His mother basically couldn't make mistakes. Not even when it came to putting on perfume.

Under her arm, she carried the purse that he and his brother had given her. Paolo had contributed nearly all the money, but it was Step who had selected it, in that shop on Via Cola di Rienzo where he'd watched his mother stop, undecided, far too many times.

"You're quite the connoisseur," she'd whispered into his ear after unwrapping it. Then she'd put it under her arm and, swiveling her hips in an exaggerated, funny fashion, she'd done a sort of runway presentation. "Well, how does it look?"

Everyone had replied, laughing. But actually, she only wanted to hear the verdict of the connoisseur. "You look beautiful, Mamma."

Step heard the kitchen door shut. When was it they'd given her that purse? Had it been for Christmas or for her birthday? He decided that, for the moment, the best thing he could do was focus on trying to remember the chemistry formulas.

Later, his decision proved to have been the right one. It was almost seven, and he was three pages short of finishing his planned course of study. He was on edge. He wanted to go to the gym—he'd already made plans to do so with Pollo—but he wasn't going to be able to make it.

Then it happened. Battisti started singing from the half-open window of the top floor of the apartment building across the way. Louder than before. Insistently. Provocatively.

Showing no sign of respect for anyone or anything. No respect for Step, who was studying and who wouldn't be able to go to the gym. This was too much.

Step grabbed the house keys and went running out the door, slamming it behind him. He crossed the street and went into the lobby of the building. The elevator was occupied so he galloped up the stairs, taking them two at a time. *Enough's enough, I just can't take it anymore.* They'd hear from him now.

He had nothing against Lucio Battisti, in fact. He loved him. But to treat him like that.

Step reached the top floor. Just then, the elevator door opened. Out came a delivery boy with a gift-wrapped package in one hand. He beat Step to it. He checked the surname on the little plaque on the door. Then he rang the bell.

Step stood beside him, catching his breath. The delivery boy looked at him with some curiosity. Step exchanged the glance with a smile and then focused on the package the delivery boy was holding. Written on the package was *Antonini*. This must be a box of the famous pastries from Caffè Antonini. His family ordered from them, too, every Sunday. His mother was crazy about their canapés. They had every flavor imaginable. With salmon, caviar, assorted seafood. At last, a voice came from behind the door: "Who is it?"

"Antonini. It's the pastries you ordered, sir."

Step smiled to himself. He'd guessed right, and maybe the guy who'd ordered them would offer him one, just to make up for the noise.

The door swung open, and a young man appeared in the doorway, about thirty years old. His shirt was half-unbuttoned, and below it he wore only a pair of boxer shorts.

"Giovanni Ambrosini?" The delivery boy started to hand him the package, but when the young man spotted Step, he threw himself against the door, desperately trying to push it shut.

Step didn't understand, but he instinctively lunged forward in response. He wedged his foot against the doorjamb, blocking it before the guy could get it shut. The delivery boy reeled backward, doing his best to keep the cardboard tray of pastries upright and level.

Step started shoving back against the door. As he was pushing, with his face pressed against the cold, dark wood, through the opening between door and jamb, he saw it. The purse sat on an armchair, next to a fur coat.

Suddenly it all came back to him. He and his brother had given their mother that purse for Christmas.

Then rage and despair and a burning wish that he could be somewhere else, that he could disbelieve what his own eyes were seeing, increased his strength a hundredfold. He threw the door open, hurling the young guy to the floor.

He stalked into the living room like a baleful fury. And his eyes wished they could be blind rather than see what they were seeing. The bedroom stood open. There she was, amid the tangled sheets, with a different face, unrecognizable to him, although he'd seen it thousands of times. His mother was lighting a cigarette with an innocent expression.

Their eyes met, and in that instant, something snapped, a flame died out forever. At the same time, that last remaining umbilical cord of love was severed, and they gazed at each other, silently screaming, sobbing, and weeping.

Then Step walked away while she remained there, on the bed, speechless and burning steadily down, just like the cigarette she'd only just lit. Burning with love for him, with hatred for herself, for the other guy, for that situation.

Step walked slowly toward the door and stopped there. He saw the delivery boy out on the landing, next to the elevator with the tray of pastries in his hand, who was staring at him in silence.

Then, without warning, a pair of hands were laid upon his shoulders. "Listen..."

Step whirled around. It was that young man. What was he supposed to listen to? He no longer felt emotion of any kind. He laughed. The guy failed to understand. He just stood there looking at him, baffled. Then Step slammed a fist right into his face. Destiny.

The strange words of Lucio Battisti, an innocent party, guilty of that unwelcome discovery, rose into the air on the landing or else, perhaps, they just chanced to pop into Step's mind. *Forgive me, for so much, if you can, Lord. I beg her forgiveness too.*

At that moment, he realized that he didn't know anything anymore.

Giovanni Ambrosini lifted his hands to his face, covering them with blood. Step grabbed him by the shirt and, tearing the fabric, hauled him out of that filthy, illicit love nest.

He punched him over and over in the head. The guy tried to run. He started down the stairs with Step right behind him. With a precisely aimed kick, Step knocked him forward, making him trip and fall. Ambrosini tumbled down the stairs.

As soon as he came to a halt, Step was all over him.

He kicked him repeatedly, in the back and legs, while the guy clung piteously, suffering, to the railing, trying to haul himself upright, to escape his wrath.

Step was slaughtering him. Step started yanking on his hair, doing what he could to make him release his grip, but even as Step's hands started filling up with tufts of hair, Ambrosini still clung there, holding on to those iron railings for dear life, shouting in terror.

The doors of the other apartments started to open. Tenants, variously curious about and scared by those screams, emerged. They huddled together in shared concern.

Step stomped on his hands, which were starting to bleed. But there was no loosening Ambrosini's grip. He held on, certain that it was his only possible salvation.

So Step did it. He swung his leg back and, with all his strength, kicked him in the head from behind. A violent, stunningly precise blow. Ambrosini's face stamped itself right into the railing with a dull thud. Both his cheekbones were shattered, the flesh lacerated. Blood jetted forth. The bones of his mouth fractured. A tooth dropped, bouncing far away across the marble. The railing started to vibrate, and that metallic noise reverberated down the staircase, along with Ambrosini's last shout before he lost consciousness.

Step ran away, galloping down the stairs, passing quickly by all those terrible, curious faces, smashing into those flaccid bodies that tried in vain to stop him. He wandered through the city and didn't return home that evening. He went over to Pollo's for the night. His friend asked no questions. Luckily, Pollo's father was away that night.

Pollo heard Step thrashing in his sleep, suffering even in a dream. But the next morning, Pollo acted as if nothing had happened, even though one of the pillows was drenched with tears. They ate breakfast together, smiles on their faces, talking about this and that, sharing a cigarette. Then Step went to school, and at the chemistry exam, he even managed to snatch a gentleman's C from the jaws of disaster. But that day, his life changed forever. No one else knew why, but nothing was ever the same after that.

Something evil had come to roost inside Step. Some filthy beast, some terrible wild animal had built its lair inside his heart, ready to emerge at any moment, ready to strike, the progeny of suffering, the fallout of a love destroyed.

From then on, life at home became impossible. Silences and fleeting gazes. No more smiles, with the one person he'd loved more than anyone else.

And then came the trial. The guilty verdict. His own mother had not testified in his defense. His father had shouted at him, denouncing him. His brother had been unable to understand. And no one had ever known a thing, except for the two of them. Hate-filled guardians of that terrible, heavy secret.

That same year, his parents had separated and Step went to live with Paolo. The first day he moved into that new apartment, he looked out the window of his bedroom. There was nothing but a peaceful meadow. He started putting his things away. He pulled a few sweaters out of his duffel bag and put them away in the back of the armoire on an empty wooden shelf.

Then he pulled out a sweatshirt. As he pulled it out, the garment tumbled open in his hands. For a moment, it seemed as if his mother was there in the room. He remembered the time he'd let her borrow it, that day they'd gone running together along tree-lined boulevards. How he'd slowed down just to be near her. And now he was in that room, so far away from her, in every sense of the word.

He clutched the sweatshirt tight in his hands and lifted it to his face. He smelled her perfume, and he started to cry. Then, foolishly, he wondered whether, that day, he ought to have told her that she'd put on too much of it.

Chapter 16

The front wheel sank slightly into the deep sand, and the motorcycle swerved rebelliously to one side. With a precisely calculated shove of his feet, Step straightened the bike. The back wheel spun free, kicking up the darker sand behind it, in a rooster tail. Babi held tight to him, scared. The motorcycle swayed a little more, fishtailing.

Then, having reached the harder sand, everything went back to normal. Step downshifted. Gently, he gave it gas, and the motorcycle broke into a stable, regular cruise along the water's edge.

Off to the right, below them, little waves slapped and slowly subsided. They came and they went, the regular breathing of the sea as, deep and dark, it watched them from afar. Babi looked around. The moon, riding high in the sky, lit up the Feniglia shore. The beach stretched out into the distance, between darker patches of the mountains. To their left and above them, the sand dunes, pounded and torn by the day's strong winds, now slept quietly in the night, covered by a wild blanket of greenery.

Step turned off the headlights. Shrouded in darkness, they continued to race along like that, on the soft, wet carpet of sand. All around them, the sound of distant trees, the suck of the outgoing waves, the silence of nature at night. When they reached the middle of the Feniglia shore, they stopped. Step picked up a chunk of wood, still wet and ravaged by the waves, and placed it under the motorcycle's kickstand, sideways, to keep it upright in the sand. Without a word, they found themselves walking along, alone and side by side, enveloped in all that peace.

Babi walked down to the water's edge. Tiny waves fringed in silver slapped down, just short of her dark blue All Stars. She walked a little closer. A wave with a little more power than the others just caught the white rubber of her shoes. Babi darted back, escaping the salt water.

She bumped up against Step. His strong arms wrapped comfortably around her, and she settled into them. Slowly, she turned around. In that nocturnal light, a smile appeared on her face. Her blue eyes, full of love, looked up at him, amused.

He leaned down and, slowly embracing her, kissed her soft, warm lips, fresh and salty, caressed by the wind off the sea. Step ran a hand through her hair. He pulled it back, uncovering her face. Her cheek, painted with silver like a tiny mirror of that moon high above, and her profile, with the straight line of her nose and her eyes half-shut, listened to his kisses on her neck.

Now they were sprawled full length on the cold beach, arms wrapped around each other, and their hands, covered with tiny grains of sand, sought each other out. Then another kiss, and yet another, and in the meantime, a smile and a slow descent and a sweet parting, just gently brushing lips.

Babi sat up, hoisting herself on both her arms. She looked at him where he lay below her. Those eyes, calm now, were staring at her. He seemed to belong to that sand, stretched out there, his arms spread wide, master not only of the beach but of everything.

Smiling, Step pulled her closer, master of her as well, gathering her into a kiss, this one longer and more powerful. He hugged her tight, breathing in her soft scent. And she let herself go, swept away by that power and, at that moment, realized that she had never really kissed anyone before.

Now he was sitting behind her, holding her in his arms, letting her rest comfortably between his legs. And he, solid backrest, amiable armchair that he had become, broke into her thoughts every so often with a kiss on the neck. "What are you thinking about?"

Babi turned to look at him, glancing back out of the corner of her eye. "I just knew you were going to ask me that."

She went back to resting her head against his chest. "Do you see that house down there on the rocks?"

Step looked in the direction her hand was pointing. Before losing himself in the distance, he stopped to consider that tiny forefinger, and it, too, struck him as something stupendous. He smiled. "Yes, I see it."

"It's my dream house! Oh, how I'd love to live in that house. Just think what a view they must have from there. A picture window looking out over the sea. A living room where you could linger in an embrace and watch the sunset."

Step hugged her close to him. Babi remained there for a short while longer, gazing dreamily into the distance.

He drew closer, resting his cheek against hers. She rubbed against him like a cat. Then, amused and playful, she tried to push him away, smiling up at the moon. She pretended she was trying to slip out of his grasp. But then she returned to him of her own volition and slipped into his kiss, repentant and lovable.

Slowly, Babi turned toward him. Step took her face in his hands, and she, pale pearl that she was, smiled, the prisoner of that human seashell.

Step watched her. "Do you want to take a swim?"

"Are you serious, as cold as it is? Plus, I didn't bring a swimsuit."

"Oh, come on. It's not really cold. And anyway, what does a little fish like you need a swimsuit for?"

Babi's face twisted angrily, and she shoved him hard with both arms, doing her best to knock him back into the sand. But Step resisted. He clenched hard with his abs, strong and compact, and supported his own weight.

Defeated, Babi got up. She started brushing the sand off her. "By the way, you told Pollo all about the other evening, didn't you?"

Step stood up and tried to put his arms around her. "What, are you kidding?"

"Then how on earth did Pallina know? She must have heard it from Pollo, so you must have told him the whole story."

"I swear to you that I never said a word about it. Maybe I could have talked in my sleep—"

"Talked in your sleep? Give me a break! And anyway, like I told you before, I don't believe it when you swear to something."

"Actually, I really do talk in my sleep sometimes, as you'll soon find out for yourself." Step went toward the motorcycle, looking back at her with a smile in his eyes.

"Wait, I'll soon find out for myself?" she asked. "You're kidding, right?" Babi hurried over to him, worried now.

Step laughed. The barb he'd launched had had the desired effect. "Why, aren't we sleeping together tonight? After all, it's just a few hours till dawn."

Babi looked at her watch, concerned now. "It's two thirty. Oh heck, if my folks get there before I do, I'm done for. Hurry up, I've got to get home."

"So you're not sleeping at my place?"

"What are you, crazy? Maybe you don't understand who you're dealing with here! Plus, have you ever seen a little fish sleeping with someone?"

Step started the motorcycle and then kept the brake on as he revved the engine. The motorcycle, obedient between his legs, swerved around in a circle and then stopped right in front of her, ready for her slightest command.

Babi climbed on, and Step put it in first. Gently, they rode away, then faster and faster, leaving behind them a precise strip of broad tire marks. Farther on was a patch of sand churned up by innocent kisses and a tiny heart. She'd drawn it without letting him know, with the tiny forefinger that he liked so well. A treacherous and solitary wave erased the borders of that heart. But with an effort of the imagination, you could still read the *S* and the *B*.

Far away, a dog barked at the moon. Babi, leaning on Step's shoulders, braced her feet on the pedals and stood up. And so, standing straight against the sky, she breathed deep.

A Nordic wind brushed back her hair, caressing her face. Then Babi leaned forward and hugged him, kissing him.

Step felt those soft lips on his neck. A strange heat surged up inside him. He felt strangely happy. He accelerated. His wheels cut quickly through a salt wave, shattering it, wounding it fatally. Tiny silvery sprays shot off in all directions, surrounding them on all sides. The water fell far away, cutting tiny round holes into the cold sand. A vengeful wave erased that tire track while the motorcycle continued along its way, in love, vanishing into the distance of the night. There was no longer even the slightest trace of that heart carved into the sand. Still, that night would live on forever in their memories.

Chapter 17

In front of Vetrine, standing parked in the deserted lot, Babi's Vespa was the only vehicle that remained. She got off the motorcycle, undid the front wheel lock, and started her scooter. She climbed on and rocked it down off the kickstand. Then it seemed as if she just remembered Step was there.

"Ciao." She smiled at him tenderly.

Step moved closer. "I'll ride with you. I'll escort you home."

When they reached Corso Francia, Step maneuvered his motorcycle around behind her Vespa and placed his foot on the taillight. He revved his engine and gave her a push. The Vespa sped up.

Babi turned around, stunned, and looked at him. "This is scary!"

"Just keep a firm grip on the handlebars..."

Babi stared straight ahead again, holding tight and determined to the handlebars. Pallina's Vespa could go faster than hers, but hers would never be able to reach these speeds.

They covered the length of Corso Francia and then

climbed the hill of Via Jacini, all the way to the piazza. Step gave her one last shove, right in front of her apartment building. Then he let her go. Slowly, the Vespa lost speed.

Babi braked and turned to look at Step. He was stopped now, sitting upright on the motorcycle, just a short distance from her. He sat there, looking at her for a second. Then he smiled at her, put it into first gear, and pulled away.

She followed him with her gaze until he vanished around the curve. She heard him accelerating, faster and faster, a rapid shift of gears, tailpipes roaring as he sailed away at top speed into the distance.

Babi waited for a sleepy Fiore to raise the gate arm. Then she rode up the ramp to the apartment building. When she turned in to the curve, she had a grim surprise. Her whole apartment was lit up brightly, and her mother was standing there, looking out her bedroom window.

"Claudio, there she is!"

Babi gave her a desperate smile. It didn't do a bit of good. Her mother slammed the window shut.

Babi put the Vespa away in the garage, barely managing to fit it between the wall and the Mercedes. As she was pulling down the rolling door, she thought about that morning's slap in the face. Unconsciously, she lifted her hand to her cheek. She tried to remember how badly it had hurt. She wasn't all that worried. She figured that she'd know exactly how badly before long.

She climbed the steps slowly, doing her best to put off as long as possible that discovery, by now inevitable. The apartment door stood open. She walked resignedly onto that gallows. Condemned to be guillotined, by no means hopeful of a reprieve, this latter-day Robespierre in overalls was going to lose her head.

She shut the door behind her and as soon as she turned around, she caught the slap full in the face. "Ouch." Always on the same side, she thought to herself, massaging her cheek.

"Go straight to bed, but first give your Vespa keys to your father."

Babi walked down the hallway. Claudio was standing there, by the door.

Babi gave him Pallina's key ring.

"Babi?"

She turned around, worried now. "What?"

"Why this *P*?" her father asked.

The rubber *P* on Pallina's key ring dangled interrogatively from Claudio's hand. Babi stared at it, stunned for a moment. Then reawakened by the slap in the face, freshly creative in the moment, she improvised. "Oh, come on, Papà, don't you remember? It's the nickname you gave me yourself! When I was little you used to call me Princess Savina, from the Smurfs!"

Claudio swayed hesitantly for a moment but then a smile appeared on his face. "Oh, of course! Princess Savina. I'd almost forgotten." Then he turned serious again. "Now go to bed. We'll talk about all this tomorrow. I didn't like it one bit, Babi!"

The bedroom doors swung shut. Claudio and Raffaella, somewhat relaxed at last, discussed that rebellious, unrecognizable daughter of theirs, that young woman who had once been so calm and untroubled but who now came home at four in the morning, took part in wheelie competitions, and wound up with her photograph in all the morning papers. They wondered what had become of her... What had happened to the little Princess Savina they once knew?

In her bedroom nearby, Babi undressed and got into bed. Her reddened cheek found cool soothing on her pillow. She lay there like that, dreaming of reality for a while. She felt as if she could still hear the sound of the waves and the wind caressing her hair, and then she remembered that kiss, so strong and tender at the same time.

She turned over in bed. She thought of him, and as she was sliding her hands under her pillow, she dreamed she was embracing him. Between the smooth sheets, tiny grains of sand made her smile. And in the darkness of her bedroom, the answer her parents had been searching for so frantically slowly unfolded. What had become of her was really quite simple. Babi had fallen in love.

Chapter 18

That morning found Babi, oddly enough, wide awake even before the alarm clock went off. She rolled up the blinds, dancing to the beat of the dance music blaring from the radio. The sunshine aggressively invaded the room.

Babi took off her pajama top and turned up the volume. She looked at herself in the mirror. She smiled, making a funny face at her own cheerful features. Then she realized that the young man who lived across the way had just stepped out onto the terrace. She hid in the far corner of the room. Her pajama bottoms flew onto the bed while her bra and panties vanished from the chair and reappeared on her body. She adjusted the shoulder straps, running her thumbs playfully up and down as if they were a pair of suspenders, and all that enthusiasm even hurt her a little bit.

She finished dressing to a tune from the radio. Elton John suited her perfectly. She put on her blouse, writhing and rocking inside it as she did. She did up all the buttons, bobbing her head. Like a daring young toreador with long blond hair, she whipped her skirt off the chair and wrapped that dark blue cape around her hips, with a simple "Olé."

The young man from across the way was staring at her

window. They looked right at each other for a second. She smiled at him, welcoming the attention. She opened the door of her closet so it covered the window, concealing her. Amused, she put on her shoes. The young man was perplexed as he found himself looking at that poster. Some huge guy was pulling a wheelie, and behind him, for all he could tell, was the same young woman who lived there. When Babi shut the door, the guy was gone. So much the better. It wasn't a great idea to bother her. In case he hadn't received the memo, she was taken already. Or was she?

She turned to look at the photograph. She looked at Step. What a shameless smart-ass, to judge from that face. As for that smile, it didn't offer any certainty to anyone. Maybe she still was unattached after all. That thought tormented her throughout breakfast. Worse than Daniela's questions, than her mother's scolding, even worse than the completely unwanted words her father came out with.

"I'd never have expected this from you... Princess Savina."

Daniela looked at Claudio, stunned. "Princess Savina? Since when do you call her that?"

"I always have. Since the day she was born. It's the nickname I gave her."

Babi watched her father leave the room, so confident, so untroubled by that tiny lie. And for her, it was the only laugh she enjoyed that morning.

In the car on her way to school, she turned around continually, hoping to spot Step. But she never saw him. Just kids on motorcycles with similar-looking jackets and haircuts. Each time she saw one, her heart raced.

Later, at her desk at school, she filled her notebook with question marks, indecisive hearts, simple letters, or else his whole name. Every motorcycle she heard passing in the distance, she wondered if it was him.

A longer bell rang. That was a relief. Recess.

Pallina walked up to her. "So, how did it go? You disappeared."

"Great, we went to Ansedonia."

"All that way?"

Babi nodded.

"And did you do it?"

"Pallina!"

"Well, excuse me very much but, if you went all the way to Ansedonia, you must have gone down to the beach, right?"

"Yes."

"And didn't you do anything on the beach?"

"We kissed."

"Yahooo!" Pallina threw her arms around Babi.

"It's not fair though! Screw you and your whole family, you landed the hottest guy in the whole city." Then she realized that Babi was a little blue. "What's wrong?"

"Nothing."

"Come on, quit lying. Tell me what the problem is. Buck up. You can confide in your wise, old friend Pallina. You did do it, am I right?"

"Noooo! We kissed, and that's all, and it was beautiful. But..."

"But...?"

"But I don't know how we left things."

Pallina looked at her, perplexed. "Wait, did he try to..." And she poked a finger into her opposite fist, eloquently.

Babi shook her head with a sigh of annoyance. "No."

"Then this is very worrisome."

"Why?"

"He's interested in you."

"You think?"

"For sure. He almost always screws his girls the first night."

"Oh, thanks, so reassuring."

"You wanted the truth, didn't you? Well, so sorry, but you ought to be happy about this. But if that's what you're worried about, you only need to wait for the second date, wait and see!"

Babi gave her a shove. "You're so stupid...By the way, Pallina, they confiscated your Vespa."

"My Vespa?" Pallina's expression changed. "Who did?"

"My folks."

"That jolly jokester Raffaella. One of these days, I'm going to have to have a talk with her. You know, the other night she put the moves on me."

"My mother? What are you talking about?"

"She did! She kissed me when I was sleeping in your bed, thinking that I was you!"

"Do you swear?"

"Yes!"

"Just think, my father took your key ring, and believed that it was mine."

"Didn't he notice the letter *P*?"

"Yes! But I told him that when I was little he always called me Princess Savina."

"And he fell for it?"

"Oh, now that's what he always calls me."

And so they went back to class. One of them tall, willowy, and blond, the other short and dark. Pretty and well prepared the first one, funny and unmotivated the second, but sharing one great thing in common: their friendship.

Later, Babi was sitting there, dreamily staring at the blackboard without seeing the numbers written on it or hearing the words the teacher said. She was thinking about Step, about what he might be doing right then. She wondered if he was thinking about her.

She tried to imagine him but she realized she didn't really know him. Sometimes he was tender and sweet. Then he could suddenly turn savage and violent. She sighed and looked at the blackboard. She knew that the equation on the board would be much easier to solve.

~

Step had just woken up. He hopped into the shower and let himself be massaged by the strong, determined spray. He placed both hands against the wet wall and let the jets of water drum on his chest.

As the water slid over his face, he thought back to her blue eyes. They were big, pristine, and profound. He smiled, and even though his own eyes were shut, he saw her perfectly. There she was, innocent and serene, right in front of him, her hair tossing wildly in the wind. He recalled that gaze full of character and determination.

As he dried off, he found himself thinking about everything they'd said to each other, the things he'd told her. She was the only kind ear he'd talked to, practically a stranger, the silent listener to his past suffering, his self-hatred, his sadness. He wondered if he might be crazy. Too late to worry about that.

As he ate breakfast, he thought about Babi's family. Her sister. Her agreeable-looking father. Her mother with her tough, determined personality. With features so similar to Babi, but softened by age. Would Babi someday be just like her? Sometimes, mothers are future projections of the young women we're dating.

He smiled as he finished his coffee. Someone rang the doorbell, and Maria answered the door. It was Pollo. He tossed the usual bag onto the side table. Step found himself eating a salmon panino while listening to Pollo's chatter. An enjoyable routine. He looked at his friend with amusement as Pollo asked him question after question.

"You need to tell me what you got up to. Did you screw her or didn't you? I can just guess, with that girl...that personality of hers, and when are you ever going to get her in bed? Never! Also, where the fuck did you two go to? I looked for you everywhere. Oh, you can imagine the state that Madda was in. Just poisonous!"

Step looked at him differently now. The amused expression had vanished from his face. Maddalena, true enough, he hadn't thought about her. He hadn't thought about anything that evening. But, after all, he and Babi had never made any promises. It was just a casual thing. He finished the sandwich, a little more relaxed, even if he knew deep down that it wasn't really true.

"Here." Pollo reached into his pocket and pulled out a crumpled sheet of paper and tossed it at him. "This is Babi's phone number." Step caught it in midair.

"I asked Pallina to give it to me. I knew you'd be asking me for it today..."

Step put it in his pocket and then went into his room. Pollo followed him. "Well, come on, Step, cazzo, are you going to tell me anything or not? Did you do it with her?"

Step turned to look at him with a smile on his face. "Pollo, why do you always ask me these questions? You know that I'm a gentleman, don't you?"

Pollo threw himself onto the bed, bent over with laughter. "A gentleman... you? Oh God. I'm laughing so hard it hurts! The things you say. Fucking hell... a gentleman."

Step looked at him, shaking his head, and then started getting dressed. As he was putting his jeans on, Step started laughing too. All the times he'd been less than a gentleman! For a minute, he wished he had some better story to tell his friend about last night.

Chapter 19

Out front of Falconieri High School, there weren't any boys selling books. It was too affluent a school for even the poorest of its female students to consider the thought of buying a used textbook.

Babi started down the stairs, looking around hopefully. Groups of boys at the bottom of the steps were waiting, looking up for new prey or old conquests. But none of them were the right boy.

Babi descended the last few steps. The roar of a motorcycle going by fast made her look up, startled. Her heart beat faster. But it was no good. A red gas tank went zipping past, weaving through the line of cars. A young couple, the girl's arms wrapped around him, leaned left in unison. For a second, Babi envied them.

Then she got in the car. Her mother was there, still angry from the day before. "Ciao, Mamma."

"Ciao" was Raffaella's terse reply. Babi didn't receive any slaps in the face that day because there was no reason for one. But she almost would have preferred one to the cold indifference.

Step and Pollo were leaning against the fence. They were watching from the field side as their soccer team trained. Nearby Schello, Hook, and a few other friends cheered, all of them enthusiastic for the same team colors. Frenzied fans, ready to cause trouble for the hell of it. Along the drive of the stadium in Tor di Quinto, a number of more moderate fans were watching the friendly match from the comfort of their automobiles.

Along the edges of the field, a roar rang out from the bystanders. One of the new team hires, a young Slav with a hard-to-pronounce surname, had just made a great goal. Young men with light blue and white headbands and small silk scarves in the same colors tied around their necks hugged and rejoiced. They sang the team anthem, gripping the fence, rocking back and forth. They called out the player's name, getting the pronunciation completely wrong.

Step was holding on to the fence with both hands. Without letting anyone else see what he was doing, he pulled back the left sleeve of his jacket, sneaking a look at his watch. One thirty. Babi must have just gotten out of school. He imagined her in her mother's car, on Corso Francia, on her way home.

Better than a goal by Stankovic. He reckoned the timing. Maybe if he left now, he could run into her.

He noticed that Pollo was staring at him. "What's wrong?"

"Nothing." Pollo threw both arms wide. "Why?"

"Then what the fuck are you looking at?"

"Why, can't I look?"

"Just watch the game, no? I brought you all this way and what are you doing?"

Step turned to look at the field. Some of the players wore training vests over their team jerseys and were passing the ball quickly from one to the other while a miserable loser in the middle was trying to take it away from them.

Step turned to look at Pollo again. He was staring at him. "Still! So you really don't want to listen to me!" Step lunged at him. He grabbed his head with both hands and, laughing, slammed it against the hurricane fence. "That's what you're supposed to look at." He pushed Pollo's head a few times. "There, there!"

"Ouch." Pollo bounced against the fence with his nose stuck in one of the holes and his mouth crammed into the hole next to it. He pushed back with both hands, trying to free himself from Step's grip.

Schello, Hook, and the others jumped onto the two of them, just for the fun of a little mayhem. A general brawl broke out. Other superfans pushed in against the gate among them, making noise. One guy with a rolled-up newspaper in hand and a whistle in his mouth pretended to be a cop, dealing out billy-club blows right and left.

After a while, the group spread, with fans running in all directions, laughing. Step climbed onto his motorcycle. Pollo jumped on behind him and they skidded away, wheels kicking up showers of gravel. Step wondered whether Pollo had guessed at what he'd been thinking about earlier.

"Hey, Step, what a pity..."

"What is?"

"It's too late now. Otherwise we could have gone by and picked Babi up at school."

Step said nothing. He could sense Pollo smiling, behind him. Even his thoughts no longer had any secrets from him. Or maybe it had been dumb luck?

Pollo drove a fist into his ribs. "And don't get smart with me, understood?"

Step leaned forward, in pain. No, it hadn't been dumb luck, and as if that wasn't bad enough, Pollo could also deliver incredibly painful punches.

The afternoon passed slowly that day for both of them, though neither knew that was true of the other.

~

Step was all alone, driving around the city on his motorcycle, when it started to drizzle. He looked up. Menacing dark clouds sailed quickly overhead, swirling. As a distant clap of thunder sounded, he accelerated. He didn't want to get soaked.

The air around him suddenly turned chilly. Another thunderclap. Bigger drops, one after another, constant, thicker and faster. Now it was really coming down, so he sped up on the wet road.

He splashed through a puddle. A few drops of water hit the hot engine, and steam swirled around his legs. His Tobacco Motorwear trousers darkened, spattered by the rain. His jacket was getting wet. He could feel the rain pour down his neck.

Via Bevagna. Step decided to pull over. He braked to a halt in front of the market, which was closed now. He rode up onto the sidewalk and stopped in front of the newsstand. Plenty of water was already rushing past in the gutter. He looked at his jeans. They were drenched below the knee. A car went past fast, leaving behind it wet patches and the reflection of its headlights.

The rain was showing no signs of stopping. Step lit a cigarette and, before he knew it, found himself in the nearby phone booth. He had a crumpled sheet of paper in his hand.

Moments after that, the phone rang at Babi's place. Daniela immediately punched the button on the little wireless handset that she kept next to her on the sofa cushion. "Hello?" She stared at Babi, stunned. She couldn't believe her ears.

"Oh, yes, I'll put her on." Babi turned unruffled to look at her sister. "Babi, it's for you." It only took that instant, a quick glance, the look on her face to make it all clear. It was him.

Daniela handed Babi the telephone, doing her best to maintain her self-control in front of her parents, who were watching TV with them on the sofa. Babi took the phone delicately, as if fearful to touch it, as if one vibration too many might cut off the call, making it disappear forever. She slowly lifted it to her lips, emotionally stirred even by the utterance of that simple "Yes?"

"Ciao, how are you?" Step's warm voice directly reached her heart. Babi looked around, appalled, worried that someone else might have noticed what she was feeling, her heart racing at three thousand kilometers an hour, the happiness that she was desperately trying to conceal.

"Fine, you?"

"Fine. Can you talk?"

"Hold on a second. I can't hear myself think in here."

She got up off the sofa, carrying the phone with her, her dressing gown fluttering behind her. It's hard to say why, but with certain telephones, you can never hear a thing when you're around your parents.

Her mother watched her leave the living room and then turned suspiciously toward Daniela. "Who was that?"

Daniela was fast on her feet. "Oh, Chicco Brandelli, one of her admirers."

Raffaella stared at her for a second. Then she relaxed. She turned back to the movie. Daniela, too, turned to the television with a faint sigh. It was over. If her mother had stared at her just a little longer, she would have collapsed. It was difficult to meet that gaze. It always seemed as if her mother knew everything. She paid herself a silent compliment for the idea of Brandelli. At last, that knucklehead had served some purpose.

Then Daniela grew emotional as she thought about her sister. Step had called her, not to be believed. She wondered what kind of a look Giulia would have on her face when she told her all about it tomorrow morning. Happy now, Daniela got comfortable on the sofa. No doubt, Giulia would eat her heart out.

The lights were off in Babi's bedroom. She was leaning against a pane of glass, streaked with raindrops, the telephone in her hand. "Hello, Step, is that you?"

"Who else do you think it could be?"

Babi laughed. "Where are you?"

"In the rain. In a phone booth. Should I come over to your place?"

"I wish. My folks are home."

"Then why don't you come meet me?"

"I can't. I'm grounded. They caught me when I came home yesterday. They were at the window, waiting for me."

Step smiled and tossed away his cigarette. "So it's actually true! There are girls in the world who are still being grounded..."

"Yep, and now you're dating one."

Babi shut her eyes in sheer terror, waiting to hear what would happen when the bomb she'd thrown exploded, but there was no taking it back now. However, there was no explosion so, slowly, she opened her eyes. Outside the glass, under a streetlight, the rain was more visible. It was starting to slow. "Are you still there?"

"Yes, I was just trying to figure out what it feels like to have been outmaneuvered by a very clever girl."

Babi bit her lip as she walked nervously and happily around her room. So it was true. "If I was such a clever girl, I'd have picked someone else to outmaneuver."

Step laughed. "All right, truce. Let's see if we can keep it up for at least a day. What are you doing tomorrow?"

"School, then I'll study, and the whole time I'll be grounded."

"Well, I could come and pay you a visit."

"I'd say that's not one of the best ideas..."

"I could dress up nice."

Babi laughed. "Not because of that. It's a slightly more general set of considerations. What time are you getting up in the morning tomorrow?"

"I don't know, ten, eleven. Whenever Pollo comes by to wake me up."

Babi shook her head. "But what if he doesn't come?"

"Then I might sleep until noon."

"Can you come get me at school?"

"At one o'clock? Yes, I think I could do that."

"I meant at the start of the day."

Silence. "What time would that be?"

"Ten past eight."

"Why do people start school at dawn? And then what would we do?"

"Oh, I don't know. We could run away..." Babi heard those words of hers, uttered in a tone of amusement. She practically couldn't believe her ears. She must have lost her mind. Still, she liked the idea of running away with him.

"All right, let's go crazy. At eight on the dot in front of your school. I just hope I can wake up."

"It won't be easy, will it?"

"Not exactly."

She laughed. Then remained silent for a while. Uncertain what to say next, how to end the call. "Well, then, ciao."

Step looked out to see that it had stopped raining, and the clouds were scudding along fast. He felt happy. He looked at the receiver. Right now she was at the other end of the line. "Ciao, Babi."

Step hung up. A few stars had appeared, timid and wet, up in the sky. Tomorrow it was going to be a beautiful day because he was going to spend the morning with her. He climbed onto his motorcycle.

Ten past eight. He must have lost his mind. He tried to remember the last time he'd gotten up that early, but nothing occurred to him. He smiled. Just three days ago, that was when he'd returned home.

In the darkness of her room with the telephone still in her hand, Babi continued staring at the glass pane for a while. She imagined him in the street. It had to be cold out. She shivered on his behalf.

She went back to the living room, handed the telephone back to her sister, and then sat down beside her on the sofa.

Careful not to be noticed, Daniela was curiously studying Babi's face. She wanted to ask her a thousand questions. She'd have to settle for those eyes that suddenly stared at her happily before going back to watching television.

For a moment, that old black-and-white film seemed to be in full, glorious color. Babi didn't understand any of what they were talking about in it, and her mind wandered off, captivated by her own thoughts. Then she suddenly returned to reality. She looked around, worried, but nobody in the room seemed to know what she was thinking. Tomorrow, for the first time in her life, she was planning to skip school.

Chapter 20

Paolo was sitting at the table, idly leafing through the newspaper. When he got to the business section, he focused a little more intently. Just then, a noise attracted his attention. The milk had boiled over, foaming over the sides of the little pot onto the burner below, partially extinguishing the flame.

He ran toward the stove. Now the coffee came gurgling up under the lid of the Moka Express coffeepot.

Paolo turned off both burners. Then he picked up the pot of milk and the coffeepot and went back to the table. Midway there, he realized that they were both burning his hands. He picked up his pace, going faster and faster, until finally he was running. When he reached the table, he was finally able to set them down.

He waved his hands in the air, now free to cool off, and sat down. He looked around. There wasn't much there for breakfast. Strange. He'd asked Maria to bake an apple pie. Naively, he supposed she must have forgotten. He opened a jar. Cookie fragments still lay on the bottom of the jar in a golden dust. He bit into one. It crumbled in his mouth without a hint of flavor. This wasn't turning out to be one of the better breakfasts in his life.

He remembered a pastry he'd bought for emergency situations. He decided that this might be one of those cases. He opened several cabinets. At last he found it. He'd hidden it well to keep it from the ravenous hunger of Step and his friends.

He set it down on the table, unwrapped it, and cut himself a slice. Just then, Step came in. "Ciao, brother."

Paolo looked up at him and then shook his head. "Does this seem like the time of the morning to come home? Now you'll spend the rest of the day in bed, then, best case, you'll go to the gym, and come evening, you'll be out and about again with Pollo and the other half-dozen criminals you hang out with. Life is good for you..."

"Very good indeed." Step poured himself some coffee and then some milk. "As it happens, though, I'm not coming home. I'm leaving."

Paolo glanced at his watch with some concern. Then he must be late. No, it was seven thirty. He heaved a sigh of relief. Everything was under control. Still, something didn't add up. Step had never left the house at that time of the morning. "Where are you going?"

"To school."

"Ah." Paolo relaxed. Then he suddenly remembered that Step had finished school the year before last.

"What for?"

"Fuck, what's with all these questions, and at the crack of dawn too?"

"Do whatever you want, just try to stay out of trouble. Wait, didn't Maria make an apple pie?"

Step looked at him with an innocent expression. "Apple pie? Not that I know of."

"Are you sure? It's not like you ate it all up, you and Pollo and those other pigs you call your friends?"

"Paolo, why do you always have to insult my friends? It's not nice. What, do I ever insult yours?"

Paolo remained silent. No, Step didn't insult his friends. But then, how could he? Paolo had no friends. Every so often a colleague or some old university classmate would call him, but Step could hardly have insulted any of them. They'd already been insulted by life. Dreary and sad. It wouldn't be fair to punish them any further.

Step put on his jacket and left. "Ciao, Pa. See you later tonight maybe."

Paolo stood there for a second, staring at the now-closed door. His brother always managed to astonish him. Who knew where he was going at this time of the morning? He decided that, when all was said and done, it really was none of his business.

He drank a sip of coffee. Then he turned to eat the slice of pastry that he'd left on the plate in front of him. He realized it was no longer there. It had vanished.

One way or another, you always came up short when you were dealing with Step.

~

"Ciao, Papà." Babi and Daniela got out of the Mercedes, and Claudio watched his daughters head off to school. One last goodbye and he drove off.

Babi took a few more steps. Then she turned around. The Mercedes was far away by now. She galloped down the steps and, just then, crossed paths with Pallina.

"Ciao, where are you running off to?" Pallina asked.

"I'm leaving with Step."

"Really? Where are you going?"

"I don't know. Around. To start with, we'll go get breakfast. This morning I was too excited to be able to get anything down. Just think about it. This is the first time I've skipped school..."

Pallina smiled at her. "I was excited my first time too. But at this point, I can sign my mother's signature better than she can!"

Babi laughed.

Step's motorcycle roared to a halt right in front of them on the sidewalk. "Shall we go?"

Babi looked at that smile, those eyes, those broad shoulders. Only then did she realize how badly she'd wanted to see him. She gave Pallina a hasty kiss goodbye and climbed up behind him, thrilled and excited. Her heart was racing at two thousand kilometers per hour.

"Take my advice, Pallina. Do your best not to flunk, and take notes on who gets tested."

"Okay, boss!"

"And keep quiet about this, okay? Not a word to anyone."

Pallina nodded in silence and smiled.

Babi looked around, worried that someone might happen to see. Then she wrapped her arms tight around Step. By this point, she'd done it.

The motorcycle shot forward, taking her far away from school, from boring hours in the classroom, from Signora

Giacci, from her classwork and the sound of the bell, that sound that sometimes seemed never to arrive.

Pallina enviously watched her friend as she vanished into the distance. She was happy for her. She said hello to a few other classmates and started climbing the steps, chatting away without realizing that someone was watching her. High above, a hand, beautified by an old ring with a violet stone at the center, as hard as the woman who owned it, let a curtain slide back into place. Someone had seen everything.

~

In Classroom 3B, all the girls were worried. The first period was Italian, and the teacher, Signora Giacci, was going to be testing them. This was definitely one of the subjects that would be on their final exam of high school.

The students sat down at their desks, exchanging hellos. One last young woman entered in haste. As usual, she was late. The girls chatted nervously. Suddenly there was an obsequious silence. Signora Giacci was at the door. They all snapped to attention.

Signora Giacci surveyed the class. "Be seated, girls."

She was strangely cheerful this morning. That didn't promise anything good in store. As she read the roll call, various girls raised their hands, replying with a respectful "Present." One young woman, whose last name started with *C*, was absent. At *F*, another young woman, hoping to distinguish herself, let go with a disrespectful "Here." She was promptly scolded by Signora Giacci, who mocked her in front of the rest of the class. As usual, Catinelli made a show of appreciating the teacher's subtle sense of humor. So subtle that it completely eluded the notice of almost everyone else.

"Gervasi?"

"She's absent today," someone replied from the back of the class. Signora Giacci put an *A* next to Babi's name in the ledger. Then she slowly looked up. Her desk was empty.

She turned her gaze slightly to the right. "Lombardi."

Pallina, who was distracted, leaped to her feet. "Yes, teacher?"

"Why didn't Gervasi come to school today?"

Pallina was slightly nervous. "Oh, uh, I really don't know. I talked to her last night on the telephone, and she told me that she wasn't feeling great. Maybe she felt worse this morning and decided not to come to school."

Signora Giacci looked at her. Pallina shrugged her shoulders. Signora Giacci narrowed her eyes until they were two impenetrable fissures. Pallina felt a shiver run down her back.

"Thanks, Lombardi. Please be seated." Signora Giacci continued calling roll: "Ilari..."

"Present." A young woman at one of the desks in front raised her hand.

Signora Giacci put a *P* next to her name. Then she looked up. Her gaze met Pallina's. A mocking smile appeared on the teacher's face. Pallina turned red. She looked away, embarrassed. Could her teacher know something? On her desk was the phrase that she herself had carved into the surface with a pen: *Pallina and Pollo forever.* She smiled. No, that was impossible.

"Marini."

"Present!"

The teacher had gone back to calling the roll, so Pallina relaxed. She wondered where Babi was at that very moment. They'd definitely already eaten breakfast. Perhaps a nice maritozzo pastry with whipped cream at Euclide, along with one of those cappuccinos that were all foam. She wished with all her heart that she could take Babi's place, but with Pollo instead of Step.

Signora Giacci shut the ledger and started lecturing. She laid out her lesson with joy and seemed particularly relaxed. As she strolled along between the desks, a ray of sunlight struck her hands. Illuminating the finger she was toying with, an antique ring glowed with a violet light.

~

From the noises of the city, just awakened, Babi and Step rode away, their lips faintly smeared with the foam of an unsweetened cappuccino and their mouths sweetened with the whipped cream of a pastry. It was easy to predict that their path had led them to the big Euclide on the Via Flaminia, farther away and more discreet, where it was less likely that they'd run into familiar faces. Then, minutes later, up the ramp and down to the right, in front of that tire repair place and then a sharp left at that green public drinking fountain, along that narrow street with the speed bumps, the cows on the right, and the bus stop on the left.

They continued on toward the tower. Enveloped in sunshine all around them, meadows, tinged in faint green, stretched out gently rolling between the edges of darker woods. They left the road. The motorcycle moved along, bending the tall, golden stalks of wheat that stood up again immediately after its passage, unfazed and bold. All around a warm wind wafted gently over the field of wheat like the hand of a delicate pianist.

The faint wake in the field of wheat slowly vanished behind them. The motorcycle was parked there, beyond the hill, a short way from the tower. Off to the right, farther down, a good-tempered dog was sleepily keeping an eye on several mangy-looking sheep. A shepherd in jeans was listening to a small beat-up radio while smoking a joint, light-years away from his comrades in the standard manger scene.

They pushed on a little farther before stopping. Babi opened her bag and pulled out a large Union Jack. "I bought it at Portobello Market when I was in London. Help me stretch it out. Have you ever been?"

Step gave her a hand. "No, never. Is it nice?"

"Very. I had the time of my life. I spent a month in Brighton and several days in London. I went with EF. Education First."

They lay down on the flag and warmed up in the sunshine. Step listened to her account of London and a few other trips she'd taken. She seemed to have been to a bunch of places but he, largely uninterested in those past adventures and by no means used to that hour of the morning, quickly fell asleep.

A bird sang loudly, and when Step opened his eyes, he barely managed to glimpse the last flutter of wings and the shadow veering away, flapping over distant stalks of tall wheat. The sun was higher now, and Babi was no longer beside him.

He stood up, worried, and looked all around. Then he saw her. Farther down, on the hill. There she sat, among the wheat.

As he walked over to her, he called her name but she seemed not to hear him. When he was close enough, he understood why. She was listening to her Sony Walkman.

Babi turned to look at him. The look in her eyes promised nothing good. She went back to gazing into the distance at faraway fields. Step sat down next to her. He, too, sat for a while in silence.

Then Babi couldn't stand it anymore and took off her headphones. "Do you think that's respectful, to fall asleep when I'm talking to you?" She was really angry now. "That's a total lack of respect!"

"Oh, come on, don't be like that." Step smiled. "It's really a total lack of sleep."

When she huffed in annoyance and turned away again, Step couldn't help but notice how pretty she was. Maybe even prettier when she was angry. She held her face high, and everything took on a special quality, chin, nose, forehead. Her hair, lit up in the sunlight, reflected its rays, golden, and seemed to exhale the fresh scent of the wheat. She had the beauty of an abandoned beach, he decided, with the wild sea fringing its distant edges. Like foaming waves, her hair framed her face.

Below her hair, thin eyebrows, dark and determined, resembled the wings of a seagull, soaring confidently. Motionless in the wind, the bird looked down at those twin blue oceans of her eyes. Then those eyelashes, lighter at the tips. Her golden skin, that sweet velvet. Her pouting lips, caressed and dried by the wind.

Step leaned toward her and gathered her soft beauty in his hand but Babi tried to elude his grasp. "Leave me alone!"

"I can't help it. It's stronger than me. I have to kiss you."

"I said leave me alone. I'm offended by you."

Step smiled and leaned closer to her lips. "I swear that from now on, I'll listen to it all. England, London, the trips you've taken, you name it."

"You should have listened earlier!"

Step took advantage and kissed Babi fast, catching her unsuspecting lips, ever so slightly parted.

But Babi was faster than him, and she clamped her mouth shut. Then there was a gentle struggle. In the end, she surrendered, slowly, and gave in to his kiss. "You're violent, and you're rude."

Words whispered between lips that were too close.

"That's true." Words that were practically muddled together.

"I don't like it when you behave like that."

"I'll never do it again, I promise."

"I've told you before that I don't believe in your promises," Babi said.

"Well, then, I'll swear it..."

"Just see if I believe it when you swear to something..."

"Okay, fine then, I'll swear on you."

Babi punched him hard but he took the punch as a joke. Then he put his arms around her and plunged with her through the soft stalks of wheat. High above, bright sun and blue sky were silent spectators. Not far away, the forgotten Union Jack. Closer still, two smiles.

For a little while, Step toyed with the buttons of her shirt. He stopped for a moment, fearful. He looked at her. Her closed eyes seemed calm and unruffled. He undid one button, then another, gently, as if even the lightest touch might be enough to shatter the magic of that moment.

Then his hand slid inside, down her waist, and onto her tender warm flesh. He caressed her. Babi let him do it, kissing him, and wrapping her arms around him even tighter. Step inhaled her perfume and shut his eyes. For the first time, everything seemed different to him. He was in no hurry, perfectly relaxed, and he felt a strange sense of peace.

His open palm slid down her back, along that soft hollow until it reached the hem of her skirt. A gentle slope, the beginning of a sweet, sweet promise. He stopped. Right then a slightly more impassioned kiss from her made him smile.

Gently, he continued to caress her, moving up until he came to an ornate elastic strap. His fingers lingered on the snap. His touch wandered curiously as it tried to solve the mystery. Two hooks? Two tiny half-moon shapes that fit one inside the other? A metal *S* that's inserted from above?

He hesitated. She broke out of a kiss to eye him curiously. Step was starting to run out of patience. "How the fuck do you open this thing?"

Babi shook her head. "Why is it you're always such a potty mouth? I don't want you to talk like that when you're with me."

Just then, the mystery was solved. Two tiny half-moons separated while Step's hand wandered all over her back, up to her neck, at last unhindered.

He leaned down to kiss her. "Forgive me..."

Step couldn't believe his own ears. He'd asked her to forgive him. He, Step, had just apologized.

Then, determined to stop thinking about it, he abandoned himself as if swept away by this new conquest. He found himself caressing her breasts, showering her neck with kisses, moving his hand to her other breast, and rediscovering there, too, that fragile hint of desire and passion.

Then he slid slowly lower down, toward her smooth belly, the hem of her skirt. Her hand stopped him. Step opened his eyes. There Babi was, right in front of him, shaking her head.

"No."

"No, what?"

"No, that..." She smiled at him.

"Why not?" He wasn't smiling now, not at all.

"Just because!"

"But why not?"

"Just because, period!"

"But there must be some reason, like..." Step gave her a small, insinuating smile.

"No, you dummy, no reason. It's just that I don't want to. Maybe when you learn not to curse so much, well then, maybe..."

Step turned onto one side and started doing pushups. One after another, faster and faster, without stopping. "I can't believe it. Tell me it isn't true. I've figured it out."

He was smiling as he spoke between one pushup and the next, slightly out of breath.

Babi fastened her bra back together and buttoned her blouse. "What have you figured out? And stop doing pushups when we're talking..."

Step did the last two pushups on just one hand. Then he lay down on his side and gazed at her with a smile. "You've never been with anyone else."

"If you're trying to ask whether I'm a virgin, the answer is yes."

That admission cost her a great deal. Babi stood and brushed off her skirt. A few stalks of wheat fell to the ground. "Now take me back to school!"

"What, are you angry?" Step took her in his arms.

"Yes. You have a highly irritating way of dealing with people. I'm not used to being treated like this. And would you let go of me..." She wriggled free from his embrace and walked briskly toward the Union Jack.

Step went after her. "Come on, Babi...listen, I didn't mean to insult you. I apologize, for real."

Babi turned around. "I didn't hear you."

"Yes, you did."

"No, say it again."

Step looked around, annoyed, and then stared at her. "I apologize. All right? Listen, I'm happy that you've never been with anyone else."

Babi bent over to pick up the Union Jack, and she started folding it. "Oh, you are? Why?"

"Well, just because...because I am. I'm happy, and that's that."

"Because you think you're going to be the first?"

"Listen, I apologized. Now enough's enough. Let's be done with it. God, you're difficult."

Babi smiled. "You're right. Truce." She handed him one of the hems of the flag. "Here, help me fold it."

They stepped apart to hold it out flat and then stepped

closer again. Babi took the other end of the flag from his hands and gave him a quick kiss. "It's just that the topic gets on my nerves."

They walked back to the motorcycle without speaking, and Babi climbed up behind him. They drove off, down the hill, leaving behind them the broken stalks of wheat and a conversation left halfway finished.

Chapter 21

Stop!" Babi shouted, and grabbed tight to Step's waist. The motorcycle practically froze to a halt at her command.

"What's wrong?"

"It's my mother."

Babi pointed at Raffaella's Peugeot, parked a short way farther on, in front of Falconieri High School's steps. She got off the motorcycle and looked at her watch. It was only a few minutes before one thirty. She had to at least give it a try.

She kissed Step on the lips. "Ciao, I'll call you this afternoon."

She hurried off, hunching low along the line of parked cars. She moved along cautiously. When she was in front of the school, she slowly stood up. There her mother was, just a few yards away. She could see her perfectly through the glass of a parked Mini. She was fiddling around with something in her lap. Then Raffaella raised her left hand and checked it. Babi understood. She was manicuring her nails. A moment later she lifted the nail file she was holding in her right hand. Sure enough, she'd guessed it.

Babi huddled against the car and checked her watch again. The other students should be coming out right about now. She looked to her right, to the end of the street. Step was gone. She smiled. She wondered what he must think of her. She'd call him later. Suddenly she remembered that she couldn't do that. She didn't have his phone number. She didn't even know where he lived.

The bell rang, marking the end of the school day. The first classes appeared at the top of the stairs. The younger girls started descending the steps. Another bell rang. Now it was the turn of the ninth- and tenth-grade girls. One of them looked at her curiously. Babi lifted her finger to her lips, in the universal command of silence. The young woman looked away. They were all accustomed to secrets of every sort.

Finally, it was Babi's class's turn. Slowly, Babi stood up again. Her mother was still distracted, so this was the exact moment to go. Babi emerged from her hiding place and mingled with the other girls. She said hello to a few and then, careful not to let herself be seen, turned back to look at the car. Raffaella hadn't noticed a thing. She'd pulled it off.

"Babi!" Pallina ran toward her.

The two girls hugged. Babi looked at her with a worried expression. "How did it go? Did anyone notice anything?"

"No, it's all under control." Pallina handed her a sheet of paper. "Here, this is the classwork and homework they handed out today. There are the names of everyone who was tested too. All perfectly accurate and precise, you could hire me as your secretary. Well, did you have a good time?"

"A *very* good time." Babi stuck the sheet of paper in her bag and smiled at her friend.

"Let me guess." Pallina stared at her for a second. "Breakfast at Euclide on Via di Vigna Stelluti. Cappuccino and pastry with whipped cream."

"Almost nailed it. Same order, but at Euclide on the Via Flaminia."

"Of course! Much more private. Perfect. Then a quick ride to Fregene and frantic sex on the beach, am I right?"

"Wrong-o!" Babi walked away with a smile on her face.

"About Fregene or all the rest?"

"All I can tell you is that you got one thing wrong."

Babi got into the car, lying to her friend and leaving her there in front of the school, dying of curiosity. In reality, she'd got both things wrong.

"Ciao, Mamma."

"Ciao." Raffaella let Babi kiss her on the cheek. Their relationship seemed to have returned to normal.

"How was your day at school?"

"Fine. I didn't get tested."

Daniela arrived too. "We can go. Giovanna says that she'll get home on her own from now on."

The Peugeot took off. While they were waiting at the traffic light on Piazza Euclide, Babi suddenly felt something pricking her. Without letting herself be seen, she stuck her hand under her blouse. Caught under her bra was a small, golden stalk of wheat. She pried it loose and put it between the pages of her notebook. Then she stared at it for a moment. That enormous little secret. Step had touched her breasts.

She smiled, and just as the light turned green, there he was, parked to the right of the piazza. Laughing, he was waving the Union Jack, her own flag. She wondered when he'd stolen it from her. Then she remembered the most important detail. Step was like Pollo: he, too, stole things. She was amazed that it hadn't occurred to her before. She was dating a thief.

Chapter 22

The first *A* was too skinny, the second one had too long a stroke, plus the letter itself was too short, and anyway the line itself was too faint. Babi tried to imitate her mother's signature again. She filled up several pages of her math notebook before she decided that the result was passable, at least.

"Dani, do you think this could pass for Mamma's signature?"

Daniela looked at that last signature for a second. She pondered, lost in thought. "Here, the *G* is too skinny. You gave it a belly that looks little. Mamma always starts the surname with a really big *G*. Here, look." She opened her notebook and showed her sister one of the authentic signatures. "See?" She pointed to the *G* of their last name the way their mother did it.

Babi stared at it for a second, checking it against the one she had done. "They look identical to me." She turned and went back to her bedroom, pleased as punch.

Daniela got up. "Do what you think is best. But to me, that *G* is too small. And another thing, I don't understand why you always ask me what I think if you're just going to go ahead and do whatever you want to." She shut the door.

Babi opened her notebook to the excused absences page. She filled one out. She wrote down the day, and then, where it said *reason for absence*, she wrote in: *Ill health.* Actually, it was true. The idea of not running away with Step made her feel sick. She smiled.

Then it was time to forge the signature. She turned serious again. She tried another one on a sheet of paper at hand, under dozens of previous attempts at *Raffaella Gervasi*. This last effort turned out even better. It was perfect. Her own mother would have had a hard time picking it out from a string of authentic ones. But at this rate, she could even fake a check to buy herself a Peugeot Metropolis scooter. She realized she'd overdone it. After all, she didn't need money. She just needed a note justifying her absence.

She picked up the pen, fearfully staring at the dotted line immediately below the printed word: SIGNATURE. Then she leaned in and went for it. She started with the *R* and so on down the line, sliding as naturally as possible until she reached that last dot on the *i*. Then, still shaking from her extreme concentration, from the grueling effort of writing perfectly just like her mother, she looked at her signature. It had turned out even better. Incredible.

Chapter 23

Later, after Babi's parents had gone out for the evening, Step came by to pick her up. The whole group was downstairs waiting for her. Schello, Lucone and Carla, Dario and Gloria, the Sicilian, Hook, Pollo and Pallina, and a couple of other guys in a VW Golf with two girls. They rode their motorcycles toward Prima Porta and then veered right toward Fiano.

By the time they got there, Babi was chilled to the bone. The restaurant was called Il Colonnello—The Colonel—and it was very far away. Babi couldn't understand why they'd picked a place like that for dinner. There were two big dining rooms with a pizza oven open to view and rows of perfectly ordinary tables. Maybe the place was especially affordable, she supposed.

They sat down, and a young waiter showed up to take their orders. There were fifteen of them, and they were all constantly changing their minds—all except for her, who had decided from the outset to have a salad without too much oil.

The waiter was confused. Every so often, he'd try to go back over the list of pasta dishes so that he could proceed to the entrées, but by the time he made it to the side dishes, there was always someone who'd come up with a different selection.

"Listen, waiter, we'll take a couple of pappardelle al cinghiale."

"Make that three." Then there was a fourth order of pappardelle, and then a fifth. After which two others decided to get polenta, or a carbonara. It was the most indecisive group Babi had ever watched order in a restaurant. As if that weren't bad enough, Pollo tried to help out every time by repeating all the orders, which only mixed things up worse.

At last, they all laughed heartily. It had turned into a sort of game. The poor waiter walked away. The only thing he knew for sure is that he needed to bring them fourteen medium draft beers and one...What was it that pretty blonde with the blue eyes had asked for? He checked his pad, covered with scratch-outs, and headed into the kitchen, reminding himself to add a Diet Coke to the list.

The dinner went on in the throes of utter confusion. Every time a dish was brought to the table, whether it was prosciutto or mini mozzarellas or bruschetta, there was a general assault on the serving dish, with everyone lunging at it, and in an instant, it was gone.

A group of girls whose eyes were too heavily made up laughed in jolly amusement. Babi looked at Pallina, in search of a smidgen of understanding. But by now her friend seemed to have merged perfectly into the group.

Babi caught Step's eye. He was smiling at her. She tried to respond, but she wasn't all that sure of herself. She dropped her gaze. Her mixed salad without too much oil had arrived, and she ate along with everyone else.

Then, no one knew how it happened, but a chunk of bread flew through the air. Then it was a hail of bread chunks, a genuine all-out food fight with leftover meat, flying potatoes, and beer.

They threw anything that came within reach of each other. The girls were the first to abandon their seats. Babi and Pallina hurried quickly away from the table, closely followed by the other girls. The boys continued to throw scraps of food at each other, hard and vicious, indifferent to the other tables in the restaurant, even though they were hitting customers sitting nearby.

The high point came when the waiter tried to stop them. He was smacked dead center in the face by a wet chunk of bread, and there was a standing ovation. That waiter had never been more popular in his life.

Then the check arrived, and Pollo offered to collect the money. Step locked arms with Babi and led her out of the restaurant. One after another, everyone else left. In pairs or little groups of three, they all started their motorcycles. The ones in the VW Golf were the first to leave.

Babi pulled out her wallet. "How much do I owe?"

Step smiled. "Are you kidding? Forget about it."

"Thanks."

"Don't thank me. Just get on."

Step started the motorcycle. Babi climbed up behind him.

"So who should I thank? I heard Pollo say that he was going to collect the money."

"No, that's a sort of password."

At that very moment, Pollo came running out of the

restaurant and jumped onto his motorcycle. "Let's go, boys!"

Pallina held on tight, and they all took off, tires screeching. The motorcycles shot forward, turning their lights off. The waiter and a few others came running out of the restaurant. They shouted, to no avail, trying unsuccessfully to read the license plates.

The sound of motorcycles echoed loudly through the narrow alleys and lanes of Fiano. One after the other, leaning around curves at high speed, they made their way out of town, taking the smaller streets, laughing and shouting, honking their horns. Then, practically flying by this point, they took the Via Tiberina, shrouded in the chill of the road. Only then did they dare to turn their headlights back on.

Pollo rode closer to Step. "Oh, that's pretty good food at this colonel's place. Too bad we won't be able to go back for a while."

"Hey, you know where we could go on Saturday?"

"Where?"

"Up to Nervi. There's a really excellent restaurant. Farinello and the others have gone to it. They say it's great."

Pollo looked at him, worried now. "How much do they charge?"

"About forty apiece."

"Too expensive!" He put on his little kid smile and then hit the gas and raced off with Pallina, laughing crazily.

Babi leaned forward. "So are you saying that we didn't pay?"

Step slowed down. "Why, is that a problem?"

"A problem? Don't you realize that they could report

you to the police? They might have read one of your license plates."

"They can't see a thing with the lights off. Listen, we've always done this, and nobody's ever caught us. So don't jinx us!"

"I don't jinx anybody. I'm just trying to get you guys to listen to reason. Even though that strikes me as quite the challenge. All right, let's say they never catch you. But don't you ever think of the people at the restaurant? Those are working folks. They're in the kitchen all day, sweating over the stoves, setting tables for you, serving you food, clearing up after you, keeping the place clean, and this is how you treat them? You humiliate them, you spit on their work. You don't give them the slightest consideration."

"What do you mean I don't give them any consideration? I just said that I really like the food they serve in that place!"

Babi remained silent. It was pointless. She'd leaned back a little on the seat of the bike, creating some distance from him. Around her, the night wind and the damp air of the woods rushed past her, giving her shudders from the chill. But that wasn't all that was making her shiver. She was dating a guy she didn't understand, whom she *couldn't* understand.

She looked straight ahead. It was a crystal clear night. The stars glittered far away. Small diaphanous clouds were caressing the moon. It would all be so lovely, if only...

"Hey, Step." Lucone pulled up beside them, with his voluminous blond girlfriend, Carla, riding behind him. "Are you ready to bet fifty thousand lire on which of us gets to the center of town first, riding wheelies the whole way?"

Step didn't have to be asked twice. "You're on." He upshifted and twisted the throttle without warning. The motorcycle reared up.

Babi was barely in time to grab hold of Step's waist. "Step! Step!" she shouted, pounding both fists hard on his back. "Stop it! Drive normally." Step gently eased up on the gas. The motorcycle touched down on both wheels. Lucone continued on a little farther, crowing in victory.

Step turned to look at Babi. "What's come over you? Have you lost your mind?"

"No more wheelies, no more brawls, no more high-speed chases, I can't take it anymore, don't you understand?" Babi was shouting now. "I want a normal, safe life. With people who ride a motorcycle like anybody else. I don't want to run out of restaurants. I just want to pay the check like everyone else. I don't want you to keep getting in fights. I hate violence, I hate fist fighters, I hate bullies, I hate people who don't know how to live right, who don't know how to talk decently, who don't know how to engage in a civil discussion, who have no respect for others. You hear me? I hate them!"

They rode awhile in silence, letting themselves be lulled by the constant speed of the motorcycle and by the wind that slowly seemed to be calming her down.

Then Step burst out laughing.

"Do you mind telling me what's so funny?"

"You know what I hate though?"

"No, what?"

"I hate losing fifty thousand lire."

Chapter 24

One after the other, they arrived. Honking their horns and revving their engines. Some of them rode their motorcycles up onto the sidewalk, others parked them there in front of the locked metal gate in front of the Euclide.

Babi dismounted from Step's motorcycle and brushed her hair back with one hand. At that moment, Pallina came up to her. "Cool, right?"

"What?"

"Well, you know, running out of that place, into the night, without paying. I've never done that. Come on, it was too much fun. Plus, they're nice, aren't they?"

"No, they're not. And I didn't think it was fun at all."

"Well, just for this one time..."

"No, it's not just one time. You know that perfectly well. It's the usual thing for these guys. Pallina, you don't seem to understand. You might as well have just held up that restaurant. If you eat their food and leave without paying, you just took part in a robbery."

"Oh, give me a break! A bowl of tortellini and beer. The robbery of the century!"

"Pallina, when you're determined not to understand

something, there's just no way around it with you, is there?"

Suddenly, a hand slapped her on the back, twice, and not lightly by any stretch of the imagination.

Babi turned around. Maddalena was right in front of her. She was chomping on a stick of gum and staring at her, with a smile on her face. "Listen, you'd better not come around here."

"Why not?"

"Because I don't want you around here."

"I don't think this place belongs to you. So you can't tell me not to come."

Babi turned back to talk to Pallina, putting an end to any further discussion. She tried to start a conversation, any old conversation. But this time a sudden, violent shove forced her to turn around.

"Maybe you didn't understand what I'm saying. You need to beat it." Maddalena hit Babi hard on her left shoulder with her right hand. "You get me?"

Babi heaved a sigh. "What do you want from me?"

Maddalena raised her voice as she turned red. "I'm the girl that's here to smash your face in." Then she leaned in and shouted just inches away from her face: "You get me?"

Babi grimaced in distaste. All around her, people had turned to see what was happening. Slowly, the people stopped talking and clustered around. Everyone seemed to know what was about to happen.

Babi knew it too. She tried to shove Maddalena away but she was standing far too close to her. "Listen, cut this out. I don't like it when people throw tantrums."

"Ah, you don't like it, do you? Then why don't you just stay home..." Maddalena stepped forward menacingly.

Babi extended her arms and put her hands on Maddalena's shoulders, trying to keep her at a distance. "Look, I told you, I don't feel like arguing with you..."

"What do you think you're doing?" Maddalena looked at Babi's hand resting on her right shoulder. "Do you think you can put your hands on me?" And she slapped hard and fast at Babi's arm, knocking it aside.

"All right, I'm leaving. Step?"

Babi turned around, looking for him. But at that very moment, she felt a stinging blow under her right cheekbone. Something had just hit her.

She turned around. Maddalena was right there, facing her. Her fists were up, clenched and menacing, and she was smiling. She was the one who'd just hit her.

Babi lifted her hand to her cheek. Her cheekbone was hot, and it hurt. Then Maddalena kicked her hard in the belly, and Babi reeled backward. Maddalena only grazed her with the punch, but it still hurt.

Babi turned around to leave. "Where do you think you're going, you ugly bitch?"

A kick from behind caught Babi right in the seat of her pants, thrusting her forward, but Babi managed not to lose her balance. She had tears in her eyes though. She continued walking slowly. All around her she heard jeering and howls, saw faces laughing, others staring at her in cold silence, and people pointing at her.

She saw a group of girls watching with worried expressions and heard the noise of distant traffic. Then she saw Step. He was standing there in front of her.

Suddenly she heard the sound of running feet behind her. She shut her eyes and slightly bowed her head. It was Maddalena. She was going to attack her again.

Babi felt her head yanked backward by the hair, practically hauled physically, and she whirled around to keep from falling. She found herself being dragged by Maddalena. By that screaming fury who was a whirling dervish of punches to Babi's head, neck, and shoulders. Her hair almost seemed to be coming out at the roots, and a stab of atrocious pain surged to her brain, driving her crazy.

That was it: Babi saw red. She tried to shake loose. But every jerk, every writhing act of resistance, just meant a new stab of pain, another lancing streak of agony. So she followed after her antagonist, practically chasing her. She held out her hands and managed to grab hold of Maddalena's jacket, shoving forward with all her strength, closer and closer, faster and faster, without seeing where she was going, without a glimmer of understanding.

Until she heard a loud clatter of metal, the sound of falling iron, and was suddenly released, free to breathe, at last at peace. Maddalena had stumbled backward into the line of mopeds and scooters and had fallen to the ground, taking with her a green Boxer. And now there she lay still, while a greasy wheel with rusty spokes was still spinning and a heavy frame and a set of handlebars pinned her in place.

Babi felt a surge of rage rise within her suddenly, like a tidal wave. She felt her face redden, her breath grow ragged, her cheekbone still stinging, and the ache all over her scalp—and in the blink of an eye, she was all over Maddalena. She started punching her and kicking her like a wild animal, unrecognizable to those who knew her.

Maddalena tried to get to her feet but Babi leaned over her and pounded her with her fists, striking everywhere, screaming, scratching, yanking her hair, and drawing long, jagged lines of blood down her neck.

Then two powerful hands grabbed Babi from behind and lifted her into the air. She suddenly found herself kicking her feet, writhing to escape in an attempt to go back on the attack, back to biting and wounding. As she was pulled back, one last accurate kick lashed out, though not with that precise target in mind, and hit another moped. An SH 50 tumbled over slowly next to Maddalena, who lay panting in exhaustion.

"Oh, my scooter...," one innocent voice called in dismay.

As she was being dragged away, Babi looked at the crowd. They weren't laughing now. Now they stood silent, staring at her. They parted to let her through. She let herself fall back, abandoning herself to the one carrying her off. And a nervous laugh rose from her lips toward the sky but she heard nothing coming out of her mouth.

A cool breeze was caressing her face, so she shut her eyes. Her head was spinning. Her heart was racing. Her breathing was ragged, and violent surges of rage rushed through her from time to time, only beginning to subside. Something underneath her came to a halt. She was on the motorcycle.

Step helped her off. "Come here."

They were on the Corso di Francia bridge. She climbed the steps and went over to the drinking fountain.

Step got his bandanna wet and placed it on her face. "Is that better?"

Babi shut her eyes. The cool wet cloth felt good on her

reddened skin, on her bruised cheek, on her still-swollen face. She nodded her head.

Step sat down on the low wall nearby, his legs wide, feet dangling. He sat there smiling as he looked at her. "Who were you again? The one who hated brawlers? Violent thugs? Well, that's good! I mean, if I hadn't got you out of there, you'd have murdered that poor girl."

Babi looked at him. She took a step toward him and then burst into tears. Suddenly, in a convulsive fashion, it was as if something had suddenly broken in her, and that river of tears had just burst forth, untamable and violent, relentless.

Step suddenly found himself holding those small, soft shoulders, racked with powerful gasps of sobbing. He stood there, staring at her, spreading both hands wide, not sure what to do. Then he hugged her close. "Come on, don't be like this. It's not your fault. She provoked you."

"I didn't want to hit her. I didn't want to hurt her. Seriously...I didn't want to."

"Yes, I know."

Step put a hand under her chin. He caught one tiny, salty tear, and then he tilted her face upward. Babi opened her eyes, sniffing and blinking, smiling and then laughing, still on edge. Sobbing slightly, she looked up at him. He smiled at her, doing his best to calm her.

Slowly, he leaned close and then kissed her on the mouth. It seemed even softer than usual, warm and submissive. And she gave in to that kiss, seeking comfort from it, at first gently and then harder and harder, desperately, until she buried her face in his neck. And he felt her wet cheeks, her cool skin, her tiny, racking sobs hidden against him.

"That's enough now." He pushed her away a little. "Come on, don't be like this." Step climbed up onto the low wall and looked over. "If you don't stop crying, I'll jump. I'm not kidding..."

He took a few precarious steps along the edge of the marble walls. He spread his arms wide, trying to keep his balance. "All right then. Are you going to stop or do I have to jump?"

He was walking along, putting one foot in front of the other, wobbling dangerously. Many yards below, the river ran calm and dark, the black water painted by the night, the banks covered with bushes.

Babi watched him, worried, but still weeping. "Please stop...don't do that."

"Then you quit crying!"

"I can't help it..."

"Then farewell, cruel world..." Step jumped in the air and with a shout went over the side.

Babi ran to the edge of the wall. "Step!" She looked down. She couldn't see a thing, only the slow current of the river, rolling along.

"Booooo!" Step emerged from under the wall and grabbed her by the lapels of her jacket. Babi shrieked.

"You fell for it, didn't you?" He kissed her.

"Oh, this is the last thing I needed. Look at the shape I'm in, and you decide it's time to play practical jokes?"

"I did it on purpose. A good scare is exactly what you needed."

"That's just for hiccups."

"Well, it sure sounded like you had the hiccups, you

know that? Come on, come here." He helped her over the low wall.

They found themselves outside of the bridge itself, suspended in the darkness of a small marble cornice. Far below that ledge was the river, and a short distance away was the brightly lit Via Olimpica. Then, enveloped in the darkness and the slow whispering of the river's current, they kissed again, passionately, with a surge of desire.

Step lifted her T-shirt and touched her breasts, freeing them. Then he undid his own shirt and pressed his smooth flesh against her chest. They remained there, breathing in each other's warmth, listening to each other's heartbeat, feeling their skin brush together, wrapped in the cool night breeze.

Later, sitting on the edge of the low marble wall, they looked up at the sky and the stars. Babi lay down, resting her head on Step's legs. She stayed there for a while, in silence. Now she was calm and relaxed while he brushed her hair back off her face.

Looking around, she spotted a piece of graffiti that struck her fancy. "You'd never do anything like that for me, would you? You'd never write here on the side of the bridge."

Step understood what she was referring to. Right in front of them, a brokenhearted spray can had etched its words of love, in English, just to be more romantic: *Bambi, I love you.*

"That's true. I don't even know how to spell, according to you."

"Well, maybe you could find someone who knows how and tell them what you want written." Babi tipped her head back, smiling back at him.

"And anyway, I'd write something like that, which seems better suited to you."

Babi looked at the words that Step was pointing to. On a white column right in front of them was a piece of graffiti to which someone had added a brash insert: *Sophia's ass is Europe's second finest*. *Second* had been added with a small arrow.

Step smiled. "That's a much more sincere piece of writing. Especially because yours is without a doubt the finest."

Babi scrambled down off the wall and punched him with her small fist. "You pig!"

"Now what? You're going to beat me up too? Oh, then you really can't help yourself..."

"I don't like this joke," she said.

Step tried to hug her, but she resisted for a little while.

"I really don't like you. It seriously bothers me."

Step hugged her tighter. "All right, I won't say it again."

In the end, she let herself sink into his arms, believing his promise for a brief instant.

Chapter 25

When Step took Babi home, her folks hadn't come back yet. He said good night to her at the front door. "Ciao, have a good night. Good job, I'm really proud of you."

Babi smiled and disappeared up the staircase. But later, as she was going to bed with a handkerchief full of ice on her right cheekbone and little uprooted hanks of hair caught in the hairbrush in the bathroom, she thought back to those words. Right then and there, she hadn't really thought about it. He was proud of her. Proud of what? That she'd beat up another young woman? That she'd punched her, hurt her, possibly disfigured her?

Babi slid between the sheets. She was suffering now, and not only because of the pain from having had her hair yanked out. Certainly it had been self-defense. It hadn't been her fault; she'd been forced into it. But where had all that rage come from? Why so much hatred? Suddenly she didn't recognize herself, she no longer knew who she was. There was only one thing she knew for sure. She certainly wasn't proud of *that* Babi.

"Alessandri?"

"Present."

"Bandini?"

"Present."

Signora Boi was calling the roll.

Babi, sitting at her desk, was worriedly checking her note. Now it seemed not quite as perfect as it had.

Signora Boi skipped a last name. A student who was present and who was determined to be accounted for stood up at her desk and pointed out the oversight. Signora Boi apologized and started calling the roll again from where she'd made her mistake.

Babi felt slightly reassured. With a teacher like her, maybe her forged note would pass muster. When the time came, she brought her notebook up to the teacher's desk, along with the two other girls who'd been absent the previous day. There she stood, her heart pounding. But everything went fine.

Babi went back to her desk and listened to the rest of the lesson, more relaxed now. She touched her cheekbone. It was swollen and tender. Her mother, who never missed a thing, no matter how groggy she might still be in the morning, had asked her what had happened first thing at breakfast.

"Oh, nothing. I hit my face last night in the dark when I went into my room. Someone had left the door half-open."

Raffaella had fallen for it. Luckily, she didn't have any other marks on her. But she'd told another lie. Her umpteenth in recent weeks. She hadn't been caught yet. But at this rate, sooner or later, it was bound to go wrong. What she didn't know was that the moment in question was hurtling dangerously toward her.

A note landed on her desk. Pallina smiled from across the way. She'd just tossed it.

Babi unfolded the paper. It was a sketch. A young woman lay unconscious on the ground, and another was standing over her, posing like a boxer. Above them, a title in large letters: *Babi III*. It was a parody of *Rocky*. An arrow pointed to the young woman on the ground. Above it was written *Maddalena*. Next to the other young woman was a different phrase: *Babi, her fists were like granite, her muscles like steel. When she arrives, all Piazza Euclide trembles.* Babi couldn't help but laugh.

At that very moment, the bell rang. Signora Boi laboriously assembled her various items and walked out of the classroom. The girls didn't even have a chance to get up from their desks before Signora Giacci came in. They all silently sat back down again.

The teacher went to her desk. Babi had the impression that when Signora Giacci came in, she'd looked around, as if in search of something. Then, when she'd spotted Babi, she'd seemed relieved, almost. She'd smiled.

While she sat down, Babi told herself that it had just been an impression. She needed to cut this out. She was starting to fixate. After all, Signora Giacci had no evidence against her.

"Gervasi!"

Babi stood up. Signora Giacci looked at her with a smile on her face. "Come up, come up, Gervasi."

Babi left her desk. It had been much more than an impression. She'd already been tested in history. Signora Giacci really had it in for her.

"Bring your notebook with you." That phrase was like a knife to her heart. She felt like she was about to faint, and the classroom began to spin around her. She looked at Pallina. She'd turned pale too.

Babi, with her notebook in her hands—suddenly a terribly heavy load, practically unbearable—trudged slowly up to the teacher's desk. In the meantime, she was struggling in vain to come up with an answer, some last hope for that strange request. Why did she want her notebook? She couldn't seem to come up with any other reasons. Her guilty conscience seemed to have nothing to suggest, save what she already knew. She set her notebook on the teacher's desk.

Signora Giacci opened it, staring at her. "You didn't come to school yesterday, did you?"

"No."

"And why not?"

"I wasn't feeling very well." And right now she was feeling decidedly unwell. Signora Giacci was getting dangerously close to the excused absences page. She found the last note, the falsified one.

"So you're claiming this is your mother's signature, right?" The teacher laid the notebook right before her eyes.

Babi looked at that attempt at imitation of hers. All of a sudden, it struck her as insanely fake-looking, incredibly tremulous, avowedly false and counterfeit. A yes emerged from her lips so faintly that it almost couldn't be heard.

"Strange. I just talked to your mother on the telephone a few minutes ago, and she didn't know anything about your absence. Much less did she have any idea that she'd signed a note. She's on her way over now, and she didn't seem very happy.

"You're done at this school, Gervasi. You're going to be suspended. A forged signature, if reported to the proper authorities, as I intend to do, amounts to an automatic suspension. Too bad, Gervasi. You could have earned an excellent grade on your final exam. That'll have to be for next year. Here you are."

Babi took back her notebook. Now it seemed incredibly light. Suddenly everything seemed different to her, her movements, her footsteps. It was as if she were floating in midair. As she went back to her desk, she saw the glances of her classmates, heard their strange silence. She felt something like joy, an absurd taste of happiness. Then, when she got to her desk, she slowly sat down.

"This time, Gervasi, it was you who made the mistake!"

She didn't really understand what happened next. She found herself in a room with wooden benches. Her mother was there, screaming at her. Then Signora Giacci arrived with the principal. They made Babi leave the room. They went on discussing the matter while she waited in the hallway. A nun went by in the distance. They exchanged a glance, without a smile or a hello. Later, her mother emerged. She dragged Babi by the arm. She was very angry.

"Mamma, am I going to be expelled?"

"No, tomorrow morning you'll go back to school. Maybe there's a solution, but first I need to hear what your father has to say about this and whether he's in agreement."

As she went down the stairs, Babi wondered what that solution could be, if her mother seemed to think that she needed her father to agree to the decision. Later, after dinner, she finally found out. It was just a matter of money. They were going to have to pay. The great thing about private schools is that everything can be settled easily. The only real question is just how easily, that is, for how much.

Daniela entered her sister's bedroom with the cordless phone in her hand. "Here, it's for you."

Babi, worn out by the tide of events, had fallen asleep. She ran a hand over her face, brushing her hair back and cradling the white telephone against her cheek. "Hello."

"Ciao. Will you come with me?" It was Step.

Babi sat up in bed. Now she was wide awake. "I'd be glad to, but I'm not allowed."

"Come on, let's go to Parnaso, or else to the Pantheon. I'll treat you to a coffee granita with whipped cream at the Tazza d'Oro. Have you ever tried it? It's magical."

"I'm grounded."

"Again? But weren't you ungrounded?"

"Yes, but today my teacher caught me for turning in a counterfeit note from my mother, and all hell broke loose. That woman has it in for me. She filed a report with the principal. She wanted to flunk me, and I'd have to repeat the whole year. But my mother managed to set everything straight."

"Your mother is powerful! Scary, no two ways about it but she gets what she wants."

"Well, it's not exactly that simple. She had to pay."

"How much?"

"Ten million lire. To charity..."

Step whistled. "Fuck! Nice act of kindness..." An embarrassed silence ensued. "Are you still there, Babi?"

"Yes, I'm here."

"I thought we might have been cut off."

"No, I was just thinking about Signora Giacci, my teacher. I'm afraid that this isn't going to be the end of it. I caught her out in a mistake in front of everybody, and now she wants to make me pay at all costs!"

"More than ten million lire?"

"That's money my mother paid, obviously. But now she's going to go after me. What a pain in the ass! Just think, my grades were so good, it would have been a walk in the park."

"So, you really can't come?"

"No, are you kidding? Just think if my mother phoned, and I wasn't here. It really would be the end of the world."

"Then I'll swing by your place."

Babi looked at her watch. It was almost five o'clock. Raffaella wouldn't be home for quite a while. "All right, come on over. I'll make you a cup of tea."

"Not a glass of beer?"

"At five o'clock?"

"Nothing better than a beer at five o'clock." He hung up.

Babi hopped quickly out of bed and put on her shoes. "Dani, I'm just going downstairs for a second. I'm running by the store. Do you need anything?"

"No, nothing, thanks. Who's coming over, Step?"

"See you soon." Babi left the door ajar and, without answering her sister's question, hurried down the stairs. She bought two kinds of beer, a can of Heineken and a Peroni. If it were wine, she would have had a better idea of what to get. But she really knew nothing about beer. She hurried back upstairs and put the beer in the fridge.

A short time later the doorbell rang. "Yes?"

"Babi, it's me."

"Second floor." She pushed the button in the intercom's receiver twice and went to the door. She couldn't help but check her appearance in the reflection in the glass of a painting hanging along the way. She looked fine.

She opened the door and saw Step coming up the stairs, taking them three at a time. He slowed down only at the end so that he could flash the smile that she liked so much.

"Ciao." Babi leaned against the door, letting him pass. He walked past her and then, while Babi was shutting the door, Step pulled a box out from under his jacket. "Here, these are English butter biscuits. I bought them near here. They're fabulous."

"Thanks, I'll eat them right away."

Step followed her in. He was slightly worried. He hadn't bought those biscuits at a shop. He'd pilfered them at home. Then, as he stopped to think it over, he relaxed. After all, he was really doing Paolo a favor. It definitely would do him no harm to go on a bit of a diet.

Daniela came out of her room especially to see him. "Ciao, Step."

"Ciao." He smiled at her as he shook hands, appearing not to notice that she'd called him by his nickname.

Babi shot a quick glance at her sister. Daniela, getting the point immediately, pretended she'd only come in to get something and went right back to her bedroom.

A short while later, the water came to a boil. Babi took out a pink box. Then she used a little spoon to sift tiny tea leaves into the pan. Slowly, a faintly exotic odor wafted through the kitchen.

Not long after that, they were seated in the living room.

She had a cup of piping hot cherry-flavored tea in her hands, and he had both cans of beer in front of him.

Babi pulled out an album of family photographs from a cabinet in the living room and started leafing through it with him. Maybe it was the Heineken, or it might have been the Peroni, but the fact remained that he was enjoying himself. He listened to her vivid accounts that came with each different photo: a trip somewhere, a special memory, a party.

He didn't fall asleep this time. Slowly, progressively, he watched her grow up as he leafed through those plastic-covered pages. He watched as her first teeth came in, as she blew out a single birthday candle, learned to ride a bike, and then there she was, just a little older, on rides at the amusement park with her little sister. On a sleigh with Santa Claus, at the zoo holding a lion cub in her arms.

Slowly, he watched her face thin out, her hair darken, her small breasts grow, and then, suddenly, after he turned the next page, she was a woman. She was no longer just a skinny little boy-child with a sulk and a swimsuit, her hands on her hips. Instead, a small bikini covered the bronzed body of an attractive young woman with smooth legs, slender now and longer. Sitting on a pedal boat, she smiled through her long, sun-bleached hair. Her shoulders showed through, golden beneath her locks, bleached almost salt white by the sea. All around her were out-of-focus beachgoers in the background, unaware that they were being recorded for posterity.

With every page that they turned, she seemed to resemble more and more closely the young woman that now sat beside him. Step, his curiosity aroused by the stories recounted by their subject, followed those photos, sipping his second beer, every so often asking a question or two.

Then, all at once, knowing what was coming, Babi tried to skip a page.

Step, amused by those countless younger versions of Babi, was faster than her.

"Hey, no, I want to see."

They play-wrestled for the album, a struggle that quickly turned into a loving hug that made them feel closer. After finally winning control of the album, he burst out laughing. Making a funny face with her eyes crossed, Babi was smiling broadly in the middle of the page. Babi had never liked that photo.

"Strange, though, of all of them, it's the one that looks most like you," Step said.

Pretending to be offended, she punched him in the chest. Then she put the album away, picked up her mug and the two empty beer cans, and went into the kitchen.

Alone now, Step roamed around the living room. He stopped in front of canvases by artists he'd never heard of. A silver Russian icon enjoyed pride of place on a low side table, painted with dark enamel. Near two sofas upholstered in a hand-painted fabric, there was a broad table with short legs. On top of that table were small silver boxes and ashtrays, scattered in no particular order. They would have made Step's friends very happy.

From the kitchen came the sound of running water. Babi was washing her mug and throwing the two empty cans of beer into the pail under the sink. She buried those empty beer cans under an empty milk carton and a crumpled Scottex paper towel. There couldn't be any traces of Step's presence in that apartment.

When she went back to the living room, Step really had disappeared. She walked down the hallway. "Step?" No answer. She walked toward her bedroom. "Step?"

Then she saw him. He was standing next to her desk, leafing through her notebook.

"It isn't very good manners to read other people's things without their permission." Babi tore the notebook out of his hands.

He let her take it. By now, he'd read all he was interested in. He had memorized it. "Why, is there anything written in there that might make me mad?"

"These are my things. It's none of your business."

Step laughed and walked over to Babi, gave her a kiss, and dragged her onto the bed with him. Then he started to lift her T-shirt.

"Come on, no, stop it. If my folks get here and catch us, they'll get mad at me. But if they catch us doing this in my bedroom, I'll never hear the end of it."

"You're right." Step picked her up and lifted her easily into the air, accustomed as he was to lifting dumbbells much heavier than that soft, supple body. "Let's go into this other room, which strikes me as nicer." Without giving her time to reply, he darted into her parents' bedroom, pulling her after him and shutting the door. Then he laid her down on the bed and, kissing her in the dim light of the bedroom, stretched out beside her.

"You're crazy, you know that, right?" she whispered in his ear.

He didn't answer. A small shaft of light from the setting sun filtered in through the lowered wooden shutter and illuminated his mouth. She saw those perfect white teeth smile at her and open before settling into a leisurely kiss.

Then, without really knowing how, she found herself in his arms without a top. She could feel his skin brush against hers, his hands gently take possession of her breasts. Babi's eyes were shut, her soft lips were opening and closing at a constant rhythm. Suddenly she felt more relaxed, freer. As if she could finally breathe.

Step's hand silently wrapped around her belt, and he eased it through her belt loops. In the darkened bedroom, Babi heard the slithering of the leather, the sound of the metal buckle abandoning its usual groove.

She was extremely aware of everything now, even as she continued to kiss him. That room seemed suspended in midair. There was only the slow clicking of a distant alarm clock, their respiration panting with love and lust.

Then a tiny tug at her waist. The belt tightened and the prong slipped out of the third hole, with its dark edges, the one that was deformed and worn, the most heavily used one. And in a flash, her Levi's opened up. Silvery buttons that had once been imprisoned were freed at the magical touch of his thumb and forefinger. One after another, lower and lower, dangerously so.

She held her breath, and something suddenly happened in those enchanted kisses. A tiny shift, almost too small to detect. That gentle magic seemed to vanish. Even if they continued kissing, it was as if there was a silent expectation between the two of them, as if both were waiting, breathless. Step was trying to understand something, a hint, a sign of her desire. But Babi was immobile, revealing nothing. And in fact, she hadn't yet made a decision. No one in her life had ever gotten this far. She could feel her jeans undone and his hand, right there, at the edge of her leg.

She continued kissing him without wanting to think about it, without really knowing what to do. At that very moment, Step's hand decided to run the risk. It moved slowly, delicately, but she could feel it all the same. She half shut her eyes in something like a sigh. He brushed his hands over the edge of the now-open jeans. She felt his fingers on her flesh, above the pink hem of her panties. And at that thought, a shiver of chill and embarrassment ran down her spine.

Then she felt that elastic band pull slightly away from her flesh and, immediately after that, slip out of his grasp and snap back into place. A second attempt, more determined and resolute this time. Step's hand under her jeans took possession of her hip and then, brazen and masterful, slipped under the elastic. Then it slid farther in, toward the center, caressing her belly, lower and lower and lower still, coming into contact with the curly edges of unexplored boundaries.

But then something happened. Babi blocked his hand.

Step looked at her in the dim half-light. "What's wrong?"

"Shh."

Babi rose up, resting on her side, and froze in place, ears pricked for a sound from outside that room, outside the shutters, down in the courtyard...a sudden sound, a revving engine that she knew very well. She heard the car put into reverse, that tense driving style. All doubts were banished.

"My mother! Hurry up, we need to get you out of here." In a moment they were more or less presentable. Babi pulled the bedcovers up. Step finished tucking his shirt back into his trousers. Someone knocked at the bedroom door. For a second, they froze.

But it was Daniela. "Babi, Mamma's home." She didn't get a chance to finish her sentence before the door swung open.

"Thanks, Dani. I know."

Babi left the room, dragging Step behind her. He put up a small show of resistance. "No, I want to talk to her. I want to clear up this situation once and for all!" Once again he had that mocking smile on his face.

"Quit kidding around. What are you, an idiot? You can't imagine what'll happen if my mother catches you." They went into the living room. "Hurry, leave this way so you don't run into her."

Babi undid the lock of the main door, and she stepped out onto the landing. The elevator ran directly down to the courtyard. She summoned it while they exchanged a hasty kiss.

"I want an appointment with Raffaella."

She shoved him into the elevator. "Disappear!"

Step pushed the button marked *G* and, with a smile on his face, obeyed Babi's advice. At that very moment, the other door swung open. In came Raffaella. She laid bags and packages on the kitchen table. Then she had a suspicion as if perhaps she heard the click of the other door. "Babi, is that you?" She went straight to the living room.

Babi had turned on the television. "Yes, Mamma. I'm watching TV." But a faint blush on her cheeks gave her away.

That was all Raffaella needed. She hurried into the other bedroom and leaned out the window that overlooked the courtyard. There was the noise of an engine going away, leaves of ivy in a corner that were still rustling. Too late.

She shut the window and ran into Daniela in the hallway. "Did anyone come to the house?"

"I don't know, Mamma. I've been in my room studying the whole time."

Raffaella decided to let it slide. It was pointless to insist with Daniela.

She went into Babi's bedroom and looked around. Everything seemed fine. There was nothing strange or out of place. Even the bedcovers were perfectly tucked. But the bed could easily have been tidied and remade. And so, with no one there to see her do it, she laid her hand atop the covers. They were cool. No one had been lying on them.

She heaved a sigh of relief and went into her bedroom. She took off her skirt suit and hung it neatly on a hanger. Then she got out an angora sweater and a soft skirt. She sat down on the bed and put them on. Blithely unaware, relaxed, unable to even imagine that right there, inches away, her daughter had been lying, just minutes before on that blanket still warm with young and innocent excitement. With her arms around that boy that Raffaella couldn't stand.

Later, Claudio came home. He had a long discussion with Babi on the subject of the forged excuse, the ten million lire he'd had to lay out, and her behavior in the past several days. Then he sat down in front of the television set, his mind finally at ease, waiting for dinner to be ready. But just as he got comfortable, Raffaella called his name from the kitchen.

Claudio immediately went to answer his wife's summons. "Now what?"

"Look at this..." Raffaella pointed at the kitchen sink.

There stood the two empty beer cans that Step had drank.

"Well, it's beer, so what?"

"It was hidden in the trash can, under a handful of paper towels."

"Big deal, someone drank a few beers. What's so bad about that?" Without really knowing why, he felt as if he was in a television commercial.

"That boy was here this afternoon. I'm sure of it..."

"What boy?"

"The one who beat up Accado, the one who convinced your daughter to skip school. Stefano Mancini. Step, Babi's boyfriend."

"Babi's boyfriend?"

"Can't you see how she's changed? Is it possible that you never notice a thing? It's all his fault. She sneaks out to go to motorcycle races, she counterfeits notes for her absences... Plus, did you see that bruise under her eye? I think he must be beating her too."

Claudio stood speechless. More problems. Could that young man seriously have beaten Babi? He needed to do something, intervene somehow. He'd have it out with him. Yes, that's what he'd do.

"Here." Raffaella gave him a sheet of paper.

"What is it?"

"The license plate number of that boy's motorcycle. Call our friend Davione, give him the number. He'll get us the address, and you can go talk to him."

Now this would mean he'd actually have to do it. He

clung to one last shred of hope. "Are you sure that it's the right one?"

"I saw the bike in front of Babi's school last time. I remember it perfectly."

Claudio stuck the slip of paper into his wallet.

"Don't lose it!" Those words from Raffaella were practically more of a threat than a piece of friendly advice.

Claudio went back to the living room and let himself collapse onto the sofa in front of the television set. A married couple was discussing things that were really their private business in front of a guy with long hair. What made them want to go and air their dirty laundry in front of everyone on television? He couldn't even bring himself to do it at home, all alone, in his kitchen.

Now he was going to have to go and talk to that young man. And he'd probably beat him up too. He thought about Accado. Maybe he'd wind up in the same hospital room as him. They could keep each other company. That thought didn't cheer him up much. He didn't really like Accado all that much.

The show was interrupted by a commercial break. Claudio got out his wallet and went over to the telephone. Stefano Mancini, aka Step. That boy had cost him ten million lire and two cans of beer. He pulled out the sheet of paper with the motorcycle's license plate number and dialed the phone number of his friend Davione.

Then, as he waited for someone to answer the call, he thought about his wife. Raffaella really was unbelievable. She'd seen that boy's motorcycle once or twice, and she could remember the tag number perfectly. While Claudio had been driving that Mercedes Benz for a year and still didn't know his own license plate number by heart.

"Hello, Enrico?"

"Yes."

"Ciao, it's Claudio Gervasi. Listen, I'm sorry to bother you but I need a favor."

"Ask away."

For a moment, Claudio wished that Enrico weren't so damned accommodating. It's really true, when you *don't* need a favor, that's when everyone's happy to do it for you.

Chapter 26

Babi couldn't figure out whether that light tapping on the wooden blind was a dream or reality. Maybe it was the wind. She shifted in bed and heard it again. A little louder, but precise, like a signal.

Babi got out of bed and went over to the window. She looked through the tiny spaces between the extended slats. Illuminated by the light of the full moon was Step. Surprised, she tugged on the cord to raise the blind, doing her best to make as little noise as possible.

"Step, what are you doing here? How did you manage to get up here?"

"It was really easy. I climbed up on the wall and then shinnied up the drainpipes. Come on, let's go."

"Where?"

"They're expecting us."

"Who is?"

"The others. My friends. Come on, don't keep asking questions. Let's get going! This time, if your folks catch us, it really is going to be a problem."

"Hold on. Let me change into something."

"No, we're not going far."

"But I'm not wearing anything under my nightgown."

"So much the better." He laughed.

"Come on, you cretin. Hold on a minute." She half shut the window, sat down on the bed, and quickly got dressed. Bra, panties, sweatshirt, a pair of jeans, her tobacco shoes, and then she was back at the window. "Let's go, but we can use the door."

"No, we'll go down this way. It's better."

"What are you, crazy? I'm scared to do that. I could slip and fall and die. You know what would happen if my folks woke up to the sound of me screaming, followed by a thud? Come on, follow me."

Babi led him through the darkness of that sleeping apartment, tiptoeing along on soft wall-to-wall carpeting, carefully turning door handles. She deactivated the burglar alarm, took the house keys, and they were out. A slight click from the front door as it shut behind them, slowly pulled closed to prevent any loud noises. Then down the steps and into the courtyard, onto the motorcycle, rolling downhill, the engine off to avoid being heard. Then, outside the gate, Step put the bike in gear, put it in second, and hit the gas. They shot forward, now far from her sleeping home, safe and free to go where they pleased, together—while the rest of the world believed them fast asleep and alone in their own beds.

"What's this?" Curiously, Babi dismounted from the motorcycle.

Meanwhile, Step pulled something out of the top box. "Follow me, and you'll see. Don't make any noise, that's important."

They were on Via Riccardo Zandonai, just above the

church. They walked through a narrow gate. They followed a dark path running between bushes.

"Here, go under this." Step lifted a piece of metal mesh that had been torn away at the bottom of the fence. Babi ducked under, taking care not to get caught in the mesh. A few seconds later, Step was beside her. They walked along in the darkness on newly mown grass. The moon lit up everything around them. They were on the grounds of an apartment complex.

"Wait, where are we going?"

"Shh." Step put his finger to his lips, urging her to be silent.

Then, after climbing over a low wall, Babi heard some sounds of distant laughter or someone talking. Step smiled at her and took her by the hand. They went around a hedge, and there they saw it. In the light of the moon, light blue, transparent, calm, edged in by the dark of night, a large swimming pool.

In it were a number of young people. They were swimming while taking care not to make too much noise. Little waves lapped at the sides, every once in a while overflowing onto the surrounding grass. A strange breathing sound could be heard, that water coming and going and then vanishing down into the void of a little grate.

"Come on."

They approached the swimming pool. A number of young people greeted them. Babi recognized their wet faces. They were all of Step's friends. By now, she'd even learned a few names. The Sicilian, Hook, Bunny. That was easier than the usual rounds of introductions where everyone was named Andrea or Fabio or Marco.

Pollo was there, too, and Pallina also swam over to the side of the pool. "Damn, I was certain you wouldn't come. I lost my bet."

Pollo pulled her away from the edge of the pool. "You see, what did I tell you?" They laughed. Pallina tried to push him under the water but couldn't do it. "Now you have to pay."

They swam off, splashing each other and kissing. Babi wondered what they'd bet, and a few vague ideas occurred to her. Then she focused on a far more serious problem. "Step, I don't have a swimsuit."

"Neither do I. Just my boxer shorts. What do you care? Almost no one does."

"But it's cold," she added, trying to come up with some other excuse.

"I brought towels for afterward, I've got one for you too. Come on, quit stalling."

Step took off his jacket. Before long, all his clothing was lying on the ground. "Look out, or I'll throw you in fully dressed, and that's just going to be worse. You know I'll do it."

Babi looked at him. This was the first time she'd seen him undressed. Brushstrokes of silvery moonlight highlighted his muscles even more. Perfect abdominals, squared-off, compact pectorals.

Babi stripped down to her bra and panties. A short while later, they were both in the water. They swam along, side by side. Babi started to shiver a bit. "Brrr, it's cold."

"You'll warm up. Just be careful not to go under the surface with your eyes open. There's a lot of chlorine in the water. It's the first swimming pool open in the neighborhood this year, you know that? So this is a sort of inauguration. Summer will be here soon. Nice, isn't it?"

"Beautiful. It reminds me of those films Bruce Weber made with the whole Dillon family, when they went pool-hopping and would go swimming on the grounds of mansions at night."

"Those films *who* made?"

"Bruce Weber..."

"Never heard of him... We've been doing this for years now. Come over here."

They swam to the side. Babi noticed that there were bottles all over the sides of the pool. They'd been opened only recently.

Step grabbed one. "Here, have some."

"But I don't drink."

"It'll warm you up."

Babi took the bottle and tipped it back. She felt the cool liquid, slightly bitter and sparkling, drain down her throat. It was good. She handed the bottle to Step, smiling at him. "It's not bad. I like it."

"I'll bet you do. It's champagne." Step took a long drink.

Babi looked around. There were at least twenty or so people in that swimming pool. They'd all formed into small groups at the edges of the basin, right there where the bottles were. She wondered if that was all champagne. Where had they found it? No doubt it, too, was stolen.

"Here." Step handed back the bottle. She decided not to give it too much thought and took a drink. But she gauged it wrong and a little too much went down her throat. She practically choked, and the champagne with all its sparkling bubbles went up her nose. She started coughing. Step burst out laughing and waited for her to recover.

Then they swam together toward a corner of the pool across the way. A larger hedge there protected that nook from the rays of the moon. It only let through the occasional glint of silver. Soon those glints were trapped in the tangles of her wet hair. Step looked at her. She was beautiful.

He kissed her cool lips, and they were immediately locked in a clinch. Their nearly nude bodies now pressed against each other completely, head to toe, for the first time. Enveloped by that chilly water, they sought out and found warmth between them, learning each other, feeling the thrill of it, pulling apart occasionally to avoid creating too much awkwardness.

Step broke away from her, took a brief sidestroke across the pool, and soon swam back with a new catch in his hands.

"This one's still full." Another bottle. They were surrounded. Babi smiled and drank from it, this time slowly, careful not to choke. It almost tasted good to her.

Then she found his lips. They continued kissing like that, sparkly and bubbly, while she felt herself floating but couldn't quite understand why. Was that the normal effect of the water or was it the champagne? She gently let her head fall back, resting it in the water, and for a moment, it stopped spinning. She could and, at the same time, couldn't hear the sounds around her. Her ears, with tiny waves lapping at them, wound up underwater from time to time, and strange and pleasant muted sounds reached her, dazing her even more completely.

Step held her in his arms, swinging her around him, pulling her through the water. She opened her eyes. Brief surges of water caressed her right cheek while small, spiteful splashes reached her mouth now and again. She felt like laughing.

High above, silvery clouds moved slowly across the infinite depth of the dark blue night. She pulled herself up and threw her arms around his powerful shoulders and kissed him passionately.

He looked her in the eyes. He put a hand on her forehead and, stroking her hair back, uncovered her smooth face. Then he moved farther down, along her cheek, down to her chin, along her neck, and then even farther, to her breasts where the water lapped against them, shivering with cold and excitement, and then still farther down, where just that afternoon he'd first dared to graze her with his fingers.

She hugged him tighter still. She put her chin on his shoulder, and with her eyes half-shut, she looked past him. A half-empty bottle was floating in the pool. It was rising and falling in the water. And she imagined the message rolled up inside: *Help. But don't save me.*

Then she shut her eyes and started to tremble, but not just because of the cold. A thousand emotions swept over her, and suddenly she realized. She was the one who was about to need rescue.

~

"Babi, Babi." She suddenly heard someone calling her name and shaking her hard, so she opened her eyes. Right in front of her was Daniela. "What's wrong, didn't you hear the alarm clock? Come on, get moving or we'll be late. Papà is almost ready."

Her sister left the bedroom. Babi turned over in her bed. She thought back to the night before and sneaking out with Step, riding on his motorcycle, and swimming in the pool with Pallina and the others. Getting drunk. Being in the water with Step. His hand.

Maybe she'd just dreamed the whole thing. She touched her hair. It was perfectly dry. Too bad, it really had been a dream after all, a beautiful one, but still nothing but a dream.

From under the covers, she stuck out her hand and fumbled for the radio. She found it and turned it on. Propelled by a happy old song by Simply Red, she got out of bed. She still felt slightly sleepy, and the strangest thing was that she had a bit of a headache.

She walked over to her chair to get dressed. Her school uniform was lying there, but she hadn't laid out the rest of her things. *How odd*, she thought. *I must have forgotten. That's never happened before. My folks must be right. I really am changing. I'll wind up being just like Pallina. She's so messy and out of control that she forgets everything. Well, I guess that means we'll be better friends.*

She opened her top drawer and pulled out a bra. Then, as she was rummaging through her underwear, searching for a pair of panties that looked good on her, she found a sweet surprise. Hidden at the bottom of the drawer, in a little plastic bag, was a wet bra and panties. A faint scent of chlorine rose around them. So it hadn't been a dream after all.

She smiled. Then she suddenly remembered being in Step's arms. It's true, she'd changed. A lot.

She started getting dressed. She put on the uniform and

then, last of all, as she was putting on her shoes, she made a decision. She would never again allow him to go past a certain point.

Finally at ease, she looked in the mirror. She was not having a good hair day, but her eyes were the same eyes that she'd made up lightly a few days ago. Even her mouth was the same.

She brushed her hair, smiling, set down the hairbrush, and left her bedroom in a hurry to eat breakfast. Little did she suspect that she'd change even more very soon. So much that she'd be able to walk by that mirror and not even recognize herself anymore.

Chapter 27

Signora Giacci walked downstairs to the conference room. She greeted a number of mothers that she knew and then went to the far end of the room. A young man in a dark jacket with a pair of sunglasses was sitting in a rather informal pose in an armchair there. He had one leg sprawled over the armrest, and as if that weren't bad enough, he was also taking a drag on a cigarette in a devil-may-care fashion. His head was tilted back, and every so often he let plumes of smoke rise toward the ceiling.

Signora Giacci came to a halt. "Excuse me?" The young man pretended he hadn't heard her, so Signora Giacci raised her voice: "Ex*cuse* me?"

Step finally looked up at her. "Yes?"

"Don't you know how to read?" she asked him, pointing to a highly visible NO SMOKING sign on the wall.

"Where?"

Signora Giacci decided to abandon that line of argument. "There's no smoking in here."

"Ah, I really hadn't noticed." Step dropped the cigarette butt onto the floor and crushed it out with a sharp rap of his heel.

Signora Giacci was starting to lose her temper. "What are you doing here, young man?"

"I'm waiting to talk to a teacher, Signora Giacci."

"That's me. And to what do I owe this visit?"

"Ah, so you're the teacher. I apologize for the cigarette." Step sat up straighter in the armchair. For a moment, he seemed sincerely contrite.

"Forget about that. Just tell me what you want."

"Well, I wanted to talk to you about Babi Gervasi. You really shouldn't treat her the way you have been lately. You see, teacher, that young woman is quite sensitive. Plus, her parents are real pains in the ass, you understand. So if you go at her like this, then they ground her, and the one who loses out is me because then I can't take her out, and that's really not okay with me, teacher. You understand my position, don't you?"

Signora Giacci was really starting to see red. How dare this young hoodlum come in here and address her like this? "No, I absolutely do not understand, and most important of all, I can't figure out what you're even doing here."

Suddenly the teacher remembered where she'd seen him before. She'd had a feeling he might be familiar from the very first, but she hadn't been able to pin down when she'd seen him. At last it became clear to her. She'd seen him from the window. This was the young man who'd ridden away from the school with Babi. She and the girl's mother had discussed this matter at some length, the poor woman. And this was a dangerous fellow.

"You aren't authorized to be here. Please leave, or I'll have to call the police."

Step got up and brushed past her with a smile. "I only

came in to talk it over. I wanted to come to an understanding with you, try to find common ground, but I can see that that's going to be impossible. There's just no reasoning with you, signora."

Signora Giacci stared at him with a superior attitude. She wasn't one bit afraid of this guy. He might have all the muscles imaginable, but he was still just a boy, a small insignificant mind.

Step leaned forward as if he wanted to share a confidential matter with her. "Let's see if you understand this word, teacher. Listen carefully, eh? Pepito."

Signora Giacci turned pale. She didn't want to believe her ears.

Step walked away. "I see that you've grasped the concept. So, now, I'd like to see if you can behave yourself, teacher. If so, you'll see that we won't have any problems. In life, it's all just a matter of finding the right words, isn't it?"

He left her there, in the middle of the room, looking older than she was, with a single shred of hope. That maybe none of this was true. Signora Giacci went to the principal's office, asked for permission to leave the school, hurried home, and when she got there was almost afraid to go in.

She opened the door. Not a sound. Nothing. She went through all the rooms, shouting, calling her dog by name, and then she collapsed into a chair. Even more weary and lonely than she already felt every day of her life.

The doorman appeared in the doorway. "Signora Giacci, how are you? You look so pale. Listen, two young men came at your instructions today to take Pepito out for a walk. I let them in. That was the right thing to do, wasn't it?"

Signora Giacci stared at him as if she were looking

right through him. Then, without hatred, resigned, full of sadness and melancholy, she shook her head. How could he have guessed? Young people were wicked and cruel.

Signora Giacci watched the doorman walk away, and then she struggled to get up from her chair and went to shut the door. Ahead of her lay days of loneliness without Pepito's cheerful barking.

You can make mistakes about people. Babi had seemed like a proud and intelligent young woman, maybe a little too full of herself, but never vicious enough to undertake this kind of retaliation.

Signora Giacci went into the kitchen to make something to eat. She opened the refrigerator. Near her salad was a can of Pepito's dog food. She burst into tears. Now she really was alone. Now she really had lost, once and for all.

Chapter 28

That afternoon, Paolo had finished work early, so he was a happy man when he returned home. Suddenly he heard the sound of a dog barking. He went into the living room to find a little white Pomeranian wagging its tail on his Turkish carpet. And right in front of the dog was Pollo, with a wooden spoon in one hand.

"Ready? Go!" Pollo tossed the wooden spoon onto the sofa across the room. The Pomeranian didn't even turn to look, utterly uninterested in where that piece of wood might be now. Instead it started to bark.

"Fuck, though, why won't he fetch? This dog doesn't work! We got a defective dog! All he knows how to do is bark."

Sitting in an armchair in the same room, Step stopped reading the new issue of the *Totem* comic. "This dog doesn't know how to fetch, you understand? He just hasn't been trained for it. What do you expect?"

Then Step noticed his brother standing in the doorway with his hat still on his head. "Oh, Paolo, ciao. How are you? I didn't see you at first. Why are you home at this hour?"

"I finished work early. But what is this dog doing in my house?"

"It's a new dog. Pollo and I went halfsies on it. Do you like him?"

"Not at all. I don't want to see it in here. Look." He walked over to the sofa. "It's already covered with white dog hair here."

"Oh, come on, Pa, don't be rude. I'll make sure he stays in my half of the apartment."

"What?"

The dog wagged its tail and started to bark.

"You see, he's happy with the arrangement!"

"Right, already I lose sleep when you come in late at night, so I can just imagine with a dog barking all the time. It's entirely out of the question." Paolo left the room angrily.

Pollo made a funny face at Step. "Jesus, he's pissed off." Then he got an idea. Pollo shouted loud enough that he could be heard from the other room. "Paolo, for the three hundred thousand lire I owe you... I'll take him away."

Step started laughing and went back to reading his *Totem* comic.

Paolo appeared in the doorway. "You've got yourself a deal. After all, I was never going to see that money again, and this way, at least, I get this dog out of here. By the way, Step, do you have any idea what became of my butter biscuits? I bought them the other day for my breakfast, and they've already disappeared."

Step acted vague. "I don't know. Maria must have eaten them. I didn't take them. You know I don't even like them."

"I don't know why it is, but whatever happens around here, it's always Maria's fault. So, shall we just fire this darned Maria? She only seems to make things worse around here..."

Pollo broke in. "Are you kidding? Maria is fantastic. She bakes these apple pies you wouldn't believe. There was one just the other day, for instance..."

"So you guys did eat it. I was positive!"

Step looked at his watch. "Damn, it's really late. I have to go."

Pollo stood up too. "So do I."

Paolo stood, all alone now, in the living room. "What about the dog?"

Before leaving, Pollo just had time to reply, "I'll swing by later."

"Listen, either you take it away or you give me the three hundred thousand lire."

The door shut behind them.

Paolo looked at the Pomeranian, in the middle of his living room, wagging its tail.

Chapter 29

Babi was riding behind Step. Her cheek rested on his jacket, and the wind was tearing at the tips of her hair.

"So are you sure this isn't going to hurt me?"

"Positive! Everyone has tattoos. You see how big mine is. If it really hurt, I'd be dead now, right? You just get yourself a really little one. You won't even notice."

"I didn't say I was going to do it. I just said I'd come in and take a look."

"All right, whatever you decide. If you don't like it, you don't have to do a thing. Agreed?"

Babi didn't answer. Step braked and parked the motorcycle. "Here we are."

They walked down a narrow lane. There was sand on the ground. It had been blown there by the wind, stolen from the nearby beach. They were in Fregene, at the fishermen's village.

For a moment, Babi started to wonder if she'd lost her mind. Who knows what she'd be able to say to her parents if they found out. She'd have to get it in some hidden spot. But where? A place that was reasonably well hidden, but not too much so. After all, the guy who'd be doing the work would have to be able to see it.

Omigod, I'm about to get a tattoo, she thought. She imagined her mother finding out. She'd start screaming her head off. Her mother always shouted at her.

Step smiled at her. "Are you thinking about where to get it?"

"I'm still thinking about whether to get it at all."

"Come on, you really liked mine when you saw it. Plus, Pallina has one, too, doesn't she?"

"Yes, I know that, but so what? She did that on her own, at home, with needles and india ink."

"Well, this is much better than that. And with the tattoo machine, you can add color and everything. It's supercool."

"But are you sure that they sterilize it?"

"Of course. Come on, how could you doubt that?"

Babi thought to herself that she didn't do drugs and she'd never had sex. It would really be the dictionary definition of bad luck to get HIV from having a tattoo done.

"Here, this is the place."

Step stopped in front of a rustic cabin. The wind was moving the reeds that covered the little building's corrugated tin roof. The window was glazed with panes of colorful glass, and the door was made of dark brown wood. It almost looked like chocolate.

Step opened it. "John, okay if I come in?"

"Oh, Step, sure. Come right in."

Babi followed him. She fearfully shut the door behind her. A strong smell of alcohol washed over her. At least there was disinfectant in the place. Now she'd just have to make sure they used it.

John was sitting on a sort of stool and was touching the shoulder of a young blond woman sitting in front of him on a bench. The sound of a little electric motor reached Babi's ears. It reminded her of the sound of a dentist's drill. She just hoped that it wouldn't hurt like one.

The young woman was gazing straight ahead. Maybe she was feeling pain, but if so, she wasn't showing it.

A young man, leaning against the wall, stopped reading his *Corriere dello Sport*. "Does it hurt?"

The young woman with extremely pale skin and the strap of her tank top pulled down over her arm replied in a faint voice, "No."

"Oh, come on. It does too hurt."

"I told you it doesn't."

The young man went back to reading his newspaper. He almost seemed annoyed that it didn't hurt. Maybe it had hurt him when he'd done it.

Babi looked around. The walls were covered with sheets of paper with drawings of all sorts: birds, fish, butterflies, dragons, tigers. Below that array, arranged over a table covered with small bottles of pigment, were a number of photos. John had had pictures taken of him with his newly tattooed customers. There were pretty blond girls and strange muscular guys with long hair. Every one of them was smiling as they displayed the new tattoo on their bodies.

In one especially big photograph, a muscular man with a bald head had covered his back with an enormous blue dragon. Farther down, a guy was displaying a rose on his chest, the same rose that could be seen on his motorcycle's gas tank. Everyone seemed happy to have been tattooed.

Babi looked at the young blond woman John was working

on. Why wasn't *she* smiling? There was a strange expression on her face. At a certain point, she made what looked like a grimace of pain. If he'd taken her picture just then, John wouldn't have known where to put the photo.

"All done." John moved the machine away and leaned over her shoulder to get a better look at his work. "Perfect!"

The young woman heaved a sigh of relief. She craned her neck to see if she, too, was in agreement with John's enthusiasm. Babi and Step moved forward, curious. The young man stopped reading and leaned in. They all gazed at each other in silence.

The young woman looked around, seeking some sign of approval. "It's nice, isn't it?"

A butterfly made up of many colors glowed vividly on her shoulder. The flesh was slightly swollen. The color was still fresh, mixed with the red of the blood, making it particularly glossy.

"Beautiful," the young man replied with a smile, clearly her boyfriend.

"Very." Babi decided to give the young woman an extra smidgen of satisfaction.

"Here, let's put this on." John applied a gauze bandage to her shoulder. "You'll have to clean it every morning for a few days. You'll see, there won't be any infection!"

The young woman clenched her teeth and inhaled sharply before letting out a sigh.

Babi smiled. One thing was certain. At least afterward, John definitely applied alcohol.

The boyfriend pulled out a hundred thousand lire and paid. Then he smiled and hugged his newly tattooed girlfriend.

"Ouch. You're hurting me, you know!"

"Oh, I'm sorry, sweetheart." He delicately moved his arm lower, to her waist, and left the cabin with her, wondering if it really had hurt her or if she was just taking revenge for earlier.

"All right, Step. Let me take a look at how things are going with your tattoo."

Step pulled up the right sleeve of his jacket. On his muscular forearm there was an eagle with a flaming red tongue. Step moved his hand like a pianist. His tendons tightened and darted under his skin, bringing those large wings to life.

"It's really beautiful." John looked at his handiwork complacently. "Maybe we need to touch it up, here and there..."

"One of these days, maybe. Today we're here for her."

"Ah, for this lovely young lady. And what would you like, signorina?"

"First of all, I'd like for it not to hurt, and then... do you sterilize the tattoo machine every time you use it?"

To reassure her, John removed the needles and cleaned them with alcohol right in front of her. Her two big blue eyes followed every tiny detail as he worked, increasingly worried about the fateful moment that was fast approaching.

"Have you decided where you want it done?"

"Well, I'd like it to be someplace where it's not too obvious. If my folks see it, I'm going to be in a world of pain."

She immediately regretted using that turn of phrase. Maybe it was going to be a world of pain in any case. She decided not to think about it.

"Well"—John smiled at her—"I've done some tattoos on people's ass cheeks and others on their heads. One time, an American girl came in here and insisted on getting one, well, yeah, you know where... right? But before I did the tattoo, I even had to shave her!"

John burst out laughing right in front of her. Babi looked at him with growing concern. *Omigod, this guy is a sex maniac.*

"John." Step's voice, slightly harsh, resounded from behind her. John's expression changed immediately. "Yes, sorry about that, Step." Now he turned back to look at Babi with a more professional demeanor. "Anyway, I don't know. We could do it on your neck, under your hair, or on your ankle, or even on your hip."

"Okay, on the hip would be just fine."

"It's just that it would have to be something small. Nothing special, because I'm guessing you'd need it to be covered up by the hem of your panties or under your swimsuit, I mean, right?" This time he wasn't being lewd.

"Oh, but I want something simple. Something brightly colored, something cheerful."

"Here, you can choose something from here." John pulled a large book out from under a table. Babi started leafing through it. There were death's heads, swords, crosses, revolvers, all sorts of terrible designs.

John stood up and lit a Marlboro. He'd figured out that this wasn't going to be quick.

Step sat down next to her. "This one?" He pointed at a Nazi swastika set on a banner with a white background.

"Are you joking?"

"Well, I didn't think it was bad... How about this?" He

pointed out a large snake done in purplish hues, its jaws wide in a sign that it was about to attack.

Babi didn't even reply. She continued leafing through the large book. She skimmed the figures rapidly, dissatisfied, as if she already knew that she wasn't going to find anything good.

Every so often, Step would interrupt, suggesting this or that terrible design. This only got on her nerves. Finally, Babi turned the last page, a sheet of hard plastic, and shut the book. Then she looked at John. "No, there's nothing I like."

John took a drag on his cigarette and blew out a plume of smoke. Just as he'd expected. "Well, then, we'll have to invent something. Would you like a butterfly like the one I did for the young woman earlier?"

Babi wrinkled her nose.

"A rose?" Babi shook her head.

"A flower in general, by any chance?"

"I don't know..."

"Well, young lady, why don't you help me out? Otherwise we could be here all night. Look, I have another appointment at seven."

"Well, I really don't know. I'd like something a little odd."

John started pacing the room. Then he stopped. "One time I tattooed a bottle of Coca-Cola on a guy's shoulder. It turned out great. Would you like that?"

"I don't really like Coca-Cola though."

"Well, Babi, why don't you tell him something that you *do* like?" said Step, trying to be helpful.

"All I ever eat is yogurt. I can't exactly get a container of yogurt tattooed on my hip!"

In the end, they came to a solution. Step had proposed it. John agreed, and Babi really liked it.

John immediately set to work. It was no easy job. First, because Babi refused to take off her jeans and, second, she was afraid of even a single injection, let alone a hundred or so, administered in rapid succession with the aid of a small electric motor. John told her all kinds of stories just to calm her down. His most absurd memories, people that had asked him to do tattoos on their head and on their eyebrows. One guy even had a tattoo done on his, well, "you-know-what."

He told her about the time that Step and Pollo came in to get their tattoos. Step had been cool as a cucumber, Pollo a complete disaster. He'd drained two beers in a row, and then, as if that weren't enough, he'd decided to smoke a joint, even though he never smoked dope. Okay, that was years and years ago, and they'd both been kids at the time, but that was clearly a case of genuine fear.

In the end, Pollo, completely wrecked, had decided that he didn't like his tattoo. He'd started whining that he wanted to get it removed right away. John had told him that it was impossible, but Pollo didn't want to listen to reason. Higher than a kite, Pollo had overturned the pigments, all the little bottles full of solvents, things John had imported from Bali. Pollo left the tattoo parlor with two hundred fifty thousand lire less than when he'd come in, and on his chest, a red tattooed heart with *Mamma* written on it.

Babi burst out laughing. She asked mischievously whether Pallina had even seen it. For a moment, she forgot about the faint stinging feeling on her hip. Then, as she noticed the droning buzz of the motor, she turned serious again. There was a risk she might hurt herself, and lying there, stiff and tense, seemed like a good way to ward it off.

She remembered when she'd gotten her ears pierced with Pallina. That piece of cork behind her earlobe and the ice to keep her from feeling anything. Oh, but she'd felt it, and how! And now, here she was, getting a tattoo. She smiled at Step.

"Everything all right?"

"Just fine."

Step paid John fifty thousand lire while Babi checked her tattoo. It had turned out perfect. A short while later, on the motorcycle, she undid the top button of her jeans, loosened the gauze dressing, and peeked at it again, happily.

Step noticed what she was doing. "Do you like it?"

"I love it."

On her delicate skin, still swollen with color, a small, newborn baby eagle, similar to Step's, a daughter of the same hand, was soaring on the cool breeze of a sunset.

~

The doorbell rang, and Paolo went to answer it. There at the door was a distinguished-looking gentleman.

"Good evening. I'm here to see Stefano Mancini. I'm Claudio Gervasi."

"Good evening. I'm afraid my brother isn't here."

"Do you know when he'll be back?"

"No, he didn't tell me when he'd be back. Sometimes he doesn't even come home for dinner. He just comes in late at night."

Paolo looked at that gentleman. What on earth could he

want with Step? *Looks like trouble*, he thought. *It must be the usual thing, something to do with a fistfight or brawl.*

"Listen, if you'd like to make yourself comfortable, he might arrive soon, or else he might telephone."

"Thanks." Claudio walked into the living room.

Paolo shut the door but he couldn't restrain himself any longer. "Excuse me, is there anything I can help you with?"

"No, I wanted to speak to Stefano. I'm Babi's father."

"Ah, I understand." Paolo flashed him a bland smile. Actually, he hadn't understood a damned thing. He didn't have the faintest idea of who this Babi was. *A young woman*, he thought, *which is worse than a brawl. More serious problems.* "Excuse me for a moment." Paolo went into the other room.

Claudio, alone now, looked around. He walked over and inspected a few posters on the walls, and then he pulled out his pack of cigarettes and lit one. *At least this whole thing has one silver lining. I can smoke without worrying about it. How strange though. This is the brother of Stefano, that guy Step who beat up Accado, and yet he seems like a perfectly respectable young man. Maybe the situation isn't as bad as I thought. As usual, Raffaella likes to exaggerate. Maybe it really wasn't even worth bothering to come. These are just kid issues. They naturally work them out among themselves. It's just a crush, a teenage love story.*

Maybe Babi would get over him soon.

~

"Hey, Babi, ciao. I need to go!" Step took her in his arms.

"Where do you have to be? Stay a little longer."

"I can't. I have an appointment."

"Tell me right away who you're going out with," Babi said.

"You'd never guess."

"Do I know her?"

"Very well indeed. Excuse me, but first of all, why don't you ask me if this is a man or a woman."

Babi heaved a sigh of annoyance. "Is this a man or a woman?"

"A man. I'm seeing your father."

"My father?"

"He came looking for me at my house. When I phoned, he was there waiting for me. We made an appointment to meet in a few minutes at Piazza dei Giuochi Delfici."

"What does my father want with you?"

Step put on his jacket. "I don't know! But once I find out, I'll call you and tell you. All right?"

He gave her a powerful, dizzying kiss. She let him do it, still stunned and surprised by that piece of news.

Step went galloping down the stairs, hurtling over the last few steps, and she watched him vanish. Then she went back inside, silent, sincerely worried. She tried to imagine the two of them meeting. What would they talk about? And what would come of it?

Then, worried especially about her father, she just hoped they wouldn't come to blows.

Chapter 30

When Claudio arrived, Step was already there, sitting on the low wall, waiting for him and smoking a cigarette. Claudio parked nearby and got out of his car.

"Hello."

"Good evening, Stefano." They shook hands. Then Claudio lit a cigarette, too, to feel more at ease. Unfortunately, it didn't work. That young man really was strange. He just sat there, smiling at him in silence, staring at him, in that black jacket.

He was very different from his brother. Among other things, he was a lot bigger, Claudio thought to himself. Suddenly, just as he was about to sit down next to him on the low wall, a sort of sudden recollection burst into his mind. That boy had beat up his friend Accado. He'd busted his nose. And now he was dating his daughter. That young man was dangerous. He'd a thousand times rather be talking to his brother.

Claudio remained standing. Step looked at him curiously. "Well, what are we going to talk about this fine day?"

"Well, here's the thing, Stefano. At my house, we've been having some problems lately."

"If you only knew how many problems I've been having myself..."

"Yes, sure, I understand, but you see, we've always been a very happy family. Babi and Daniela are two very good girls."

"It's true. Babi is a special young woman. Listen, Claudio, is it okay if I call you Claudio? I'm already not that much of a talker. If I have to be all formal, well, then I really lose touch."

Claudio smiled. "Certainly." Deep down, this young man was likable enough. If nothing else, he still hadn't tried to hit him.

Step stood up from the wall. "Listen why don't we go sit somewhere else? We could talk more comfortably and maybe we could even drink a little something."

"All right. Where are we going?"

"Not far from here is a little place some friends of mine opened up. It's like being at home. No one is going to bother us there." Step got on his motorcycle. "Follow me."

Claudio climbed into his car. He was happy. His mission was starting to look easier than expected. *That's a relief*, he thought.

He followed Stefano down toward the Via Farnesina. At the Ponte Milvio, they turned right. Claudio took care not to lose sight of that small red taillight as it raced through the night. If he made that kind of stupid mistake, Raffaella would never forgive him.

Step turned to look back every so often, making sure that Claudio was still behind him. Luckily, he thought to himself, this guy wasn't one of those drivers who cling fearfully to the steering wheel and are terrified of using the gas pedal.

A short while later, they stopped on a small street just behind Piazzale Clodio. Step pointed Claudio to an empty spot where he could park his car while Step left his motorcycle right in front of the door to Four Green Fields. They went downstairs. The place was jumping. There were plenty of young people perched on stools in front of the long bar. Other people, some of them older, were seated at round wooden tables scattered throughout the room, talking animatedly.

The walls were painted dark brown, and light-colored columns divided the big room into sections. All around were paintings and logos of brands of beer from various countries. A guy with round wire-rimmed glasses and unkempt hair was moving frantically behind the counter, making fruit cocktails or simple gin and tonics.

"Ciao, Antonio."

"Oh, hey, ciao, Step. What can I get you?"

"I don't know. We'll talk it over and decide. What'll you have?"

As they were going over to sit down, Claudio remembered that he hadn't had anything to eat yet. He decided to go easy. "A Martini spritz."

"So a nice blond beer and a Martini spritz."

They sat down at a table in the back of the place, on the left, where things weren't quite so loud and crazy. Almost immediately a beautiful, dark-skinned young woman named Francesca came over. She brought what they'd ordered, and she stayed at the table awhile to chat with Step.

He introduced her to Claudio, who politely stood up to shake hands. Francesca was surprised at this show of chivalry. "This is the first time I've seen a gentleman in this place."

She held Claudio's hand a little longer than was normal.

He looked at her, slightly embarrassed. "Is that a compliment?"

"Certainly! You are distinguished, courtly, and charming." Francesca laughed. Her long raven-black hair danced cheerfully around her dazzling white teeth. Then she walked off, sensually, well aware that his eyes would be following her.

Claudio took a seat, careful not to sit on the tail of his jacket. He decided he didn't want to disappoint her.

Step picked up on that. "Nice ass, eh? Brazilian girls all have incredible asses. At least, that's what I hear. I really wouldn't know because I haven't been to Brazil yet, but if they're all like Francesca..." Step laughed and tossed back half his beer.

"Yes, she really is quite attractive." Claudio drank his Martini spritz, slightly annoyed that his mind had been so easy to read.

"So, what were we talking about? Ah, yes, we were saying that Babi really is a remarkable young woman. Very true."

"Yes, that's right, and my wife, Raffaella..."

"Hmm, yes, I've met her. She's a little powerhouse, shall we say."

"Yes, true enough." Claudio finished his Martini spritz. He was in full agreement with Stefano on that point too. At that moment, Francesca went by again. She tossed her hair, laughing, and shot a provocative glance at their table.

"You made a good impression, you know that, Claudio?

Listen, shall we get something else to drink?" He didn't give him time to answer. "Antonio, would you bring me another beer?" Then he turned to Claudio. "What'll you have?"

"Why, no thanks. I don't really want anything else..."

"What do you mean, you're not having anything? Come on, now..."

Claudio decided that, at least for the moment, it wouldn't be a good idea to push back too hard. "All right, then I'll have a beer too."

"Two beers and a bowl of olives, some potato chips, you know, bring us something to munch on."

A short while later, their order arrived. Claudio was a little disappointed. Serving them now wasn't Francesca but a black guy, slightly overweight, with a kind face.

Step waited for him to leave. "He's Brazilian too. But a completely different kind of Brazilian, eh?"

They exchanged a smile. Claudio tasted his beer. It was good and cold. He drained another gulp. Stefano was a good guy. Maybe he was even more likable than his brother. In fact, no two ways about it.

And he took another drink of beer. "Anyway, like I was saying, Stefano, my wife is very worried about Babi. You know, this is her last year, and her final exams are coming up."

"Yes, I know. I heard about her teacher, too, and the problems she's been causing." Step decided that it was probably wise not to mention the money they'd had to pay.

Claudio seemed surprised. "Oh, so you heard..."

"Yes, but I'm pretty sure that things will settle down."

"I certainly hope so..." Claudio threw back a long slug

of beer, thinking back on the ten million lire he'd been forced to pay out.

Instead, Step thought about Signora Giacci's dog and Pollo's efforts to teach it to play fetch. "You'll see, Claudio, everything's going to turn out fine. Signora Giacci is going to stop pestering Babi. That problem no longer exists, take it from me."

Claudio tried to smile. How could he tell Step that the real problem was him?

Just then, a group of young guys came in. Two of them saw Step and came over to say hello. "Oh, ciao, Step! What the fuck happened to you? You have no idea, we've been looking for you everywhere. We're still waiting for our rematch."

"I've had other things to do."

"Scared, are you?"

Step seemed slightly annoyed. "What are you talking about? Scared of what? We thrashed you two. And you're still talking?"

"Hey, calm down, don't lose your temper. We just haven't seen you since then. You took our money, and then you disappeared."

The other young man worked up his nerve a little too. "Plus you had a piece of luck on that last ball."

"Just be glad that Pollo isn't here. If not, I'd be glad to take the same amount of money from you, and we wouldn't be talking about luck. We just made a series of incredible shots, one pocket after another."

The two young men put on dubious expressions. "Yes, okay." They went over to the bar to order a round of drinks.

Step saw them chatting. Then they looked over at him and started laughing. Step couldn't stand it. "Listen, Claudio, do you know how to play pool?"

"There was a time when I played frequently. I was pretty good too. But now I haven't picked up a pool cue in, like, forever."

"Come on, please, you need to help me out. I can beat these guys like a drum. I just need you to set up the shots for me. I'll take care of getting them into the pockets."

"I don't know though. We were supposed to talk."

"Come on, we can talk later. All right?"

Claudio nodded. Maybe after a game of pool it would be easier to talk to him. But what if they lost? He preferred not to think about that.

Step stood up and went over to the bar, where he spoke to the two guys. "All right, you're on. Come on, Antonio, give us the table. We'll win the same amount of money off these two."

"Wait, who are you playing with? That guy?" One of the two boys pointed at Claudio. He was sitting at the table, finishing his beer.

"Yes, why, are you good to play with him?" Step asked.

"Hey, if you're happy with him as a partner, you must know what you're doing."

"Well, no doubt if Pollo was here, it would be quite a different story. You both know that. It's just going to mean I'm willing to give you some money today. All right?"

"No, if you're going to be like that, then we're not playing. Afterward you'll just say that we won because Pollo wasn't there."

"Ah, I can beat the two of you by myself," Step said.

"Yes, of course you can!" The two guys broke out laughing.

Step gazed at them seriously. "You want to raise the stakes? You want to make it two hundred thousand lire? You in? But just one game, I've got things to do."

The two guys exchanged a glance. Then they looked at Step's partner. There Claudio sat, at the far end of the room, playing awkwardly with a pack of Marlboros on the table. Maybe that was what finally made up their minds for them.

"Okay, you're on. Let's go on in." The guys picked up the box of pool balls.

Step went over to Claudio. "Do you know how to play American-style? One game, two hundred thousand lire. Come on, Claudio, don't worry. Those guys are delusional. We can take them!"

"No, Stefano, no thanks. We really ought to have this talk."

"Come on, just one game. And if we lose, I'll pay."

"That's not the issue—"

"So what are you two going to do? Are you going to play some pool?" It was Francesca. She stood facing Claudio, a smile on her face. "Come on. I'll come watch, and I'll root for you. I'll be your cheerleader."

Step looked at Claudio, curious now. "Well?"

"Okay, but just one game."

"Yahooo! Let's go over there and beat them silly." Claudio put the cigarette pack in his pocket, and then he stood up.

Cheerfully, Francesca locked arms with him, and all three of them walked over to the poolroom. The balls were already racked on the green felt. One of the two young men lifted the triangular rack. The other one went down to the far end of the table and took a precise shot, breaking the rack. Balls of all colors scattered across the felt, rolling silently. Then some of them smashed together with flat clacks and then, slowly, came to a halt.

The game started in earnest. At first, it was simple, carefully calibrated shots, then harder and harder, more demanding and difficult. Claudio and Step had the striped balls. Step made the first pocket. The other guys put in two balls, with a third pocket that was just dumb luck.

When it was Claudio's turn, he took a long shot. He was out of practice. He came up short. It didn't even come close to the pocket. The other two guys exchanged a look of amusement. They could already feel that money in their wallets.

Claudio lit a cigarette. Francesca brought him a whiskey. Claudio noticed that she had small but perky and firm breasts under her dark T-shirt.

A short while later, it was his turn again. His second shot turned out better. Claudio hit the ball square on, and with a nice lag, he left the cue ball in the middle of the table. The ball was the fifteen, and the two young men had left it open for him, certain that he'd miss.

"Nailed it!" Step slapped him on the back. "Nice shot!"

Claudio looked at him, beaming, and then tossed back another gulp of whiskey and bent over the pool table. Concentrating, he struck the cue ball just slightly to the left, hitting the cushion and running down along the edge, with a sweet effect on the ball. A perfect shot. In went the target ball.

The two other guys exchanged a worried look while Francesca clapped her hands. "Nice!"

Claudio smiled. He dabbed the tip of his tongue onto the light blue chalk and rapidly buffed the end of his cue stick. "I really used to be good!"

They went on playing. Step put in a few balls, but the other two guys were luckier. After a few more shots, they had nothing left to pocket except for the red ball and the yellow ball.

But now it was Claudio's turn. There were still two striped balls on the table. Claudio crushed out his cigarette. He picked up the chalk, and as he was quickly buffing the tip of his pool cue with it, he studied the situation. It was hardly ideal. The thirteen ball was pretty close to the far pocket, but the ten was practically in the middle of the table. He'd have to place the ball perfectly, make it stop on the spot, while still knocking the ten ball sideways into the left middle pocket. Back in the day, he might have been able to pull that off, but now...

How many years had it been since he'd last played pool? He threw back the last gulp of whiskey. Putting down the glass, his eyes met Francesca's. As many years as that gorgeous young woman had been alive, most likely.

He felt vaguely dazed. He smiled at her. Her skin was the color of honey, setting off her dark hair and that incredibly sensuous smile. She was a kind person too. He assumed she must be about eighteen. For an instant, it occurred to him that he might have overestimated, maybe she was even younger. *Oh my God*, he thought, *she could be my daughter. Why did I even come here? To have a talk with Stefano, my new friend Step, my good buddy.* He opened and then shut his eyes.

He was starting to feel the effects of the alcohol. *Well, I'm in the game now, might as well go ahead and play.*

He braced his hand on the table's edge, laid the pool cue down on it, and slid it back and forth in the groove between thumb and forefinger, testing it. Then he focused on the cue ball. There it was, motionless at the center of the table, cold. Just waiting to be hit.

He took a deep breath and then exhaled completely. One more test run and then he took his shot. Precise. With just the right amount of force. Side cushion and then the cue ball just touched the thirteen ball—pocket. Perfect.

Then the cue ball started its trip back. Going fast, much too fast. *No, stop, stop, stop.* He'd hit it too hard after all. Maybe it had been his excessive alcohol-fueled enthusiasm or else his forbidden desire for that honey-hued young woman. The cue ball rolled past the ten and stopped, right there, just past the middle of the table, in front of Claudio, spiteful and cruel.

Their two adversaries exchanged a glance. One of them raised an eyebrow; the other heaved a sigh of relief. For a moment there, they'd been afraid they were about to lose the game. Now they smiled.

From that position, Claudio really had an impossible shot. He walked around the table. He studied all the relative distances. Difficult. He'd have to make a four-cushion shot. He stood there in a corner, leaning on the edge of the table with both hands.

"What do you care? Give it a try." Claudio turned around. Step was right behind him. He'd understood what Claudio was thinking as if he'd just read his mind.

"Yes, but four cushions..."

"So what? Worst case, we lose...But if you make it, just think how bad they're going to feel!"

Claudio and Step looked at their two adversaries. They'd ordered a couple of beers, and they were sitting there, at a table nearby, already drinking, certain of their victory.

Claudio started to laugh. "Right, what do we care, worst case, we lose!" By now, he was drunk. He went over to the other side of the table. He chalked his cue stick and took the shot. The cue ball seemed to fly over the green felt.

First cushion. Claudio thought back to the many afternoons he'd spent shooting pool.

Second cushion, he thought of his old friends and how they'd hang out together all the time.

Third cushion, the girls, the money he didn't have, and how much fun they all had.

Fourth cushion. His lost youth, Francesca, and when he was still seventeen...

Just then the cue ball hit the ten ball full on from behind with power, confidence, and precision. A dull *thwack*. The ten ball shot forward, into the middle pocket.

"Nailed it!"

"Yahooo!" Claudio and Step hugged in delight.

"Fuck, look at the luck you had. Look where you left the cue ball," Step said.

The cue ball stood directly in front of the yellow one ball, just inches from the far pocket. Claudio knocked it in with an easy shot.

"We won!" Claudio hugged Francesca and even managed to swing her through the air. Then, dancing with his arms around her, he bumped into one of their two adversaries.

"Get the fuck away from me." The guy gave Claudio a

shove, knocking him against the pool table. Francesca leaped right back up onto her feet. Claudio, slightly stunned, took a little longer.

The guy grabbed him by the lapels and hauled him up. "Smart guy, huh? 'It's been years since the last time I played'... 'Guys, I'm all out of practice,'" he mimicked.

Claudio was terrified. He just stood there, uncertain what to do. "I haven't played in years, for real."

"Oh, sure! Well, from that last shot I wouldn't say so."

"It was dumb luck."

"Hey, that's enough. Let go of him." The guy pretended he hadn't heard Step. "I said let go of him."

Suddenly Claudio felt himself being dragged backward. He found himself free now, with his jacket loose again.

He caught his breath while the other guy was slammed up against the wall. Step had one hand around his throat. "What are you, deaf? I'm not looking for an argument. Come on, out with the two hundred thousand lire. You guys insisted on playing."

The other guy stepped forward with the cash in his hand. "You tricked us though. That guy plays ten times better than Pollo."

Step took the money, counted it, and put it in his pocket. "That's true, but don't blame me. I didn't even know the guy."

Then he locked arms with Claudio, and together they emerged from the pool hall, victorious.

Claudio ordered another whiskey. This time, it was to get over his fright. "Thanks, Step. Heck, that guy wanted to knock my teeth out."

"No, he was just acting. He was just furious about losing!"

"No, no, thanks, for real."

Step smiled. "Here, Claudio. This is your hundred thousand lire."

"No, seriously, I can't accept it."

"Why not? Fuck, you basically won the game! And you were even taking the beating for it."

"All right, in that case, let's have a nice drink to it. On me."

Not long after that, seeing the condition Claudio was in, Step walked him to his car. "Are you sure you can drive home?"

"Absolutely, don't worry about it."

"You're sure, aren't you? It doesn't cost me anything to ride along with you."

"No, seriously, I'm fine."

"All right, if you say so. Nice game, huh?"

"Wonderful!" Claudio smiled and then he started to shut the car door. Suddenly, someone started shouting.

"Claudio, wait!" It was Francesca. "What are you doing, leaving without even saying goodbye?"

Claudio apologized. "You're right. It was just that so many things happened all at once."

Francesca pushed her head in the car and gave him a kiss on the lips. Then she pulled away and smiled at him. "All right then, ciao. See you around. Come see me sometime. I'm always here."

Claudio looked at her, stunned. "Sure I will."

Then he shut the door, started the car, and pulled away. He opened the car window. The cool night air was pleasant. He pushed a cassette tape into the stereo and lit a cigarette.

Then, completely drunk, he slammed both hands hard

on the steering wheel. "Wow! Fuck, what a shot! And what a babe..."

Suddenly he felt happy in a way he hadn't in a long, long time. Then, as he got closer to home, he grew sad again. He started trying to think of what he could tell Raffaella. He pulled into the garage, still undecided about the official version to supply.

Backing into that narrow space, already difficult when sober, proved impossible when drunk. As he got out of the car, he looked at the scratch along the side and the Vespa knocked over against the wall. He lifted it upright, apologizing aloud. "Poor Princess Savina, I dented your Vespa."

Then he went upstairs. Raffaella was there, waiting for him. It was the worst interrogation of his life, worse than the third degree in a cop movie. Raffaella was playing bad cop and nothing else. The good cop, the one who acts like your friend and offers you a glass of water or a cigarette, that role had been abolished in this movie.

"Well, do you mind telling me how it went? Come on, tell the story!"

"It went fine. In fact, it went fantastic. Step is a very decent guy, deep down, a good boy. There's nothing to worry about."

"What do you mean, there's nothing to worry about? He broke Accado's nose."

"Oh, maybe he was provoked. How are we supposed to know? Plus, Raffaella, let's face facts. Accado is a real pain in the ass..."

"What are you talking about? Didn't you tell him to stay away from our daughter, that he can't see her, talk to her, or go pick her up at school?"

"Well, no, actually, we never got to that point."

"Then what did you say to him? What have you done all evening? It's midnight!"

Claudio gave in and confessed. "We played pool. Just think, sweetheart, we beat a couple of boasters! I sank the last two balls. I even won a hundred thousand lire. Cool, right?"

"Cool? You're the same idiot as always, you're incompetent. You're drunk, you reek of tobacco, and you didn't even manage to put that criminal in his place." Raffaella left the room, furious.

Claudio made one last effort to calm her down. "Raffaella, wait!"

"What now?"

"Step says that he'll go to university."

Raffaella slammed the door and locked herself in her bedroom.

Not even that last lie had done a bit of good.

Chapter 31

And you won?" Pollo couldn't believe his ears.

"We took two hundred thousand lire off them!"

"I can't believe it. So this guy, Babi's father, is actually a nice guy?"

"He's incredible! Just think, Francesca told me that she really likes him."

"He struck me as a loser."

"Why, when have you ever seen him?"

"When I went back to your house to pick up the dog."

"Ah, right. By the way, how is Arnold doing?"

"Just great. Believe me, that dog is really intelligent. I'm sure that, before long, I can teach him to fetch and retrieve. The other day I was out front, I threw a stick, and he went and got it."

Step stopped in front of an apartment house door. "We're here. Listen, don't make a ruckus."

Pollo glared at him. "Why, do I usually make a ruckus?"

"You always do."

"Oh, really? You know, I just came along to do you a favor."

They went up to the fourth floor. Babi was babysitting

Giulio, the Mariani child, five years old and hair as fair as his skin.

Babi was waiting for him at the door.

"Ciao." Step kissed her.

She was a little surprised to see Pollo too. He muttered something that must have been meant as a "ciao" and then sat right down on the sofa, next to the little boy. He changed the channel in search of something better than those stupid Japanese cartoons.

Giulio, of course, promptly objected but Pollo tried to persuade him. "No, believe me, now they're going to show even better ones. Now you're going to see the flying turtles." Giulio fell for it hook, line, and sinker. He sat watching the soccer postgame show in silence, trusting that turtles would start flying any second.

Babi went into the kitchen with Step. "Do you mind telling me why you brought him?"

"I don't know, he kind of insisted. Pollo has a weak spot for little kids."

"I don't think so! The minute he got here, he already had the kid crying."

"All right, then. Let's say that I did it so I could be alone with you." He put his arms around her. "You have to admit, I'm quite the truth teller. You seem to bring out the best in me. Come to think of it, why don't we take our clothes off right now?"

He dragged her, laughing, into the first bedroom he found. Babi tried to resist, but in the end, she allowed herself to be convinced by his kisses. They both wound up on a small bed.

"Ouch." Step reached around behind his back. A sharp-edged toy tank had poked him right between the shoulder blades. Babi started laughing. He threw it on the carpet as he cleared the bed of some other electronic warriors and several transformable figures.

Then, finally comfortable, Step pushed the door shut with his foot and devoted himself to his favorite pastime. He stroked her hair, kissed her lips, and raced to the buttons of her blouse, systematically undoing them. He lifted her bra and kissed her where the skin was paler, sweetly softer, and rosy pink.

Then, all at once, something stabbed his neck. "Ouch." Step slapped at the spot where he'd been stabbed. In the darkness, he saw her laugh, still holding a strange action figure with pointed ears. And that fresh young smile of hers, that naive way that she had about her, hit him where he lived.

"You hurt me!"

"We can't stay in here. This is Giulio's room. Just think if he comes in."

"But Pollo's with him. I gave him very specific orders. That terrible child is basically done for, bound and gagged. He can't even get up from the sofa."

Step dove back in and focused on her breasts. She caressed his hair and let him go on kissing her. "Giulio is a good boy. You're the one who's a terrible child."

~

Pollo was eating a sandwich that he'd found in the kitchen and drinking a nice, ice-cold beer when Giulio got off the sofa.

"Where do you think you're going?"

"To my room."

"No, you need to stay here."

"No, I want to go to my room."

Giulio started to leave but Pollo pulled him back by his little red woolen sweater, practically dragging him over to sit by him on the sofa. Giulio tried to struggle but Pollo pinned him down with an elbow to the belly.

Giulio started to whine. "Let go of me, let go of me!"

"Come on, the cartoons are coming on any minute."

"That's not true." Giulio looked at the television set again and burst into tears.

Pollo released him. "Here, you want to try this? It's delicious. Only grown-ups are allowed to drink it."

Giulio seemed slightly interested. He grabbed the can of beer with both hands and took a sip. "I don't like it. It's bitter."

"Okay, then look what Uncle Pollo has for you..."

A short while later, Giulio was playing happily on the floor. He was bouncing the little pink inflatable balloons that Uncle Pollo had given him. Pollo watched him with a smile on his face. *After all, it really doesn't take much to make a kid happy. Just two or three condoms.* After all, he wasn't going to be needing them that night.

He turned around. Not a sound from the bedroom. *And for that matter, Step's probably not going to need them either*, Pollo thought, laughing inwardly.

Then, since he was starting to get bored, he started making phone calls.

~

In the dim light of that bedroom full of toys, Step caressed Babi's back and her shoulders. He ran his hand down her arm, and then he took that arm and brought it up to his face. He brushed his mouth over it, the length of that arm, every inch of flesh. Step delicately opened her hand, kissed her palm, and then laid it on his own naked chest, abandoning her to her own thoughts.

Babi lay immobile, suddenly frightened. *Omigod, now I understand. But I'll never be able to do it. I'm not ready.*

Step continued kissing her neck tenderly, behind her ears, on her lips. All the while, his hands, more confident and relaxed, more experienced, were taking possession of her like soft waves, leaving stranded on that unknown shore a shipwrecked pleasure.

Then, all at once, dragged along by that current, she, too, finally moved. Babi gathered her courage. She slowly moved away from where she'd been lying and started caressing him too. Step hugged her close, instilling trust, reassuring her, and Babi let herself go. Her fingers lightly explored his skin. She felt his powerful abs.

Every step along this path was a plunge into the depths, a tumble into the abyss, a difficult—almost impossible—leap forward. And yet, Babi was determined to do it, and holding her breath in that darkened room, she took the leap. And so she found herself with her fingers gingerly stroking the edge of that little patch of soft curly hair, and then farther and deeper into his jeans, and then that button, the first such button for her, in every sense of the word.

And at that very moment, without knowing why, she thought of Pallina. Her friend, already more confident and more experienced. She thought of when she told her the story. *You know, after that I couldn't do it, I just didn't have the nerve.* Perhaps that is what gave her the courage, the final impetus. Suddenly she did it. She unfastened that button. His first golden button popped out of the buttonhole with a faint, jeansy sound. In the silence of the room, she heard it clearly; it came sharp and bright to her ears. She'd done it. She almost sighed. Now everything would be so much easier. It was as if they'd said something to each other, acknowledged it. They both knew what was happening, what she was doing. Her hand, more confident now, moved on to the second button and then the third and so on, farther down, as the jeans opened wider, growing free. Step rolled gently away from her, letting his head fall back. Babi reached out for him again, taking shy shelter in that kiss, unhappy at that tiny separation.

Then there was an unexpected noise. Doors slamming.

And as if it were some fragile enchantment, the magic spell was shattered. Babi pushed his hand away and sat up. "What was that?"

"How would I know? Hey, come on back." Step threw his arms around her and pulled her close to him.

Another noise. Something breaking.

"No, darn it, something bad is going on out there!" Babi got off the bed. She brushed her skirt back into place, buttoned up her blouse, and hurried out of the room.

Step fell back onto the bed, arms thrown wide. "Fuck that Pollo!" Then he zipped up his jeans, put on his T-shirt, and left the room too.

When he arrived in the living room, he couldn't believe his eyes. "What the fuck are you doing?"

They were all there. Bunny and Hook were having some

sort of wrestling match on the carpet. Nearby lay an overturned lamp. Schello was sitting with his feet on the sofa, eating a bag of potato chips and watching *Colpo grosso*, the TV show that featured housewives doing stripteases.

Babi lunged at them in a rage. "Get out! Get out of here. Immediately!"

At the sound of that shouting, Dario and another guy came out of the kitchen with beers in hand. The Sicilian arrived, too, with a young woman. They were both red-faced. Step figured they must have just done what he and Babi hadn't even attempted. Well, so much the better for them!

Babi started pushing them all out the door, one by one. "Get out of here, every last one of you... out!"

Amused, they allowed themselves to be herded out, making even more noise on their way. Step helped. "Come on, guys, out you go."

Last of all, he shoved Pollo out the door. "I'll deal with you later."

"But all I did was call Hook. It's his fault that he passed the word to all the others."

"Shut up." Step gave him a kick in the ass and sent him staggering out the door.

"Look, just look at what a mess those vandals made of the place." Babi pointed out the broken lamp and the sofa stained with beer. Potato chips were scattered everywhere. Babi had tears in her eyes.

Step didn't know what to say. He hugged her. "Forgive me. Come on, I'll help you clean up."

"No, thanks, I'd rather do it alone."

"Are you mad at me?"

"No, but you'd better get out of here. The parents will be back soon."

At the door, Step turned around one last time. "Are you sure you don't want me to help you?"

"Positive."

They exchanged a hasty kiss. Then she shut the door.

Step went downstairs. He looked around but there was no one in sight. He got on his motorcycle and drove off.

Babi collected the shattered pieces of the broken lamp, threw them in the trash, and then mopped the floor and cleaned up the stains on the sofa. When she was done, she looked around. *Well, it could have been worse. I'll just say that the lamp fell over while I was playing with Giulio.*

The little boy couldn't contradict her story in any case. He was lying there, fast asleep, exhausted by all the excitement.

Chapter 32

The next morning, Step woke up and went to the gym. But he wasn't going to train. He was looking for someone. And in the end, he found him. His name was Giorgio. He was a young kid, about fifteen, who had boundless admiration for Step. He wasn't alone in that admiration. Giorgio's friends also spoke of Step as a sort of god, a myth, an idol. They knew all the stories about him, everything that people said about him, and they did nothing but add even more to what had become a sort of urban legend by now.

That boy was a trusted accomplice. The only person Step could have asked a favor like this without running the risk of looking like an absolute fool. In part because, where admiration left off, sheer terror began.

After talking with Step, Giorgio was inside Falconieri High School. He walked along, shoulder brushing the hallway walls, and finally managed to sneak into Classroom 3B, Babi's class. Signora Giacci was teaching a lesson, but strangely, she said nothing.

Babi was speechless. She looked at the enormous bouquet of red roses on her desk. Amused, she read the note: *My friends are a bit of a disaster, but I promise that this evening, when we have dinner at my house, we'll be all alone. From: Someone Who Had Nothing to Do with It.*

The news soon made the rounds at school. When the principal learned about it, she flew into a complete rage. No one had ever done anything like it before.

After the school day was over, Babi descended the front steps of the school with that enormous bouquet of red roses in her arms, sweeping away any remaining doubts. Everyone was talking about her. Daniela was proud of her sister. Raffaella got even angrier, and Claudio, naturally, received another dressing-down.

That afternoon, Step was organizing a collection of drawings by Andrea Pazienza, when someone rang the doorbell.

It was Pallina. "Oh, first I was the cupid in this affair, and now I'm the mailman. Next time, what role am I going to have to play?"

Step laughed. Then he took the package from her hands and thanked her. He opened it. In it was a pink-flowered apron and a note. *I accept, but only if you cook, and especially if you do it while wearing this little gift of mine. PS I'll be there, but at eight thirty, no earlier, because that's when my folks go out!*

A short while later, Step was in his brother's office.

"Paolo, I absolutely need the place to myself tonight."

"But I already invited Manuela over."

"Well, you're just going to have to change that invitation to some other day. Come on, you can see Manuela whenever you want. Darn it, Babi can only come tonight."

"Babi? The daughter of the guy who came to our house?"

"Yes, why?"

"That guy seemed pretty mad to me. Did you finally talk to him?"

"Of course I did. We went and played pool together, and we even got drunk."

"You both got drunk?"

"Yes, or, well... actually, he got drunk all by himself."

"Did you get him to drink?"

"What do you mean, did I get him to drink? He did the drinking all on his own. Come on! We're agreed, right? Tonight, you go out. All clear?"

Then, without waiting for an answer, he hurried out of the office. He was so caught up in the things he had to do that he didn't even notice the especially sunny smile that he got from Paolo's secretary.

From his house, he phoned Pollo. He warned him not to come by, not to call on the phone, and especially not to start trouble of any kind. "Listen, your life depends on not screwing this up. Actually, it's more serious than that. Our friendship depends on it, and I'm not kidding!"

Then he drew up a grocery list, went to the supermarket downstairs, and bought just about everything that came to hand, even a box of those English butter biscuits his brother liked so much. After all, Paolo deserved it. All things considered, he was a good brother.

By eight o'clock, everything was ready. Step had listened to the latest American hits on the radio. He hadn't put on Babi's apron, but to make up for that, he'd laid it out on a chair nearby, ready to lie brazenly when the time came.

He looked at the results of his hard work. Carpaccio with Parmesan cheese and arugula. A mixed salad with avocado and a fruit salad seasoned with maraschino liqueur.

Memories surfaced. He'd eaten that fruit salad often when he was a boy...

He let the memories slip away. He was happy now. This was going to be his special evening, and he didn't want anything to ruin it.

Pleased and satisfied, he checked the table, adjusting the placement of a napkin. He really was quite the chef.

He started wandering around the apartment, a little nervous now. He washed his hands. He sat down on the sofa. He smoked a cigarette, and then he turned on the television set. He brushed his teeth. A quarter after eight. Time didn't seem to be passing at all.

In fifteen minutes, she'd be here, they'd eat dinner together, and they'd chat comfortably. They'd have the sofa to themselves without anyone to disturb them. Then they'd go into his bedroom and then...

No, Babi would never do it. It was too soon. Or maybe she would. There's no such thing as too soon for certain things. They'd spend some time together, and then maybe it would happen.

He tried to remember the words of a song by Lucio Battisti. How did it go? *"What a sensation of faint madness I feel coloring my soul, the record player, the lights down low, and then... iced champagne and the adventure can..."* *Damn it. That's what I forgot! The champagne! It's essential!*

Step went quickly into the kitchen and pulled open all of the cabinets. No good. There was nothing but a pinot grigio. He put it in the freezer. *Well, that's still better than nothing.*

At that very moment, the telephone rang. It was Babi. "I can't come." Her voice was cold and annoyed.

"Why not? I've prepared everything. I even put on the apron you gave me," Step lied.

"Signora Mariani called. She's missing a gold necklace with diamond settings. She blames me. Don't ever call me again." Babi hung up.

A short while later, Step was at Pollo's house. "Who the fuck could it have been? Do you realize? Nice fucking friends I have."

"Come on, Step, don't talk like that! How many times have we all gone to someone's house and stolen things? Practically at every party we've ever been to."

"Yes, but never at one of our girlfriends' houses!"

"Well, that wasn't Babi's house..."

"No, but she's being held responsible for it. You need to help me make up a list of everyone who was there..."

Step pulled out a sheet of paper. Then he frantically hunted around for a pen.

"Oh, don't you ever have anything to write with around here?"

"There's no need. I know who took the necklace."

"Who?"

Then Pollo said a name, the one name that Step really wished he hadn't heard. It was the Sicilian who'd stolen it.

~

Step was riding his motorcycle in the night. He'd chosen not to ask Pollo to come with him. This was a matter between him and the Sicilian, and no one else.

Going to his house and demanding that necklace back was tantamount to calling him a thief. No one would be especially happy to be accused of such a thing, least of all the Sicilian. He was especially touchy about things like that.

When the Sicilian came downstairs, his smile promised nothing good.

"Ciao, Sicilian. Listen, I don't want to fight with you."

A fist hit Step right in the face. Step staggered backward. This was definitely not what he'd expected. He shook his head, trying to see clearly. The Sicilian came right at him but Step stopped him with a straight-on kick.

Then while he was catching his breath, Step thought about the dinner he'd prepared, the flowered apron, and how he had wanted everything to be different tonight. He wanted a relaxed evening at home with his girlfriend in his arms. But that's not how it had turned out.

The Sicilian was there, in front of him, in position. He was gesturing with both hands, urging him to come forward. "Come on, then, let's do this."

Step shook his head and took a deep breath. *Fuck*, he thought, *I don't know why it is, but my dreams never seem to come true.*

At that very moment, the Sicilian lunged forward. This time, Step was ready for him. He darted to one side and smashed his fist into the Sicilian's face with a powerful, precise punch. He felt the Sicilian's nose crumple as his fist dug in, the already soft, battered cartilage crunching again. The Sicilian's eyebrows furrowed in pain. Then Step saw his face, that grimace, the lower lip as he tasted his own blood. He saw him smile, and, at that moment, realized how difficult this was all going to be.

~

Babi was sitting on the sofa. She was listlessly watching TV while sipping a rosehip herbal tea when someone rang the doorbell. She got up to answer the door.

"Who is it?"

"Me."

Step was there in front of her. His hair was tousled, his shirt was torn, and his right eyebrow was still bleeding.

"What happened to you?"

"Nothing. But I found the necklace." He raised his right hand. Signora Mariani's gold choker was there, glittering in the dim light of the landing. "Now can you come out to dinner?"

Babi, after giving Signora Mariani her necklace back and inevitably losing her position as a babysitter, let Step take her to his house. But when they opened the door, they were faced with a terrible surprise. At the little table in the middle of the living room, illuminated by a romantic candle, sat Manuela. A moment later, Paolo came in from the kitchen. He was carrying the fruit salad that Step had prepared and, as if that weren't bad enough, he was also wearing the flowered apron that Babi had given him.

Paolo looked at Step, who was standing, frozen in disbelief, at the door. "Ciao, Step. Sorry, eh... but I called, and there wasn't any answer. So we came home, and we waited awhile but by then it was ten o'clock. So we said to ourselves, 'They're not coming, after all.' So we started to eat. Isn't that true?"

He sought out Manuela's confirmation, and she nodded and gave him a feeble smile.

Step looked at his plate. There were still bits of his fruit salad. "And you polished it off, too, I see. Well, how was the dinner, at least? Was it good?"

"Delicious." Manuela seemed to mean what she said. Then she fell silent again. She'd realized that it was a question that wasn't really asking for an answer.

"Okay, Paolo, just lend me your car then, and we'll go out for something to eat."

Paolo set the fruit salad down on the table. "Well, actually..."

"Actually what? Don't you dare, okay? You ate everything I made for our dinner, and now you're arguing?" Step stepped closer. "Come on. Out with the keys."

Paolo decided that, all things considered, Step had a point. He pulled the keys out of his pocket and entrusted them to his brother's hands with a timid "Take it easy, though, okay?"

Step headed for the door. "By the way, I bought you your butter biscuits. If you want dessert, they're in the kitchen cabinet."

Paolo gave him a faint smile, but by now his thoughts were focused entirely on his silver VW Golf and what was likely to become of it.

Step and Babi went to a small crêperie over near the Pyramid of Cestius. Then, even though they were giddy with the bubbles of the beer they'd drunk, they dismissed the idea of going back to his house. Babi didn't want to because his brother was there.

At that point, Step, cursing Paolo and his girlfriend, turned left and headed up Gianicolo Hill. Spread out before them, the city lay sleeping. They parked at the fork in the road where the gardens were, surrounded by other cars whose windshields were already fogged up with lovemaking.

Step changed the radio to 92.7, the romantic station. He reached out to Babi and started kissing her. Despite the pain in his dislocated shoulder, his aching sternum, and his ribs still sore from the pounding the Sicilian had given them, desire erased all his bruises. Impassioned kisses overcame any physical difficulties.

But then the hand brake got in the way and the knob to lower the seat back stuck. Step smelled her soft, sweet-smelling skin and made another attempt to lower the seat back. Nothing doing, it was still stuck. And so, while he used his right hand to turn the knob, he braced his foot against the dashboard and pushed with all his strength. There was a *crack*, and the seat back went straight down and Babi went with it. Step went with Babi, and they both laughed.

Each of them grabbed the other's jeans, madly unbuttoning as if it were a race. Then Babi slowed down, inexpert and embarrassed, shutting her eyes, and in the end, holding him tight.

When she realized that Step wanted to go further, she stopped him. "No, what are you doing?"

"Nothing." Step smiled. "Just seeing what I could get away with."

Babi pushed him away, annoyed now. "No, seriously, here in the car?" She looked dreamily out the car window. "My first time has to be something beautiful, in a romantic place with the perfume of fresh flowers and the moon."

"The moon is out." Step opened the sunroof a little. "You see? It's a little cloudy, but there's a moon. And also just take a whiff of that..." He inhaled. "There are lots of flowers around here. What more could you ask for? This location is romantic. Come on, we're even tuned to Tele Radio Stereo. It's perfect!"

Babi started laughing. "I had something else in mind." She looked at her watch. "It's really late. If my folks get home and I'm not there, they'll ground me again. Let's go."

She pulled up her jeans. Step got dressed again, too, and then together they tried to fix Babi's seat. Nothing doing. They drove back, laughing, with the seat back sagging. Every time the car accelerated, Babi wound up flat on her back. They imagined all the possible excuses he could offer his brother.

Step shook his head thinking back over that evening's events. With this finale, it had turned tragic.

He walked Babi to the door and said good night. Then he drove fast through the night.

Chapter 33

Babi was holding on tight to Step as she rode, head resting on his back and eyes half-shut. But even if they hadn't been, she still wouldn't have been able to see a thing. Step had blindfolded her. Suddenly it felt as if she were flying, a cool wind caressing her hair and the scent of broom plants redolent in the air.

She wondered where she was. How long had it been since they left? She tried to calculate in terms of the cassette tape she was listening to. The first part had just ended. Now she was on the B side. About a quarter of the way through. The best she could remember, it must be a C90 tape. So it had been a little over an hour since they'd left. Where were they heading?

She thought about when Step had come to pick her up. She'd been in Fregene, dining at Mastino with the rest of her class. They were celebrating the last hundred days of school. They'd only just finished eating and were taking a stroll on the beach. A few of her friends were playing capture the flag while she was sitting on a pedal boat chatting with Pallina.

Then she'd seen him. Step was walking toward her with

that smile on his face, with those sunglasses and that jacket. Babi's heart leaped to her throat.

Pallina noticed immediately. "Hey, don't die on me, okay?"

Babi had given her a quick smile, and then she'd taken off at a dead run to meet Step. And she'd left with him without even asking him how he'd managed to track her down or where he was taking her now.

She'd waved goodbye to her classmates with a distracted "Ciao." Some of them had stopped playing and had watched her go. Envious and dreamy, they wished they could take her place with their arms wrapped around Step, a solid A-Plus.

When she got to the motorcycle, Babi looked at it curiously. "Where are we going?"

"That's a surprise." Step walked around behind her, bracing her shoulders, and pulled out the green bandanna he'd brought in his pocket to cover her eyes. "No cheating now, eh... You're not supposed to see."

Laughing, she adjusted the blindfold. "Hey, I think I know this handkerchief..." Then she gave him an earphone from her Sony Walkman, and they listened to a song by Phil Collins while they rode.

Yes, an hour or so must have passed... "How much longer?"

"We're almost there. You're not peeking, are you?"

"No." Babi smiled and laid her head on his shoulder again, holding on tight. Deeply in love.

Step felt that embrace and experienced a strange sense of tenderness and happiness. Then he gently downshifted and veered off to the right and then up the hill, wondering whether she'd guessed.

Step slowed down and then turned right. "Here we are, safe and sound." He switched off the motorcycle and leaped off. "No, don't take off the bandanna. Just wait for me here."

He helped Babi off the motorcycle and left her standing next to it. Babi stayed there, obediently, with the bandanna over her eyes. She turned off her Sony Walkman and took out the headphones. She rolled up Step's earphone, which was dangling loose, with hers. As she gathered up the cable, she tried to figure out where she was.

It was afternoon by now. The wind, softer now, caressed her face, and the strong scent of nature surrounded her. She could hear a faraway sound, muffled and repetitive, but she couldn't figure out what it was. Suddenly, she heard a louder noise, as if something had just been broken. It reminded her of the sound of a tree branch snapping. She listened closely.

"Here I am." It was Step, and he took her by the hand.

"What happened?"

"Nothing. Follow me."

Apprehensively, Babi let herself be led. She took great care where she put her feet, fearful she might trip and fall. Now that noise could no longer be heard. Her leg hit something. "Ouch."

"It's nothing."

"What do you mean, it's nothing? It's *my* leg!"

Step started laughing. "And you never stop complaining, do you? Stay right here."

Step abandoned her for a minute. Babi's hand hung, all alone, dangling in the void. "Don't leave me..."

"I'm right here, close to you."

Then there was a loud, continuous, mechanical, wooden noise. Blinds were being cranked open. Then Step gently took off the bandanna blindfold. Babi opened her eyes, and suddenly she saw it all.

The sunset over the sea was glowing before her. A warm, red sun seemed to be grinning at her. She was in a house.

She walked out onto the terrace, passing under a wooden roller shutter pulled all the way up. Down to the right lay the beach where they'd first kissed. Far off, her favorite hills, her sea, the familiar rocky shore, and Porto Ercole. A seagull soared past, calling out a greeting.

Babi looked around, deeply moved. That silvery sea, the yellow sprays of broom plants, the dark green bushes, that house standing solitary on the rocks. Her house—her dream house. And she was there, with him, and she wasn't dreaming.

Step hugged her. "Are you happy?"

She nodded her head. Her eyes were wet with tiny transparent tears, glistening with love, beautiful.

He looked at her. "What's wrong?"

"I'm afraid."

"Of what?" he asked.

"That I'll never again be as happy as I am right now..."

Then, crazed with love, Babi kissed him again, luxuriating in the warmth of that sunset.

"Come on, let's go inside."

They started wandering through that unfamiliar house, opening unknown rooms, inventing histories for each bedroom, imagining the owners, blithely unaware of their presence.

They pulled up all the shutters, found a big stereo, and turned it on. "You can get Tele Radio Stereo here too." They laughed.

They wandered through that house, opening its drawers, uncovering its secrets, enjoying themselves enormously. When separated, they'd call out to each other now and again to show off even stupid little discoveries, and everything seemed magical, important, unbelievable.

Step went outside, took off the motorcycle's storage box, and brought it inside. A little while later, he called to her. Babi entered the bedroom. The big picture window overlooked the sea. Now the sun seemed to be winking at them. It was vanishing in silence behind the distant horizon. That last polite sliver of sunlight was tingeing the soft clouds with pink high in the sky. Its sleepy reflection was running along a golden wake in the sea. It crossed the salt water to fade and die on the walls of that bedroom, in her hair, on the new sheets, across the freshly made bed.

"I bought them myself. Do you like them?"

Babi said nothing as she looked around. A small bouquet of red roses stood in a vase next to the bed.

Step tried to make light of it now. "I swear I didn't buy them at a traffic light..."

He opened the motorcycle's storage box. "*Et voilà!*"

Inside the box was a slush of melted ice cubes, with a few cubes still bobbing in the cold water. Step pulled out a bottle of champagne and retrieved two glasses wrapped in newspaper. "To make sure they don't break," he explained.

Then he pulled a small radio out of his jacket pocket. "I didn't know if there would be one here." He turned it on, tuned it to the same frequency as the stereo in the house, and set it down on the nightstand. A faint echo of "Stay" reverberated in the room.

"It almost seems as if it was chosen on purpose."

Step stepped closer, took her in his arms, and kissed her. That instant seemed so wonderful that Babi forgot everything, her resolutions, her fears, her scruples. She even forgot that she'd entered a house that didn't belong to her, where she had no right to be, that they'd smashed open a door, that she was lying there on a bed that also wasn't hers, drinking champagne.

Slowly, she allowed him to take her clothes off, and in turn took off his. She found herself in his arms completely naked for the very first time while a magical light, shimmering over the sea, faintly illuminated their bodies. A curious young star glittered high above in the sky. Then—amid a sea of caresses, the sound of distant waves, the cry of a cheerful seagull, and the perfume of the flowers—it happened.

Babi opened her eyes. Step looked down at her. He gave her a small smile and ran his fingers through her hair, reassuring her. At that moment, from the little radio nearby and throughout the house, Spandau Ballet struck up, innocently enough, "Through the Barricades," but neither of them even noticed. They didn't know that it was going to become "their song."

Babi shut her eyes and held her breath, suddenly swept away by that incredible excitement, that magical feeling of becoming her own person for the first time in her life. She turned her face to the sky, sighing, clutching Step's shoulders, embracing him with all her might.

Then she let go, relaxing. She was his. She opened her

eyes, and there he was, on top of her. That soft smile swam lovingly over her face, kissing her from time to time. But she wasn't there anymore. That young woman with scared blue eyes, filled with doubts and fears, had vanished.

She thought back to when she was little and how stories about butterflies had fascinated her. That cocoon, that tiny caterpillar that suddenly becomes tinged with a thousand splendid colors and then learns to fly. Again, she saw herself, a fresh, delicate butterfly, newly born in Step's arms.

She smiled at him and hugged him as she gazed into his eyes. Then she gave him a kiss, a soft, new, impassioned kiss. Her first kiss as a woman.

Later, stretched out under the covers, he was stroking her hair while she held him tight, her head resting on his chest. Then Babi lifted her head and gazed at him, with a smile. "I'm not very good, am I?"

"You're very, *very* good."

"No, I feel kind of klutzy. I need you to teach me how."

"You're perfect. Come on."

They got out of bed, Step took her by the hand, and they went into the other room. Between the flowered sheets, a little red rose, newly bloomed, stood out from the others, the purest and most innocent of them all.

Soon Babi and Step were once again intertwined in the bathtub. They were drinking champagne, chatting cheerfully, slightly tipsy and in love. Soon, drunk with passion, they were again in the throes of lovemaking. This time, without fear, with more impetus and greater desire.

Now it seemed even nicer to her, easier to move her wings, now that she was no longer afraid to fly. Suddenly she understood the beauty of being a young butterfly.

Then they took the bathrobes hanging on the door and went down to their private inlet. They amused themselves by dreaming up names that could go with the two unknown sets of initials stitched on their chests. After competing to come up with the strangest ones, they abandoned the bathrobes on the rocks.

Babi dove in second. They swam like that, in the cool, salty water, in the wake of the moon, pushed along by small gentle waves, embracing from time to time, splashing each other, swimming away only to turn around and catch each other for another taste of those lips that smacked of maritime champagne.

Later, sitting on a rock—wrapped in the bathrobes of Amarildo and Sigfrida, they guessed—they gazed dreamily up at the thousand stars overhead, at the moon, the night, and the dark and peaceful sea.

"It's beautiful here."

"This is your home, isn't it?"

Babi shook her head. "You're crazy! But I'm so happy. I've never felt so happy in my whole life. How are you?"

"Me?" Step wrapped his arms around her, hugging her tight. "I'm great."

"So great that you could reach up and touch the sky?"

Step smiled at her and shook his head. "No, not like that."

"What do you mean, not like that?"

"Much, much more than that. At least three meters higher than the sky."

~

The next day, Babi woke up at home at the usual time. As she rinsed the last traces of salt water from her hair in the shower, she thought back with fondness to the night before.

She ate breakfast, said goodbye to her mother, and climbed into the car with Daniela, ready to go to school like any other morning. Her father stopped at the traffic light before the Corso di Francia bridge.

Babi was still sleepy and distracted when it suddenly caught her eye. She couldn't believe what she was looking at. High up, well above all the other graffiti, on the bridge's white column, was a string of words that dominated all the others, indelible. There it was, on the cold marble, as blue as her eyes, and as beautiful as she'd always dreamed it would be.

Her heart started racing. For an instant, she thought that everyone else could hear it, that everyone could read those words, just as she was reading them at that moment.

They rose high, unattainably so. Up there, where only lovers can reach: *You and me, three meters above the sky.*

Chapter 34

Step was awake. Actually, he'd never gone to sleep at all. The radio was playing, tuned to Rock Dimension. His head hurt, and his eyes were tired. He turned over in bed.

Sounds were coming from the kitchen. His brother was making breakfast. He looked at the clock. It was nine in the morning. Who could guess where Paolo was going at that hour of the morning on Christmas Eve.

He heard the door slam. Paolo had left. He felt a sense of relief because he needed to be alone. Then a strange feeling of suffering swept over him. He didn't *need* to be alone. He *was* alone.

At that idea, he felt even worse. He wasn't hungry, he wasn't sleepy, he didn't feel anything at all. He lay there like that on his belly. He couldn't say how much time had passed. Little by little, he glimpsed that room in happier times. How often had he awakened in the morning and found Babi's earrings on his nightstand, how many times had he found her watch, how many times had they been there, together on that bed, embracing in love, lusting for each other?

He smiled. He remembered her icy feet, those frozen

little toes that Babi laughingly wedged under and between his much warmer legs. After they'd made love, when they were just lying there, talking, looking at the moon out the window, or else the rain or the stars, equally happy whatever the case. Caressing her hair, whatever might be happening outside, in spite of the problems of the world.

He had watched Babi head for his bathroom, and deeply in love, he admired the light patches on her skin, the shade of a swimsuit just removed or a bra undone. He had heard her laugh through that shut door, saw her walk in that funny way of hers, her hair hanging down, running embarrassed to his bed, diving onto him, still cool from the water, from shy washings, still scented with love and passion.

Step turned over again on his bed, looking up at the ceiling. How many times, reluctantly, had he seen the time arrive to get dressed again, to take her back home. And then, silent and close together, they'd sit on that bed and start to get dressed again, slowly, occasionally one handing the other something that belonged to them. Exchanging a smile, a kiss, slipping on a skirt, chatting as they bent over tying shoes, leaving the radio on, just for a few minutes, just the time to run her home.

He wondered where Babi was at that moment. He wondered why. He felt a stab of pain to his heart, knowing all the answers already.

~

During the holidays, people feel either sadder or happier than usual. And people don't know what to do with certain thoughts.

"Dani, do you want this? If not, I'm getting rid of it."

Daniela looked at her sister. Babi was standing in the door to her room with a dark blue jacket in her hand.

"No, leave it here. I'll wear it."

"But it's coming all unstitched."

"I'll have it mended."

"If you want it." Babi left it on the bed, and Daniela watched as she left the room. Given all the times that she and Babi had fought over that jacket, it never would have occurred to her that Babi might just toss it out one day. Her sister certainly had changed. Then she dismissed that thought and started packing the last few gifts.

Babi was almost done clearing out her closet when her mother came in.

"Good girl. You've gotten rid of a lot of stuff."

"Yes, here, take this. It's all the stuff I'm throwing out. Even Dani doesn't want it."

Raffaella took a few outfits that were lying on the table. "I'll make a package for the poor. The charity should be coming around later today for a pickup. Shall we go out together later on?"

"I don't know, Mamma." Babi blushed slightly.

"Whatever you prefer. Don't worry about me." Raffaella smiled and left the room.

Babi opened a few more drawers. She was happy. She'd really been getting along well with her mother recently. How strange, she thought to herself. Just six months ago they couldn't look at each other without fighting.

She remembered the end of the trial, when she had left the courthouse and her mother had come running after her, catching up with her outside. "Have you lost your mind?

Why didn't you tell them what really happened? Why didn't you tell them that that juvenile delinquent beat up Accado without any justification?"

"As far as I'm concerned, things went exactly the way I said they did. Step is innocent. He had nothing to do with any of it. How do you know what he's been through? What he felt at that moment? You don't know how to justify, you don't know how to forgive. The only thing you're capable of doing is judging others.

"For you, life is like playing a game of gin. Everything you don't know is just an inconvenient card that you wish you'd never drawn. You don't know what to do with it; it's burning a hole in your hands. But you don't stop to ask why someone is violent, why someone does drugs. What do you care?" Babi asked. "Instead, this time it does mean something to you, Mamma. This time your daughter is dating a guy who has some real problems, who isn't only interested in driving a sixteen-valve VW Golf GTI, wearing a Rolex Daytona, or vacationing in Sardinia. He's violent, that's true, but maybe it's just because he can't figure out so many things in this life, because he's been told so many lies, because that's the only way he has of reacting."

"What are you saying? This is all nonsense... Plus, can you just imagine? What are people going to think? You're a liar. You lied in front of everyone," Raffaella said.

"I don't give a damn about your friends, about what they might think or how they judge me. You always say that they're all self-made men, people who have achieved something. What have they achieved? What have they done with their lives? Made money and spent it. They don't talk to their children. They really don't give a damn about what they do or how much they're suffering. You don't give a fuck about us."

That's when Raffaella hauled off and slapped her right in the face. Babi put one hand to her face and then smiled.

"I said it intentionally, you know? Now that you've given me a slap in the face, your conscience is at rest. Now you can go back and chat with your girlfriends and sit playing cards with them. Your daughter has been brought up right. She knows right from wrong. She understands that you shouldn't say bad words and you should always try to use good manners. Don't you see how ridiculous you are, how laughable?"

Babi turned and left. Then she climbed onto Step's motorcycle and rode away with him.

How long ago had that been? How many things had changed? Babi sighed and opened another drawer.

Poor Mamma, the things I put her through. In the end, she was right. Maybe I only realize that now. But there are more important things in life. But she couldn't actually think of a single one of those things, so much more important, maybe because she preferred not to think about it, because it was just easier this way. Perhaps it was because there really aren't that many things that matter.

"You look so sexy this evening." One after another, the memories came back to Babi, implacable, melancholy, sad, and distant now. The weekends they'd spent together, fleeing on the wings of this lie or that. Always the four of them, with Pollo and Pallina, at the beach or in the mountains, at little restaurants, out on delightful moonlight strolls, standing somewhere chatting at night, or sitting on a low wall, lying on a beach, lost in the shadows on some uncomfortable cot.

Her eighteenth birthday party in Ansedonia. Ten at night, a sudden roar of motorcycles. All the guests rushing over to the edge of the terrace. Finally something to talk about. Step, Pollo, and all his friends had arrived. They dismounted from the motorcycles and strode into the party, laughing, brash, bold, and confident, looking around, his friends on the hunt for some pretty girl or other, and he on the hunt for her.

Babi had run to meet him, losing herself in his arms, between a loving "Happy birthday, sweetheart" and an irreverent deep French kiss. "Hey, hey, my folks are here..."

"I know, that's why I did it! Come on, come away with me...," Step said.

After the birthday cake with the candles and the Rolex her folks had given her, they'd run away together. She'd allowed herself to be captivated by his laughing eyes, by his fun ideas, by his fast motorcycle. Away, racing downhill, toward the midnight sea, through the scent of broom, far away from those pointless guests, escaping Raffaella's contemptuous glare and the chagrined expression of Claudio, a father who just wanted to dance a waltz with his daughter like any other father.

But Babi wasn't there anymore. She was far away. A little more grown-up now, she was lost in another world, dancing amid Step's kisses, to the music of soft, salty waves, a romantic moon, her young love.

"Here, this is for you." Around her neck there gleamed a gold necklace studded with turquoise stones, the blue of her happy eyes. Babi smiled at Step, and as he kissed her, he even managed to convince her the following was true.

"I swear to you that I didn't steal it."

It was the eve of her final exams. How funny that time had been, at home studying until late. Continual guesswork about the subject of the main exam, exchanging secretive tips. Everyone thought they knew the subject of the written essay. They'd share confident phone calls, all of them certain that they'd nailed the topic.

"It's the sesquicentennial of Leopardi's death...a new essay by Manzoni has just been found...it's about the French Revolution, for sure."

Some said they'd received the news from Australia, where the test had been given to Italian students there the previous day. Others had heard it from a friend who was a teacher or a member of the examination board, and some talked about having consulted a medium. When, the next day, the future turned into the present, they learned that the teacher wasn't such a good friend after all, that the medium was nothing but a con artist, and that Australia was too far away to bother with their problems in Italy.

But then, when the scores were posted, that enormous surprise. Babi had achieved a sixty. Sixty out of sixty. A perfect score. She'd run happily to tell Step, thrilled at her achievement.

He'd laughed, needling her good-naturedly. "You're a grown-up now. You're so mature. In fact, you might even be overripe, like a squishy peach..."

He'd undressed her, laughing as if he'd known, as if he'd expected that result. Then they'd made love. And she'd gloated over her victory. "Would you ever have thought it? Here you are, a humble forty-two out of sixty, enjoying the unrivaled honor of kissing an eminent sixty out of sixty. Do you even realize how lucky you are?"

He'd smiled at her. "Yes, I fully realize." And he'd embraced her, in silence.

Sometime later, Babi had gone to see Signora Giacci. In the end, after all their disagreements, her teacher seemed to have taken a shine to her. She'd started treating her well, with kindness and with an almost excessive modicum of respect. That day, when she went to visit her at her home, Babi had learned why.

That respect was nothing more than fear. Fear of being forced to live alone, fear that she'd never get back her one and only friend and companion. Fear of never seeing her dog again.

Babi was left speechless. She'd stayed to listen to her teacher's furious outburst, her rage, her vicious words. There Signora Giacci sat, facing her, with her little Pepito back in her arms. The older woman seemed even wearier than before, more bitter and disappointed in the world and, especially, in its young people.

Babi had hurried away, apologizing, not knowing what else to say, no longer knowing who she even was, who she was surrounded by, what her score would be—her real score, the one she'd truly deserved.

Babi went to the window and looked out. An array of Christmas trees were blinking on and off on the terraces of the other apartments, in the elegant drawing rooms of the mansions across the way. *It's Christmas*, she thought. *It's a time to be kind. Maybe I should call him. But all those times I've been kind though. All those times I've forgiven him.*

She remembered the differences in the way they saw the world, their screaming fights, and then the sweet truces that followed in blithe hope that everything could change. But that's not what had happened. Arguments and more arguments, day after day, and her folks waging war on her. The phone ringing late at night, her mother picking up, Step hanging up. And her, grounded, more and more frequently.

That one time that Raffaella had thrown a dinner party at their house, forcing her to attend. She'd invited an array of respectable people and the son of a very wealthy friend of the family. A good catch, Raffaella had told her. Then the doorbell had rung again. Daniela had opened the door without thinking twice, without calling out to ask who it was. Step had shoved the door open, hitting her in the head. "Sorry, Dani. It's not you I'm mad at, you know that!"

He'd grabbed Babi by the arm and dragged her off, amid Raffaella's useless shouting and the best efforts of the good catch to stop him. That good catch had found himself suddenly flat on his ass with a fat and bleeding lip.

Babi had fallen asleep in Step's arms, weeping. "How difficult it's all become. I so wish I could be somewhere far away, without any more problems, without my folks, without all this craziness, someplace quiet, outside of time."

He'd smiled at her. "Don't worry. I know where we can go. No one will bother us there. We've been there plenty of times before. It's enough just to want to go."

Babi looked at him, her eyes full of hope. "Where?"

"Three meters above the sky, the place where people in love live."

But the next day, she went back home, and it was from that point that everything started, or, perhaps, ended.

Babi had enrolled at the university. She'd started attending courses in business and finance and spent her afternoons studying. She'd started seeing less and less of Step now.

One time, she went out with him in the afternoon. They'd gone to Giovanni's to get a vitamin shake. They were standing outside the café chatting when suddenly two horrible guys rolled up. Step wasn't fast enough to realize what was happening. They were all over him in a flash. They started headbutting him, holding him helpless in their combined grips, taking turns slamming their foreheads into his face in an appalling, bloody seesaw ride. Babi had started screaming.

In the end, Step had managed to struggle free, and the two guys had made their escape on a souped-up Vespa, vanishing into traffic. Step was just lying there on the sidewalk, dazed. Then, with her help, he'd gotten to his feet. He'd tried to stem the flow of blood from his nose with paper napkins, but his Fruit of the Loom T-shirt was a bright red mess.

Later, he'd driven her home in silence, uncertain what to say. He'd talked about retaliation for a brawl long ago, before they were even dating. She'd believed him, or maybe she'd just badly wanted to.

When Raffaella saw her come home, her blouse covered with blood, she nearly had a heart attack. "What happened to you? Babi, are you hurt? What's all this blood? This is all that hoodlum's fault, isn't it? Can't you see that this isn't going to end well?"

Babi had gone to her room and changed her clothes in silence. Then she'd lain down, all alone, stretched out on her bed. It had become clear to her that this wasn't working. Something was going to have to change. It wouldn't be as easy as taking off a bloody blouse and tossing it into the laundry hamper.

A few days later, she'd seen Step again. He had a new cut on his face. He'd been given stitches to his eyebrow.

"What else happened to your face?"

"Well, you know, to keep from waking up Paolo, I didn't turn the light on in the hallway when I came home. I walked right into a door. You can't imagine how it hurt. It was really painful."

Exactly what she had invented as an excuse that other time. She'd learned the truth later from Pallina, by pure chance, while chatting on the phone. They'd gone for Talenti to Zio d'America. They were all carrying clubs and chains, and they were led by Step. A gigantic brawl, a genuine vendetta. There was even an item in the newspaper.

Babi had hung up the phone. There was no point in arguing with Step. He was going to do what he wanted to do. He was stubborn. She'd told him a thousand times that she hated violence, fighting, and bullies.

She'd started sorting out her bookshelves, pulling down a number of notebooks and dropping them on the wall-to-wall carpeting without any interest. Notebooks from years gone by, from high school of course, and old textbooks.

"What do you want to do tonight? Should we go to the motorcycle races? Come on. Everyone else is going," Step had said.

"I certainly hope you're joking. It's out of the question! I never again want to set foot in that place. Maybe I'd run into Maddalena and I'd have to punch it out with her again. There's an after-dinner party, if you feel like coming."

Step had put on a navy-blue blazer. He'd spent the whole time sitting on a sofa, looking around, doing his best to find anything amusing in the things he heard and saw, but failing utterly. He'd always hated those college people. He'd crashed parties like that only to smash everything up, having the time of his life with all his friends as they stole things from the bedrooms, throwing things out the windows.

His friends. Who even knew where they were right now. At the Greenhouse, popping wheelies at eighty-five kilometers per hour, on their motorcycles with friends all cheering them on, with Siga taking bets, with the chamomiles riding on back and all the rest.

What a bore this party is. *His eyes met Babi's. He smiled at her. She wasn't happy because she knew perfectly well what he was thinking.*

Babi even managed to get her hands on the book that was higher than all the others. Then she remembered as if it had just happened.

The intercom buzzing insistently, insanely. The lady of the house rushing through the living room, the door opening and Pallina standing there, pale, horrified, bursting into tears.

It had been a terrible night. Babi stopped thinking about it. She just started picking up the books that she'd tossed onto the floor. She pulled out others and set them down on the table, and then, when she bent over again, she saw it.

There it was, light colored, brittle, yellowing, as faded as the times gone by. Broken, lying on the dark wall-to-wall carpeting, lifeless now for all this time. The little stalk of wheat that she'd put in her notebook the first time she skipped school with Step. That morning, in the wind that was announcing the arrival of summer, those kisses that smacked of skin with the scent of sunshine. Her first love. She remembered how certain she was that there could never be another one like it.

She picked it up. The stalk of wheat crumbled between

her fingers, like some old thought, like gossamer dreams, like feeble promises.

~

Step leaned over the stove and examined the espresso pot. The coffee still wasn't bubbling up. He turned the flame a little higher. Nearby, there was still a small pile of ash and one last piece of yellowed paper. His beloved drawings, the graphic novel panels, from the hand of Andrea Pazienza. They were originals. He'd stolen them from the newsroom of a new newspaper, *Zut*, when Andrea was still alive and was contributing to the paper.

One night, he'd broken a pane of glass in an upstairs window with his elbow and then climbed in. It had been easy. He'd only stolen the panels drawn by the legendary Paz and then made a quick escape out the door.

But just as he was leaving, someone had emerged from the adjoining room and had grabbed him by the shoulders. "Stop!"

Step had the panels pressed against his body, and he'd given whoever it was a shove, shaking them off and then throwing a punch. A hard, straight right to the face, followed by a bitter surprise. It was a woman. Her name was Alessandra, and she was an unfortunate graphic artist, an unlucky volunteer. She was working late, laying out the publication. That night she'd thrown in the towel early, but certainly through no fault of her own.

Step leaned over and picked up the panel that was supposed to be coming out in that week's issue and made his way into the night, happy, with the drawings of his idol clutched tightly in his hands. It wasn't long after that that Andrea Pazienza died.

That was in June. A photograph of Andrea in a newspaper. Gathered around Andrea was the whole newsroom staff, including the graphic artist that Step had punched. That photo must have been taken a few days after his burglary. In fact, Alessandra was wearing a large pair of sunglasses.

Step picked the scrap of paper out of the metal grate over the burner. He wondered which panel it had been. It must have been the one with Zanardi's face. It no longer really mattered. He'd taken them all and burned them that night, after the phone call.

He'd watched those colors burn, the faces of his heroes crumple up, embraced by the flames. The legendary words of unknown poets vanishing into slow fades of smoke.

Then his brother had walked in. "What are you doing? Have you lost your mind? Look, you're burning the kitchen hood, the fan..." Paolo had tried to put out the flames that were leaping too high but Step had stopped him.

"Step, what's going on? I'm going to have to pay for this. Go do this bullshit outside."

That was it. Step had seen red. He'd slammed his brother against the wall next to the window. He'd placed his hand around his brother's throat, practically suffocating him. Paolo had lost his eyeglasses. They'd flown far away, landing on the floor and shattering.

Then Step had calmed down. He'd set his brother down and let him go. Paolo had collected his broken eyeglasses and left the room without a word. Step had only felt worse at that point. He'd heard the front door slam. While he'd stood there, staring at his drawings as they burned, ruining the hood over the stove, he'd suffered like he'd never suffered before. Was lonely like he'd never been lonely before.

He was reminded of a song by Lucio Battisti. *To punch a man in the face just because he's been a little rude, knowing that what burns most are never the insults.* It was true, Lucio had been right. And it only burned harder. That man was his brother.

The coffee came up suddenly, burbling, as if it wanted to chime in with its own two cents. Step poured it into the cup and then threw it back in a gulp. It left a hot bitter taste in his mouth, the same taste as the memories abandoned in his heart.

August. Riding on a motorcycle to go see Babi when the air was still cool from the night wind. Stopping on the highway to call her. A cappuccino and then he was off, back on his motorcycle, accelerating, devouring the kilometers, starving for her kisses, for her embrace, still warm from sleep. Tapping at her window, hearing the sheets rustle, her bare feet on the floor, her light footsteps. Seeing her appear behind a wooden blind, just rolled up into the morning light. There Babi would be, in the dim light of the bedroom, rubbing her eyes, thinking that this, too, might still be a dream, only nicer, sweeter than her other dreams.

September. Babi's parents had bought her a ticket for London. They'd made an arrangement with Pallina's mother. They wanted to get their daughters away from these bad new friendships.

It hadn't taken much to foil that project. A well-devised plan. A visit to a friend at police headquarters. A new set of passports. And on that charter for England, the two of them *did* board, but the tickets, changed just a few days earlier, now featured different names. The two of them who boarded were Pollo and Pallina.

It had been fifteen unforgettable days for everyone. For Babi's parents, laboring under an illusion but happy there, with their minds finally at rest. For Pollo and Pallina, rocking around London, in pubs and discos, sending everyone postcards purchased back home in Rome at the Lyon Bookstore. English postcards, already signed by Babi.

And meanwhile, Step and Babi, far from them all, on the Greek island of Astypalaia. It had been an epic journey. By motorcycle to Brindisi and then the ferryboat, arms around each other under the stars, lying on the bridge in their colorful sleeping bags, singing English songs with foreigners from everywhere, working to improve their pronunciation, but definitely not in the setting her parents would approve.

Then white windmills, nanny goats, rocks, a little house overlooking the sea. Fishing at dawn, sleeping in the afternoon, out at night, strolling on the beach. Masters of their location, their time, all alone, counting the stars, forgetting what day it was.

Step sipped his coffee. It seemed even more bitter now. He started to laugh remembering that time that Babi had invited all his friends to dinner. An attempt to get to know them. They'd sat down at the table and behaved reasonably well, just as Step had asked and cajoled them. Then they hadn't been able to resist any longer. One after another, they'd stood up, picking up their plates, draining their beers, heading into the living room. Never invite them over on a Wednesday. And never during championship season.

Naturally, it all ended tragically. A. S. Roma had lost, a few

S. S. Lazio fans had started making mocking comments, and there had been the beginnings of a brawl. Step had been forced to kick them all out. Disagreements, differences, difficulties.

He'd tried to make it up to Babi. They went to a masquerade party. They'd dressed up as Tom and Jerry, and then it turned out that Pollo and the others showed up at the same party. A mere case of the mockery of fate? Or more simply a tip from Pallina? They'd all pretended not to recognize him. They'd said hello to Babi, that little blue-eyed Jerry, and they'd ignored Tom, laughing every time that big old cat with bulging muscles walked past.

The next day, in the piazza, Pollo, Schello, Hook, and a few others came over to him with somber expressions. "Step, there's something we need to tell you. You know, last night, we were at a party, and Babi was there."

Step had looked at them, acting nonchalant. "So what?"

"Well, here's the thing. She was dressed as a mouse, and there was this big tomcat that was coming on to her... like a pig. The guy in the costume seemed pretty big, too, like he was a hitter. If you want a hand, we can help you take care of him. Just say the word. You know, it's a real problem. There are big cats that have certain..."

Pollo didn't even get a chance to finish his sentence. Step jumped on him, getting his neck in a headlock, scrubbing the back of his neck with his hard knuckles. To the laughter of his friends, to Pollo's laughter, to his own laughter. What friends he had!

Suddenly he felt sad. That night. Why had he gone to that party instead of going to the races? Babi had really insisted. All the things he'd done for her. Maybe it wouldn't have happened. Maybe.

The intercom started ringing crazily. The lady of the house went running through the living room to open the door. Pallina, her face white as a sheet, shaking, appeared in the doorway. Her eyes were sad, glistening with tears and suffering. As Step walked toward her, she looked at him, struggling to choke back that first sob.

"Pollo is dead." Then she'd hugged him, seeking in him what she could no longer find anywhere else. His friend and her boyfriend, that laughter, so loud and robust.

They'd raced out to the Greenhouse with Babi in the Autobianchi Y10 that her parents had recently bought for her. All three of them together, with the new car smell now tinged with sorrow and silence.

Then he'd seen it. Blinking emergency lights around that one point. His friend's motorcycle. Police uniforms and squad cars massed around Pollo, flat on the pavement, with no more strength, no more laughter, no more jokes, no more mockery, no more streams of mindless bullshit.

One man was holding a tape measure and taking measurements of something. A few other young men stood watching. But no one could see or measure everything that had just vanished within him.

Step bent over him in silence and touched his good friend's face. That gesture of love that they'd never once exchanged in all their years of friendship, that he'd never dared to express. Then, weeping, he'd whispered, "I'll miss you." God only knows he'd meant it.

~

Babi looked at the gift she'd bought for Pallina. There it was, on her worktable, in red giftwrap with a gold ribbon. She'd chosen it with care—she'd even like one for herself—and it hadn't been cheap. And yet, here it still was. She hadn't called her; they hadn't talked.

How many things had changed with Pallina. She wasn't the same anymore. They didn't get along. Maybe in part because their paths had diverged so sharply after school. Babi studying business and finance and Pallina studying at a school of graphic design. She'd always loved to draw. Babi was reminded of all the notes Pallina had sent her during their hours in class. Caricatures, funny phrases, comments, the faces of friends. *Guess who this is?* She was so good at it that it never took Babi long. A quick glance at the drawing and Babi would look up, and there the subject was, in front of her. That classmate with the strong chin, the prominent ears, the beaming smile. And they'd laugh from a distance, ordinary classmates, great close friends.

Then came that tragic evening and the days that followed and the month after that. Extended silences and crying jags. Pollo was gone, and Pallina couldn't reconcile herself to that fact. Until the day that Pallina's mother had called Babi. She had rushed over to Pallina's house and found her there, sprawled on her bed, throwing up. She'd drained a half bottle of whiskey and swallowed a small bottle of valerian root tablets. The Poor Man's Suicide is what Babi had called it when Pallina finally seemed capable of understanding spoken words. Pallina had started laughing, only to burst into tears in her arms. Pallina's mother had left the two of them alone, not really knowing what else to do.

Babi stroked her hair. "Come on, Pallina, don't be like this. We all go through terrible moments. We've all thought about ending it at least once, felt like life wasn't worth living. But don't forget pastries from Mondi, pizza from Baffetto, or gelato from Giovanni's."

Pallina had smiled, wiping away her tears with the back of her wrist, sniffing loudly, and Babi gave her a Kleenex to dry her eyes. Still, though, after that day, something had started to change, something was broken. They spoke less and less frequently, and even when they did, it never seemed like they had much to talk about.

Maybe it was because letting a friend who's doing better see us in our moment of weakness is so uncomfortable. Or perhaps because we always think that our own pain is unique, impenetrable, like everything that concerns us.

No one else can love the way that we love, no one else can suffer the way that we suffer. Maybe Pallina never forgave her for going to that party with Step. If Step had been at the races that night, he never would have let Pollo race. Step would have saved him, he wouldn't have let him die; Step was his guardian angel.

Babi stared at her gift. Maybe there were other reasons, hidden ones, difficult to understand. She really ought to call Pallina. At Christmas, everyone's a little kinder.

"Babi!" It was Raffaella's voice.

She'd have to call Pallina later. "Yes, Mamma?"

"Could you come here for a second?"

Babi went into the other room. Raffaella was smiling at her. "Guess who's here?"

Alfredo was there, standing in the doorway. "Ciao."

Babi turned a little red. She hadn't changed, at least not

where blushing was concerned. As she walked forward to greet him, she realized, maybe she never would change.

Alfredo tried to put her at ease. "It's warm in here."

Babi smiled. "Yes."

Her mother left them alone.

"Would you care to go see the nativity scene at Piazza del Popolo?"

"Yes, hold on. Let me put on something warm. It's nice and toasty in here, but I bet it's chilly outside."

They exchanged a smile, and Alfredo clasped her hand. She looked at him with complicity. Then she went back to her room. How strange, they'd lived in the same apartment building for all these years, and they'd never met.

"You know, I've mostly been studying lately. I was doing my thesis, and then I broke up with my girlfriend."

"Same here," Babi said.

"Are you doing your thesis?" He'd smiled at her.

"No, but I did break up with my boyfriend."

Actually, Step didn't know that yet, but she'd already made up her mind. A difficult decision, the product of fights, arguments, problems with her folks, and now also the matter of Alfredo.

Babi was putting on her overcoat and walking down the hallway when the phone rang. She stopped for a second and looked at it. One ring, then two.

Raffaella went to answer it. "Hello?"

Babi stayed close to her, looking at her quizzically.

Raffaella gently shook her head and covered the receiver with her hand. "It's for me..."

Babi said goodbye, relieved. "I'll be back later."

Raffaella watched her leave and responded to Alfredo's polite farewell with a smile.

The door shut.

"No, I'm sorry. Babi is out. No, I don't know when she'll be back."

~

Step hung up the telephone. He wondered if Babi really had gone out. If she would even have told him so. Alone, on that sofa, remembering, next to a silent telephone. Happy days of the past, smiles, days of sunshine and love. Slowly he imagined her closer to him, in his arms, right on that sofa, the way it had been.

A momentary illusion, then arguments of passion, and now, a solitary vigil. Afterward, he felt even more alone, without even his pride.

Later, leaving the apartment to walk anonymously through the crowded streets of Rome, he saw cars with happy loving couples inside, in the holiday traffic, the car seats piled high with presents. He smiled. It's hard to drive when a woman has her hands all over you, when she absolutely insists on shifting gears but doesn't know how, when you only have one hand to steer with, but at the same time, you need that hand to express your love.

He continued walking through a stream of fake Father Christmases and the scent of chestnuts roasting on an open fire. Traffic cops whistling and people loaded down with packages and shopping bags. Looking for Babi's hair, her perfume, mistaking another woman for her and then being forced to stop and try to still his disappointed heart.

Someone bumped into him, and he didn't even notice that it was a good-looking young woman. Wherever he looked, he saw memories. The T-shirts that they'd bought, identical, an extra large for him, a sweet little medium for Babi.

Summer. The beauty pageant at Monte Argentario. Babi had entered the competition as a joke really, and he'd taken a comment some guy had made far too seriously—*Oh, would you just look at the fabulous ass on that girl*—creating an instant brawl.

Step smiled. He'd been promptly tossed out of the disco and hadn't been able to watch Babi win. But all the times he'd made love with Miss Argentario. By night at Villa Glori, under the cross to the fallen, on a bench hidden behind a hedge, high above the city. Their sighs kissed by moonlight.

In a car, that time that the police had interrupted their surreptitious kisses, and she, exasperated, had had to provide her ID to prove her age. Step had bidden farewell to the policemen, once he was at a safe distance, with an amused "Jealous bastards!"

They say that you see all the most significant moments of your life flash before your eyes when you die. So Step tried to push away those memories, those thoughts, that sweet suffering. Then, all at once, it became clear to him. It was pointless. It was all over.

He continued walking for a while after that. Almost by chance, he found himself looking at his motorcycle. He decided to go to Schello's house. His friends were all there, celebrating Christmas.

His friends. When the door swung open, he had a strange sensation.

"Hey, ciao, Step! Fuck, I haven't seen you in forever. Merry Christmas. We're playing horsie. You know how to play?"

"Yes, but I'd rather just watch. Is there any beer?"

The Sicilian handed him one, already open. They exchanged a smile. Water under the bridge.

He took a sip as he sat down on a low step. The television was on. Against a festive background, competitors with colorful ribbons were playing some idiotic game. An even stupider host took far too long to explain the rules of the game, so he lost interest. He noticed music was coming from a stereo hidden somewhere. The beer was cold but it soon grew warm.

He looked around. His friends. They were all dressed up nice, or had at least made the effort. Lots of oversized navy-blue blazers over pairs of jeans. This was them in fancy outfits. A few of them wore suits; another guy wore a pair of too-tight corduroy trousers.

Suddenly he remembered Pollo's funeral. They'd all been there, and plenty of others as well. Better dressed, with a more serious look to them. Now they were laughing, joking around, tossing fresh figs and colored paper, burping, eating huge slices of Christmas panettone.

That day, at the funeral, they'd all had tears in their eyes. A farewell to a real friend, a sincere, sorrowful goodbye from the bottoms of their hearts. He saw his friends again in that church, their muscles aching, in shirts that were too tight, with serious faces as they listened to the priest's sermon, and then walking out in silence. In the background, girls who had skipped school to be there were weeping. Friends of Pallina, companions for nights out or midnight escapades or just beers at the local stand.

That day, everyone had really mourned. Every tear shed had been heartfelt. Concealed behind Ray-Ban Baloramas or Wayfarers, mirrored sunglasses or dark Persols, their gazes had all glistened as they looked at that wreath of pink chrysanthemums spelling out *Ciao Pollo*. Signed *Your Friends*. God how he missed him.

His gaze turned clear for an instant, and he recognized a smile. It was Madda. She was in a corner, her arms around a guy that Step had seen regularly at the gym. She smiled at Step but then looked away.

Step drank another slug of beer. He missed Pollo so bad. That time in front of Club Gilda when, pretending to be valet parkers, they'd made off with a Maserati with an onboard telephone. They'd driven around all night, calling everyone, phoning friends in America, women they barely even knew, and cursing out relatives who were still half-asleep.

When they went to return the dog to Signora Giacci, Pollo didn't want to give it back. "Fuck, I'm just too crazy about Arnold. This dog is a legend. Why do I have to give him back? I'm certain that, if Arnold had any say in the matter, he'd stay with me. Fuck, that dog has never had so much fun in his life. He sleeps in my bed, he eats like a king, what more could he want from life?"

"Yes, but you never could train him to fetch..."

"Another week and he would have had it down cold. I'm sure of it."

Step had laughed and then buzzed Signora Giacci's apartment. They left the dog for her fastened to the front gate with a rope around his neck. Then they'd hidden nearby, behind a car. They'd spotted Signora Giacci come running out the front entrance, free the dog, and hug him tenderly. She stood there, sobbing, clutching Pepito to her chest.

Then the unbelievable happened. Signora Giacci had taken the makeshift leash off the dog and thrown it as far as she could. And that's when it happened. Pepito bounded out of her arms and took off at a furious run, barking like a nut. A short while later, he had returned to Signora Giacci with the rope in his mouth, tail wagging, proud of his perfect fetch.

Pollo couldn't contain himself. He'd leaped out from behind the car shouting with joy. "I knew it! Fuck, I knew it! He mastered it!"

Pollo had wanted to take Pepito back but Step hauled his friend onto the motorcycle, pulling him by the arm. And then they were off, escaping at top speed, shouting like a thousand other times. By day, by night without headlights, shouting at the tops of their lungs, bold and brazen, the masters of all they beheld, the heroes of their lives. They felt immortal.

"How are you?"

Step turned around. It was Madda. Her smile was hidden behind the rim of a glass full of bubbly, her hair as wild as her eyes.

"What are you doing tonight? Where are you having dinner?" She stepped a little closer.

"I don't know yet. I haven't decided."

"Why don't you stay here? All of us together. Like in the old days. Come on!"

Step stared at her for a minute. Then he saw a young man in the distance looking at him curiously, wondering whether he needed to intervene. And he saw a young woman even farther away, somewhere in that city, in a car, at a party, with some other man at her side. He wondered how that could be. And yet it was all there, in his heart.

Step ran his hand through Madda's hair but shook his head and smiled at her.

She shrugged her shoulders. "Too bad."

Madda went over to the guy with the hard look in his eyes. When she turned around, Step wasn't there anymore. Where he had been sitting, there was just an empty can of beer.

Outside it was cold now. Step zipped his leather jacket nice and snug and pulled up the lapels, covering his neck.

Then, almost without meaning to, he started his motorcycle. By the time he switched it back off, he was in front of Babi's apartment building.

He stayed there, sitting on his Honda, watching the people going by, hurrying along, loaded down with packages. A woman stopping to satisfy her curiosity, looking at the shop windows. A young man and woman holding hands pretended they were interested in something behind a plate glass window. Their gifts were certainly at home, already wrapped. They laughed, both certain that they'd chosen the right thing, and then walked away, leaving the window to a mother with her daughter, with the same noses but different ages.

The doorman came out of his booth, took a few steps in front of the gate, and nodded hello to Step. Then, without a word, he went back to his warm perch inside. Step wondered if he knew. What a fool, he thought to himself. Doormen always know everything. He must have seen Babi's new boyfriend, no doubt. *He must know the person that I've only heard about over the phone.*

"Hello?"

"Ciao."

He'd remained silent for a moment, uncertain what to say, giving his heart room to run wild. It hadn't pounded like this in more than two months. Then, the most banal question imaginable: "How are you?"

Then a thousand other questions, full of enthusiasm. Then, that enthusiasm had slowly subsided in the face of her pointless words, full of local news, old developments in her life, once considered interesting, at least by him. Why had she phoned? He listened to her pointless chatter, asking himself that same question over and over. Then, suddenly, he knew.

"Step... I'm seeing another guy."

He'd remained silent, struck harder than ever before in his life, a life that had suffered thousands of punches, injuries, falls, headbutts to the face, bites, and hanks of hair ripped out of his scalp. At last, struggling, he'd managed to summon his voice. He'd found it there, at the bottom of his heart, and he'd forced it to come out, gaining some modicum of self-control.

"I hope he makes you happy."

Then that was all. Only silence remained. The telephone receiver hung up, put back in its place, mute now. *This can't be. It's a nightmare.* Wishing he could travel back in time and, right before hearing the news, hover and remain there, halting time and stopping his own life, never to advance another second. Caught in a magical, terrible equilibrium.

He'd lain there, alone in his bed, a prisoner of his own mind, of hypotheses, vague, formless ideas. He imagined her in the arms of someone else. Faces of people glimpsed, possible lovers appeared and mingled, swapping noses, eyes, mouths, bodies. Her face, close to the face of some imaginary man who was still, unfortunately, all too real.

Step felt a hot shiver run through his body, and he trembled slightly. Then he got off his motorcycle and started strolling. There was something in a shop that he liked. He went in to buy it. When he came back out, he felt like he was dying. A Lancia Thema went by, right in front of him. But not so fast that their eyes didn't have time to meet. At that moment, their eyes told each other everything, suffering deeply, and this time, once again, together. Babi was right there, behind that electric-powered car window.

They maintained eye contact for a little while longer, with their old memories and with a new, added sadness. Then Babi vanished into the apartment building.

He remained there, walking slowly toward his motorcycle, thinking as he went. He couldn't say what it was he was feeling. Babi was there, close to him, in that home where they'd spent afternoons and clandestine nights when her folks were out. But now that other guy was beside her. Who the fuck was he? What did he have to do with her life? Why?

He sat down on his motorcycle. He'd wait for him. He remembered everything Babi had always told him. "I hate violence. So if you continue doing whatever you want, we won't be together much longer, I swear it."

He'd accepted her demands. "All right, I'll change."

Like that time at Club Classico. A guy had bothered her—he'd asked someone else to tell him her name, and then he'd called out to her from his table: "Babi! Come on over here. Sit with us." He was acting the clown with his friends, the idiot.

Step hadn't batted an eye. He'd stood beside her, calm and smiling. He'd finished his beer in silence.

At that point, Babi had leaned toward him and whispered in his ear, "I love you! Shall we go to my house?" Instead they'd gotten no further than making out for a while outside the front door downstairs. Unfortunately, her folks had come back early.

Babi had complimented him. "There, that's the way I like you. You were so good, you didn't fight with that idiot. You've changed. You seem like another person."

He'd smiled at her and walked her upstairs to her apartment door. He'd waited for it to shut behind her, and then he'd hurled himself down the stairs, leaped onto his motorcycle, and raced to Club Classico.

The idiot never even knew where that fist came from. He'd found himself outside the club, over by the drinking fountain with his friends, but now with a broken nose, laid open like a grapefruit. He was sobbing. He no longer felt so much like being a smart-ass now.

Step had driven home and gone to bed. He couldn't have gotten a wink of sleep with the thought of that guy having so much fun acting the fool with his girlfriend, but now that buffoon had paid the price, so Step fell asleep peacefully. He didn't like being that other person. And Babi would never know about it. As far as she knew, he'd changed, and he was no longer a violent thug.

But now it was the state of things that had changed. They were no longer together. He had no reason to hide anymore. He no longer needed to be someone else. He could be himself, whenever and however he wished. He was free now. Violent and alone. Again.

The Lancia Thema was exiting the building. It waited for the gate arm to rise and then drove out onto the street.

Step started his motorcycle and put it in first. He drove fast off the sidewalk and followed the car. The guy was alone, and he was driving fast. Step poured on the gas. *At the stop sign, he'll have to stop.*

Before Via Jacini there was traffic, cars in line, brake lights. The Lancia Thema stopped. Step smiled and pulled up next to the car. He started to get off the motorcycle but just then he understood. What good would it do to smash his face in, see his blood, hear his moans of pain? What good would it do to kick him across the pavement and shatter his car windows, ramming his head through the glass? Could that possibly bring him new happy days with Babi, bring back her loving eyes, her wild enthusiasm? All it would do is help him to sleep with some satisfaction that night. And maybe not even that...

He already thought he could hear her words. "You see? I was right about you. You're just a violent thug. You'll never change!"

And so, without even looking inside, Step revved the engine and passed the car calmly, a free man on his motorcycle, weaving in and out of traffic on this major holiday. Alone, without curiosity, without anger.

He continued accelerating, feeling the cold wind on his face and the night air slip under his jacket.

You see, Babi, it's not the way you think. I have changed. And anyway, as we know, everyone's a little kinder at Christmas.

Chapter 35

Step walked into the apartment and crossed the living room. Then suddenly he stopped. From the next room came the cheerful sound of someone singing. He opened the kitchen door, and there was Paolo, standing at the stove, busy with the pots and pans.

When he saw Step, he smiled at him. "Hey, nice to see you. I was afraid you'd never come back! Are you ready for this fabulous Christmas banquet?"

Step was in no mood for joking around, but he was also happy to see that his brother had forgiven their quarrel from the night before.

"What are you doing here? Weren't you supposed to have dinner with Manuela?"

"I put that commitment off. I'd prefer to spend the night with my brother. But let's have an understanding. Even if the meal isn't any good, you leave my glasses alone."

Paolo reached into his jacket breast pocket and pulled out a pair of brand-new eyeglasses. "I won't tell you how much these cost, otherwise you'll say that I only ever think about money. Anyway, it's really true, before Christmas the shopkeepers really gouge you on the prices."

Paolo set down an enormous bowl of salad with arugula, Parmesan cheese, and bits of light-colored mushrooms. "*Et voilà!* French cuisine!"

Step noticed that Paolo was wearing a normal white apron. The flowered apron that Babi had given him was hanging up next to the sink. He wondered what his brother had thought about that.

"All kidding aside, why aren't you having dinner with Manuela?"

"What is this tonight, the third degree? It's Christmas, we ought to be happy. Let's talk about something else. It's not a happy subject."

"Sorry to hear that." Step picked up a piece of cheese from the salad bowl with his fingers and popped it in his mouth.

"Yes, thanks for that. But try not to finish off the whole bowl of salad, okay? Listen, why don't you go in the other room and set the table? The tablecloth is down there."

Step stood up, opened the drawer, and pulled out a random tablecloth.

"No, use the red one. It's cleaner, and after all, it's Christmas. By the way, Papà and Mamma called... They wanted to wish you Merry Christmas. Why don't you call them back?"

"I tried. The line was busy." Step went into the living room.

"Why don't you try again now?"

Step decided not to answer that question.

"Do as you think best... I told you to call." Paolo burned a finger trying to see if the pasta was done. He decided not to insist.

Later, they were sitting across from each other. A small Christmas tree was blinking on a piece of furniture nearby. The television was turned on, but with the sound off, and Christmas presenters were talking over the cheerful music on the stereo.

"Jesus, Paolo, this pasta is incredible. For real."

"It needs a little more salt."

"No, if you ask me, it's perfect like this." In an instant, Step turned into a prisoner of his thoughts and memories again. Babi always put a little extra salt on everything. He'd make fun of her because she always did it, indiscriminately, with every dish, no matter what, even before tasting it.

"Why don't you try it first?" he would ask her. "Maybe it's already super salty."

"No, you don't understand," Babi said. "The part I like is actually salting the food, putting it on..." Sweet and stubborn. No, he didn't understand. He couldn't understand. How had the breakup happened? How could their relationship have simply ceased to exist? How could she be with another guy? He imagined them together in an embrace.

Step was a masochist for love, eager and willing to suffer. *He could never love her the way I loved her. He won't be able to adore her the same way. He won't know how to appreciate all her tiny movements, those fleeting signals on her face.* It was as if he, and only he, had been given the right to see, to understand the true flavor of her kisses, the real color of her eyes, that sweet awakening as they opened with fluttering eyelids. *No other man will ever be able to see what I saw. He least of all.*

He imagined him like that, incapable of loving her, of truly seeing her, understanding her, respecting her. He wouldn't be amused by her sweet caprices. He wouldn't love her little hand, the gnawed fingernails, her slightly pudgy feet, that tiny hidden flaw, though not all that well concealed. Perhaps he'd seen her tattoo, a terrible thought, but he'd never be capable of loving it. Not as much as Step had when he'd first kissed it and now just at the memory of it. Sadness filled his eyes.

Paolo looked at him, worried now. "The pasta's disgusting, isn't it? If you don't want any more, just leave it. There's a fabulous main course."

Step looked up at his brother and shook his head, trying to smile.

"No, Pa, it was great, seriously."

"Do you want to talk about it?" Paolo asked.

"No, it really is a sad story."

"Sadder than mine?"

Step nodded. They smiled at each other. A brotherly gaze in the true meaning of the word, perhaps for the first time, only now.

Then, suddenly, the doorbell rang, a long, determined sound that split the air, bringing with it joy and hope. Step ran to the door and pulled it open.

"Ciao, Step."

"Oh, ciao, Pallina." He tried to hide his disappointment. "Hey, come on in why don't you?"

"No thanks. I just came by to wish you Merry Christmas. I brought you this." She gave him a small package.

"Should I open it now?"

Pallina nodded.

Step turned it over in his hands until he found the top side and then quickly unwrapped it. It was a wooden picture frame and, in it, the best gift he could ever have hoped for. It was a picture of him and Pollo on his motorcycle, arms around each other, short hair, legs up, laughter in the wind. Something hurt inside him.

"Pallina, it's beautiful. Thanks."

"God, Step, I miss him."

"So do I." Only then did he notice how Pallina was dressed. How many times had he seen that jean jacket behind him on his motorcycle, how many times he'd slapped it, with friendship, with force, with glee. They smiled at each other.

"Step, can I ask you to do something for me?"

"Name it."

"Give me a hug," Pallina said.

Step moved closer to her awkwardly, opening his arms and enveloping her in a bear hug, thinking about his old friend and how in love with him she'd been.

"Hug me tight, harder. The way he used to do. You know, he always used to say... 'This way you won't be able to get away from me. You'll stay with me forever.'" Pallina put her head on his shoulder. "But instead, he ran away from me."

She started crying. "You remind me of him so much, Step. He adored you. He always said that you were the only one who got him, that the two of you were identical."

Step looked into the middle distance. The door was slightly out of focus. He hugged her tight and then even tighter. "It's not true, Pallina. He was much better than me."

"Yes, that's true." She smiled as she sniffed loudly. Pallina pulled away from Step. "Well, I'm going home now."

"Do you want me to drive you?"

"No, thanks. Dema's downstairs waiting for me."

"Give him my regards."

"Merry Christmas, Step."

"Merry Christmas."

He watched Pallina enter the elevator. She smiled at him one last time, shut the doors, and pushed the G button for the ground floor. As she was riding down, she reached into her jacket and pulled out her pack of Camel Lights. She lit her last cigarette, the one that was upside down. But she smoked it sadly, hopelessly. She knew that her one true desire, her only wish, could never come true.

Step went into his bedroom and put the photo on his nightstand and then went back to the table. Next to his place was a giftwrapped package. "Hey, what's this?"

"Your Christmas present." Paolo smiled at him. "Haven't you heard that people give each other presents at Christmas?"

Step started to unwrap the package while Paolo watched him in some amusement. "I saw that yesterday you burned all your panels, and I thought that now you wouldn't have anything left to read."

Step finished unwrapping the present. He practically had to laugh. *Il mio nome è Tex.* Tex Willer. The comic book series he hated most.

"If you don't like it, you can always return it."

"Are you kidding? Paolo, thanks. I seriously didn't have this one. Hold on a second, I have something for you too."

A short while later, Step came back from his bedroom with a small case. He'd bought it that afternoon while he was waiting downstairs from Babi's house. Before he saw her. He preferred not to think about that too carefully.

"Here."

Paolo took the gift and opened it. A pair of Ray-Ban Balorama sunglasses appeared in his hands.

"They're just like mine. They're tough as nails, they'll never break. Even if someone knocks them onto the floor." Step smiled at him. "Oh, by the way, you can't exchange these."

Paolo put them on. "How do I look?"

"Great! Fuck, you look like a tough guy. You're almost scaring me."

Then it suddenly popped into his mind, clear, perfect, and amusing.

"Listen, Pa, I have an idea, but you can't say no to me the way you usually do. Today's Christmas, so you can't turn me down!"

~

The cold wind was messing up Paolo's hair.

"Could you slow down, Step?"

"I'm only going fifty."

"In the city, you're not supposed to go faster than thirty."

"Cut it out. I know you like it." Step accelerated.

Paolo held on tight, clinging closer. The motorcycle was running fast through the streets of the city, crossing intersections, whipping through yellow stoplights, silently and deftly. The two brothers rode along in a fraternal embrace. Paolo's tie broke loose of his jacket and fluttered cheerfully in the night, flaunting its argyle pattern. Above the tie, behind his new sunglasses, Paolo was watching the road in sheer terror, ready to pick up on any impending danger.

In front of him, Step was driving confidently, unruffled. The wind was caressing his Baloramas.

There were people hastily double-parking in front of a church. Christmas prayers weighed down by the flavor of panettone. For a moment, he, too, was tempted to go in, to ask for something, to pray.

But then he wondered how God could ever care about someone like him. He looked up, into the sky. The stars appeared crystal clear, sparkling and glowing in their thousands. Suddenly that midnight blue seemed so far away, farther than ever, unattainable. He accelerated, and the wind stung his face as his eyes slowly began to glisten, and not only because of the chill.

He felt Paolo clinging tight to him. "Come on, Step. Don't go so fast. I'm scared!"

I'm scared, too, Paolo. I'm scared of the days to come, that I won't be able to keep it up. I'm scared of what I've lost, of what is going to be blown away by the winds of time.

Step let up on the gas a little and gently downshifted. For a moment, he thought he heard Pollo's laugh. That powerful, giddy laugh. He saw his face again and heard his fond voice.

"Fuck, Step, we're having fun, aren't we?" And more beer, and more late nights, always together, always giddy, with an overwhelming lust for life, for fighting, sharing a cigarette and so many dreams.

So he twisted the throttle all at once, sharply. Paolo screamed while the motorcycle's front wheel reared up. Step continued like that, accelerating on a single wheel, popping a wheelie just like in the old days.

Far away, much farther away, on a sofa in an elegant home, two nude bodies were caressing each other.

"You're so beautiful."

Babi smiled, shy, ashamed, still slightly absent.

"But what's this?"

A hint of embarrassment. "Nothing, just a tattoo."

"It's an eagle, isn't it?"

"Yes, I got it with a girlfriend." A bitter lie.

A sense of sadness filled her heart. And fate clearly had it in for her, as if to punish her, when "Through the Barricades" came on the radio. Their old song. Babi started crying.

"Why are you crying?"

"I don't know."

She couldn't come up with any answers. Maybe because there really were none.

~

Slowly the wheel lowered back to the pavement, just as smoothly as it had reared up.

Paolo started breathing again. Step slowed down and smiled.

Very slowly, the motorcycle leaned into the curve. It was time to go home now. It was time to start over, little by little, without thinking about it too much. With just one thought. *Will I ever go back up there, in that place that is so difficult to reach? Three meters above the sky, where everything seems so much finer, so beautiful.*

And at the very instant he asked that question, he already, sadly, knew the answer.

YOUR BOOK CLUB RESOURCE

READING GROUP GUIDE

Dear reader,

This novel was born long ago in 1992, when I first took on the challenge of becoming a writer. The manuscript was rejected by every major publisher in Italy, except for Il Ventaglio, a small independent publisher in Rome. The first two thousand copies disappeared very quickly from the shelves, and the publisher became bankrupt, so no reprints could be put in place and my book was nowhere to be found. At that time, I thought my career as a writer was over before it had even started.

Still today, I owe everything to my enthusiastic readers. The incredible happened, a real story inside a story. They were the ones who started talking about *One Step to You* and making photocopies to pass it to their friends. They were reading it in secret, and slowly, slowly, by word of mouth, they were learning about Babi and Step's love story thanks to a novel that didn't exist as such anymore. Eventually, ten years later, one of those copies fell into the hands of a filmmaker who realized its potential and decided to make a movie out of the story I had written.

That very same year a big Italian publisher acquired the rights to the novel, and it quickly became one of the biggest Italian bestsellers, topping the bestseller lists for three years in a row. My dream had come true.

But more exciting news was waiting for me around the corner. As soon as the Italian edition came out, a Spanish translation was published, and *One Step to You*'s success was even bigger, when a Spanish film based on the novel was also produced and premiered in Spain.

Babi and Step's love story has been translated into fifteen languages and sold more than ten million copies worldwide, with the novels never out of print: A bestseller became a long seller. So much so that it has inspired the 2020 Netflix series *Summertime*.

The edition you are now holding in your hands is beautiful to me because it is the very first time this love story is told in English. You, too, will be able to live all the emotions of Babi and Step's love story that also continues in the two other novels in the trilogy, *Two Chances with You* and *Three Times You*.

I feel so incredibly humble, thankful, and proud of how my love story has grown throughout the years. It was a book that no publishing house wanted and ended up touching millions of hearts. I now hope it will touch yours, too, and that you will fall in love with my story, *One Step to You*.

Arrivederci from Rome, with love,

Questions and Answers with Federico Moccia

Q: This is the first time that you've gotten to tell your story to English-language readers. What would you like to say to them?

A: I'd like them to know this is a true story I wrote when I was still young. This was a love story that was quite similar to one I had lived, and I tried to write about it because, when a love story ends, especially when you are young, you think it's unbelievable that this has happened, that this love has come to an end... I was trying to find closure and get rid of my great pain. A little bit like when Kevin Costner in *Message in a Bottle* writes a letter full of grief for the death of his wife, puts it in a bottle, and throws it into the sea. *One Step to You* had all this: my passions, my love for Babi, the bike races, everything I had lived with my ex...

I'd like each of you to find all the moments of happiness and pain in my first love story. Every time my books have been translated in a different language—and it has happened fifteen times—I am very curious. I want to see the effect my stories have, stories thought of and written in Italian and full of our atmosphere, on readers from different parts of the world. When I have seen the response in the countries I've traveled to to promote my books, I've been left in shock. It has been amazing how each love story I wrote multiplied and transformed according to the contexts, the habits, and lifestyles of the people who have read them. It has always evoked a very strong emotion for me; it has been literally a discovery for me. I have seen how far love can go and how, after all, love is a universal language.

It's now time for the United States to read it, a country that I love for its many facets, always diverse, always surprising. You cannot tag the US with a single label, definitions fit it badly, and that's what I most love about it. During college, I spent some time working in New York while I was studying at university to become a film director because I felt I needed different perspectives from the Italian ones I was used to. New York City blessed me with the most wild and amazing gifts and helped me grow a lot despite the short time I spent there.

Thinking now that, in that very same city, there will be people reading my stories and—why not?—growing fond of Babi, Step, and Gin (in book two of the trilogy), and I hope telling me what they think of it, thrills me just like thirty years ago when *Tre metri sopra il cielo* came out for the first time. Babi, Step, and Gin are not fictional characters but three real friends who have taught me so much during these past years and are now about to surprise me once again in the English world.

Q: Step and Babi have been called a modern-day Romeo and Juliet. What other stories influenced you as you were writing this book?

A: Certainly, there have been many because a writer is nothing but a person who learns by reading more than with writing courses. One gets used to writing by reading, by assimilating other writers, by loving paragraphs, sentences, passages, and scenes told in a certain way that help you find your own voice. It's like having digested their writing and creating your own as a result. Paul Auster, Truman Capote, and Raymond Carver were influences, but also Thomas Pynchon, Donald Barthelme, and John Barth were my food, with books like Jack London's *Martin Eden*, and especially *Tender Is the Night*, *The Love of the Last Tycoon*, *The Great Gatsby*, and *The Beautiful and Damned* by F. Scott Fitzgerald. I loved every sentence, I read every passage, and I tasted all the moments, the pains, the peculiarities, the characters, his love for his wife Zelda, his mental fragility, everything he loved about her and fell in love with. At the same time, I loved a writer who was his most total opposite, Ernest Hemingway, with his hunting and fishing trips, his strong and extreme ways; all these I loved. I loved his writing and how he loved life. For example, in the beautiful book that is *Islands in the Stream*, I appreciated how Hemingway loved the beauty of the sea and how this somehow confirmed his love for life, bullfights, and people.

Here these writers were fundamental to me. I love to find out where the authors I love will take me. I tie their stories to people, to facts, a normal moment in everyday life. It is a real satisfaction for me to go out now in the

States, given my love for great American literature, contemporary and otherwise, which I have always devoured. So often love is intertwined with the social issues of a complex, multicultural country, full of different influences, which therefore produces diverse, poignant, and always surprising books.

With *One Step to You*, I wrote the story I wanted to read. Two characters of today with two family stories only apparently different, but certainly similar in complications with parents and siblings. Two teenagers who unwittingly found themselves dealing with each other and who continued to choose each day against the opinion of practically everyone, because few have bet on their love. In there, you will find all my passion as a reader, the authors I loved and love.

Q: Rome has the "Moccia route," where sentences from your books are written on the walls of the city. If we are lucky enough to travel to Rome, can we see *three meters above the sky* written?

A: Indeed you can. I passed by, just the other day, as I was cycling under the bridge in Corso Francia located in the northern part of Rome known as Roma Nord, which is where *One Step to You*, *Two Chances with You*, and *Three Times You* are set. Still today, under the bridge that takes you from Ponte Milvio to Labaro, heading north in Roma Nord, you can see the *Tre metri sopra il cielo* graffiti. Both in the movies and in my novels, the bridge in Corso Francia is in important love scenes and moments of our characters, as well as in the races.

Q: Step is a very cool character. Were you part of the cool kids growing up? Or were you studious like Babi?

A: Step is a very interesting and difficult character. My group of friends was a very miscellaneous group because I never liked to hang out with people I didn't like just because they were cool. I used to spend time, and I still do, with special and worthy people with whom I feel we can share some meaningful time together.

I enjoyed studying things that amused me. I was no nerd; my graduation score in high school was high just because I was more mature than the average guy. At the exam, I debated about the ancient Greek authors I had to translate into Italian. Teachers were amused watching me criticize the school system and pointing out those authors' different points of view. That's how I got full marks.

I loved school because I was conscious it was the most beautiful and peaceful time of our lives, with very few problems, unlike the years that follow. I remember many of my schoolmates trying to squeeze two years into one in order to get to college sooner. I used to tell them, "Are you crazy? What for?" Why were they in so much of a hurry if time was passing by anyway? One must enjoy life with no rush and a certain dose of carefulness, savoring the beauty of each moment.

Q: There is a lot of violence in the book. Do you think this is a rite of passage for most young males? Do you think readers have been shocked by it?

A: Sometimes it's inevitable, mostly during high school, as kids try to assert themselves in any way they can, which often leads to mistakes. That's how the issue of bullying arises, the need for one to overshadow the other in order to find one's place and be the best you can be.

I tried to write about how Step is full of anger and resentment toward his mother, something he found out at his own expense and a truth that he doesn't want to admit or discuss with either his brother or his father. Step is angry toward life until he finds love.

My intention was to explain how love has the incredible ability to cure people of their anger. Love triumphs over violence. Hopefully this message reaches my readers, which can be an important answer to the whole issue.

Q: You convey a wonderful sense of freedom while riding motorcycles. Do you like to ride? Do you own a motorcycle that is a particular favorite?

A: I'm really fond of motorbikes. They allow you to wriggle between traffic and escape chaos easily and quickly, by visiting the coast, for instance. Motorbikes are freedom, wind, speed, and independence. I've been passionate about them since I was young.

I used to have a Honda 350, then a Honda 750, and now I navigate the city on my Honda 300. It's my secret pleasure to get out at night, surrounded by silence, as I watch the moon high in the sky, illuminating the road. It's wonderful to just drive slowly with no rush, with the low humming of the engine, breathing in the scent of the flowers, especially during this season just before summer begins. Every time, the fragrance of the night amazes me as if I forgot it...I love rediscovering it again and again.

Q: One of the best action scenes takes place at the Greenhouse. Is the Greenhouse a place that exists in real life? Did you ever attend any illegal races while you were growing up?

A: The Greenhouse really existed. When I was young, I used to watch illegal street races. The place is named after a dip along the road where riders can pick up speed very easily. They could reach two hundred kilometers per hour, and sadly there were lots of accidents. Both sides of the road were covered with flowers in memory of those who had lost their lives. That's why we called it the Greenhouse; it was packed with flowers. I never took part in a race; kids under fourteen years old weren't allowed to. Only the older ones, like sixteen and up—a few years make a huge difference at that age. Despite all this, I've been a huge fan of those races, and every time I could, I escaped my home to go and watch them.

Q: One of Step's most romantic gestures is to give Babi a night in her dream house. Is the dream house based on a real place?

A: Yes, it is indeed a real place. Along Feniglia beach, where I used to go when I was young, there's still a house, an amazing villa standing alone on a cliff facing the sea. It's incredibly beautiful and hard to get to. As a matter of fact, it's enclosed by a fence that runs along the street and has a very high gate. It's unique because it's exposed to the summer sunset, which turns orange in the evenings.

I remember watching it while passing by on the long beach—over six kilometers—in the direction of Ansedonia and thinking how much I would have liked to visit there. That's why I decided to let Step do it, by breaking in through the window. I thought it was the perfect spot for Babi and him to make love for the first time.

Many years after the success of *Tre metri sopra il cielo*, I was sailing nearby with some friends, and I got closer to the house to take a better look. The landlords peered out, recognized me, and invited me in. We docked the boat and entered the villa. The owners asked me if I had ever been inside, if by any chance the housekeeper who manages it in the winter had allowed me in, because many of the things I imagined and depicted in the book were real. They were amazed by the resemblance and invited me to take a tour. It was really remarkable, and I felt the same amazement Step felt when he took Babi there for the first time.

Q: There are a lot of fun cultural references from the 1980s, like going to the discotheque. Did you spend a lot of time in clubs as a young person? Are you a good dancer? Did you have a favorite dance song?

A: I used to love dancing and still do, I usually have great fun; it's an incredible moment when you close your eyes and stop thinking about the people staring at you. You just let go and dance, and the more you let go, the better you dance. I cannot say I'm a good dancer, but I do love dancing and I don't care about the people around me.

All my favorite songs are from the late 1970s, like the songs from the film *Saturday Night Fever*, the Bee Gees or Duran Duran, Spandau Ballet, "Disco Inferno," mostly 1980s music. I believe it's the best, and it's no coincidence that it's still popular today. You can find some of my favorite tracks in the book...such as Spandau Ballet's "Through the Barricades." It was the perfect song for a very difficult moment in the story.

Q: Babi's parents are quite strict, while Step's parents seem more lenient. And you dedicate this book to your own parents. In what ways do your parents resemble the parents in the story? Or are they completely different?

A: My parents are just like Step's parents, but they never split up. I dedicated the book to them because it seemed like the natural thing for me to do. In the trilogy, there's a big part of my family, the things I observed, what I felt and lived through as a kid. I changed it slightly in the story so that it fit, but it's there. My mom and dad loved each other very much and continued to do so. So I tried to imagine through Step's eyes what it would be like to witness the end of such a great love, very much like the one my mother and father had, and then the pain of watching your parents getting a divorce.

Q: A teacher plays a major role in this story. Do you think you would make a good teacher?

A: A teacher is a very important person, the person we meet at school who enables us as we grow up and someone with the power to change our life. What I said may seem trivial, but it is not. I remember one of my high school professors, his name was Giuseppe Gioia, he taught religion, Latin, and Greek. Thanks to him, I learned to outline, to make a script, and to organize my time in order not to be frightened when facing big projects and to be able to deal with difficulties by structuring them. So in addition to teaching me his subjects, he showed me how to deal with problems.

I like to teach a lot. I often do internships with young people who want to become actors. We talk about acting, directing, the history of cinema, and what I have done in my career, in order to show the differences between the big and small screens and also what it means to be a television writer. I try to give them many ideas. In addition to the theoretical part, practice is the best way to teach something, experimenting by implementing what has been studied. Teaching also means investigating the person, what his characteristics are, his difficulties, and seeing what he can actually create not only as an actor but also in regard to his approach toward life.

Q: The story is very romantic. Do you feel the Italian culture, particularly for men, may be more open to discussing their feelings? Or was writing a romantic story something that made you work at expressing your emotions? Do you have your own great love story?

A: Novels talk about lives, my protagonists' lives, their families' lives, the life of a young girl and a boy falling in love for the first time and almost touching the sky. One could say I told a story that happens to everybody. Your first love story is a big deal; it's the best you can have because it's the first time you feel something so powerful. You are amazed and realize for the first time what loving another person means, a person that suddenly becomes more important than you, that comes before anybody else, whose happiness is more important than your own.

You'll try everything to make that person happy. I remember when I was in school and had the best score on my finals, but I was feeling miserable because Babi, the girl I was dating at the time, didn't do so well. She had a passing grade, and despite being the one who believed she always knew everything, she was the one who got marked a 36 when I got a 60. I was wrecked, and I wanted to tell the teachers, "No, please, give her my sixty, and I'll take her grade." She couldn't accept the fact she'd done so badly while I couldn't care less about my score. Love works like this; the one you love comes first.

Q: You now have a family of your own. Have your children read this book? What were their thoughts? If one of your children chooses to rebel like Step, do you think it will be easier or harder for you because of the empathy you have for Step's character?

A: No one teaches you how to be a parent. When you have kids of your own, you learn by living through it, day by day. I'm proud of my family, and my kids are still young, eight and ten years old, so they haven't read *One Step to You* yet. Just like my father did with me, I talk to them about my life and let them see that I'm not perfect but just a man. I share with them my mistakes, my failures, and the ways I always got back on the right path again. I want them to know me as a real man. I know they will eventually rebel some day or another, like we all do, but if dialogue, conversation, and no fear of conflict are the basis of our relationship, we'll always find a way to be a family.

Q: Most English-language readers probably learned the most about Italian culture through food. Are you a good cook? What Italian dish would you recommend that readers may not have tried before? When in Rome, can we enjoy pastries from Caffè Antonini?

A: I love eating but I'm not a good cook, although every now and then I give it a try. If I were to give you a piece of advice on food, I would say that traditional Roman dishes are really delicious, such as carbonara with short rigatoni or long spaghetti. It is traditionally prepared with eggs and pancetta, and in my opinion, it is a truly exceptional pasta when made in the right restaurants because sometimes people make mistakes with the wrong ingredients or technique.

In the Prati district, they serve Antonini's canapés, the ones I describe in *One Step to You*, when Step realizes that the delivery boy is taking them to his mother, who is crazy about them. They are very special small sandwiches with oil that are cut in half, but only the lower part is used, and above there's mayonnaise all around and in the center are oysters, shrimp, caviar, porcini mushrooms, or octopus, and many other flavors. You're given slices of lemon to squeeze on the ones you like. They are really delicate and delicious canapés.

Q: There are two more books in this series. Can you give readers a hint about what is in store for Step and Babi in the future?

A: I cannot reveal too much because the good thing about the books is that you follow the protagonists and see what happens to them page after page. Babi and Step's future is full of incredible things to come and that's because he's hopelessly in love with her. Although Babi's family will try to keep them apart, and that's when everything happens. There are big surprises waiting for you. Maybe love will not be able to counter the will of Babi's parents, or it will keep Babi and Step together forever, but I cannot tell you more. But you can find out...it's all there, written in the books.

Discussion Questions

1. Federico Moccia has often been praised for writing stories that pull at readers' emotions. Looking back on the story, discuss the moments that were the most emotional for you. What moments made you cry? What moments made you laugh? Were there moments that made you angry?

2. This story celebrates the power of first love. Can you remember the intensity of your feelings the first time you fell in love? Do you think most people could be happy forever with their first love? Do you know where your first love is now?

3. What made Step so irresistible to Babi? What kind of partner do you find irresistible? Would you date a person that others don't find suitable for you? Is it better to be in a long-term relationship with someone larger than life or with just a normal person who makes you happy?

4. Initially, it's physical attraction that draws Step to Babi, but by the time he brings her to her dream house, he feels something deeper. What is it about Babi that causes Step to pursue her so relentlessly? What makes Step feel that their relationship can last forever?

5. The common saying that there's a fine line between love and hate seems to apply early in Step and Babi's relationship. What would you describe as the turning point in their relationship? When does Babi stop hating Step and start loving him?

6. When Step writes *three meters above the sky* on the wall, is that the most romantic moment in the book? If not, what do you see as the most romantic gesture Step makes for Babi?

7. Step and Babi both grow over the course of the story, breaking free of long-standing assumptions about school, life, and family. What are the most significant ways they change? What risks do they each take to be together? How do insecurity and jealousy influence their actions? What actions or decisions did you disagree with?

8. The story touches on the concept of forgiveness in many ways. The most obvious is when Step experiences a big betrayal by his mother. Do you think Step will ever be able to fully forgive his mother? Who should have helped Step? Do you think his father knew? Do you think the lawyer knew? Which character has the

most to be forgiven for? Step or his mother? What other characters need forgiveness throughout the story and why?

9. After Step has been legally prosecuted for his violent behavior, everyone who knows this seems to view him differently. Do you think that society is treating him too harshly or not harshly enough? Did it make you angry when they assumed that Step was responsible for other bad acts? Do you think that Step can break the circle of violence? In what ways is Step's story one of hope?

10. Step lets being a bad boy define who he is. Do you see this as an issue related to his self-worth? Do you think he will eventually attend college? What defines Babi? Being a good daughter? A good student? Is the answer about what defines them different for either of them by the end?

11. In a famous scene from the American film *Rebel Without a Cause*, the young men also engage in illegal street racing. Do you understand the need for speed? Do you think Babi enjoys any of the time riding behind Step on his bike? Do you think the risks of daredevil acts are outweighed by the thrill?

12. Babi rebels by getting a tattoo. Do you have a tattoo? Did you consider your tattoo an act of rebellion when you got it? Would you change anything about your tattoo?

13. This story was written more than twenty-five years ago and reflects the relationship between men and women at that time. Do you think we have made big advances in equality since then? What do you think equality between men and women really means, and how can we get there?

14. The city of Rome and its culture plays a big role in the story. Have you been to Italy and, if so, what did you enjoy most about it? How big an impact does the place where you live have on you—your personality, relationships with others, and world outlook?

15. The story uses many fun elements of 1980s pop culture to convey a sense of time and place including songs by Phil Collins, discotheques, and Walkmans, to name a few. Are you old enough to remember these things from the 1980s? Which of them did you enjoy?

16. How will having known Step impact Babi throughout her life? Has Babi changed for the better or worse since Step entered her life?

17. Is Step destined to lead an unhappy life, or has his relationship with Babi led him to a point where he can turn his life around?

18. At the book's conclusion, do you think Step regrets dating Babi? Do you think Babi regrets dating Step? Are they stronger as individuals for knowing each other?

19. Are Step and Babi ultimately a good match? Do you think Step and Babi could have a successful marriage at some point in the future? Which makes the best match—a marriage of opposites or a marriage of similar personalities?

20. What do you think happens to Step and Babi's relationship after the end of this book? Do you think Step will truly let Babi go? Do you think Babi will successfully move on? Why or why not?

About the Author

FEDERICO MOCCIA is one of Italy's publishing phenomenons, and his emotional stories have been compared to the works of Nicholas Sparks and John Green. The first two Babi and Step books were blockbuster bestsellers in Italy, spending three full consecutive years on the Nielsen bestseller list. His books have been published in fifteen languages worldwide and have sold more than ten million copies, and there are feature films in Italian and Spanish based on the first two books in the trilogy.

Learn more at:

FedericoMoccia.es
Twitter @FedericoMoccia
Facebook.com/FedericoMocciaOfficial

ABOUT THE TRANSLATOR

ANTONY SHUGAAR is a translator and writer who lived for many years in Italy, France, and Spain. He has received two translation fellowships from the National Endowment for the Arts. He has translated close to forty books for Europa Editions and has worked for many of the most prestigious publishers, trade and academic, in the United States and the United Kingdom. He has translated extensively for the *New York Review of Books* and has written for the *New York Times*, *The Times* of London, and many other publications.